A French Affair

Susan Lewis is the best selling author of twenty novels. She is also the author of *Just One More Day*, a memoir of her childhood in Bristol. She lives in France. Her website address is www.susanlewis.com

Also by Susan Lewis

A Class Apart
Dance While You Can
Stolen Beginnings
Darkest Longings
Obsession
Vengeance
Summer Madness
Last Resort
Wildfire
Chasing Dreams
Taking Chances
Cruel Venus
Strange Allure
Silent Truths
Wicked Beauty
Intimate Strangers
The Hornbeam Tree
The Mill House
Missing
Out of the Shadows

Just One More Day, A Memoir

A FRENCH AFFAIR

Susan Lewis

arrow books

Published by Arrow Books 2009

2 4 6 8 10 9 7 5 3 1

First published in Great Britain in 2006 by
William Heinemann
The Random House Group Limited
20 Vauxhall Bridge Road, London, SW1V 2SA

www.rbooks.co.uk

Addresses for companies within The Random House Group Limited can be found at:
www.randomhouse.co.uk/offices.htm

The Random House Group Limited Reg. No 954009

A CIP catalogue record for this book
is available from the British Library

The Random House Group Limited supports The Forest Stewardship Council (FSC), the leading international forest certification organisation. All our titles that are printed on Greenpeace approved FSC certified paper carry the FSC logo. Our paper procurement policy can be found at www.rbooks.co.uk/environment

ISBN 9780434019755

Typeset by SX Composing DTP, Rayleigh, Essex
Printed and bound in Great Britain by
CPI Mackays, Chatham ME5 8TD

To Jenny

Acknowledgements

My biggest thanks of all go to Raphael Vigneau, who so patiently and expertly guided me through the complex journey of wine-making – from the planting of the grapes, right through to the opening, pouring and tasting of an exceptional Grand Cru. If there are any mistakes in this book, please know they are all mine. I also warmly thank Julian Faulkner for his additional help with the wine-making process, and for the very enjoyable time we spent at his vineyard in the Var.

A very big and warm thank you to Cathy Hubert for the French translations, which give the book so much more colour and authenticity than it might otherwise have had. Again, if there are any mistakes, please be assured they are mine.

There are three people to thank for their invaluable help with the sections on sculpting – first and foremost Maria Gamundi, whose sculptures are amongst the most elegantly beautiful I've seen. Secondly, Martin Foot who very kindly showed me around his studio and explained many intricacies of his exceptional work. And thirdly, much love and thanks to my dear friend Fanny Blackburne, for giving me the experience of sitting as a sculptor's model.

Lastly, I would like to thank my editors, Susan Sandon and Georgina Hawtrey-Woore for all their patience, forbearance, encouragement and support during the writing of this book – it was greatly needed, and hugely appreciated.

A French Affair

Prologue

'There's a secret hiding place in here,' the little boy said, leading the way. 'My uncle showed me where it is. He used to keep all his special things here when he was young, so did my granddad. Even Elodie doesn't know about it.'

'Do you think there are spiders?' Natalie asked, keeping close behind.

'Oh yes, lots. I can catch some if you like and you can give them names.'

Natalie's eyes were searching the darkness. 'There are beds in here,' she said. 'Does someone sleep in them?'

'Only me and Elodie, when we want to.'

The little boy, Antoine, stumbled on the corner of a frayed rug, then stopped in front of a large mahogany chest that was mistily lit by a few rogue rays of daylight coming in through a small roof window. 'Are you ready?' he asked as Natalie joined him, his voice resonating importance.

'You're not going to do anything nasty, are you?' she asked. 'If you do, I shall scream and hit you.'

'Don't be silly. Watch,' and kneeling in front of the bottom drawer he used its fancy iron handles to ease it forward. There was a bump as the drawer fell onto the floor.

Natalie looked down at it, then back to Antoine who seemed swollen with mystery. 'So? It's just a drawer,' she scoffed. 'We've got drawers all over our house.'

'Yes, but I bet you don't have one hidden away behind another,' he said, and reaching into the empty space he pulled another drawer forward.

More interested now, Natalie dropped to her knees to inspect it. 'It's empty,' she said, annoyed and disappointed.

'Yes, because I took my secrets out before you came, in case you found them.'

Slightly bored again, Natalie looked around the dim attic space. 'I've never been up here before,' she said. 'I think Harry and I should sleep here.'

'You can't in the summer, it's too hot.'

It was summer now, and the drawer had no secrets, so they didn't hang around for long.

The next time Natalie came was at Christmas, so it was too cold for her and her brother Harry to sleep in the attic then, and at Easter, when her grandmother brought her, she was too afraid to sleep there alone. However, she wasn't afraid in the day, so it was where she sometimes went to write her secrets in her very own diary which she kept tucked away in the hidden drawer.

One rainy morning, as she sat under the roof window, writing down her most private thoughts about Antoine, she heard a car pull up outside, and a moment or two later her grandmother called out for her to come down and see who'd arrived. Quickly she wrote a few more words in her diary, then after sliding it carefully into the secret drawer she went downstairs. The kitchen door was open and because she didn't mind the rain she skipped outside. She would go back to her diary later, she decided, and write about everything they did today.

But Natalie never went back to the diary again.

Chapter One

'Jessica? Jessica Moore?'

Jessica turned round, half-expecting to see someone she knew, but the flush on the age-crushed cheeks in front of her and the soulful look in the watery old eyes were enough to tell her that she'd never seen this woman before.

Jessica smiled at her vaguely. She didn't want to be rude, particularly when the old lady looked quite a dear with her fluffy white curls and warming smile, but nor did she want to engage with the air of tragedy that was emanating through the kindness in what Jessica felt to be almost suffocating waves.

As the woman began to speak Jessica continued to smile, and even nodded once or twice, but her mind had quickly switched to another place, another time, where she could no longer be reached.

They were standing halfway down the pet-food aisle in Sainsbury's on the Cromwell Road. It was odd for Jessica to be there, since there were no animals at home, nor had there ever been. When she was a child she'd been so desperate for a dog that she used to walk around pulling a ball of string behind her, calling it Timmy. The memory flitted through her mind now as softly as a whisper. She was seeing a lonely little girl with no brothers or sisters, a father who was unknown and a strikingly beautiful mother who sometimes wanted her, but usually didn't. Her grandparents, with whom she'd lived most of the time, would have allowed her a dog, but her mother, from the end of a phone, or during one of her sweeping, gift-showering visits, would never permit it.

'She'll be coming to live with me any time now,' her

mother used to gush, all corkscrew curls and cherry-red lipstick, 'and I'm sorry, but I can't have a dog too. They're the worst kind of tie, and with all this quarantine business... What if we go to live abroad? No, no, a dog is just another complication, and that is something I really don't need.'

They did go to live abroad, she and her mother, for two agonisingly lonely years, during which Jessica had missed her grandparents so much that in the end she'd stopped eating and even speaking. She'd known, in her eight-year-old way, that her mother didn't really want her there, that she was a liability every bit as inconvenient as a dog, probably even more so, and the man her mother was living with didn't seem interested in her either.

In the end, her mother and her French-Canadian lover had broken up, and Jessica had been packed off back to Dorset to her lovely gran and big, strong grampy. And that was where she'd stayed, discounting a couple more disastrous attempts on her mother's part to be a full-time parent, until she and her best friend, Lilian, had left for university at the age of eighteen.

All best forgotten now, though. It was a long time ago, and really had no bearing on today at all.

Feeling a slight pressure on her arm, Jessica looked down to see the old lady's arthritic fingers touching her kindly. Jessica's eyes came up to the woman's gentle gaze. She smiled again, then after whispering a polite thank you, she began wheeling her trolley on down the aisle. For the next few minutes she focused only on what she'd come for: Greek yoghurt, muesli, fresh pasta, artichokes . . . She'd made a list and most items were ticked off by now, so it only remained to pick up some bread before she could join a queue at the checkout.

It was a Thursday morning in early July. There weren't many people around, but even so, as she moved quietly about her business she could feel the glances following her like ghosts, seeming to cling to her even after the curious, sympathetic and even embarrassed eyes had turned away. This was one of the very worst parts about being 'known': it allowed her no refuge in anonymity, nor any real privacy to call her own. At least not while she was out in public, and this was the first time she'd braved even a supermarket trip since the terrible event that had shattered her life. Had three months really gone by already? Sometimes it felt as though it was only three days, while at others it might have happened a lifetime ago.

Should she get a French stick, or a *pain de compagne*? She was thinking about Charlie now and wishing she'd let him come with her. He'd offered, but he hadn't really had the time, and Nikki, their seventeen-year-old, had merely looked at her and shrugged, as if to say, don't ask me, I don't know what you're making all the fuss about anyway, it's only a supermarket, for God's sake.

Jessica hadn't told her she was afraid of breaking down in public. Nikki didn't need to know that. For a few crazy minutes she'd considered keeping eight-year-old Harry home from school so he could come with her, but apart from being a selfish and even cowardly idea, it would have totally defeated the purpose of this visit, which was to start getting back to normal.

Strangely, now she was here the only thing she really felt was vaguely distanced from herself, almost as if she were another shopper watching Jessica Moore's progress and wondering what it was like to be her. Do well-known people feel things as deeply as everyone else? Is it easier for them because they've got money, or fame, or beauty, or successful husbands, to fall back on?

'It's not her,' she heard someone whispering nearby.

'I'm telling you, it is.'

'Who? What are we talking about?' a third voice asked.

'Jessica Moore,' came the reply.

'Jessica who?'

'Moore. You know, the one who does the arts programme on Wednesdays, after the news. She's on the radio too, I think, but I've never heard her. It's terrible what happened. Makes you want to go up and hug her, doesn't it?'

'Why, what happened?'

'Don't you ever read a paper? Honestly, I wonder if you even know what day of the week it is sometimes.'

Jessica dropped a French stick into her trolley and turned towards the checkout. That was another thing about being 'known', people seemed to discuss you as though you were unable to hear.

As she waited to pay she picked up a magazine, opened it and stared down at the words. She didn't want to catch anyone's eye, or hear any more whispers, she just wanted to be left alone. If she could, she'd tell them how she was trying to get her life back together, and coming here was one of the first small steps. *So please don't look at me any more, just try to pretend you've never seen me before.*

She detested self-pity, but she knew that the envy she felt of those around her was rooted in it, for she longed to be free to go about her business in a normal, unnoticed way, untouched by curiosity, barely even registering in people's consciousness, except as a tall, slim woman in white jeans and a plain T-shirt, who was paying for her groceries in cash, and taking a little too long to pack her bags.

As she wheeled her trolley across the upper level of the car park she could feel the summer sun on her skin and hear the nearby roar of traffic. Then someone whistled – a long, tunefully appreciative note, swooping up, and then down, before ending in a small staccato burst that made those around him laugh.

Though she didn't look up, she guessed the whistle had come from the scaffolding nearby, where a small group of men with bare chests and hard hats were, apparently, not paying too much attention to their work. Of course, the whistle might not have been for her, but instinct, and the fact that no-one else was around, told her it was.

At thirty-nine she might have felt flattered by the attention, but she didn't. In fact, it almost upset her to be reminded of how attractive she was. It seemed so superficial and irrelevant, and so very out of kilter with the way she felt inside. Who cared that her lithe figure and subtly exotic looks could still turn heads? Certainly not her. As far as she was concerned nothing could matter less.

As she approached her husband's Jaguar she caught a glimpse of her reflection and felt a moment's surprise. Then a small flutter of emotion broke into the numbness of her heart, like the tiny wings of a moth making ready to fly. She'd cut her hair so radically that she almost hadn't recognised herself. She didn't mind – she felt she'd like to be a stranger – but it seemed odd to see this different person looking back at her. She wondered if she'd been trying to make herself less attractive by chopping off the sleek blonde mane she'd always had. If so, she wasn't sure it had worked, because the wispy strands that now curved and curled like feathers around her face and scalp seemed to make her dark, almond-shaped eyes appear even deeper and more lustrous, while lending a new softness to the precise symmetry of her delicately flared nostrils and sumptuously wide mouth.

Nikki had cut her hair short first. In fact, Nikki had gone a step further and totally changed the colour, so now she was a brunette, instead of the scrumptious teenage blonde her father had so adored. It was a rare event to hear those two quarrel, but Charlie had been so upset by Nikki's new look that he'd been unable to hold back.

'It doesn't suit you at all,' he'd shouted, his pale, handsome face darkening with fury – though Jessica had known it was pain. He didn't want anything to change, even though everything already had, irrevocably, and suddenly Nikki's new hairstyle was too much for him to bear.

Was it really only a week since that explosion? It seemed so much longer, but time had lost all meaning since Natalie, their younger daughter, had been so cruelly taken from them.

Because of the way Charlie had reacted to Nikki's new hair, Jessica had been sure to warn him about her own plans to cut hers. Instead of protesting, as she'd expected, he'd merely nodded, as though already half-expecting it.

'Just please don't change the colour,' he'd said, lifting the hair from her shoulders and letting the cool softness of it run through his fingers. So she hadn't, but even so, Charlie's angels, as he'd teasingly called his three blondes, were no more.

As she loaded her shopping into the boot of the car the sound of rap music suddenly crescendoed beside her. She took a quick step to one side, as though to avoid a collision, then half-smiled when she realised it was the mobile phone in her pocket.

'Hello, Charlie Moore's number one fan,' she said into it.

'Jessica?' Charlie said. 'Is that you? Where are you?'

'In the supermarket car park. Where are you?'

'At the office, looking for my phone.'

Humour was lighting her eyes. 'Well, seems you found it,' she said. 'You left it in the car when I dropped you off earlier. Sorry, I should have called to tell you.'

'No problem. Has anyone rung?'

'No. You're your own first caller and it's already past ten o'clock.'

'No-one's rung me at all?' he said incredulously.

'Seems you're not quite as much in demand as you thought,' she responded dryly.

He chuckled. 'So how did it go? Was Sainsbury's as bad as you feared?'

'I'm not sure. It felt odd, but I'm glad I did it. I need to get back to normal. You and the children need me to get back to normal.'

'You've done a lot better than you give yourself credit for,' he told her. 'It's been a difficult time.'

'For you too,' she reminded him, while thinking 'difficult' had to be the understatement of the year. However, there was no point in trying to put it into words any grander than that, because no matter how descriptive, accurate, or cleverly metaphorical they might be, they wouldn't lessen the pain, or change it in any way. If anything they were more likely to make it worse, so it was best to keep to the trusty old euphemisms which they were now becoming quite good at.

'So what are you doing?' he asked.

'I'm on my way home. I've decided to write a couple of reviews. It'll keep me busy.' Her career as a presenter was over. She'd been unable to continue as though nothing had happened, so she'd withdrawn from the limelight completely, though lately she'd realised that for the sake of her own sanity she must do something to help fill her days. Book and art reviews were an obvious choice, but staying focused was hard, so a few days ago she'd applied for a full-time job in TV that would make her part of a team again – behind the scenes though, because nothing in her wanted to return to the public eye. 'What shall I do about your phone?' she said. 'Do you want me to bring it over?'

'No. If anyone rings, just tell them I'm at the production office all day, so they can get me here. Unless you want to bring it, and I'll take you for lunch.'

'You have time for lunch?' she teased.

'No, but I'll make some if you want me to.'

She was touched by the offer, not only because they didn't always find it easy to be together these days, but because his commitments to the news channel, as well as to his own independent company, meant that he rarely had time to grab a sandwich in the middle of the day, never mind break for lunch. She was about to respond when she realised she was being watched, and her expression instantly sobered. She was afraid the woman in the next car would be thinking that someone in her position should have nothing to smile about – unless, of course, it was true that celebrities, even minor ones such as Jessica Moore, simply didn't feel things as deeply as the rest of the world.

The sun suddenly seemed too hot, burning into her skin with the same scalding intensity as the guilt that all too often blazed in her heart. Then the blessed numbness returned and sliding into the driver's seat, she said to Charlie, 'I'd love to have lunch with you, darling, but that would hardly make it a normal day, and as that's what we're trying for now, I shouldn't duck out at the first opportunity.'

She wasn't sure if he'd heard, until he came back on the line and said, 'Sorry, Carl just put his head in. So, was that a no I heard? You're turning me down?'

'Try not to sound too relieved,' she chided. 'Are you in the studio tonight, or will you be home for dinner?'

'Definitely home for dinner. I'll try to get Nikki to join us. It'll be nice for us all to sit down together.'

Would it? No, of course not, because one of the angels was missing, creating a hole in their lives and an empty space in the house that nothing would ever fill, but since it was all about getting their lives back on track, and somehow accepting that they were four now, instead of five, perhaps it was a good idea.

After ringing off Jessica drove carefully out of the car park, onto the Cromwell Road, then turned up towards Kensington High Street. There were closer supermarkets to their home in Notting Hill than this one, but it was the Sainsbury's she'd come to know while she was working, so it had seemed easier to go back there for her first venture out alone.

As she turned into the crowded shopping street full of trendy boutiques, mobile phone shops and open-top buses, she was mulling over Charlie's invitation to lunch and wondering if he'd guessed the real reason she'd turned him down. Probably he hadn't given it a second thought, but if he had, he'd be likely to realise that it was his fame, much more than her own, that was making her head for home instead of an expensive eatery in Knightsbridge or Soho. As a newsreader his face appeared on television screens on an almost daily basis, so he could go virtually nowhere without being recognised, and whilst he seemed to handle the attention perfectly well, even now, after 'the tragedy', Jessica was growing increasingly resentful of the consequent intrusions into their lives.

'I'm just not cut out for fame,' she'd informed him on several occasions during the last few years. 'I never was. In fact, I could almost be tempted to give it all up and become a full-time housewife. Or better still, I'd like to go back to Dorset to live the same kind of normal, uncomplicated life my grandparents had.'

'If that's what you want,' Charlie sometimes replied, 'let's get a house there and go as often as we can.'

His answer could be annoying, because it showed that he'd failed to understand that no matter where she went with him, recognition would always be theirs. Or maybe he deliberately avoided the issue, since there was really nothing he could do about it, for not even changing jobs would allow him to blend in with the crowd now.

Their home in Notting Hill was a four-storey townhouse in one of the white stucco crescents that made the area so desirable. They'd moved in a little over eight years ago, from a much smaller end-of-terrace in Chiswick, mainly because Charlie had fallen in love with the place. And who wouldn't, when it was so stylish and spacious and full of light, even on the gloomiest day. Of course it had cost a fortune, and they'd only been able to afford it because Charlie's mother, Rosa, had died, leaving them her large house in Kew. It was where Charlie and Jessica had lived for the first six years of their marriage, with Rosa taking care of Nikki while her youthful and ambitious parents made a start in the world. Jessica missed Rosa a lot, probably as much as her grandparents who'd both died before Nikki was three.

Since Notting Hill was where many of the up-and-coming were setting up home these days – and the Moores were certainly part of this elite – it had come as no surprise to Jessica when Charlie had focused his search there. And it wasn't that she didn't love the house too, or the glittering social life that had come with it, she'd just never really felt as comfortable with it all as Charlie seemed to. Perhaps if she could have bonded with one or two of the women, or seen something worthwhile in their astonishing need to be considered important, it might have helped her feel more at home, but she never quite managed this. Charlie, on the other hand, had no problem fitting in at all, though he insisted it was because he had no need for any bonds beyond the one he had with her and the children.

'But I understand it's different for women,' he readily conceded. 'I know how much your friendships mean to you, so I won't take offence that you need something more than me.' Could she have been so generous, she wondered, if she'd felt he needed something more than her? Once, she knew she'd have found it hard to take, now it was different.

If only Lilian hadn't moved to Paris. She'd never needed her best friend more than she had these past months. Of course Lilian was always there, at the end of the phone, and whenever she could she'd talk for hours, but she was generally so busy and anyway, it wasn't the same as having her here. However, she mustn't begrudge Lilian her new life, for if anyone deserved to be happy it was her, even though it could be said that were it not for Lilian's new life none of it would have happened. She wouldn't allow herself to think that way though, because when Lilian had married Luc Véron, last Christmas, she couldn't possibly have known what a terrible route fate was opening up for them. No-one could have known, which was why no-one was to blame. Jessica told herself that over and over. It wasn't anyone's fault that Natalie had died – but still the guilt ate at her like a cancer, for she knew in her heart that she should never have allowed her mother to take Natalie to France. If she hadn't Natalie would still be with them, she was in no doubt about that, because she of all people knew how selfish and irresponsible her mother could be, how incapable she was of putting a ten-year-old's needs before her own.

So why, dear God, *why* had she agreed to let Natalie go? It didn't matter that Natalie had begged to show her grandmother the quaint little village where Lilian and Luc had married, to be able to stay in the same grape-picker's cottage they'd occupied for the big occasion that Natalie had loved so much. What Natalie wanted and what was wise for her to do were two different things, and being put into the care of her maternal grandmother was definitely not wise. Which was why, in spite of Charlie's support for the scheme, she, Jessica, should have put her foot down and refused to let Natalie go.

And she might have, had it not been a convenient answer as to who was going to take care of Natalie during the first part of the Easter break. Both she and Charlie were working, Nikki was studying for her A levels and Harry was going camping with the school.

So Jessica had put her job before her daughter, farmed her out to a woman she knew she couldn't trust, and now, God help her, she would never see her little girl again.

'Who was that on the phone?' Jessica asked, coming in from the garden just as Harry went on tiptoe to put the receiver down.

'It was Dad,' he answered, turning his impish, freckled face up to her. With his deep blue eyes and unruly mop of sandy hair, he could be no-one else's son but Charlie's, he even pulled the same expressions as his father and was fast developing, Jessica had noticed, a similar sense of humour. 'He said,' Harry continued, trotting back across the kitchen to his art homework, 'that he's just picked up your car from the garage and he'll be home . . . Um, I forget what time he said. No, I know, he said in about ten minutes.'

'Did he mention if Nikki was with him?' Jessica asked,

starting to rinse the handful of tarragon she'd just picked from the herb pots she kept on the patio.

When she received no answer she glanced over to the long, ten-seater table that took up most of the kitchen's conservatory extension and smiled to see how engrossed Harry was in the choosing of another crayon. They were spread out all over the place, along with his pencil cases and a drawing pad, while for once his Gameboy lay idle on top of his school bag beside him.

The conservatory, with its tall succulent plants and assortment of toys, was where the children ate their meals, often did their homework, occasionally watched TV and threw boisterous parties for friends on their birthdays. When they were just family Jessica and Charlie generally ate there too, since it was much easier than carrying meals upstairs to the formal dining area that was part of the large, elegantly furnished drawing room that ran from front to back of the house.

Harry's head suddenly came up. 'Did you say something?' he asked, frowning curiously.

'I asked if Nikki was with Dad?'

He shrugged. 'I don't know.' His frown deepened. 'Is she going to be reading the news too?' he asked.

Jessica smiled. 'No. She's just helping out at the studios to earn some money for the summer.'

'Oh,' he said, then put his chin in his hand and stared thoughtfully into space. 'Mum?' he said after a while.

'Yes,' she answered, selecting a knife from the heavy wood block to start chopping.

'I've been thinking.'

'What about?'

'Getting married.'

'Really?' she replied. 'Do you have anyone in mind?'

'No, but it's up to me to carry on the family name, because I'm the only boy. So if I'm going to have children I have to get married.'

'There's no rush,' she assured him.

He was clearly still deep in his reverie. 'I think I'm probably into older women,' he said, quite seriously.

Jessica choked back a laugh. 'Why do you say that?' she asked.

He shrugged. 'Girls my age are just stupid. I mean, Sophie Towers is all right, sometimes, and I suppose Elinor Curtis is OK, when she's not picking her nose or trying to make me say I love her . . .' His dark eyes moved to his mother's. 'I want to marry someone like Natalie,' he declared. 'She was the best person in all the world, when she wasn't beating me up, and locking me out of the bathroom. And I didn't really mind when she bossed me around. And that's what wives do, isn't it? They boss their husbands around, and then the husband lays down the law and they have a fight. You know, like you and Dad.'

Jessica laughed through the tears in her eyes. 'You think I boss Dad around?' she said.

He nodded earnestly. 'All the time. I think he's a bit scared of you, actually.'

There was such a light of mischief in his eyes now that Jessica dropped the knife and went to scoop him up in her arms. 'You are a terrible little rogue, Harry Moore,' she told him, hugging him hard.

'That's what my teacher said,' he cheerfully replied, hugging her back.

Jessica's eyes closed. 'And what did you do for her to say that?' she enquired, standing him on his chair so they were eye to eye.

He was a picture of innocence. 'I don't know,' he answered, 'she just said it.'

Jessica regarded him suspiciously.

'Honest,' he cried. 'I didn't do anything.' A moment later his eyes went down. 'Well, it might have been because I told her she should stand in the corner for swearing. She said bloody, Mum, and that's swearing, isn't it?'

'It could be, depending on the context.'

Harry's eyes opened wide with indignation. 'She said that we were all going to visit the Bloody Tower next term. Honest, that's what she said. So I put up my hand and told her she should stand in the corner.'

Jessica watched him and waited for the grin. It wasn't long in coming. 'You knew very well she wasn't swearing, didn't you?' she said, starting to tickle him.

'She thought I was serious though,' he laughed, and

yelped as he tried to break free. 'Let me go, or I'll fart,' he cried.

Jessica laughed again and pulled him into a bear hug. 'You are such a boy!' she told him as he howled with laughter. Then suddenly he was leaping to the floor as the front door slammed upstairs. 'Here's Dad,' he shouted. 'Dad! Dad! Guess what?'

As he thundered up to the hall Jessica turned back to the chopping board, still smiling, but aware of the constant heaviness in her heart that she knew would never go away. Natalie should be running up there with him, fighting to get to her father first, the way she always had. Then, hearing Charlie's shout of triumph as Harry told him how many runs he'd scored in cricket that day, Jessica found herself almost resenting the way they were able to behave as though nothing bad had happened to their family at all.

Looking up as Nikki came into the kitchen, she said, 'Hi darling, how did it go today?'

Nikki was scowling down at her mobile phone, then her cheeks suddenly turned crimson as she shouted, 'Dad! Did you send this?' She spun round as Charlie came down the stairs behind her.

'Send what?' he asked, all innocence.

'It was you,' she cried, laughing in spite of herself. 'Oh Mum, he is like soooo embarrassing.'

The fact that Nikki had stormed off in a strop this morning, without even saying goodbye to her mother, was clearly forgotten, and Jessica found herself smiling at the twinkle in Charlie's blue eyes as he looked at his daughter. As usual he seemed to be filling the room, not only with his imposing physique, but with the very energy of his presence. She'd often thought how everything felt safe when he was around, and almost anything seemed possible. That was before, of course, because now almost nothing felt safe. However, that still didn't change the fact that he was a strikingly good-looking man, with strongly defined features that even in repose showed his inherent good nature, while the unruly thickness of his lustrous sandy hair was the delight of many a cartoonist – and apparently an irresistible magnet to female fingers, an imposition Jessica had been forced to live with over the years, to the point that she barely even noticed it any more.

'What is it?' Harry was demanding, jumping up and down as he tried to grab the phone from Nikki's hand. 'Let me see.'

'No way.' Her deep brown eyes darted back to her father. 'That is so not true,' she told him.

'What isn't?' Harry wanted to know. 'What did he say?'

'It's got nothing to do with me,' Charlie informed her.

From his expression Jessica knew that whatever it was, it had everything to do with him.

'How do you know that, when I haven't even told you what it is?' Nikki challenged.

Jessica laughed as Charlie staggered back. 'I walked right into that,' he conceded, his eyes full of mischief and his smile as roguish as his son's.

Nikki banged his arm with her clenched fist. 'It is so not true,' she said through her teeth.

'Then what are you getting so worked up about?'

She blushed again. 'I'm not. When did you send it? Oh my God, no-one saw you taking his picture, did they? Dad, please tell me no-one else knows, or I'll never be able to go back there.'

'I was very discreet,' Charlie promised.

'But he's looking straight at the camera!' Nikki protested. 'He must have known you were taking it.'

'Of course he did. I told him it was for me.'

Nikki's head fell back as she groaned. 'That is it. I'm never setting foot in those studios again. Mum, he's totally out of order this time. You've got to speak to him. Look!' she demanded, shoving the phone at Jessica.

When Jessica saw the heart-framed picture-text of Freddy Crossland, the new trainee reporter on the programme Charlie presented, though she understood Nikki's embarrassment, she had to smile. 'He is pretty gorgeous,' she said, handing the phone back.

Before Nikki could take it Harry grabbed it. 'That's Freddy!' he declared. 'He's really cool, Nik. I think you should marry him.'

Charlie's eyes were brimful of laughter, but as they met Jessica's she couldn't help noticing how they sobered again.

Was her expression unwelcoming, she wondered, or had the pain stolen into her eyes without her realising? He hated to see it because it reminded him of his own, and though she had not a moment's doubt about how much he was suffering, he was becoming quite practised now at avoiding it. In fact, they almost never talked about what had happened, at least not in a direct sense, and it sometimes scared her to think of the grief he had bottled up inside, for he had still barely allowed any of it to come out.

'Hi, honey, I'm home,' he drawled, in a bad American accent.

'Cue the gin and tonic,' she replied, rolling her eyes.

'Don't forget the pipe and slippers,' he reminded her, as Harry darted to the fridge to dispense some ice.

'If you really smoked a pipe I'd leave home,' Nikki told him. 'I think they're revolting.'

Charlie was opening the drinks cupboard as Jessica filled a bowl with nuts. 'It's time you left home anyway,' he told Nikki. 'You're eighteen next month, and I can't afford you any more.'

'Take no notice of him,' Jessica said, unable to tolerate even a joke about Nikki going.

'Mum, what am I going to do about this picture?' Nikki wailed, her lovely gamine features drawn and desperate. 'If Freddy knows Dad took it for me . . . Oh God, I can't bear it. I mean, I am like so not interested in him . . .'

'Oh yes you are,' Harry informed her, plonking a bowl of ice down next to his father. 'I heard you telling Sonya the other day how fit you think he is . . .'

'You little devil, you've been eavesdropping again!' Nikki cried, advancing on him.

'I was not,' he shrieked, running round the table. 'Your bedroom door was open, so I couldn't help hearing. Mum! Mum! Get her off, she's going to kill me and I can't help it if she's in love with Freddy Crossland, can I?'

As he dashed out into the garden with Nikki hard on his heels, Jessica took the drink Charlie was passing her, saying, 'Well, what do you know? She seems to be speaking to me again.'

Charlie smiled and touched his glass to hers. After they'd

both taken a sip he said, 'She's in the throes of first love. Remember what that feels like?'

'Mm, I think so,' Jessica responded, looking at him.

To her dismay his eyes moved away, showing again his reluctance to engage with her, so going to put her arms around him she said, 'Don't I get a kiss?'

As his mouth came to hers she was aware of how tense he was, but he didn't try to pull away, nor did he protest when she tightened her embrace, he merely held her and kissed her until she broke away.

'So is Freddy interested in her?' she asked, turning to watch Nikki rolling Harry about on the grass.

'When she bends over in front of him like that, exposing a pink lacy thong and all that ripe young flesh,' Charlie answered, 'I think it would be hard for him not to be.'

'So you decided to help things along?'

'Let's just say I sensed he was having a bit of a problem with me being her father, so I thought I'd set him straight. I took the picture, told him she'd asked me to, and now he knows I'm cool with it he'll probably get round to asking her out.'

'Subtlety was never your strong point,' she commented, turning aside to check the chicken she had slowly poaching on the hob. 'Anyway, I thought you were at your own office today, not the studio.'

'I was, I just popped across the road to pick up Nikki when we'd finished.' Then, eyeing her critically as she bent over to put a bowl in the dishwasher, he said, 'Have you lost more weight?'

'I don't know,' she said, straightening up. 'Do I look as though I have?'

He shrugged, and took another sip of his drink. 'Incidentally, I ran into Pru Janssen outside. She invited us over for supper tonight, if we want to go. Just a few of the gang. Impromptu, dead casual.'

Jessica turned to him in surprise. 'I thought you wanted to have dinner as a family,' she said. 'I've started preparing it now.'

'It's OK. I told her we probably weren't free,' he replied. 'It was just if you didn't feel like cooking . . .'

'Do you want to go?' she said, feeling herself starting to tense.

'No. I'm just saying . . .'

'If you want to go, I'll happily eat with the children.'

'Don't be ridiculous. Of course I don't want to go without you.'

'But you do want to go.'

'Just leave it, Jessica. We're having dinner as a family and that's fine. God knows we get little enough opportunity, with my schedule and the children's social lives.'

Jessica was shaking her head in confusion. 'I'm sorry, but am I missing something here? It was your idea. You asked me earlier . . .'

'Mum!' Harry shouted, racing in the door. 'She's confessed. She really, really likes him and she wants to snog him, you know, like they're going to eat each other all up, the way you and Dad do . . .'

'I've got to be out of my mind ever to tell you anything,' Nikki declared, coming in behind him. 'You are totally incapable of keeping a secret.'

'I know,' he answered cheerily.

Nikki's smile suddenly drained as her eyes moved from her mother to her father and back again. Then grabbing her phone from the table she stalked past them, heading for the stairs.

'Nikki, what's the matter? Where are you going?' Jessica demanded.

'It's you!' Nikki cried, spinning round. 'You think I'm stupid, don't you? Well, I know what's going on here. You can't hide it from me, so you're wasting your time trying.'

'Darling, don't talk to your mother like that,' Charlie said. 'No-one's trying to hide anything from you . . .'

'She is!' Nikki shouted, pointing at Jessica. 'She thinks I don't know what's going on in her head, well you're wrong, Mummy dearest, because I do. You're planning to go back to work, aren't you?'

Jessica's eyes darted to Charlie.

'I didn't say anything,' he assured her.

'He didn't have to. It's all over the studios, and now you're blaming him because they don't want to give you a job. Well, it's not his fault. It was your decision to give up your own programme, and now you're trying to push your way into his and you shouldn't be doing it, because we all know what happened the last time you were working. *Don't* we?'

As Jessica's face paled, Nikki pounded up the stairs, leaving a stunned silence behind her. Jessica started after her, but Charlie pulled her back.

'I'll go,' he said. 'She's obviously got hold of the wrong end of the stick, so it's for me to straighten her out.'

Still shaken by the outburst Jessica stood aside, then seeing Harry's bewildered expression she put on a smile and went to fold him in her arms. 'It's all right,' she soothed, as he hugged her back. 'Nikki's just a bit overwrought. Like Dad said, she's misunderstood something . . .'

'Yes, she always does that,' Harry said, clearly wanting to cheer his mother up. 'You mustn't take any notice when she gets angry. It's probably the time of the month.'

Jessica had to laugh. 'Who on earth told you about that?' she asked, tilting him back to look into his cheeky face.

'You did,' he reminded her. 'Remember the little chat you had with Natalie, before, well,' a flush spread under his freckles, 'you know before . . . You let me join in too, remember, even though I'm a boy, because you said it was important for me to know about girls.'

As a lump formed in Jessica's throat she said, 'You're right, I'd forgotten about that.'

'So what I want to know,' Harry said, 'is if I can have a time of the month too.'

Again Jessica laughed. 'You, my darling,' she told him, 'can have anything you like.'

'Oh cool! Can I make a list?'

'As long as it only covers one sheet of paper.'

In a flash he was back at the table, and as he opened up his A3 drawing pad Jessica stood smiling down at him, watching him write as fast as his clumsy little fist would allow. She was barely registering the words, however, for her mind was still full of Nikki's outburst, and the shock of finding out that her job application had been turned down. She hadn't mentioned it to Nikki, because she'd judged it wiser to break it to her once she knew what she'd be doing.

That way she'd be in a much better position to calm Nikki's fears, and reassure her that no matter what her commitments, Nikki and Harry would *always* come first.

Well, there didn't seem to be an issue now, did there, at least not of the kind she'd expected. She put a hand to her head and pressed her temples. It had never even occurred to her that the news channel would turn her down, not only because of Charlie, but because Melissa Kingsley, the executive editor, was a close friend of theirs who'd frequently said what a great asset she'd be to their schedule. So what had changed? It was true she hadn't offered herself up as an on-screen presenter, which was what she was known for, but her skills as a producer and interviewer would be just as valuable behind the scenes, so she couldn't think why Melissa had taken a negative decision. More to the point, at least right now, was the fact that if Nikki knew she'd been turned down for the job then surely Charlie must have known too, so why was she finding out like this?

Chapter Two

'I don't know what else to say, except I'm sorry,' Charlie told her later.

By then dinner was over and Nikki had gone to take a shower, while Harry was revising for a spelling test the next day. 'I didn't expect it to come out like that, obviously,' he continued. 'Christ, it didn't even enter my head that people would talk about it . . .'

'How did they even know?' Jessica demanded, embarrassment heating her anger. 'Whatever happened to confidentiality?'

His eyes sharpened as he looked at her. 'I hope you're not accusing me . . .'

'Don't be ridiculous, but someone must have told them, and as Melissa was the only one I spoke to . . .'

'She's not a gossip and you know it.'

'All I know is that she led me to believe there was a job waiting for me any time I wanted one, so I asked if she'd consider me as a producer, or even a researcher, something low key and not on camera, and as far as possible, not on the same shift as you. I have to get out of this house, Charlie. I'm driving myself crazy, sitting here thinking and hurting and longing for her in ways I can hardly even begin to describe.'

His face immediately paled, the way it always did when any mention was made of Natalie. 'I know, and I understand,' he said, 'which is why you've got my full backing . . .'

'Really?' she challenged. 'Because frankly I don't think you want me to go back to work any more than Nikki does. In fact, you probably blame me too, for putting my job before Natalie.'

At that he jerked up from the table and stormed over to tear open the fridge. 'I'm not going there again,' he growled angrily. 'No-one blames you . . .'

'You know damned well Nikki does.'

'Because you put it into her head. You've got to stop this, Jessica. You're punishing yourself for something you had no control over . . .'

'But if I hadn't put my job first she'd still be here . . .'

'And now you want to work again,' he cried, throwing out his hands.

'You see, you do want me to stay at home.'

'No, I just don't understand your reasoning. You keep reminding me of how it's too late for Natalie, but there's still Harry. He needs you too.'

'Which is why I asked Melissa for something undemanding and flexible, something I could even do from home if need be.'

'What about your own programme? I'm sure Derek would give you a job producing, instead of presenting, if you asked.'

'How many times do I have to tell you, I can't go back to how it was before,' she exclaimed. 'It would be as though nothing had happened, and though you might be able to carry on like that, I can't. Besides, it wouldn't be fair to Felicity. She's done a fantastic job stepping into my shoes. It'd make her uncomfortable to have me around and she doesn't deserve that.'

Charlie took a deep breath, and bringing the wine back to the table he refilled both their glasses. 'There are other options,' he reminded her, sitting down again. 'I know the radio show's off the air until October, but there are still reviews you can write . . .'

'I don't need you to tell me what my options are,' she snapped. 'I just thought the news would work, since Melissa offered . . . Anyway, I clearly thought wrong, so let's forget it.'

'I can have a word with her,' he said. 'If that's what you want.'

'Oh, for heaven's sake, I don't want a job because you forced someone to hire me.'

Sighing, he sat back in his chair and stared at her in something close to helplessness. After a while he said, 'Am I allowed to change the subject?'

'Of course,' she replied, more stiffly than she'd intended.

'Actually, I'm not sure this is going to do much to improve your mood, but I had a call today from someone called Rufus Keane.'

She looked at him blankly. 'Am I supposed to know him?'

'Not necessarily, though it's you he's trying to get hold of. Apparently he's a friend of your mother's. He wanted to know if we've heard from her lately.'

At the mention of her mother the light vanished from Jessica's eyes. 'So what did you tell him?' she asked.

He shrugged. 'The truth, as far as I know it, that we haven't had any contact with her for at least two months, so we've no idea where she might be.'

Jessica looked away. 'You could have added that we don't even care where she is, but we hope she's rotting in hell.'

Charlie took a breath.

'OK, conversation over,' she snapped, before he could go any further, and jumping up she started to clear the table.

Though he kept his silence, he knew very well there was more to come, and it didn't take long. 'My mother is hiding something about what happened that day and you know it!' she suddenly shouted. 'She says Natalie fell down the stairs . . .'

Struggling to hold onto his temper he said, 'All the findings are consistent with that . . .'

'But Natalie called me, seconds before it happened . . .'

'You only think it was seconds. You weren't there . . .'

'I heard her fall, for Christ's sake . . .'

His face was chalk-white now. 'Jessica, please stop torturing yourself like this. Your mother might have been a hopeless parent, but you know she was trying to make it up with her grandchildren. She cared about them . . .'

'Don't defend her to me. Something's not adding up about that fall and you know it.'

'No, I don't. It's only you who thinks so . . .'

'No! You do too!' she shouted. 'You just won't admit it.'

'That's absurd,' he cried. 'Of course I accept what she's

saying, and everything in the police and paramedics' reports bears her out.'

'So where is she now? And why didn't she come to the funeral?'

'You told her to stay away,' he reminded her. 'You made it very clear she wouldn't be welcome . . .'

'Because she was lying. I don't want her anywhere near me until she's prepared to tell the truth. *Don't look at me like that!*' she yelled. 'I'm not crazy and I'm not in denial. I know there's more to it – call it a mother's instinct, a suspicious mind . . .'

'I wish you'd stop this!' he exclaimed. 'Whatever you're telling yourself, nothing can bring her back . . .'

'*I know that*, but if we knew what really happened we might at least be able to stop blaming ourselves . . .'

Immediately he looked away.

'You see,' she cried, 'you can't even talk about how guilty you feel, but it's eating you up, Charlie. It's there with you, every minute of the day. You keep telling yourself you should have been there for her, or you shouldn't have talked me into letting her go . . .'

'That may be true,' he growled, 'but no matter how I might feel inside we can't change the past, and punishing yourself and your mother like this . . .'

Her eyes flashed. 'For Christ's sake, you know what she's like. She's only ever been interested in herself, and now she's trying to protect herself, or someone else for all I know, by lying about what happened that day in France.'

Since they'd been down this road too many times before for him not to know where it would lead, Charlie bit back his anger and took refuge in a silence that they both allowed to simmer on until the phone suddenly rang. 'Are you going to answer, or shall I?' he said.

'It's bound to be for you or Nikki,' she replied brittlely, and pulling open the dishwasher she started to load.

A few minutes later Charlie put the phone down, and going to pick up his wine again, he said, 'That was Paul Kingsley wanting to know if we'd like to watch the big match over at his place. A few of the guys are already there. Girls are invited too, obviously.'

'How lovely,' Jessica responded tartly. 'I'll go and fetch my knitting.'

He cast her an exasperated look.

'Well what do you want me to say?' she cried. 'The boys sprawl out drinking beer and watching rugger, or football, or whatever the hell it is, while the girls sip wine in the kitchen, talking kids, recipes and all kinds of domestic goddess stuff.'

'You know very well it's not like that,' he retorted. Then with a sigh, 'They're decent people, Jessica. If you'd just give them a chance . . .'

She stopped what she was doing and pushed her hands through her hair. 'I know, and I'm sorry,' she said, forcing herself to calm down, 'but honestly, I really don't feel like it tonight. You go. You'll enjoy it.'

'Not if I'm thinking about you sitting here on your own.'

'I've got plenty to occupy me. I still haven't finished the reviews I started today, and I promised to have one ready by five tomorrow.'

Though he was looking at her anxiously, he was clearly keen to go. 'Are you sure?' he said.

She smiled. 'Of course I am. You'll enjoy it, and it'll do you good to chill out with the guys for a couple of hours. You work too hard, so you deserve some down time.'

He glanced at his watch. 'Kick-off's in ten minutes so I should be going.'

She was about to answer when Harry came bouncing down the stairs in his ink-stained pyjamas and a flowery shower cap. 'I've done my revision,' he announced. 'Will you come and test me, Dad?'

Charlie pulled a face as he looked at Jessica. 'Son, I've just arranged to go and watch the game with Tom Kingsley's dad.'

'Oh cool, can I come? We can have beer as well. I like beer, don't I, Mum?'

'I've no idea, but I hope not,' she answered. 'And I'm afraid it's too late for you to watch the match. You've got school in the morning . . .'

'So's Tom and I bet he's watching it.'

'Tom happens to be fourteen.'

Harry gave a shrug. 'Then will you come and test me, Mum?'

'Of course. Now, kiss Dad goodnight before he goes . . .'

Even before she could finish he'd rushed into his father's arms to embrace him brutally, then in response to Nikki's, '*Harry!* What have you done with my shower cap?' he raced back up the stairs again.

'Are you sure you don't mind?' Charlie said, going to the fridge to collect some beer to take with him.

'Sure, just promise not to go on the rampage after the match,' she teased, and linking an arm through his she walked out to the back gate with him. As they stepped out into the lane she reached up to put her arms around his neck. 'We're going to be all right, aren't we?' she said, looking up into his eyes. 'You're not starting to think you want out?'

Meeting her gaze, his expression softened as he said, 'You talk such rubbish sometimes. We're fine, and no I don't want out. I love you, remember?'

She smiled. 'I love you too,' she said, 'but you have to talk about what happened. You can't keep carrying it around inside the way you are . . .'

'Darling, I have to do this my way,' he interrupted. 'I know you're not finding it easy to cope with, but not everyone's as able to open up as you are.'

'I accept that, but maybe if you'd just listen to what I have to say . . .'

His expression instantly closed down. 'I've heard it,' he said. 'I know you can't accept the real version of events so you're trying to make your own, but whatever it is it won't be real. It can't be, because I saw the reports and spoke to the emergency teams myself, so I know what happened . . .'

'But did you ask the right questions?'

He groaned and let his head fall back. 'Jessica, please *please* let it go,' he implored. 'You're just making it harder for yourself and I can't bear to see it.'

Swallowing her next words, she said, 'I'm sorry.' Then she added, 'The last thing I want is for this to come between us.'

'It won't,' he promised, touching the tip of his nose to hers. 'We'll get through it, it's just going to take some time.' Kissing her gently on the mouth, he started to turn away.

'Please don't mention anything to Melissa about the job tonight,' she said. 'Not with everyone there.'

'Of course not,' he assured her, and after kissing her again he headed along the lane to the Kingsleys' place, just four houses away, while she stood watching him until he disappeared through their gate.

As she wandered back into their garden she was thinking glumly of how many marriages broke down after the death of a child, and though she didn't really believe theirs was in too much trouble yet, she was all too aware of the cracks that were starting to weaken it. She just wished Charlie wasn't finding it so hard to trust her instincts, or was at least prepared to listen to why she believed her mother was hiding something, but he was as resolutely determined not to indulge her on that as he was not to give in to his grief. It was as though he was shutting everything out, keeping it all at a distance, which was something that had never happened between them before. However, they'd never even come close to experiencing anything like this, so they really had no idea how to handle it, or one another – and though his withdrawal might be causing a part of their problems, she knew that her fear of some kind of cover-up concerning Natalie's death was only increasing the pressure.

'Mum!' Harry called from his window. 'Are you coming?'

Breaking out of her reverie, she abandoned the hose she'd started to unravel and shouted back, 'On my way,' then after stopping to rinse her hands in the kitchen she ran upstairs to test him.

Everything was going to be fine, she told herself firmly. Like Charlie had said, it would take time, obviously, and there were probably many more difficult and unexpected phases for them to get through yet, so she should try to stop worrying so much and keep on reminding herself that come what may she wasn't going to allow her family to fall apart.

It was past midnight by the time Charlie came home. Jessica was already asleep, but as he clambered into his side of their six-foot bed she stirred awake and turned drowsily towards him. He smelled of beer and toothpaste and the uniquely musky male scent that was him.

'Did you win?' she murmured as he drew the sheet up around him.

'Mm,' he responded. 'Three—two.'

They lay quietly for a while, listening to the night and feeling the comforting presence of one another, even though neither of them made a move to close the small gap between them.

Soon she fell into the rhythm of his breathing and found her thoughts drifting back over the years they'd been together, how they'd been introduced at a student party, and how mad she'd been about him from the start. Within a week they were sleeping together, and a month after that she'd left the small flat she'd shared with Lilian to move in with him. He'd always sworn that even if she hadn't fallen pregnant with Nikki ten months into their relationship he'd have asked her to marry him anyway, and though she doubted he'd have done it quite that soon, she had no reason not to believe him. They'd always been good together, sharing the same kind of temperament as well as ambitions, supporting each other's careers and never seeing their children as anything other than the most wanted additions to their lives.

They still were, it was just that there were only two children now, instead of three.

She turned her head to look at him, then reaching across she felt for his hand.

As he took it he lifted it to his lips. 'I'm pretty tired,' he said, 'and I've got an early start tomorrow.' To her dismay he turned away, though keeping her hand in his so she was snuggling into his back.

This was another part of how things had changed between them, because in the past they'd never shied away from making love. If anything, it had been one of the mainstays of their marriage, but now he'd become almost as resistant to it as he was to his grief. On a couple of occasions he'd actually been unable to work himself up to it, which hadn't so much surprised her as enraged him, particularly when she'd tried to explain how emotional issues could manifest themselves physically. She hadn't made the same mistake the next time the problem occurred, instead she'd done what she was doing now, holding him close wanting him to feel her love, while reassuring herself that was another phase that would pass. She didn't really crave the physical release herself, it was enough just to feel him there as she fell asleep, and to know he'd still be there when she woke up.

'Mum! *Muuuum*!'

'Natalie, no!'

Jessica came awake with a start. Her heart was pounding, her limbs trembling as sweat broke from her pores. The words had torn with such clarity through her dream that even though she knew she was awake now, their echo still resounded in her head. They were the last words she'd heard Natalie utter, shouting down the phone. 'Mum! Mum!' And then had come her mother's voice yelling, 'Natalie, no!'

After that there had been some kind of muffled banging before the line went dead.

She'd called back immediately, but there was no answer from Natalie's mobile, nor from the phone at the cottage where they were staying. She'd been about to go into the studio, the guests were assembled, the cameras were ready, so she'd had little choice but to hand her phone to her assistant, telling her to keep trying until she got a reply. By the time the recording was over, an hour later, her assistant still hadn't got hold of anyone, so, worried – though nowhere near as worried as she now knew she'd needed to be – Jessica had called Lilian at her office in Paris to ask for Luc's father's number. He owned the cottage, along with the nearby *manoir* and surrounding vineyards.

As it turned out Luc himself was at the *manoir*, and had wasted no time in going to the cottage to find out what he could. It seemed an interminable time before he'd called back, and the instant Jessica heard the graveness in his tone her insides had turned to ice.

'I am afraid Natalie has had a fall on the stairs,' he'd said, speaking fluent English with a pronounced French accent. 'The police and paramedics . . .'

'But she's all right!' Jessica cried, as though her words could make it so. 'She's not badly injured.'

There was a pause before he said, 'I am very sorry . . . her neck was broken.'

In all her life Jessica would never forget those words, or the terrible silence that followed them. It was as though the world fell away, leaving her stranded, unable to function. She tried to hold on, but there was nothing to hold onto. She told herself she hadn't heard correctly, that he'd got something wrong in the translation, but even if he hadn't, it didn't necessarily mean . . .

'Is she . . . Is she . . .?' she'd whispered hoarsely.

His voice was cracked with emotion as he'd said, 'I am afraid so.'

The next hours were blurred in her mind now – all she really remembered was the overpowering need to get to her baby, to make it all right, as though the combined power of her will and her love could somehow bring Natalie back to life. Since Charlie was filming it had taken a while to reach him, but luckily he'd been in Paris, so he'd been able to get there much quicker than she could.

In the end Jessica hadn't arrived until the following day, taking Nikki and Harry with her, because they hadn't wanted to be left at home. All three of them were still in deep shock when Lilian collected them from the airport in Lyon. Charlie, accompanied by Luc, was at the local *gendarmerie*, dealing with the formalities surrounding the death.

When Jessica walked into the *manoir* her mother, Veronica, was sitting in a capacious fireside chair in the vast open kitchen appearing agitated and upset, but Jessica noticed right away that her make-up was unsmudged, and not a strand of her immaculate silvery blonde hair was out of place. A dangerous fire immediately leapt into Jessica's eyes, for she knew her mother well enough to see straight through the facade of a shocked and grieving grandmother to the nervous, guilty woman lurking behind.

'What happened?' Jessica demanded, having to struggle for breath. 'What did you do to her?'

Her mother's bewitching eyes grew wide with alarm. 'I didn't do anything,' she cried, her hands fluttering upwards as though to ward off an attack. 'It was an accident. She fell . . .'

'She called me,' Jessica seethed. 'She was afraid, and I heard you scream. So what the hell happened?'

'She was on the phone,' Veronica sobbed helplessly. 'I saw her going towards the stairs . . . There was a pile of newspapers . . . I realised she hadn't seen it and I shout . . . Shouted to her . . . But it was too late. I wasn't quick enough . . . Oh God, Jessica, I'm sorry. I'm so sorry . . .'

She reached for Jessica's hands but Jessica slapped her away. 'You're lying!' she cried. 'She was afraid when she called me – something was wrong, so what was she calling me about?'

'I don't know,' her mother insisted.

'Who else was in the house?'

Veronica looked stunned. 'No-one,' she cried in confusion. 'There was only us. We'd been for a walk and got caught in the rain, so we were upstairs changing our clothes . . .'

At that moment the door opened and as Fernand, Luc's father, came in, Jessica saw her mother's glance in his direction and the little coquettish light that peeped into her eyes. That was when Jessica lost it completely.

'What's the matter with you?' she screamed, grabbing her mother's hair. 'Even now you can't stop flirting . . . You think it's all a game . . .'

'No, no, let me go,' her mother protested, struggling to break free.

'I want to kill you,' Jessica seethed. 'You've taken away my baby . . .'

'It was an accident! An accident!'

As Jessica's hands closed around her mother's throat, Lilian took her firmly by the shoulders, while Fernand prised her fingers apart.

'Come and sit down,' Lilian said, leading her away. Then, whispering in her ear, 'You're frightening the children.'

Jessica had forgotten Nikki and Harry, and seeing their pale, anguished faces she'd gathered them to her, and asked Fernand if he could suggest somewhere for them to stay, because she couldn't remain under the same roof as her mother.

In the event Veronica had been the one to leave, moving into another of the nearby cottages, while Jessica, Charlie and the children had stayed at the *manoir* until they were able to take Natalie home.

Now, as Jessica pushed back the sheet and slipped soundlessly out of bed, she was still finding it hard to shake the horror of the hours and days that had followed that terrible scene with her mother. And it hadn't been the only one, for there had been plenty more as Jessica had struggled to get to the truth of what had happened, forcing her mother to go over and over it, needing to know every single detail, no matter how difficult it was to hear. Veronica had never deviated from her story, but Jessica had seen the panic that kept coming into her eyes, and heard the fear in her voice. It didn't matter that the police and everyone else believed her, Jessica had known there was more to it, but it seemed nothing would drag it out of Veronica. In the end, half-mad with despair, Jessica had told her to get out of her life and never come back until she was ready to tell the truth.

The day after Veronica had left the tiny hamlet of Valennes the press had arrived, flocking in to cover the tragedy that had befallen one of Britain's best-known couples. Even the children had been unable to go out without being photographed or having questions thrown at them, so in the end Luc and Lilian had taken them to Luc's sister's, where their privacy was restored. Jessica would always be grateful to Luc and Lilian for the way they'd stepped in then, since she'd been so beside herself with grief it had been almost impossible for her to deal with Nikki and Harry herself.

Worst of all though, during those nightmare days – worse than anything she'd ever experienced in her life – was the morning Charlie had taken her to see their little girl laid out in her coffin. Even to picture it now unsteadied her, for Natalie had looked so perfect. Not broken at all, or even bruised. Just as if she were sleeping.

Struggling to push the image away, Jessica wrapped a robe around her and started quietly down the stairs. Her and Charlie's bedroom was on the first floor, along with two guest rooms, while the children's rooms were all on the top level. There were no sounds coming from up there, but as she stepped into the wide marble entrance hall down below she realised that someone was either in the den, or had gone to bed forgetting to turn off the TV.

Finding Nikki huddled into the corner of one of the sofas watching a pop channel with the sound down low, she said, 'Are you OK? What are you doing down here?'

Keeping her eyes on the screen, Nikki said, 'I couldn't sleep and Harry's in my bed – and since you won't allow him to have his own TV yet, I had to come down here.'

'Harry's in your bed?' Jessica said, going to perch on the arm of the sofa.

'He comes in sometimes,' Nikki replied with an offhandedness that didn't quite work. 'He has dreams . . . about dying.'

Jessica's heart turned over. 'I didn't know that,' she said. 'Why doesn't he come to me?'

'Because I told him not to. It'll only upset you and anyway, I don't mind him coming in to me.'

Appalled to think they'd kept this from her, Jessica made a mental note to check with Harry's teachers that there were no problems at school, and said, 'You know, darling, if either of you ever want to talk about Natalie . . .'

'I don't,' Nikki cut in.

Jessica flinched at the abruptness.

Nikki's eyes darted to her, then away again.

Jessica waited to see if she'd look again, but she didn't, so she said, 'Nikki, why are you so angry with me? Is it because . . .'

'I said I don't want to talk,' Nikki growled, her face growing taut.

Jessica looked around the room, as though searching for another way to approach her.

'Anyway, it's not your fault,' Nikki suddenly snapped.

Jessica looked at her.

'It's mine,' Nikki said. 'If I hadn't been so wrapped up in my exams she could have stayed home here . . .'

'No, no,' Jessica interrupted, going to sit beside her. 'You had to study . . .'

'Like it was more important than her?'

'We didn't know it was going to happen,' Jessica said, trying to hold her.

Nikki pulled away. 'I told you, I don't want to talk about

it,' she said, and hugged her knees to her chest so Jessica couldn't come any closer.

Jessica looked at her fresh young face and felt her torment as though it were her own – sharp and harrowing, deep and relentless. If only she could take the pain from her completely, instead of sharing it, then Nikki could be free, and not have to carry this terrible burden any more.

'Do you think she's all right where she is?' Nikki whispered brokenly, and as tears welled in her eyes Jessica had to blink back her own.

'Yes, of course,' she responded. In truth, she wasn't sure if she believed it, for the days were long past of having trust in a merciful God and his heaven, but it was what she had to tell herself, and what Nikki needed to hear.

'I keep thinking what if she didn't die straight away?' Nikki said shakily. 'What if she was crying and needed us . . .'

'Sssh,' Jessica said, pulling her into her arms. 'They said it was instant. That she didn't feel anything . . .'

'But she must have known she was falling.'

'Of course, but you can't torment yourself like this. It won't bring her back, and it's not helping you at all.'

'I know, but I can't seem to stop,' Nikki replied, tears rolling down her cheeks. 'I keep thinking about all the times I was mean to her . . .'

'And she was mean to you. Sisters are like that.'

'But I was older . . .'

'And what about how lovely you were to her? The way you used to take her shopping, help with her homework, keep her secrets, show her how to do her hair . . . Think of all the happy times you shared, when you used to laugh and laugh, and Dad and I never knew what you were laughing at . . .'

A smile wavered onto Nikki's lips. 'She was such a giggler, wasn't she? It was always so easy to make her laugh.'

Jessica smiled too. 'I remember you telling her that a comedian should have an audience full of Natalies, he'd think he was a massive success.'

Nikki chuckled. 'She was really noisy too,' she said.

'Everything she did . . . We all knew about it . . .' Her voice faltered. 'I suppose that's why we miss her so much, it seems so quiet without her.'

'Quiet? With Harry?' Jessica teased.

Nikki rolled her eyes. 'Maybe not.' She took a breath that came out shakily. 'Did you see him in my shower cap earlier?' she asked. 'He's got it on now, while he's asleep. He's such a fool.' She swallowed hard, then her voice was ragged again as she said, 'I love him so much, Mum, I just couldn't bear it if we lost him too.'

'Oh darling,' Jessica said, holding her tightly. 'That's not going to happen.'

'I know, I mean, I think I know, but I feel so afraid sometimes. Don't you?'

'Of course. We all do, but it doesn't mean there's anything to be afraid of. It's only natural that we'd be feeling insecure now – something happened that shocked us deeply, and it's hard to trust after you've had your world shattered like that. But it will get better. I promise. Soon we'll be able to put it behind us, and live our lives normally again. In some ways we already are.'

'But I don't want to leave her behind.'

'Oh no, we'll never do that,' Jessica assured her. 'It's only the grief we need to let go of, not the love. That will always be with us.'

Nikki sighed and rested her head on her mother's shoulder.

They sat quietly for a while, barely listening to the music, simply feeling the comfort of one another.

'Mum?' Nikki said finally, twisting her fingers round Jessica's. 'Can I ask you something?'

'Yes, of course.'

'Well, is . . . I mean, like is everything OK with you and Dad? You're not going to break up or anything, are you?'

Startled, and disturbed that Nikki should be thinking that way, Jessica said, 'No, of course not. Whatever put it into your head?'

Nikki shrugged. 'I don't know. It's just . . . I suppose you don't seem as close as you used to.'

Jessica smoothed her hair. 'Like I said just now, we need

time to get back to normal, all of us, including me and Dad, and I promise you, we're not going to break up.'

Nikki lifted her head and looked uncertainly into her mother's eyes. Then seeming reassured by what she saw there, she changed the subject again. 'You know, I'm really worried about my results. If I don't get the right grades . . .'

'I'm sure you will,' Jessica said soothingly, 'so your place at uni will be safe.'

'But what if I don't?'

'You know we've made arrangements for you to resit, if the worst has happened. Everyone understands what pressure you were under, how difficult it was for you to sit them at all considering what you were going through.'

Nikki sighed. 'Actually, they were kind of like a life-saver at the time,' she confessed. 'It gave me something else to think about, but now they're over . . .' She shook her head, apparently at a loss.

'What about Freddy?' Jessica ventured. 'Isn't he something else to think about?'

A blush accompanied Nikki's smile. 'He really is cute, isn't he?' she said. 'I mean, I know he's like nearly four years older than me, but I really think he might be interested.'

'Dad seems convinced of it.'

Nikki glowed. 'You know, I really love Dad,' she said. 'I mean, he gets on my nerves sometimes, but he's usually so cool with everything.'

'He'll be very glad to hear you love him,' Jessica smiled. 'I'll be sure to tell him. In fact, I've been thinking about doing something to let him know how special we think he is.'

'Really?' Nikki responded, intrigued. 'Like what?'

'Well, you know how much he loves to entertain and it's been a while since we had anyone round, I mean in any kind of numbers.'

'You're thinking about throwing a party?'

Jessica grimaced. 'Not a party, exactly, a dinner. It's more his kind of thing to sit around the table with lots of wine and friends, putting the world to rights.'

Nikki nodded. 'So how many are you thinking of?'

'Well, we can seat fourteen comfortably, so why go any higher? Will you help me put together a guest list? I was thinking we could start with you and Freddy, if you don't think us oldies will be too boring.'

'Oh my God, you are like so ahead of yourself,' Nikki gasped, flushing deeply. 'He hasn't even asked me out yet.'

'But he will, I'm sure. So now we need to come up with another ten . . . But not tonight. It's past three already, and if you're getting a lift with Dad in the morning you'll need to be up at seven.'

As they walked up the stairs with their arms round one another, Nikki said, 'Do we have to invite Melissa to this dinner?'

Jessica's eyebrows rose in surprise. 'I think it would look a little odd if we didn't,' she said. 'Why? Is she coming on a bit strong with you at the office?'

'No, it's not that exactly, but she didn't give you a job and I think that really sucks when she knows what a hard time you've been having.'

Jessica laughed. 'I can hardly keep up with you, Nikki Moore. I thought you blew up at me earlier because you didn't want me to go back to work.'

'Yeah, well, I had a chat with Dad after, didn't I, and he made me see how important it is for you to have something to do. So I think it's really mean of Melissa to turn you down.'

'Actually, so do I,' Jessica conceded, 'but I'm sure she has her reasons, so before we strike her off the guest list, let's wait and find out what they are.'

Chapter Three

The following morning they were all in the kitchen, Harry wolfing down Coco Pops, Nikki begging to borrow one of Jessica's more daring tops, Charlie reading the paper while listening to the radio, when the phone started to ring.

Jessica and Charlie immediately looked at one another. 'Who's that at this hour?' Harry demanded for them.

'It'll be for you,' Jessica said to Charlie, and returned to the packed lunch she was preparing for Harry.

'Hello,' Harry sang cheerily into the phone. He listened, then said, 'Um, I think you've got the wrong number.' His eyes moved uncertainly to Jessica, then to Charlie as he listened again. 'We don't know anyone called Ronnie,' he said.

Jessica's face darkened.

'Grandma,' Charlie reminded him, and reaching across the table he took the phone.

'Hello, Charlie Moore here,' he said. 'Can I help you?'

'Sorry to bother you so early,' said the voice at the other end. 'It's Rufus Keane again. We spoke yesterday.'

'I remember,' Charlie responded, 'but I'm afraid the answer's still the same, we've no idea where Veronica is, and I don't wish to be rude, but how did you get this number?'

'I found an old phone book of Ronnie's in her desk,' he replied. 'I really am sorry to bother you so early, but I have a flight to catch and I was hoping to speak to your wife before I leave . . .'

'She won't be able to tell you anything different,' Charlie interrupted. 'We haven't had any contact with Veronica for over two months.'

'I understand that, but I was wondering if your wife might

be able to put me in touch with some of Ronnie's other friends, to see if they could shed some light on where she might be.'

Charlie was starting to look troubled. 'You're making it all sound mightily mysterious,' he commented darkly.

'I rather think it is,' came the reply.

Charlie's eyes moved to Jessica, and putting a hand over the receiver he relayed the message.

'Oh, all right, give me the phone,' she snapped, and aware of Nikki and Harry watching her with some apprehension she tried to temper her tone as she said, 'I'm afraid, Mr . . .?'

'Keane.'

'. . . that I can only repeat what my husband's just told you, I've no idea where my mother is – and at the risk of sounding rude, if you are as close a friend of hers as you say you are . . .'

'Actually, I didn't . . .'

'. . . then you'd know how unlikely it is that I would.'

'I'm aware of the difficulties between you,' he said, still sounding perfectly polite in spite of her tartness, 'but it's not like her to take off without . . .'

'Once again,' Jessica cut in, 'if you know her at all, then you'll be aware that she has a long history of taking off without telling anyone where she's going, or how long she'll be, so rest assured she'll turn up sooner or later, bad pennies always do. Now I'm sorry if she's run out on you . . .'

'Mrs Moore, I should tell you that I'm not one of your mother's more intimate friends, as you seem to be thinking. My wife and I live next door to her, here in Oxfordshire. We generally check her mail and keep an eye on things when she's away, and it's usual for her to give us a number where we can contact her, should we need to. We're worried because she left here ten days ago saying she'd be gone a day or two, and we haven't heard from her since.'

Feeling suitably abashed at having presumed he was one of her mother's conquests, Jessica adopted a much gentler tone as she said, 'I see, but I'm afraid I still can't help you. I have no idea where she might have been going.'

'Well, that's just it – she left us a note saying she was going to London for her usual check-ups and things, and that she was hoping to see you while she was there.'

Jessica turned to look at Charlie. 'Even if she intended to come here,' she said, 'we still haven't seen her.'

'Then I don't understand what could have happened to her. Please don't think I'm objecting to taking care of the house, it's simply that we started to worry when we realised how long it had been since she'd been in touch. Oh, excuse me, they're announcing my flight, I'll have to go. I should be in Rome by midday – if it's all right with you, I'll ring again once I've checked into my hotel to see if you can give me some other names and numbers to call.'

'By all means,' she replied, 'but I can tell you now that I know virtually no-one in my mother's social circle, so I doubt I can be of any help.'

After putting the phone down she turned to find the children staring at her expectantly, while Charlie was behind the paper again.

'Well?' Nikki prompted.

She pulled a face, and going back to making Harry's packed lunch she gave them a quick precis of what had been said.

When she'd finished Nikki said, 'So aren't you worried?'

Jessica shrugged. 'Why should I be? You know very well what she's like. She probably met someone on the train and got herself whisked off to Rio de Janeiro or Timbuktu or some tumbledown pile in Totnes.'

'But aren't you at least interested to know what she was coming to see you about?' Nikki pressed.

Though Jessica was, she ignored the question, for they all knew, without her having to tell them, that there was only one thing about her mother that interested her now.

Nikki looked at her father as he said, 'Maybe we should tell this guy to try getting hold of Maurice. If anyone's likely to know where she is . . .'

'Do you have a number for him?' Jessica interrupted tersely. 'No, nor do I.'

Nikki said, 'Are you sure she didn't come here?'

'If she did, we must have been out,' Jessica replied.

Nikki's eyes turned playful. 'Wow, you haven't offed her, have you?' she asked.

Jessica threw her a distinctly unamused look.

'What? It was just a joke,' Nikki responded sulkily.

'Which wasn't even close to funny,' Jessica informed her. 'Now unless you two want to be late, I suggest you get going. And yes, you can wear my pink lacy top, seeing as you already have it on, but it had better come back in the same pristine condition it's in now, or you're buying me a new one – and just so's you know, it cost a hundred and fifty pounds.'

At that Charlie's head came up. 'That little scrap of a thing cost a hundred . . .' Seeing Jessica's face he bit back the words. After all it was her money, not his – and when had he ever refused her anything anyway? But really . . . It was no bigger than a couple of ten-pound notes with a couple of sparkly chains and some floaty sort of gauze stuff holding it all together. Well, if nothing else, Nikki was going to go down a treat at the studios today, which, now he came to think about it, was very probably the intention.

'So,' Nikki said, busy pressing a text into her phone as she and Charlie inched through the morning jam on Holland Park Avenue, 'what did you make of all that?'

'You mean about Grandma?' he replied. 'I'm not sure. What did you make of it?'

Nikki shrugged. 'She definitely didn't seem too bothered about it, did she?'

'Well, you know how she feels where her mother's concerned.'

'But if this bloke Keane's worried, maybe as family we should be too.'

'Perhaps,' Charlie conceded, 'but I guess it has to be her call.'

Nikki no longer seemed to be listening as she started another text, so letting the subject drop Charlie turned on Radio 4, only to have it changed seconds later to some pop station.

'You might have asked,' he commented.

Nikki looked at him blankly.

He rolled his eyes. 'So, do you think there's any chance

you might go back to your natural colour some time soon?' he enquired, turning into Campden Hill Road.

'Oh don't start again,' Nikki grumbled. 'I like it like this. Everyone says it really suits me.'

'Then they're wrong, but what do I know, I'm just your father who happens to prefer blondes.'

'Really?' she responded mildly.

He glanced at her in surprise, but her head was down as she read an incoming text so he was unable to see her face. Thinking better of asking her what she was implying, he hooked on his earpiece to answer his phone.

By the time he ended the call another was coming in, followed by another, then another, until they were almost at the studios, and his mind was full of the day ahead.

'So are you enjoying your job?' he asked, as he steered the Jaguar into the underground car park.

'Yeah, it's cool. Everyone's really nice. Elsa's letting me do some research on inner-city housing today for some features they've got coming up.'

Charlie was impressed. 'Well, I'm glad they're making good use of you,' he commented. After pulling into his reserved space he said, 'I hope you're not taking too much notice of any gossip you might be hearing.'

Nikki shrugged. 'What, you mean like about Mum and the job?'

'Well, yes,' he answered, though it wasn't actually where his mind had been. 'How did you hear about that?'

'Someone was talking in the canteen. I don't think they realised I was there, or maybe they didn't know I was your daughter . . .'

'Who was it?'

'I only know one of them – Frances, Melissa's PA. Oh my God, there's Freddy,' she gasped, and immediately sank down in her seat.

Charlie rolled his eyes. 'You're not going to make much progress if you start hiding from him like that,' he told her, pushing open his door.

'I don't want to see him while you're there, not after you took his photo. Are you sure you didn't tell him it was for me?'

Charlie grimaced. 'Well, I suppose I might have mentioned . . .'

'Oh Dad, no!' she cried, ready to be mortified. 'You did, didn't you?'

'It'll be fine,' he told her. 'Now come on, I'm due in a meeting at eight thirty and it's already twenty-five past.'

'I am like so mad with you,' she said furiously, as she loaded her phone, make-up and magazines back into her bag. 'Everyone's going to know. They'll all be talking and laughing . . .'

'They won't,' he said irritably. 'Besides, you shouldn't listen to gossip.'

'Oh, like, when it's about me I'm not supposed to mind? Get a life, Dad.'

'When it's about anyone,' he retorted, slamming his door closed and starting towards the lift. 'People often make things up, you should know that by now,' he said as she joined him.

'So are they making things up about you? Is that what you're worried about?'

He turned to her sharply. 'Are they?' he demanded.

'Depends what you think they're saying.'

Though his expression showed he'd like to take that further, as they were joined by one of the subs at that moment he had to let the subject go.

A few minutes later, having parted from Nikki outside the Ladies in reception so she could finish preparing to dazzle Freddy, Charlie diverted from his usual route straight to the newsroom to his personal suite on the first floor. It was luxuriously fitted out with expensive fawn leather sofas either side of a glass coffee table, a large desk in front of a picture window that was protected by vertical blinds, a 55-inch plasma screen across one wall invisibly connected to a small bank of technology in the sideboard below; a fully stocked bar, a spacious corner wardrobe and an adjoining kitchen and shower room at the far end.

After closing the door behind him he took out his mobile, pressed in Melissa's number, then hit the remote to tune into the studio's current output.

Melissa answered on the fourth ring. 'Good morning,

Charlie,' she drawled in her soft Scottish accent.

'Good morning,' he responded, almost curtly. 'Where are you?'

'At home. I'm not due in until three. Is there a problem?'

'Yes and no. Nikki found out, apparently from overhearing Frances gossiping, that you're not giving Jessica a job.'

'Oh dear,' Melissa commented, sounding suitably bothered. 'Well, that's Frances's employment at an end. Now, what to do about Jessica. Has Nikki told her?'

'She has.'

'Oh. Definitely not good. I was going to pop along and see her this morning anyway – obviously I still will, but I'm glad you told me she already knows. How did she take it?'

'She was upset, as you might expect. Naturally, she wants to know why you're turning her down when you've been actively trying to persuade her to join the channel.'

'Yes, well, of course she wants to know. So maybe you'd like to help me out here, Charlie. Tell me why I don't want her to join us, and please don't give me all that bullshit about her not being ready yet, because she's not going to swallow it any more than I do. So I'd like the truth, Charlie, whatever it is.'

Charlie remained silent, his face taut with anguish.

There was a note of reassurance in Melissa's voice as she said, 'Don't worry, it'll stay between us, but if I'm going to lie, my friend, I'd like to hear from you why I should.'

'OK,' he said abruptly, 'the long and short of it is I have to get away from her sometimes. She's suffering so badly I can hardly bear to see it, and I think it's the same for her, so it won't do us any good to be in each other's pockets.'

'Mm,' Melissa responded, not sounding fully convinced. 'So what do you want her to do?'

Charlie felt a tight band closing around his head as he said, 'I wish I knew, but thank you for supporting me over this. I won't forget it.'

'Then let's hope you won't regret it either,' Melissa retorted, and a moment later she was gone.

*

Having performed her scheduled carpool duty, Jessica was back at home and still not entirely sure what she was going to do with her day – apart from finish the DVD reviews which she sorely wished she'd never agreed to now. She had a pile of books in her study too, all of which she'd have to take a pass on, because it simply wasn't fair to the authors to assess their work when she was finding it all but impossible to stay focused. Unfortunately there was still the mountain of sympathy letters to be got through, but since she was more inclined to throw them away than read them, there wasn't much chance of her filling the time with that.

What she'd really like to do was spend the day with Lilian, just talking and being together, the way they always used to, but she couldn't even call her friend – at least she wouldn't – because Lilian's job as chief auctioneer at Summerville's Paris salerooms meant that she was almost never available, and right now Jessica wasn't even sure what she wanted to say.

Were she of a mind to, she could try sorting through Natalie's room, but she knew very well she didn't have the heart for that. She'd have to get round to it sooner or later, of course, but she still couldn't bear even the thought of going through her daughter's cherished possessions, never mind parting with a single one of them. So for now the room remained as it had always been, pink and lavender covers and curtains, with shelves crammed full of Care Bears, a hopelessly cluttered dressing table, an overstuffed wardrobe and all kinds of perfumed candles, dancing mobiles and books numerous enough to stock the children's section of WH Smith. There were her diaries too, with pretty padded covers and tiny little locks, and somewhere, presumably, their keys. Jessica hadn't even looked. She didn't want to read them, but nor would she ever part with them.

By ten o'clock the temperature outside was rising fast. It seemed summer was finally with them, which reminded her that a decision still had to be taken on what they were going to do about a holiday. Were it left to her they'd return to the grape-picker's cottage in France, but she knew Charlie would immediately veto that, and maybe revisiting the place Natalie had died wouldn't be good for her either. She had a feeling it would make her feel closer to Natalie though, which was what she wanted more than anything. Also, if Lilian was able to take some time off, she'd be at the *manoir*, so they could spend some days together too. However, there was no point even fantasising about it, for she knew Nikki would be as reluctant as Charlie to go back to Valennes. In any case, now Nikki was almost eighteen and currently earning her own money, she might not want to go anywhere with them.

Sighing to herself, Jessica dried her hands on a tea towel and reached for the phone as it rang. 'Hello, Jessica Moore speaking,' she said, tucking it under her chin as she started to make some fresh coffee.

'Jessica, hi. It's Karina here. Karina Rutherford.'

'Oh yes, hi, how are you?' Jessica responded, guessing already what the publishing director of one of the major houses was calling about.

'I'm fine. How are you? Is this a bad time?'

'Not at all. You want to know if I've managed to take a look at William Koby's new book yet. I'm afraid I haven't got round to it and I'm not sure I'll be able to . . .'

'Please don't worry. I'm sure you're inundated with review requests – we count ourselves lucky when you take one on, but no, that's not why I'm calling. Would you happen to be free for lunch sometime next week? I have a proposal to put to you that I think – hope – might interest you.'

Intrigued, Jessica said, 'Would you like to give me an idea of what it is? That way I can be thinking about it before we meet.'

There was a wry note in Karina's voice as she said, 'I had a feeling you were going to say that. The trouble is, you might turn me down flat on the phone, whereas if we meet there's a chance you'll at least enter into a discussion.'

Jessica's eyebrows rose. 'What if I say I promise not to turn you down on the phone?' she replied.

Karina took a moment. 'Well,' she began, drawing out the word, 'I'd like to commission you to do a book.'

'Really?' Jessica couldn't help feeling flattered. 'What about?' But even as she asked the question she could feel her defences rising, for she was fairly certain now that she knew the answer.

'About Natalie, and how you've coped,' Karina answered, confirming her suspicions. 'Before you reject it completely,' she went on quickly, 'I want you to consider how helpful it might be for other women in your position to hear from you at a time like this. It could provide them with enormous comfort and strength to learn how you've dealt with it . . .'

'Karina, I have to stop you there . . .'

'You promised not to turn me down on the phone.'

Jessica's eyes closed. 'Listen, I'm really not dealing with it very well, and it's still too early to be submerging myself in it all over again.'

'I understand, and you probably hate me for even bringing it up, but there's no rush. We can publish in a year, even two years from now.'

'Karina, I'm sorry . . .'

'At least say you'll come and have lunch.'

Jessica sighed. She liked the woman, and it would be good to get out, so why not?

'Will Wednesday work for you?'

Jessica nodded. 'Wednesday's fine.'

'I'll email you time and location when I've made a reservation – unless you have a preference?'

'No, I'll leave it to you,' Jessica replied, starting as the buzzer sounded at the back gate. 'And please know I feel bullied already.'

Karina laughed. 'Till Wednesday,' she responded, and rang off.

A few minutes later Jessica was pouring a coffee for Melissa, who was talking into her mobile phone, while grimacing apologetically for taking the call. Jessica gestured for her to continue, then watched her walk back out into the garden where the reception was better. As usual Melissa's voluptuous figure seemed to be staging a winning battle with its prison of buttons and seams, yet despite the strain her pale blue shirt and matching pencil skirt still contrived to look as expensively cut as they no doubt were. Her hair, a luxuriant mass of ebony curls, was bouncing about her shoulders in its habitual haphazard way, while the generous features of her elongated but nonetheless attractive face were as colourfully rouged, lipsticked and shadowed as ever. The only thing different about her this morning was the missing high heels, presumably because she'd thought better of them for the short trot down the back lane. Then Jessica smiled to herself as, still talking into the phone, Melissa reached into her voluminous bag and pulled out a very elegant pair of pale blue Manolos, which she stumbled about exchanging for the rubber gardening shoes she'd arrived in.

Her call finished and outfit complete, Melissa breezed back into the kitchen, air-kissed Jessica on both cheeks, and took her coffee with a satisfied sigh. 'I'd treat you to genuine smackeroos if I thought you'd appreciate my lip prints,' she declared, with a playful twinkle. Then, after giving Jessica the once-over, 'You look good. Very good. Why is that everything you put on looks as though it's about to go swanning off down the catwalk?'

'Charlie thinks I'm too thin at the moment,' Jessica informed her, picking up her own coffee, 'and he's probably right.'

With a dismissive wave Melissa went to perch on the edge of the table. 'Charlie tells me my assistant was less than discreet,' she began, taking a sip of her coffee. 'She will, of course, find herself out of a job by the end of the day, but I'm sure what you're more interested to know is why I came to the decision I did.'

'I have to say, it surprised me,' Jessica said, keeping her tone neutral.

Melissa smiled, showing two neat rows of perfectly capped teeth. Then, pulling out a chair, she sat down and crossed her ample legs. Jessica couldn't help glancing at the expanse of smooth, lightly tanned thigh and thinking that for a woman who was essentially overweight, she flaunted herself with admirable style. She wondered how much she liked her, and thought perhaps reasonably well. She was direct, usually even-tempered, fiercely intelligent, and of course, given her position, extremely powerful. As was her husband, a senior Downing Street advisor with burgeoning parliamentary ambitions of his own.

'I want you to understand,' Melissa began, 'that my decision in no way reflects what I think of your ability. We both know how good you are, so I won't sit here flattering you when it goes without saying that I'd never have offered you your own programme if I considered you anything but the best. And therein lies the rub. When it comes to presenting, Jessica, you are it. The ultimate. People want to be interviewed by you, or reviewed, or even remembered. You're admired and respected by both sexes, though perhaps men more than women, which is exactly what we want for a news channel. So, in a nutshell, I want you on camera, not behind it.'

Jessica's expression tightened. 'But you know . . .'

'That it's not what you want. Yes, you made that very plain when you came to see me. You don't like being famous, you never have, and you don't want to be famous any more – that's going to be difficult with Charlie as a husband, but we don't need to go there. I respect your feelings, Jessica, and I understand how hateful it can be having people recognise you all the time, blundering into the middle of conversations in restaurants, feeling free to offer advice you don't want, or photographing you when you'd rather they didn't. I'm sure it's uncomfortable in a hundred ways I don't even know about, and you've come to a time when you want your privacy back – particularly after what happened. And you deserve it, which is why I'm not going to try to make you change your mind about presenting. The trouble is, bringing you in as the producer of a topical arts programme would mean pushing aside those who are currently doing the job. If there were a vacancy, obviously there would be less of a problem, but I would still have to explain to the board why Jessica Moore is not doing what she does best to pull in the ratings. However, that's academic, because there isn't a vacancy. If that changes, obviously we can talk again.' She flashed another smile. 'You have my support, Jessica, please believe that, but as much as I'd like to have a completely free hand in these matters I'm afraid I am answerable to those above me.'

Jessica nodded. 'Of course,' she said quietly, not sure how much of the diatribe she believed, even though she could think of no reason for Melissa to lie. 'I really appreciate you coming to see me,' she said. 'It couldn't have been easy, with us being friends and . . . Well, thank you.'

Melissa got to her feet. 'It's for me to thank you,' she said, putting a hand on Jessica's arm. 'You've taken it very well. You know if there's anything else, anything at all . . .'

Jessica smiled and turned towards the open French doors. As they walked across the garden she considered telling Melissa about her book offer, but decided not to. It wasn't something she was going to do, so what was the point in bringing it up?

At the gate Melissa changed back into her garden rubbers. 'By the way,' she said, popping her Manolos into her bag once more, 'Nikki's doing extremely well. Everyone's very impressed with her,' and with a friendly squeeze of Jessica's arm she started back down the lane.

As she closed the gate Jessica could feel tears burning in her eyes and was angry with herself for minding about the bloody job, when she hadn't really wanted it anyway. Or was it that Melissa's praise for Nikki had been a reminder that she would never hear anyone talk about Natalie that way now?

Hearing the phone ringing inside she hurried back across the garden and picked it up, hoping it would be Charlie, but knowing it couldn't be, because he was on air now.

'Jessica?' a wonderfully familiar voice cried from the other end. 'It's me. How are you?'

'Lilian,' Jessica gasped, feeling more emotional than ever.

'I'm sorry I haven't been in touch for a few days,' Lilian said, 'it's been a madhouse here. Still is, so I can't stay long I'm afraid. I just wanted to check in, find out how everything's going?'

'It's OK, I think. I've just been turned down for a job . . .'

'What? Are you serious?'

'Long story, I'll tell you another time. I've braved the supermarket and been whistled at. Someone's asked me to write a book . . .'

'Stop there, that sounds interesting. What about?'

'What do you think?'

'Ah, I see. Not something you want to get into?'

'No.'

'And how are things with Charlie?'

'The same. Maybe worse, I'm not sure. To tell the truth, I don't know what's happening between us. We seem OK on the surface, but underneath it's different. At least, sometimes it is . . . Anyway, don't let's talk about that. Tell me about you. Are you and Luc still wildly happy and madly in love?'

Lilian's voice was full of laughter as she said, 'Absolutely. He's so wonderful I haven't come up with enough words yet to describe him. He sends his love, by the way. I spoke to him just now, and told him I was going to call you.'

'That's nice of him,' Jessica replied. 'How is he?'

'OK, I think. His father's not too well, so he's in Burgundy at the moment.'

'Nothing serious, I hope.'

'We hope not. He's having some tests. We should get the results next week.'

'Then I'll keep my fingers crossed. And speaking of parents, it seems my mother's done a disappearing act again.'

'Well, there's a surprise. But how do you know? Have you been in touch with her?'

'Absolutely not. I had a call from her neighbour this morning. Apparently she took off ten days or so ago and hasn't been seen or heard from since.'

'Really?' Lilian sounded genuinely concerned.

'Oh come on, you know my mother,' Jessica protested. 'She's probably in Hollywood somewhere thinking she's about to star in some movie, or sailing the South Seas with some besotted billionaire.'

'Actually, come to think of it,' Lilian said, 'I'm sure Luc's father heard from her quite recently. I'm trying to remember when it was, and what he said.'

'Please don't tell me she's making a play for him,' Jessica sighed, feeling her insides starting to sink.

'Well, he's a handsome man with lots of money, so he'd be her type. I can't imagine she'd be in much of a hurry to go back there though, can you?'

'I wouldn't put anything past my mother. Anyway, have you been back lately?'

'Not for a couple of weeks, but I'm trying to get down there tomorrow. Luc and I are hardly seeing each other these days, thanks to our various commitments. This could hardly have been a worse time for my workload to virtually double, because I feel as though I haven't been there for you anywhere near enough. I really want to ask you to come for the summer, but I don't suppose you will, which I understand, of course, but I miss you so much and the cottage is free. Oh listen, I'm being summoned. Sorry. I'll try to call again at the weekend.'

'OK. It's lovely to hear you. As usual, your timing was perfect.'

Lilian immediately sounded concerned. 'Are you having a bad day?' she asked softly.

'It was just a tearful few minutes, nothing more. Go on, you'd better go. Let's speak again soon. Love you.'

'Love you too.'

After ringing off Jessica stood with the phone in her hand staring out at the garden, thinking of Lilian's bright blue eyes and the ready warmth in her smile. She was such a special person, so full of life, yet so calming too – and empathetic in a way Jessica had rarely come across in anyone else. They'd been friends since their childhood in Dorset, so were as close as sisters. They'd even read French at university together, and Lilian was godmother to all – both – her children. They adored her, as did Charlie – in fact everyone loved Lilian, because it was impossible not to, she was just that kind of person, which was why it had never seemed to make any sense that she'd found it so hard to meet the right man. Over the years she'd been far too hurt by far too many unsuitable lovers for it ever to be considered fair. But then, at the ripe old age of thirty-eight, she'd been posted to Paris, and two weeks later Luc Véron had wandered into the saleroom. Six months after that they were married.

And now Jessica missed her so much it hurt.

Chapter Four

Charlie was about to remove his earpiece when a voice from the production gallery said, 'Melissa's asking to see you before you leave.'

He nodded into one of the cameras, letting the director know he'd heard, then pocketing his pen and closing down his laptop, he got up from the newscaster's chair to begin winding his way through the tangle of cables, cameras and booms towards the door. The channel's transmission had now been switched to studio 2, where one of his colleagues was hosting the weekly *Left, Right and Centre* show, while this studio stood down for an hour – though for him it was the end of the shift.

As he headed towards his dressing room one of the subs caught up with him, but he was only half-listening to what the guy was saying as his mind was more occupied with the debate he was to chair at the London School of Economics later that evening. Since it wasn't due to start until nine, he'd have time to go home for dinner, he was thinking, unless he could persuade Jessica to meet him at a restaurant in the centre of town.

Once in his dressing room he dropped everything on the bar, discarded his jacket and tie, and headed for the shower room to rinse off his make-up. He was just dabbing his face with a towel when someone knocked on the door.

'It's open,' he called out.

'Are you alone?' Nikki asked tentatively as she put her head round.

'I am,' he confirmed.

At that the door was flung open and she all but exploded

into the room. 'Oh my God, Dad, you are so not going to believe this.'

'I think I am,' he responded dryly as she made sure the door was closed behind her.

Her smile was pure rapture. 'He's asked me to go for a drink after work,' she declared, squeezing her hands into fists and all but jumping up and down. 'Oh my God, I just can't believe it. I mean, what are we going to talk about? He's so brainy, and up with everything . . . I mean I know he's only just out of uni, but I haven't even started yet, and he's already a reporter . . .'

'Trainee.'

'Yeah, well, same thing. Oh God, I'll just die if I make a fool of myself.'

'You won't,' he assured her, throwing down the towel and going to fetch a clean shirt from the wardrobe.

'But what if I fall over, or choke on my drink, or say something stupid? Oh Dad, I don't know if I want to go now. I mean, I do . . .'

'Have you told Mum?' he interrupted.

'Of course. We've been on the phone for hours. She says I have to stop panicking, because it's not like he's my first boyfriend or anything, but I am like, sooooo nervous. You've got to tell me what to talk about,' she pleaded. 'You're clever, you know everything that's going on in the world. Do you think I should bring up about the report he did today, on education reforms?'

'No, I do not,' Charlie laughed. 'If he wants to tell you about it, let him, but he'll be a dull dog if he does.'

'Then help me out here!' she cried.

'Just let it flow,' he advised. 'And if you feel yourself getting stuck, tell him about your own ambitions to become a reporter.'

'Foreign correspondent,' she stated hotly.

'I stand corrected. Or ask him about himself. But be warned, it's most men's favourite subject, so once you get him started on that you might not be able to shut him up.'

Nikki laughed. 'That's exactly what Mum said.'

'Now why doesn't that surprise me?' he said wryly. 'How was she when you spoke to her?'

'She seemed OK.'

'Did that guy Rufus Keane call back?'

'No idea. I forgot to ask.'

Knowing how self-involved kids were at her age, especially in the first throes of romance, Charlie wasn't even close to surprised. Belatedly remembering that he still didn't know how it had gone between Melissa and Jessica that morning, he picked up his mobile, wanting to hear from Jessica what had happened before talking to Melissa.

However, he was too late, for he'd barely switched the phone back on before there was a knock on the door and Melissa put her head round. 'Are you decent?' she asked. Then seeing Nikki, she came right on in. 'Hi sweetheart,' she drawled, in her habitually lazy tone, 'how are you? I've been hearing great things about the research you did on the housing situation today.'

Nikki glowed.

'I'd like you to attend the morning meeting tomorrow and talk us through it,' Melissa told her. 'And I'm thinking of attaching you to the forward-planning desk starting next week, if that interests you.'

'Absolutely,' Nikki gushed. Her eyes were shining as she turned to her father, but before either of them spoke Melissa said, 'Do I hear you have a date tonight?'

Nikki's cheeks turned crimson as her mouth fell open. 'How do you know?' she demanded.

Melissa laughed. 'Very little gets past me. You should learn that before we go any further.'

'Oh my God, the whole world knows,' Nikki cried, turning in panic to Charlie. 'This is like soooo embarrassing. Oh Dad, I can't go now. Everyone's going to be watching us leave and . . .'

'Get him to meet you in the car park,' Melissa advised. 'Anyway, you don't need to worry too much, I only know because Freddy told me himself that he'd asked you out.'

Both Charlie and Nikki stared at her in amazement. That a trainee reporter would even mention his love life to someone in Melissa's position wasn't only shocking, it was unthinkable.

Melissa's eyes were dancing. 'He's my godson,' she told

them. 'But that really is to stay within these walls. At least for the time being. He doesn't want anyone thinking he got the job because fairy godmummy waved her magic wand, especially when it's not strictly true. He wouldn't be here if he wasn't good, and he went through all the right procedures – but obviously our connection didn't do him any harm. Now, Nikki darling, if you don't mind I need to have a chat with your father before he leaves.'

Nikki looked at Charlie, but he'd already turned towards the bar. 'Wish me luck,' she said.

'You'll knock him off his feet,' Charlie assured her, and glanced over his shoulder as he took two glasses from the cupboard. 'Do you have money for a taxi, if you need one later?'

'Yeah, I'm cool. Um, don't forget to call Mum, will you?' she said. 'She's waiting at home.'

Charlie's eyes widened in surprise, but before he could say anything Nikki had gone.

'Such a lovely girl,' Melissa commented as the door closed behind her. 'She's going places, that's for sure.'

'Just as long as she's not in too much of a hurry,' Charlie responded, pouring two generous shots of vodka into the glasses.

Melissa sauntered over to take the drink, then leaning against the bar she raised her glass to salute him. 'So, a good day in the studio,' she said, letting her eyes run over his face. 'You handled the lost link to Afghanistan with your usual cool.'

'It was just lucky we had the American ambassador sitting right there, already miked up,' he replied. 'It was the obvious place to go.'

She chuckled. 'I don't think he was quite prepared to be hauled over the coals about their . . . disastrous occupation – is that what you called it?'

His eyebrows arched. 'Actually I was quoting Yuri Romanov from *The New York Times*.'

'Well, it certainly rattled him, and it was a great off-the-cuff interview as it turned out, particularly as he'd come in to talk about US handling of racial tensions. It was a pity you let your irritation show when he kept trying to change the subject. Not like you, Charlie.'

A dark colour began spreading over his neck. 'I apologise. It won't happen again.'

'But it's not the first time lately . . .'

'I'm not a schoolboy,' he cut in angrily.

'And I'm not reprimanding. I'm just pointing out that you're still under a great deal of strain, personally, so if you need to take more time off . . . Of course, it'll give us a bit of a problem with summer holidays coming up . . .'

'The last thing I need is time off,' he said sharply. Then added more gently, 'But thanks for the offer.'

'You're welcome.'

Looking down at his own drink, he gave himself a moment to pull back from his anger. After a generous sip, he said, 'I take it you've spoken to Jessica.'

'She didn't tell you?'

'Not yet. So how did it go?'

'Very well. She accepted my decision extremely gracefully – as one would expect from her. As a point of interest though, what would you have done if she'd decided to take an on-screen position?'

'I knew she wouldn't.'

Her chin came up, but she didn't pursue it. Instead she said, 'So, now I've done as you asked, perhaps we can discuss your real reason for not wanting her here.'

His eyes shot to hers as he frowned. 'I've already told you . . .'

'I know what you said on the phone, but I don't think you're being strictly honest with me, Charlie.'

Though his expression remained harsh as he stared back at her, inside he was feeling the heat of discomfort as he realised where this could be going.

'Would your reason for not wanting her here be in any way connected to what you were doing in Paris three months ago?' she asked mildly.

At that his eyes widened in amazement. 'What the hell's that supposed to mean?' he demanded. 'You know exactly what I was doing.'

'Do I? I know you say you were interviewing the leader

of the Syrian Opposition, but I've never seen it.'

'Because it's part of a series of interviews that isn't complete yet,' he informed her. 'What are you driving at? Exactly what are you trying to say?'

She smiled and shrugged. 'I take it you are intending to offer this series to me?' she said, avoiding the question.

'Of course. Who else?'

'I merely wondered, as I haven't seen anything yet.'

His hostility was growing as he looked back at her, while inside he felt sick to his very soul, not because he was lying, but because for some reason she seemed to think he was.

She took a sip of her drink, then smiling again, she said, 'I apologise if I've misunderstood, it's just that I'm getting this feeling you're not giving me the full picture, and I can't imagine your reason for wanting to keep Jessica away from here is because you're afraid she'll find out about our little fling . . .'

His face immediately tightened. 'That was over six years ago . . .'

'Precisely. However, people still talk.' Her eyes were narrowing suspiciously, and as her head tilted to one side he glanced away. 'You know, I rather think I could be on the right track now,' she said, watching him closely. 'But it's not the past you're afraid of, is it . . .' Her eyebrows rose as enlightenment dawned. 'Would you like to sleep with me again, Charlie?' she asked. 'Is that what this is really about?'

'For Christ's sake, Melissa!'

Smiling, she put a finger to his lips. 'It's OK,' she told him. 'I understand perfectly. You've been under a great deal of pressure lately, so if things aren't going too well for you and Jessica on that front . . .'

'Melissa, I'm not going to tolerate this. My private life with Jessica . . .'

'Is your business, of course it is, and I wouldn't dream of asking you to discuss it, but I can quite see now why having Jessica around would complicate matters if I were to . . . How shall we put it? Agree to help you take your mind off things once in a while?'

He took a step back from her, as though repulsed. 'Are

you at all in touch with what you're saying?' he cried angrily. 'After what we've just been through, you can't seriously think I'd cheat on her now.'

'Maybe you wouldn't, but it doesn't mean you don't *want* to.'

'I think we should end this conversation now,' he said abruptly.

'OK, have it your way. But for the record, if you do want to . . .'

'For Christ's sake! How clear do you want me to make this?' he snapped, suddenly exploding. 'I don't want an affair. I'm happy with Jessica, I'd rather die than do anything to hurt her . . .'

'Believe me, it's not my intention either, so maybe we should change the subject. We need to discuss coverage for the upcoming conference on climate change. I issued a preliminary schedule three days ago, so have you had a chance to read it yet?'

'Of course, and I've drafted an email with my suggestions, but we can always discuss it now, if you prefer. I just don't have much time . . .'

'Send me the email, and we'll schedule a meeting,' she said. Then, glancing at his mobile as it started to ring, 'I'll leave you to take that, and I apologise if I've caused any offence. Just bear in mind that I'm your friend, Charlie, not your enemy.'

He watched her walk to the door, open it, then close it behind her, but left alone in the room he still didn't reach for the phone, even though he felt sure it was Jessica. He needed a few moments to get himself together before he spoke to her, to remind himself nothing had actually happened with Melissa. Nor would it. Not now, not ever.

Finally, as the call went through to messages, he picked up the phone and speed-dialled home.

'Sorry,' he said when she answered, 'I was in the shower. Everything OK?'

'I think so,' she replied. 'Have you spoken to Nikki since coming off air?'

He smiled. 'Seems like she's up for a hot date tonight. Did you know Freddy's Melissa's godson, by the way?'

'No. Really? I'm not sure how I feel about that. It sort of makes her family, but not.'

He laughed. 'They haven't even been on their first date yet,' he reminded her.

She laughed too.

'Tell me, were you that nervous the first time we went out?' he asked.

She took a moment to remember. 'I know I kept going to the loo a lot,' she confessed. 'What about you?'

'Actually, I think I was drunk. Jeremy Rockwell was pouring Scotch down me to keep me calm, and then I threw up. So I was either hung-over, or loaded.'

'It didn't show. You must be a better actor than I took you for. Anyway, I was ringing to find out if you're coming home for dinner. Harry's gone off to guitar class with the Fenton twins and won't be back till nine, so it's just us, unless you're not able to make it.'

Before he could answer there was a knock on the door and his assistant put her head round. 'Next week's schedule,' she told him, leaving a copy on the arm of a sofa, then with a wave she went out again. 'Sorry,' he said to Jessica, 'that was Maggie. So where were we? Yes, dinner. How about coming into town?'

'I'd rather not,' she replied.

Unable to stop the dismay he said, 'Won't you at least think about it?'

'I don't need to. We'll only be stared at, or sympathised with, or asked for autographs . . .'

He took a breath to push down his frustration, but it was no use, he was annoyed. 'Jessica, we can't go on like this,' he protested. 'It's crazy, the way you're hiding yourself away . . .'

'I'm trying, OK? I just don't find it easy.'

'I know, darling, but life has to go on, whether we like it or not.'

'I tried to get a job . . .'

'Hiding behind the scenes, instead of going on camera where you belong.'

'No, Charlie, where you belong. I'm over it. I don't want it any more, but please don't let's argue. Just tell me if you're coming home for dinner.'

'Are you going to be mad with me if I say no?'

'Not mad, just disappointed. You've got this LSE thing tonight, haven't you? So what time will you be in?'

'Around midnight. I'll try not to wake you.'

After ringing off he tossed the phone onto a sofa, poured himself another vodka and downed it in one. He wondered how much longer they could go on like this, pretending they weren't drifting apart when they both knew they were. It was his fault, and he knew it, but he didn't know what the hell to do to stop it. He found it so hard to be with her, to see her pain and feel his failure so intensely that he was barely able to function any more. He was letting her down on every front, but worst of all was how he'd been unable to keep their daughter alive. Though he knew in his rational mind that there was nothing he could have done to save Natalie, it didn't change the fact that he'd failed as a father, as surely as he was failing now as a man.

Sighing heavily, he stared down at his glass and resisted the urge to fill it to the brim. His inadequacy was with him every minute of the day now, and starting to show in ways that was making it worse. And all the time Jessica was tying herself up in knots with this damned obsession that her mother still hadn't told the truth about what had happened to Natalie. He wondered if he should find Veronica and get her to try one more time to convince Jessica that nothing sinister had happened that day. But even as he thought it, he knew already he wouldn't do it – and not only because Jessica was incapable of believing a word her mother said, but because having been through the terrible nightmare of it once, he simply couldn't bear to go through it all over again.

Two days later Jessica was at her desk in the study she and Charlie shared, sitting very quietly, not moving, hardly even breathing. Luc had rung a few minutes ago, looking for Charlie, and though she'd only spoken to him briefly, she still couldn't disconnect from the images his call had conjured. She was seeing the *manoir* at Valennes, the vineyard and the grape-picker's cottage where Natalie had died. She could smell the earthy air, see the endless expanse of sky and the vines, neatly planted in tiers over the slopes of the valley. All of it rippled through her in a way that seemed to fuse the broken pieces of her heart, as though Natalie was still there, captured in its beauty, breathing, laughing, running – waiting for her to come.

Catching her breath on a sob she covered her face with her hands, but the images were still there. Natalie as a bridesmaid at Luc and Lilian's wedding, her shining blonde hair streaming down her back, her mischievous eyes glowing with excitement. Natalie dancing at the party afterwards with Luc's niece and nephew, Antoine and Elodie, silly show-off dancing that Charlie had joined in, embarrassing Nikki and making Natalie shriek with delight. Then there was Christmas at the *manoir*, Natalie decorating the tree, opening presents and helping Fernand in the kitchen. The long bike rides they'd taken through the winter-white terrain, Natalie always charging on ahead, so full of life, leading the way, or chasing Antoine and Elodie through the vines while Harry struggled to keep up. They played hide and seek in the *cave*, knock down ginger on Luc's studio where he sculpted, and went searching the woods for birds and bears. Then Natalie was snuggling into Charlie's lap at the cottage, happy and tired, her face smeared in dirt, dry leaves in her hair and a thumb trying to sneak its way into her mouth.

In the end Jessica just let the tears flow. The longing didn't get any easier, it only got worse, and knowing it was the same for Charlie didn't seem to help any more. She didn't know why, she only knew that she wanted her baby back so badly that she was starting to wish her own life was over just so she could be with her again.

Charlie was carrying a pile of Sunday papers out into the garden ready to read after lunch, whilst half-listening to the radio news that was on in the kitchen.

'By the way,' he said, glancing over to where Jessica was planting the begonias she'd bought that morning while he'd had a lie-in, 'did that guy Rufus Keane ever call again? Your mother's neighbour.'

Jessica put down her trowel and gently popped a small plant into the hole she'd scooped into the soil. 'I was wondering when you were going to ask,' she responded.

A brief look of impatience crossed his face – clearly he'd failed again, since she'd obviously been waiting for him to mention it instead of just volunteering the information herself. 'Does that mean he has?' he asked.

As she sat back on her heels his annoyance increased, but then faded. She'd been crying again, he could see it in the redness of her eyes, but there was nothing he could say or do that would give her what she wanted, so he made no comment, only felt trapped in the same wretched sense of helplessness that always came over him when he was aware of her pain.

Before she could answer the phone started to ring inside the house, so being the nearest he went to find out who it was.

Watching him go, Jessica took off her gardening gloves, and used the back of her hand to push the hair from her face. She wasn't surprised, only dismayed, that he'd taken more than a week to ask if Rufus Keane had called back, since it seemed to be almost second nature to him now to avoid any mention of either her mother or Natalie. However, at least he had got round to asking in the end, which she might be able to view as some kind of a breakthrough if she didn't already know better.

Since he continued talking to whoever was on the line, she returned to her planting. Instead of allowing her thoughts to linger on Natalie, she pushed them on to Nikki who was currently not speaking to her, even though it was Charlie who'd told her off for coming home so late last night. As far as Nikki was concerned Jessica had betrayed her by telling him, because only Jessica had been up at that hour, and since she wasn't a child any more they could both just get over themselves and stay out of her face, because she was going to come home any time she liked, thank you very much. In fact, she wouldn't come home at all if they didn't stop going on at her like this, at which point she'd stormed out, leaving Jessica to thank God for Harry, who seemed so happy and uncomplicated compared to the rest of his family that he was probably the only sane one amongst them right now.

Thinking of her son made her heart melt, even as it twisted with unease. He'd been invited to Devon for two and a half weeks starting almost as soon as he broke up from school, which was only eight days away, and she had yet to say he could go. He'd often been away from home before, but this would be the first time since they'd lost Natalie and she didn't know if she could take it. But he so desperately wanted to go – Kieran Grant was his best friend these days, and Kieran's dad had a boat in Salcombe which they could all go sailing on, and Kieran's mum was really cool, because she did things like hang-gliding and potholing and all the things Harry really, really, really wanted to do. 'Please Mum, please, please, please.'

Of course she would have to say yes, and nothing in her wanted to deny her son such an action-packed holiday, but the dread of something happening to him was so huge, she was finding it almost impossible to imagine him coming back in one piece.

'Jessica, you've got to stop this,' Charlie had told her last night, 'or you're going to bring the whole damned world crashing in on us.'

'And exactly what is that supposed to mean?' she'd demanded angrily. 'That the power of my one little mind can make things happen, or is that some kind of prelude to you abandoning us because you can't stand living with me any longer? You think *you're* the whole damned world?'

Holding onto his temper, he'd said, 'I was referring to self-fulfilling prophecies, and I'm beginning to wonder which one you're going to pull off first, because I'm getting the distinct impression you don't want me around here any more.'

'That's just ridiculous.'

'Is it?'

Seeing the confusion in his eyes she'd immediately backed down and gone to put her arms around him, assuring him he had no need to feel like that, because no matter what else was going on between them she still loved him and always would.

'Are we having lunch today?' he asked, coming back into the garden, 'and if so are Harry and Nikki with us?'

'No, they're both out until later,' she replied, 'so it's just us. There's a spinach quiche in the oven. We can have it with salad and new potatoes, if you like.'

'I'll put the potatoes on,' he said, and disappeared back inside.

Sighing, she dropped her trowel, then picking up the discarded plant trays she carried them over to the bin.

'It's OK, I've got everything under control,' he told her as she joined him in the kitchen. 'There's a glass of wine for you there that I was just about to bring out.'

'Thank you,' she said, going to wash her hands. Picking up the glass, she stood watching him chopping tomatoes before slicing into an avocado. She was thinking of how much she'd always loved his hands, so large and masculine, how they could make her feel safe, or sexy or just plain happy. Today she wasn't sure how they were making her feel. 'The answer's yes, Rufus Keane did call back,' she told him.

He carried on arranging avocado slices on a plate, then sprinkled them with lemon juice and black pepper.

'I told him that nothing had changed since the last time he'd called, I still didn't know who else he could contact to find out where my mother might be, apart from Maurice whose number we don't have.'

Charlie glanced at her, then reached past her to the mesclun he'd emptied from a plastic bag into a bowl. 'Are you at all interested in where she might be?' he asked.

'Are you?' she countered.

Pouring a dressing over the leaves he said, 'That's hardly relevant, is it, when she's your mother, and you're the one who doesn't believe her.'

Feeling her temper starting to rise, she said, 'I think we should drop the subject or we're going to end up falling out,' and putting down her glass she began collecting cutlery and plates to set the table outside.

'Did he leave a number?' he asked when she came back in again.

'Who? Rufus Keane? Actually, yes, but . . .'

'Then I'll give him a call.'

'What for? You don't know who her friends are any more than I do.'

'I was thinking,' he responded, 'that at least one of us should share his concern about where she might be.' She started to protest, but he cut across her. 'Have you ever stopped to think what it was like for her, Jessica?' he demanded. 'She was there, she saw it happen and was helpless to do anything about it.'

As her face darkened his voice rose.

'She might be a lot of things, Jessica, but she's not without feeling. She cared for Natalie – she loved her . . . You can't seriously think she'd do anything to harm her . . .'

'I'm not accusing her of murder, for Christ's sake. I'm just saying that the whole truth isn't being told.'

'Then I can't begin to imagine what you think it might be . . .'

'Because you won't ever listen, that's why.'

'I'm not encouraging you in your paranoia . . .'

'You can call it what you like, but remember, you only sleep easier at night because you didn't receive that phone call seconds before she fell. You didn't hear her . . .'

As he looked down at her his face was paling with anger, but she could see the pain in his eyes. Reminding herself that the wrenching loss was his too, and that he really didn't sleep easy at night, she softened her tone as she said, 'I'm sorry. I didn't mean to suggest you don't care.'

'I know. And I'm sorry too.'

She tried to smile, then going to him she slipped her arms around him and rested her head on his chest. 'Do you think we can manage lunch without erupting into another row?'

'I'm definitely up for trying.'

Tilting her head back to look at him, she said, 'Sometimes I feel as though I'm losing you, or at least a sense of who we once were, and it scares me so much.'

Pulling her in close again he said, 'I've told you before, we will get through this, it's just important not to keep trying to push one another away.'

'You're right,' she whispered, feeling certain he was the only one doing that, but not wanting to criticise or upset him again she kept her thoughts to herself.

For the next hour or so, as they sat in the sun, enjoying the food, and drinking a little too much wine, she could sense the easy familiarity between them finally reasserting its hold. Ordinarily on a Sunday, should they find themselves alone like this, they'd go upstairs for a siesta after lunch, but it didn't seem likely they would today, since neither of them was willing to risk it not working, and bringing back the tension between them. Instead, she told him how she was glad the publisher, Karina Rutherford, had postponed their lunch, since it would give her more time to work on the proposal she was planning to put to her. She'd like to do a book, but not the one Karina was suggesting. Instead she'd like to write a part-fact, part-fictionalised biography of Modigliani and his muse, Jeanne Hébuterne. It wasn't a new idea, as she'd been toying with it for years, but until now she'd never had enough time to pursue it.

His response was encouraging enough, though she guessed it wasn't so much the idea that interested him as the hope that any new project might provide the distraction she needed. Since Jeanne Hébuterne's passion for the artist who'd immortalised her had always been a source of great fascination for her, Jessica was ready to believe that she could stay focused for long enough to lose herself entirely in the work she'd have to do.

'By the way,' he said, coming back into the garden with two coffees and a handful of chocolates, 'have you looked at my schedule this week? We're transmitting from Manchester on Wednesday and Thursday.'

'Yes, I noticed that. What's the event?'

'An all-party conference on climate change. I don't suppose you feel like coming?'

She shook her head. 'I have to be here for Harry.'

'I'm sure he'd be only too happy to stay with the Grants, if we asked them.'

Her eyebrows arched. 'They're having him for over two weeks when school finishes,' she reminded him, 'so I don't think we can ask them to take him now. Besides, I'm going to miss him enough when he goes away, so please don't ask me to part with him even sooner than I have to.'

'Well, at least that sounds as though you're allowing him to go to Devon,' he commented mildly.

'Of course I am. He'd never forgive me if I didn't.'

'So why not tell him, instead of putting him through all this angst?'

She frowned. 'What angst? He hasn't said anything to me.'

'But he has to me, and I've already told him he can go.'

Her eyes widened with surprise.

'By holding back your decision you were making him suffer unnecessarily,' he informed her, and picked up one of the tabloids.

Though she was about to deliver a cutting retort she stopped herself as she realised he was right, she had been withholding her decision unnecessarily, thanks to an inability to commit to anything that would take her children from her side. 'I should have realised you had when he stopped plaguing the life out of me,' she said, attempting a sardonic tone.

His eyes flicked in her direction, then returned to the paper.

'So, what time are you due at the studios?' she asked, a while later. 'I thought we might go for a walk in Holland Park.'

'I'm happy sitting here,' he responded, keeping his eyes on the page. 'Why don't you read the papers? You haven't picked one up today.'

A playful light came into her eyes. 'Is it safe?' she asked.

He frowned and looked at her. 'What do you mean, safe?'

She shrugged. 'Well, I'd hate to find out you were playing away through one of the Sundays.'

At that his expression turned thunderous, and putting down the paper he got to his feet. 'That has to be one of the stupidest things I've heard you say yet,' he snarled.

Her face turned crimson. 'Of course it was. I'm sorry,' she cried. 'I just didn't think. Charlie, come back, please . . .'

But he was already inside the house, and a few minutes later she heard the front door slam shut behind him.

Guessing he'd go straight to the studios, she decided to give him a while to calm down before calling to apologise again. It really had been the stupidest thing to say, and she couldn't even think now what had made her come out with it, especially when she didn't suspect him of being unfaithful at all – she never had. They'd always been far too close for that, and considering the problems he was having lately she could only cringe now at having shown such an atrocious lack of sensitivity. Still, she barely knew what was driving her these days, so it wasn't likely she could understand what had got into her then, she only knew that she mustn't let him go on air with this still simmering between them – nor was she going to allow Harry to go on not knowing that he had both parents' permission for his holiday. As soon as he came in she'd make a big deal about having to hurry up and buy everything he needed to take with him, which, she realised with sinking dismay, was going to mean another journey out to the shops alone – unless she ordered everything via the Internet, as she'd started to do for the groceries again.

Deciding to do a spot of surfing ready for when he came in, she carried the dishes into the kitchen, loaded them up, and was just climbing the stairs to the study when the phone started to ring. Surprised Charlie was calling her so soon, she ran the rest of the way and grabbed the cordless on his desk before he had time to ring off.

'Jessica! Hi, it's me.'

'Lilian!' Jessica replied delightedly. 'What a lovely surprise. You've got the most wonderful knack of calling at just the right time.'

'More bad moments?' Lilian said darkly.

'Not the kind you're thinking. Anyway, where are you? Did you manage to get down to Burgundy for the weekend?'

'That's where I am,' Lilian confirmed. 'And Luc's in Paris, would you believe, but he'll be back tomorrow. Talk about ships in the night, but I've managed to wangle the week off, so we'll at least get to spend Monday and Tuesday together – and then, my darling, I'm going to be there, with you. If you're free.'

Jessica's heart leapt with joy. 'Oh my God, that's fantastic news,' she cried. 'I haven't seen you for so long. Are you sure Luc doesn't mind?'

'He's fine with it,' Lilian assured her, 'but I'm afraid it'll only be for one night. I want to be back here on Thursday, because his father's test results are due on Friday.'

'Of course. One night is more than I'd dare hope for, and as luck would have it Charlie's going to be away on

Wednesday, so we can do exactly as we please. I might even venture out to a restaurant, because I'm less likely to be recognised if I'm with you. Oh, Lily, this is so wonderful. I can hardly wait.'

'Me neither. I've missed you so much these past few months.'

At that Jessica's smile wavered. 'Do you realise we haven't seen each other since Natalie's funeral?'

'Of course I do,' Lilian responded. 'And I feel absolutely terrible about it . . .'

'I didn't say it for that reason,' Jessica jumped in. 'Honestly, just talking to you on the phone makes me feel more able to cope. So tell me where you're flying into and I'll pick you up.'

'There's a flight from Lyon straight into Heathrow arriving at eleven twenty. Is that OK?'

'I'll be there.'

'Great, now is there anything you'd like me to bring? Fernand has already boxed up a few bottles of his best wine.'

'Fantastic. We'll definitely see a couple of those off. Incidentally, did you ever ask him about that call from my mother?'

'As a matter of fact I did. He thinks it was around the beginning of June, because he remembers it was when he first started feeling unwell. Apparently she was asking if she could stay at the grape-picker's cottage for a few days. He said yes, but then he never heard from her again.'

Jessica was frowning. 'Why did she want to go there?' she asked. 'I'd have thought she'd never want to see the place again.'

'So would I. Maybe it seemed like a good idea, some kind of therapy or something, but in the end she decided she couldn't face it.'

'Mm,' Jessica responded, wondering how to voice her suspicions.

'Anyway, this is just a fleeting call,' Lilian told her. 'I'm taking Fernand over to Daniella's for the evening. Between you and me I think the poor guy's terrified of what might be wrong with him, so he's making the most of his grandchildren while he can.'

'Then please send Daniella my love,' Jessica said. 'As sisters-in-law go, I think you struck gold. Actually, with husbands too, but don't tell Luc I said that or it might go to his head.'

Lilian laughed. 'You haven't done so badly yourself,' she reminded her. 'I'm sorry I won't see him on Wednesday, but hopefully all four of us can get together soon.'

After ringing off Jessica quickly connected to the Internet, then picked up the phone to call Charlie.

'Can you talk?' she said when he answered.

'Not for long, but I'm sorry I walked out on you.'

'Oh darling, it's for me to apologise, not you,' she told him earnestly. 'It really was the stupidest thing to say, and it wasn't meant to hurt you . . .'

'I know. These things just come out the wrong way sometimes, and when I consider some of the things I've said and done that have hurt you in the past . . .'

'You've never hurt me,' she assured him.

Instead of laughing, as she'd expected, he sounded almost sad as he said, 'I only wish that were true, but it was never intentional, I hope you know that.'

'Of course I do. Now, before you go, I've some good news. Lilian is coming over on Wednesday and you know how she always manages to cheer us up. It's just a pity you won't be able to see her too.'

'What's important,' he responded, 'is that you do – and with any luck she'll be able to talk some sense into you about what happened that day.'

Jessica immediately tensed. 'Maybe you're right,' she replied, 'or maybe she'll be able to tell me by then why my mother contacted Fernand at the beginning of June with the intention of going back there, because frankly I find that a little odd, even if you don't.'

There was only silence from the other end.

'Are you still there?' she asked.

'Yes, I'm here,' he answered. 'I should go now though, I'm due on air in five minutes.'

'OK, let's avoid the issue,' she retorted. 'We might as well, because we're clearly never going to see eye to eye.'

He sighed wearily. 'Give me Rufus Keane's number when

I get home,' he said. 'I'll do what I can to find Veronica, and we'll speak to her again. Will that make you happy?'

Only slightly mollified, she said, 'I wouldn't use the word happy, but I'm glad you're finally prepared to accept I might have a point.'

Though he hadn't actually said that, he didn't argue. 'I'll call you when I take a break. It should be around seven.'

'OK. But before you go . . .'

He waited.

'I love you,' she said.

After a pause he said, 'I love you too,' and a moment later they both hung up.

Chapter Five

'Hey, Mum! Have you seen this?' Nikki cried, grinning all over her face as she bounded into the kitchen clutching one of the morning tabloids. 'Dad's only made it into the list of the nation's sexiest men. I mean, there have got to be a lot of weird people out there to have voted for him, don't you think?'

Charlie's head came up from *The Times,* as Jessica chuckled into her cornflakes.

'Has he got his clothes on?' Harry demanded. 'If he hasn't everyone's going to see his willy.'

As he sniggered and spluttered Jessica patted his back, while reminding him that everyone had seen his at the pool last night, when he'd dived in and lost his trunks. Then to her surprise Nikki treated her to a resounding kiss on the cheek as she passed, making her wonder what she'd done to find herself back in favour after the sulking and backchatting of the past few days.

'So where do I rate?' Charlie wanted to know, clearly ready to enjoy his new status as a sex symbol.

'Ninety-eight out of a hundred,' Nikki informed him.

Charlie's face dropped.

'Just joking,' Nikki grinned. 'You're at number seven. Can you believe it?'

'Out of how many?' Jessica asked, reaching for the paper.

'Twenty, which isn't bad. It means you're a hunk, Dad.'

'Is that like the Incredible Hunk on UK Gold?' Harry wanted to know.

Jessica and Nikki burst out laughing. 'Exactly like that,' Nikki informed him, planting a kiss on the end of his nose.

'You can mock,' Charlie grumbled, 'but at least I have a public out there who appreciate me, even if you lot don't.'

'But they don't have to live with you,' Nikki reminded him. 'We know what you're really like.'

'Yeah, because you're always bursting out of your trousers,' Harry piped up.

At that even Charlie had to laugh, and it was quite some time before Nikki and Jessica could keep a straight face.

'Did you speak to Lilian last night?' Jessica asked Nikki, going back to her breakfast.

'Oh yeah, and she was totally cool about me not being here today. I explained I had to go to Manchester with Dad, because I'm helping out on the programme . . .'

'With me?' Charlie interrupted. 'I think you mean Freddy, don't you?'

'OK, he's going too,' Nikki conceded, 'but that's got nothing to do with it. Jackie Brazier, the producer, thought I did a very good job with the background I prepared on America's stand on environment issues, so it was her idea for me to go.'

Charlie eyed her sceptically.

'That is so true,' she cried. 'Mum, tell him it's got nothing to do with Freddy.'

'He knows,' Jessica assured her. 'He's just winding you up.'

'Can I come too?' Harry asked, spilling Weetabix on the paper that declared Charlie's sexiness.

'You've got school,' Jessica reminded him. 'And it's the final practice for sports day, which you won't want to miss.'

'Yeah, yeah,' Harry shouted, standing on his chair and being the champ. 'You're coming, aren't you Dad?'

'Not today,' Charlie responded.

'No, for sports day next week.'

'Of course. Maggie's already put it in my schedule.'

Harry's mind did one of the leaps Jessica adored – except in this instance she'd have preferred it not to. 'Mum, can we have a dog?'

'Not today,' she answered.

'No, but like soon. I want one the same as Lilian and Luc's. I'm going to call it Alan.'

'Alan?' Nikki scoffed. 'You can't call a dog Alan.'

'Well it's better than having a ball of wool called Timmy, like Mum did when she was little,' Harry retorted.

Nikki's eyes moved to Jessica's. 'He's got a point,' she said, as Charlie got up and kissed Jessica on the top of the head as he passed.

'That wasn't very sexy,' Jessica commented, winking at Nikki.

'The hunk can't be incredible all the time,' he responded smoothly. 'Now, if you're coming with me, Nikki, the car should be here any . . .'

'Mum's taking me,' Nikki jumped in.

Charlie stopped and turned back. 'You get a lift and I don't?' he enquired.

'I've got some things I need to talk to her about,' Nikki explained. 'I'll meet you at the airport. No, don't start insisting on coming with us. It's girl stuff and you won't be interested.'

He glanced at Jessica, then getting a picture of what was going on, he said, 'Terminal One. You'll find me easily enough when you get there, I'll be the one being mobbed by blondes.'

'In your dreams,' Nikki mumbled, rolling her eyes.

'Come on you,' Jessica said to Harry. 'Upstairs and dress. Barry Kenn's mum is carpooling today and you know she's always early.'

'Can I take the paper in for show and tell about Dad?' he asked, brushing off the milk and Weetabix.

Jessica hesitated. 'Maybe not,' she replied.

'Why don't you take Timmy instead,' Nikki suggested, 'and show everyone all the tricks you've taught him?'

Harry looked perplexed.

'Whose side are you on?' Jessica muttered.

'Always yours,' Nikki assured her. 'That was a momentary lapse. I'll go and finish my packing.'

An hour later Jessica was at the wheel of her Mercedes 4×4 speeding along the M4. Nikki sat beside her, alternately texting and talking and repeating herself ad nauseam, as was her wont these days. 'So like, you're totally OK about me doing it with Freddy,' she was saying, 'I mean if it turns out that way? I mean, it's not like I need your permission or anything, but you're so brilliant, I can talk to you about anything and this is like, really important.'

'I didn't say I was OK about it,' Jessica corrected, 'I said you should make sure it's what you really want before you do it, and don't even think about it unless you've got some form of protection. Frankly, I think you should wait a bit longer. You've only been seeing him a couple of weeks, and I'm not . . .'

'Oh Mum, you are like so in the Dark Ages,' Nikki groaned. 'Everyone does it on the first night now. Some of my friends even have shag-buddies.'

Jessica cast her a look.

'I'm not saying I do,' Nikki cried. 'For God's sake, I'm still a virgin, which like makes me such a freak. I mean, everyone's already done it, except me. I came really close with Dan Avery when I was seeing him, well you know that, but we never went the whole way. I wish I had now, maybe then I wouldn't be so nervous about doing it with Freddy. Oh Mum, I bet he's been with loads of girls already, he's going to end up thinking I'm such a child . . .'

'Does he know you're still a virgin?'

'No way!' Nikki exclaimed in horror. 'He thinks I'm like really out there, and dead cool for my age.' She turned to Jessica with an expression of anguish, though nothing could hide the glittering excitement in her eyes. 'What if I can't go through with it, Mum? I mean, I know I will, but what if I can't?'

'You're really not sounding very ready for this,' Jessica ventured, already bracing herself for the response.

'I so am,' Nikki almost shouted. Then in an urgently plaintive voice, 'I really, really like him, Mum. He's so cool and intelligent and funny. And you and Dad like him too, so it's not as if I've chosen someone like totally unsuitable.'

'If you do go through with it, he's going to know you're a virgin,' Jessica reminded her.

Nikki's eyes closed. 'I am so going to die if that freaks him out,' she declared. 'Do you think it will?' Before Jessica could answer her hands flew to her face. 'Oh Mum, this is like so complicated. I can't do it. I just can't.'

Jessica's only response was to cast her another look, which

Nikki seemed not to notice, and for a while she went back to texting her friends.

'Do you think he'll have condoms?' Nikki suddenly blurted. 'I mean you're right about protection, so do you think I should get some myself? Will you buy them for me when we get to the airport? I can't buy them myself. Oh God, that would be so embarrassing.'

'What happened to the ones I gave you on your sixteenth birthday?' Jessica asked.

'Oh, like nearly two years ago,' Nikki retorted. 'Have you never heard of sell-by dates? Anyway, I donated them to worthy causes, namely Sonya, Marina, Leila . . .'

Jessica's eyebrows rose. 'Well, I'm sure Freddy will have some,' she said, 'but just in case I'll ask Dad to get . . .'

'Are you insane? You can't ask him,' Nikki shrieked. 'He'll go ballistic if he finds out they're for me, and you can hardly say they're for you.'

'He'd rather you had some than you didn't,' Jessica pointed out, though she had to concede, as liberal as Charlie was, he'd probably rather not play even a peripheral role in his precious daughter's big event. 'There might be a machine in the Ladies when we get there,' she said hopefully. 'Anyway, you were most insistent earlier that this trip had nothing to do with Freddy, which is not how it's sounding now.'

'I'm just preparing for all eventualities,' Nikki retorted, reading a text. 'Mostly it's going to be about work, obviously. I am so into this environment thing. It's really scary. Didn't you chair some debate about it a few months ago? I wish I'd remembered that sooner, I could have asked you to help with my research. Oh my God, Freddy's just sent me a text saying good morning. Isn't that cool? He is like so romantic.'

Jessica started to laugh.

'What's so funny?' Nikki demanded, looking at her.

'Nothing,' Jessica replied, indicating to pull onto the Heathrow slip road. 'I'm going to miss you while you're away.'

Nikki's mood instantly changed. 'Oh, no, please don't start with all that,' she begged.

'All what?'

'Making me feeling guilty about leaving you. You'll be fine, and Lilian's going to be here . . .'

'I was just saying that I'll miss you,' Jessica interrupted.

'But what you were meaning is you're scared something might happen to me, so really you'd rather I stayed at home where you can take care of me. Well, I'm going to be fine. And Dad'll be there, for heaven's sake, so you don't have to keep worrying.'

'Actually, I wasn't saying it for any other reason than the house is going to seem a bit empty without you.'

Nikki let her head fall back against the seat. 'Now I feel really guilty for being mean to you,' she grumbled. But clearly her mind was darting about like lightning for she suddenly said, 'Have you and Dad ever used condoms? Do you know how to put one on? And don't you dare say ask Dad.'

Jessica gave a splutter of laughter. 'Nikki, I dread to think what kind of state you're going to be in by the time this evening comes round,' she replied. 'Just try to calm down, because if you end up irritating Dad while he's working it could spoil the entire two days for you.'

'That is so true,' Nikki conceded. 'Oh God, just imagine if he told me off in front of Freddy.' The very prospect of it sobered her completely. 'I wish I wasn't going now,' she said glumly. 'I'd rather stay at home with you and Lilian. I wonder if she knows how to put a condom on a man.'

'I think,' Jessica replied, her eyes twinkling, 'you'd better let Freddy take care of the condom business. And tell him up front that you've never done it before. It'll probably mean quite a lot to him.'

Nikki gawped at her as though she were mad. 'Yeah like, which fairy tale are you living in? It doesn't work like that any more. People just do it. It's no big deal.'

'Then what are you getting so worked up about?'

Nikki stayed silent then, giving no indication where her thoughts might be going, until they were out of the car and walking into the terminal. 'So what you're saying is just be honest?' she said, as they looked around for Charlie and the others.

'It usually works best,' Jessica told her.

'So like, you and Dad are always honest with each other?'

'I think so,' Jessica replied. 'At least we try to be.'

When Nikki didn't answer Jessica turned to look at her, and seeing how her expression had tightened she said, 'What's the matter?'

Nikki shrugged. 'Nothing,' she answered. 'There's Dad, over there. Come on, let's go and join him.'

Seeing them coming, Charlie interrupted what he was saying to Melissa and moved round her to meet them. 'So you made it,' he said, handing Nikki a copy of the schedule. 'I know this isn't about Freddy,' he murmured as Jessica and Melissa greeted one another, 'but he's with the crew in Costa, if you're looking for him.'

'It's OK, thanks,' she said haughtily, 'I'll catch up with him later,' then making sure no-one was looking she poked out her tongue as she tucked an arm through her mother's.

'Charlie says you're here to pick up a friend,' Melissa was saying to Jessica.

Jessica grimaced. 'I've got a bit of a wait, but madam here wanted her own personal service to the airport. I'm surprised to see you. You don't normally go on the OBs, do you?'

'Absolutely not, but there are going to be several influentials at this conference that it'll be, let's say politic, to catch up with. Having them all in the same place for a couple of days saves me the time and trouble of tracking them down individually.'

'Of course,' Jessica responded. 'Is Paul taking part?'

'No, he's in Washington until Saturday, so fortunately I don't have to mess about with wifely duties, I can just be the big boss for forty-eight hours.' Then after waiting for an airport announcement to end, 'I hear you've decided to write a book on Modigliani's muse.'

Jessica looked at Charlie. 'Well, nothing's definite yet,' she replied, not thrilled that he'd discussed it with someone already.

'They'll jump at it,' Charlie assured her, clearly wishing Melissa hadn't brought it up.

Melissa was watching them closely, until noticing Nikki's scowl her eyes narrowed slightly.

'Actually, I'm glad to see you,' Jessica said, 'we're hoping you and Paul might be free for dinner on the 30th.'

Melissa looked pleased. 'I'll have to check the calendar,' she responded, 'but if we are, we'd love to come. Your dinner parties are always such fun. I've often remarked to Charlie that of all of us, you're absolutely the best hostess.'

Slightly taken aback by such effusiveness, Jessica shot a look at Charlie, but he was answering a call on his mobile and seemed not to have heard. 'Thank you,' she mumbled, perhaps a touch ungraciously, but it wasn't an accolade she'd ever particularly desired, unlike many of their more competitive friends.

'And as usual you look gorgeous today,' Melissa informed her, with a sweeping glance over the neutral-coloured shirt and jeans with a white string-strap T-shirt underneath.

Blinking, Jessica said politely, 'So do you,' though striking as Melissa looked in her tight red dress with halter neck and matching high heels, she knew very well it wasn't an outfit she'd have chosen for herself.

With a grin Melissa glanced down at her cleavage, 'Yes, well, I do my best,' she replied. Then, taking Charlie's arm as he finished his call, she said, 'I guess it's time we were off. I'd like to say I'll deliver him back in the same condition I found him in, but I'm not making any promises,' and with a bawdy wink she started to lead Charlie towards the self-check-in.

Jessica stared after them, dumbfounded, until Charlie gently eased his arm free and turned back for a proper farewell. 'I should think so,' she muttered, as he pulled her into an embrace.

'Don't tell me you're jealous,' he teased, looking down into her eyes.

'Of Melissa? I don't think so.'

He chuckled, and after kissing her briefly on the mouth, he said to Nikki, 'Come on, Miss Blue-eyed Girl, you can start by carrying my bag and fetching me a coffee.'

Nikki turned to her mother. 'Don't worry, Mum,' she said, 'I'll make sure he comes back in the exact same condition he's leaving in.'

Jessica's eyes were dancing. 'Ah yes,' she responded, 'but will *you*?' and as Nikki blushed and laughed, she gave her a hug before heading off to the bookshop for a nice leisurely browse before Lilian's flight came in.

The strangest thing happened in the moments after Jessica and Lilian virtually ran into each other's arms – for the first time in all the years they'd been friends, Jessica sensed a slight awkwardness in Lilian. It passed quickly and within minutes it was as though it hadn't happened at all, but it had been enough for Jessica to feel afraid that even her best friend was going to start treating her like some damaged and delicate soul, the way so many others had since Natalie had gone. However, Lilian's vivid blue eyes and engagingly ironic smile were soon convincing her that the awkwardness was no more than a fleeting stab of her friend's conscience for not being around more often, or perhaps it was even a trick of Jessica's imagination, for all the closeness they'd shared over the years was very quickly starting to work its magic.

'You look fantastic,' Jessica told her, as they walked arm in arm through the crowded arrivals hall to the car park. And Lilian did, for the energy that seemed to flow from her creamy soft skin and abundant glossy brown hair was as radiant as it was infectious, while the sumptuous curves of her figure showed that French life was suiting her well.

'And you've lost weight,' Lilian stated bluntly. 'Charlie told me you had, but you still manage to look gorgeous, God damn you.'

'You've spoken to Charlie?' Jessica asked in surprise.

Lilian's smile was sheepish. 'I call him from time to time, just to check how you are,' she confessed. 'I feel I might get a more honest answer from him.'

Jessica rolled her eyes. 'I might have known,' she said, and opening the boot for Lilian's overnight bag she struggled to help her lift it in. 'What on earth have you brought with you?' she gulped.

'Wine,' Lilian reminded her, 'and gifts for Harry and Nikki. I'm sorry I won't see her, but I believe there's an important event she simply has to be there for.'

Knowing it was absurd to mind that there was no gift for Natalie, Jessica hid the pang with a laugh, and said, 'She told you about Freddy?'

'At length. Were we like that at her age? Short on vocabulary and repeating the bit we knew a thousand times over?'

'No, we were erudite, scintillating and altogether perfect,' Jessica assured her. 'Now, what would you like to do? Straight to the house, or lunch at Harvey Nicks followed by a big spend, or . . . anything at all.'

'Paris takes care of all my shopping needs,' Lilian replied. 'So let's go home and get smashed in the garden.'

Less than an hour later they were popping the cork of a crisp dry white burgundy to accompany one of Delia's scrumptious summer salads, and setting it all out in the garden. 'Oh God, it's so blissful here,' Lilian sighed dreamily, as she flopped into a chair under the sun-dappled leaves of a silver maple. 'Remind me why I left London. Oh yes, I remember, it was something to do with a job.'

'And look what happened,' Jessica responded, her eyes glowing with affection. 'So tell me about Luc. Is it still wonderful between you – as if I need to ask?'

Lilian's expression softened in a way that conveyed even more than her words as she said, 'I can still hardly believe it. He's everything I ever dreamed of, and more.'

Easily able to picture Luc's unmistakably Gallic features and the sheer romance the couple seemed to exude when they were together, Jessica sipped her wine and felt the warmth of pleasure for the happiness that was making Lilian so captivatingly lovely.

'I know you know this, and I've said it a thousand times before,' Lilian continued, 'but I'd virtually given up hope of ever meeting anyone. And now to think of how my life has changed . . . Did I tell you they're thinking about promoting me to managing director, by the way?'

Blinking at the sudden change of subject, Jessica said, 'No, but that's wonderful. Isn't it?'

Lilian laughed. 'Of course. The only trouble is it's going to mean more travelling and I already don't see enough of Luc.'

'And what does he think about that?'

'He understands what a fantastic opportunity it is, so he's right behind me.' Though dimples showed as she smiled, she looked away with what seemed to be the tiniest flicker of doubt in her eyes. 'I only need to take it for a couple of years,' she continued. 'As Luc says, at least then I won't look back and regret giving up the opportunity to go to the top.'

Frowning, Jessica said, 'Why am I getting the impression you're not overjoyed by the prospect?'

Lilian seemed surprised. 'Oh no, I am,' she assured her. 'I'd just prefer it if he were free to travel with me.'

'Doesn't it help with him being freelance?'

'It would if he were still a photojournalist, but he's having to spend a lot of time in Burgundy now, helping his father take care of the vineyard. But he loves to be at home, doing his thing with the wine, creating his art, reading his books, you know what he's like, so it's no great hardship for him to be away from Paris.'

'But it is to be away from you?'

Lilian nodded and twinkled. 'However, we certainly make up for it when we're together,' she declared with a waggle of her eyebrows. 'I'm here to tell you that everything they say about Frenchmen is true, they are wonderful lovers – well, Luc is, and as far as I'm concerned, he's the only one that counts.'

Jessica swallowed as she smiled. 'So do you still plan to have a family?' she asked, as Lilian drank.

To her surprise Lilian coloured slightly, and didn't quite meet her eyes as she said, 'Yes, but . . . Well, you know . . . I'm sure it'll happen soon enough.'

Jessica waited for her eyes to come to hers, but they took too long. 'Lily? Is there something you're not telling me?' she probed gently.

Lilian seemed startled. 'No, why?' she responded brightly.

'You just seem . . . I'm not sure . . . There is something, isn't there?'

As Lilian looked down at her glass some of the warmth seemed to drain from her smile.

'Lily,' Jessica prompted, 'we've always shared everything, so whatever it is, you know you can tell me.'

Lilian's mouth trembled slightly as she shook her head.

'Oh no,' Jessica said, reaching for her hand, 'were you pregnant again?'

It took Lilian a moment to fight back the tears. 'It's OK,' she said, 'these things happen.'

'But why didn't you tell me?'

Lilian took a breath. 'In the face of what you were going through, it seemed so . . . unimportant, and the last thing I wanted was to burden you with my problems. I'll get over it.' She forced a smile. 'I already am. I just think about it now and again . . . Well, it's best not to really. Like the first time it happened, it was probably meant to be.'

'How did Luc take it?'

'He didn't say much, but I think he was pretty devastated. He wants children almost as much as I do . . . Well, you've seen him with his niece and nephews – I'm sure that's half the attraction of being in Burgundy.'

Jessica was watching her closely, certain she was still hiding something, but then Lilian was dabbing her eyes and laughing as she refilled their glasses. 'I'm afraid it's the time of the month,' she confessed, 'which is why I'm so emotional – another missed opportunity, and I've been working so hard, I'm exhausted, so please take no notice of me. I'm really happy to be here. I've missed you so much.'

Jessica picked up her glass. 'The feeling's mutual,' she assured her, and deciding not to push her any further for the moment, she said, 'So tell me about Fernand, and these tests he's having.'

As Lilian talked, moving from Fernand to Daniella, Luc's sister, to Luc and everything that was happening at the vineyard, Jessica could feel the pull of it stirring warmly inside her. She'd completely fallen in love with Valennes on the two occasions they'd visited, before they'd lost Natalie. It had seemed so idyllic, and set apart from the madness of the world that surrounded it – and once again she started to feel that she might reconnect with Natalie there in a way she'd been unable to here.

'Tell me,' she said to Lilian, as they pushed aside their plates and sat back to enjoy the rest of the wine, 'do *you* think my mother was entirely truthful about what happened to Natalie?'

Lilian took a breath and let it out slowly.

'You do, don't you?' Jessica prompted, hearing the

stiffness in her voice as she uttered the words. Then, aware of how difficult she was finding Lilian's failure to support her, she said, 'I thought you of all people would back me on this. I know what I heard in Natalie's voice, Lily. Something wasn't right. She was afraid . . .'

'But of what?' Lilian implored.

'That's what I need to find out. I keep hearing her . . . I know you're going to think I'm crazy, but sometimes I feel as though she's still trying to reach me . . . OK, that sounds like the deluded ramblings of a bereaved mother – a guilty mother even, because I should never have let her go without me – but I'm telling you, something happened to scare her, or at the very least upset her and I need to find out what it was.'

Lilian's eyes were warm with sympathy as she looked at her.

'I'm missing something, Lily,' Jessica said, her hands clenching on the table. 'I feel certain of it. It's as though it's right there, staring me in the face, but I'm just not seeing it. Of course, my mother could tell me what it is, and if I thought she would, believe me, I'd be out there looking for her now.'

'So still no news on where she is?'

Jessica shook her head. 'Charlie called her neighbour the other day, this Rufus Keane guy, and asked him to let us know if he hears anything, but we haven't had a call back.'

An even deeper concern was showing in Lilian's eyes. 'I know it's always been like her to drop off the radar for a while,' she said, 'but I'm with Charlie on this, I think she was devastated by what happened to Natalie . . .'

'And now she can't face me any more,' Jessica cut in. 'Well, let her stay wherever the hell she is, because I never want to see her again, unless she's prepared to tell me what really happened to my baby.'

Lilian looked away for a moment, but she was clearly still troubled. 'Jessica, this isn't doing you any good,' she said gently. 'There was a full investigation . . . Everyone accepts that she fell . . .'

'I accept that too,' Jessica cried. 'It's what happened prior to the fall that concerns me. Why was she afraid, and why did my mother shout "no"?'

'Because she could see what was about to happen. It's a very natural thing to do.'

Jessica turned her head sharply away as though rejecting the very words, and for a while there was only the sound of the birds, mingling with the musical tinkling of wind chimes that Natalie had hung the summer before, and the distant purr of traffic two blocks away. Then Jessica became aware of the same tightness in her chest that always came when she was close to the edge. The grief and longing were so intense they seemed to be tugging at the very core of her, as though Natalie was right there inside her, an unborn child again, needing her, depending on her, and convincing her that they were still an intrinsic part of one another. They shared a bond that only a mother and child could. It was beyond anyone else's comprehension, and in some ways perhaps it was beyond hers too.

'Go and sit in her room,' she said to Lilian in the end. 'See if you feel anything. You were always so close to her . . .'

Lilian swallowed hard as the light dimmed in her eyes. 'Oh Jessica,' she murmured, 'I don't think . . . I'm not as tuned into that kind of thing as you. You were her mother . . .'

'Then will you accept that as her mother I might feel something the rest of you can't?'

Lilian nodded slowly. 'But I still have to remind you that the police and paramedics . . . No, OK, I know you know that . . . But unless you talk to your mother again . . .'

After a beat Jessica's eyes came back to Lilian's. 'I could go back to the grape-picker's cottage,' she said. 'I was so distraught the last time I was there . . . I might have overlooked something . . .'

Lilian's expression showed her dismay. 'You know you can come any time you like,' she said, 'but I've been into that cottage a dozen times since . . . If there were anything to find, I'm sure I'd have seen it.'

'But how could you, when we don't even know what we're looking for?'

Lilian had no answer to that.

Jessica watched her empty the last of the wine into their

glasses. 'You think I'm losing it, don't you?' she said with a flatness that conveyed her pain.

'No, but I do know it's virtually impossible to get over the death of a child, and it's not even four months yet.'

'Do you think it's odd that I want to go back to the cottage?'

Instead of answering, Lilian said, 'Have you mentioned it to Charlie?'

Jessica sighed. 'No, I haven't,' she answered, 'because I already know that he never wants to set foot in the place again.'

'Which is perfectly understandable. It's how a lot of people would feel, in the circumstances.'

Jessica rose abruptly to her feet. 'But I don't,' she said shortly.

As she walked into the house to answer the phone Lilian sat back in her chair, watching her with a heaviness in her heart that was hard to bear. Never before had they had secrets from one another, but this was one Lilian had to keep because if Jessica ever did find out the truth, it would almost certainly end up destroying her – and without Jessica Lilian had to fear for them all.

Chapter Six

Charlie was alone in his suite at the Lowry Hotel, going through the evening's bulletin sheet which, apart from the rest of the day's domestic and international news, featured several live interviews with conference delegates, a satellite link-up with a US senator who apparently had plenty to say about climate change, and a videophone chat with a reporter who was calling in from Greenland's melting ice cap.

Since there was nothing beyond the expected, he dropped the running order on the bed and went to stand at the floor-to-ceiling window, his hands stuffed in his pockets as he stared down at the river that was glistening silvery-white in the late afternoon sun. His mind was so full of the conference, and its opening speeches, that he'd all but forgotten he was due to have drinks with Melissa in her room – at least, that was what he was telling himself. In truth, he knew very well she was waiting for him now, that there was every chance she'd already poured the vodkas, and might even have told the switchboard to put her calls on hold.

Of course, he could have read her invitation wrongly. After all, tomorrow's schedule had to be discussed at some point, and there was every possibility she was calling for a full presenters' meeting in her suite, not just a one-on-one with him. If that were the case, it would be very remiss of him not to show. On the other hand, if she was intending to deliver on the promise she'd been throwing out all day with her innuendoes as well as her eyes, it would be like announcing it to the world if he were to ask anyone else if they were going, and they knew nothing about it.

He wasn't surprised when the knock came on his door, but

it filled him with dismay. If it turned out to be her, he'd have to find a way of letting her down without incurring her wrath, for the last thing he needed right now was to make an enemy of his executive producer. However, any misplaced desire he might have had to try to prove himself with her had well and truly vanished, because he really didn't want to have sex with her at all.

Going to the door, he pulled it open and was about to step outside rather than take the risk of letting her in, when the wind was all but knocked from him as Nikki came breezing in, saying, 'Hey Dad, I've got Mum on the phone. If you ask me she's a bit tipsy, but I thought you'd like to say hi.'

Still blinking, Charlie took the mobile she was handing him and watched her kick the door closed behind her before making off to the bathroom. Then putting the phone to his ear he said, 'Hi darling, are you and Lilian having a good time?'

'Fantastic,' Jessica answered. 'How about you? How's it going up there?'

'So far, so good. I think I'd rather be there with you two though. How's Lilian?'

'She's great. I'll put her on in a minute. I just wanted to warn you that Harry's sports teacher is going to be in touch to ask if you'll officiate at the sports day next week.'

'I've already agreed to it,' he reminded her.

'I know, but I think they're a bit nervous after Jonathan Cowley let them down at the eleventh hour last year. Anyway, how's Nikki getting on?'

'Haven't you just spoken to her?'

'Yes, but I wanted to get your take on it.'

'Well, if we're talking about her performance as a back-up researcher-cum-gofer, she's making her father proud. She's showing a real knack for getting to the heart of an issue and putting it into as few words as possible. Everyone's really impressed with her. Or so they're telling me.'

'I hope you're passing it on, it'll help her confidence no end.'

'Of course I am.'

'Good. And what about things with Freddy?'

'You'll know more about that than I do, I've been on air

most of the afternoon. She seems to be doing a good job of staying professional though.'

'That's my girl. And has Melissa exploded out of her red dress yet?'

He laughed. 'Not yet, but we live in hourly expectancy of it.'

It was Jessica's turn to laugh. 'Here you are, I'll put you onto Lilian now,' she said. 'We're going out this evening, by the way, so if you need to get hold of me for any reason I'll be on my mobile.'

'What's happening to Harry?'

'He's going to stay at the Cowleys.'

'So it's OK to go out with Lilian, but not with me?'

'Lilian's not famous.'

'Right, so I need to give up my job and everything I do in order to get a date with my wife?'

'Don't be silly. Now I'm not going to argue. Here's Lilian, and Harry will want to speak to you after, so don't ring off.'

A moment later Lilian was saying, 'Hi Charlie, how are you? I'm sorry to have missed you.'

'Likewise,' he responded tonelessly. 'It sounds as though you two are having a good time.'

'Don't we always?'

'How does she seem to you?'

'The way you might expect, considering what she's going through.'

He sighed and looked up as Nikki came out of the bathroom.

'How about you, how are you coping?' Lilian asked.

'I'm fine,' he lied. 'Nikki's here, if you want to have a word, but before you go, thanks for coming over. I know you've got a lot on at the moment, so I really appreciate you taking the time.'

'You know how much she means to me, so I'm glad you asked.'

As Nikki took the phone back from her father, she flopped out on the bed and spread out her limbs. 'Hi, Lilian,' she cried with a happy smile. 'You two are so blitzed, and don't pretend otherwise, because I've already spoken to Mum.'

Charlie looked down at her as she laughed at Lilian's

reply, then picking up his files and mobile phone he said, 'I'll see you downstairs.'

Quickly putting a hand over the mouthpiece, Nikki said, 'If you're off to the meeting with Melissa, it's cancelled. Sorry, I meant to tell you when I came in.'

Slightly thrown to discover that the meeting had been official after all, Charlie reminded himself that he'd had no intention of going to Melissa's room anyway, he'd just wanted to escape his own in case she came to find him. However, he might as well go now, so blowing a kiss to Nikki, he told her to tell Harry to call his mobile before he went off to the Cowleys, and left her to it.

He took the lift down to the lobby where scores of journos, conference delegates and general public were milling around before the next session began. His mobile rang, and seeing it was Rufus Keane returning his call he immediately clicked on.

They didn't speak for long. With so much noise going on around him Charlie had a job to make himself heard, but in the end he managed to let Keane know that he should check Veronica's phone book for the number of her lawyer, Maurice Halden-Bligh.

'He's an old friend of hers,' Charlie told him. 'Retired now, but they're almost certainly still in touch, so there's a chance he might know where she is.'

'It'll be a great relief if he does,' Keane responded. 'I've heard her talk about a Maurice from time to time, but I didn't know his surname.' Then he added something that Charlie didn't quite catch.

'I'm afraid I have to go,' Charlie told him, 'but please feel free to call me any time if you have some news.'

Almost before he'd rung off he was accosted by one of the producers, who drew him into a group of highly animated Japanese delegates, most of whom appeared more interested in being introduced to him than they did in their reason for being there. It wasn't difficult for him to be polite and charming, he'd been in his position for so long it was second nature, but when Melissa sauntered up to join them and murmured in his ear that he was looking tired, he excused himself much more abruptly than he'd intended, and all but collided with a Cabinet minister as he headed away from her, back into the conference hall.

'So how are things going between you and Charlie now?' Lilian was asking as she and Jessica handed their menus back to the waiter. 'Any improvements?'

Jessica's vision was slightly blurred as she looked past Lilian to the scattering of other diners in the small Thai restaurant which she'd chosen because she'd eaten here before without running into anyone she knew – or who presumed to know her. So hopefully they'd be spared any interruptions in their small, candlelit corner. 'No, not really,' she answered, wishing now that she hadn't drunk so much wine. 'I mean, we're OK on the surface, life goes on more or less as normal, but underneath . . .' Her eyes went to Lilian, then dropped to her hands as she said, 'He still won't discuss what happened, not in any detail, and as far as I'm aware he hasn't even allowed himself to cry yet. He's just blocking it all out, or trying to, and to be honest it's starting to scare me, because it's obviously not good for him to bottle it all up like this.'

Lilian's eyes showed how concerned she was. 'What about things on the physical front?' she asked gently. 'Any change there?'

Jessica shook her head. 'I know he feels terrible about it, but instead of trying to deal with it he's internalising it, the way he is his grief, and I don't know what to do to help him.' She sighed shakily. 'He's suffering so much inside, and I know seeing me suffer is making it worse, because he can't do anything about it. He feels he's let me down, he even says so sometimes, and the awful thing is, there are times when I feel as though he has too. Not over Natalie, there was nothing he could do to prevent that, but in the way he's refusing to deal with it, or to accept that my mother's hiding something. It feels like such a betrayal. Not only of me, but of Natalie too.'

Lilian sat back in her chair, a pale flush staining her cheeks. After a while she said, 'I know this isn't what you want to hear, but grief can play strange tricks on the mind . . .'

'You're right, it's not what I want to hear,' Jessica interrupted. 'You're going to tell me I'm not thinking straight, that I'm in my own kind of denial, or searching for someone to blame. I don't want to start falling out with you too, so maybe we should talk about something else, because things always seem to turn ugly when my mother's name comes up.'

Lilian sighed and looked down at her wine. 'You're going through a difficult enough time without avoiding issues with me too,' she said, 'so even if I don't always agree with you, you should feel free to say whatever you want to me.'

Jessica smiled, then in an attempt to move past her despair she said, 'I keep reminding myself that I have so much to be thankful for, my children, my marriage – provided it doesn't end up falling apart, and please God don't let that happen, because if I lost him too . . .' Her eyes closed as the horror of it settled around her heart like a cold fist.

'You won't,' Lilian assured her.

'Then there's my health,' Jessica pressed on, 'my financial security, my lovely home . . . Thousands of people out there would give anything to be in my shoes, while all I want is to kick them off and run away to a place where no-one will ever find me again. Sometimes it's like I just don't want to be *me* any more, but if I somehow managed to stop I'd lose Charlie and the children and . . . Oh God, listen to me, I hardly even know what I'm talking about any more. Maybe I am losing my mind and I haven't quite realised it yet.'

Seeming to feel herself on more comfortable ground now, Lilian said, 'You know, this is all a very natural reaction to what you're going through. Something inside tells you that if you can escape from reality, and give up being you, the pain will stop.'

Jessica nodded agreement, then glanced up as the waiter arrived with their first course. As he set about explaining the dish, lifting small terracotta lids from scooped-out platters to reveal succulent crayfish in seaweed wrappers beneath, she was aware of how closely Lilian was watching her.

When they were alone again, Lilian said, 'I think you and Charlie need a holiday. Just the two of you, far from here, where nobody knows you, and you've got all the time in the world to work this through.'

Jessica nodded. 'I'm sure you're right, but I'm afraid holidays seem to be on the list of subjects we're not discussing at the moment.'

Lilian was about to respond when a voice beside them said, 'Jessica? Is that you?'

Frowning, Jessica looked at the woman's enquiring face, trying to recognise her, but the woman's next words confirmed that they'd never met before.

'I hope I'm not interrupting,' she said, 'but I wanted to tell you how sorry I am for your loss.'

Jessica forced a smile. 'Thank you,' she responded.

The woman glanced at Lilian, then said, 'I lost a child myself a few years ago, so I understand how it feels.'

Lilian looked at her sympathetically, as Jessica said, 'I'm very sorry to hear that.'

The woman attempted a smile, but there were tears in her eyes, and for the next few minutes she told them how her son had died of leukaemia aged seven and a half.

As she left Jessica turned back to Lilian, tears in her eyes too. 'There's so much pain in the world,' she said, 'and now everyone seems to want to share theirs with me. I suppose it's quite touching in its way, but it makes me feel so useless when I can do nothing to help.'

Lilian's expression softened as she reached across to put a hand over Jessica's. 'It's probably more of a comfort than you realise just to be able to tell you,' she said.

Jessica smiled, then looked at Lilian's mobile as it started to ring.

Seeing who it was Lilian apologised, then hurriedly clicked on, and Jessica could almost feel the change that came over her as she moved from being supportive friend to loving wife. 'Hello darling,' she said. 'Did you get my message?'

As Lilian listened to the reply Jessica picked up her chopsticks and tried to eat. She had very little appetite though, nor did she seem able to shake the melancholia that was enveloping her. All she could do was think of the place Luc was calling from and wish she was there – with Natalie.

It was filling her up like the grief, making her long for the impossible, even as she longed for Charlie and the way things used to be. Suddenly she wanted to call him, just to hear his voice, but he was on air now, and Lilian would be ringing off soon.

She tried again to eat, and this time managed a small mouthful. It was funny, she was thinking to herself, how no-one ever asked her what she thought her mother might be hiding. They all seemed perfectly ready to accept the official version of events, and showed no willingness even to entertain the possibility that there might have been more. The truth was, she was glad they didn't ask, for she had never put her suspicions into words, not even to herself. They were just there, dark and terrible, like shadows moving across a window, or the warning of a storm that might devastate everything in its path if it ever arrived. And it might not, she told herself firmly, because she wanted desperately to believe that it never would.

'He says hi,' Lilian said, putting her mobile down.

Jessica picked up her wine again. 'How is he?' she asked, letting go of her fears as she pictured Lilian's handsome husband.

'Fine. Struggling to stop his father from overdoing things, and annoyed with an editor in Paris who's handing out an ultimatum – take the assignment or there'll be no more – but other than that, I think he's missing me.'

Seeing how her eyes were sparkling, Jessica raised her glass. 'Thank God one of us is happy,' she said.

'And you will be again,' Lilian assured her. 'You're under a lot of pressure right now, but you and Charlie love one another far too much not to work this out. So you'll get past it. I promise.'

'Of course,' Jessica responded, feeling certain it was true, yet still finding it hard to believe.

Lilian regarded her with gently laughing eyes, and finally Jessica returned her smile. 'That's better,' Lilian said. 'Now let's see if we can at least get through this first course without any more interruptions, because I don't know about you, but I'm starving.'

Wishing she were too Jessica picked up her chopsticks

again, but had hardly taken a mouthful when her mobile started to ring. 'Nikki,' she announced, recognising the ringtone.

Lilian rolled her eyes. 'How many times is that today?'

'I've stopped counting. In fact, I'm starting to wish Freddy would hurry up and do the flaming deed, or I'll never get any peace. Hello darling,' she said sweetly into the phone.

'Hey Mum,' Nikki replied. 'How's everything with you?'

'Great. Lilian and I are having dinner at the Thai place. What are you up to?'

'Not much. Dad's on air, and Freddy's had to go down to interview someone in the lobby.'

'Oh, I see. You're sounding very relaxed compared to the last time we spoke.'

'I'm cool. It's all like totally fantastic.'

Jessica's eyes narrowed. 'What is?'

'Sex, Mum. Getting laid. Making love.'

Jessica's heart skipped a beat. 'You've done it? It's already happened?'

Nikki gave a screech of excitement. 'It was all like totally brilliant, Mum. He was so romantic and caring and he took care of everything . . . And he called me just now, while his interviewee was being miked up, to say he thought I was really special and that he can't wait for it to happen again. Oh Mum, I am so in love.'

Though Jessica couldn't feel entirely thrilled, she was smiling as she looked at Lilian. 'Have you told Dad?' she asked.

'Don't be insane. I can't talk to him about that sort of thing. But it would be kind of OK if he knew, so I was hoping you'd tell him when he comes off air. It'll be at one o'clock.'

'I'll be in bed . . .'

'No, no. You've got to call him, or he might end up finding out through someone else, and that would be so . . .'

'How many people have you told?' Jessica cut in.

'Only you! But you know how things get around, and they will if Freddy spends the night in my room. You can tell Dad everything you and Lilian have been talking about today too, if you like, that'll probably slow down his adrenalin and bore him off to sleep.'

Jessica's eyebrows rose. 'Charming,' she commented.

'Whatever. Just promise me you'll call him.'

'OK. If that's what you want.'

'I do. So don't forget. One o'clock. Love you,' and the line went dead.

'Well, there's someone else who's happy,' Jessica commented, putting the phone back next to her plate. 'Apparently the deed is done.'

Lilian clapped her hands, then peering at Jessica she said, 'So how do you feel about it?'

Jessica laughed self-consciously as tears began glistening in her eyes. 'The truth? I want her to stay a baby so I can keep her close for ever, and make sure nothing bad ever happens to her. But now here she is, already blossoming into a woman.'

Smiling, Lilian said, 'A natural reaction. Are you going to tell Charlie?'

Jessica nodded. 'It's what she seems to want, though it might not be what he wants at one o'clock in the morning, or at any other time come to that. However, I guess she's right, it would be better coming from me than from the crew grapevine.'

Charlie was waiting in front of the lifts with Melissa, still wearing his studio make-up and carrying the earpiece which he'd forgotten to hand back to the sound guy as they'd come off air. With them was a handful of delegates from the conference who'd stayed up late either drinking or continuing private debate, before everything started up again in the morning. The crew was nowhere in evidence, since they'd barely had time to wrap yet, while the producers were still signing off with their counterparts in London, who'd now taken over transmission.

When the lift came Charlie stood aside for Melissa and the delegates to step in ahead of him. He intended to let the doors close and make his escape without having to come up with an excuse that she'd probably see through immediately. However, it wasn't to be. A grey-bearded man with kindly eyes pressed the hold button to make sure no-one was left behind.

As the lift started to rise Charlie exchanged small talk with the delegates, managing to sound pleasant and friendly, even though he was tired and querulous and angry with himself for being in this position without even knowing how he'd managed to get here. He thought of Jessica and Lilian who were probably asleep by now, and Harry staying over with his friend, and Nikki . . . Perhaps he wouldn't think about Nikki, considering what she might be up to . . .

'By the way, have you rescheduled the presenters' meeting?' he asked Melissa, who was only partly visible behind the suited men.

'Yes, haven't you been told?' she replied. 'It's at seven thirty in the morning, before I fly back to London.'

Surprised, he said, 'You're flying back early?'

'I've achieved what I came here for, and since I've been asked to speak at a forum on the future of news media tomorrow night, I have to get back.'

'That's very last minute,' he commented.

'Apparently the ITN chap's had to cry off.'

The lift stopped and there was a general murmur of goodnight as the delegates got out.

When the doors slid closed again Melissa remained in the far corner, gazing up at the numbered lights. Since both their suites were on the same floor, he was already feeling anxious about what was going to happen when they got out.

'I wonder if there are any hidden cameras,' she said as the lift started to go up again. 'I can't see any, can you?'

Charlie looked around, saying nothing, though his heart was sinking for he had a horrible suspicion of where this was leading.

'Could it be worth the risk?' she said, tilting her head curiously to one side.

His eyes flitted across the glittering black halter top that was cleaving gamely to as much of her breasts as it could.

'Probably not,' she decided. Then with a saucy look at him, 'Do you remember what they look like, Charlie? Would you like to touch them now? Would you dare?'

'Melissa . . .'

To his relief the lift came to a stop and as he stepped out behind her he was preparing to tell her he needed to go and check on Nikki when she said, 'It's very kind of you to see me to my room. If you'd like to come in for a nightcap . . .'

'No really, that's fine,' he said. 'I'm dead beat. Ready to hit the sack.'

Her eyes were laughing as she looked up at him. 'Charlie,' she said softly, 'why are you being so hard on yourself?'

He could feel the colour suffusing his neck as he said, 'Melissa, you've got this all wrong . . .'

Putting a finger over his lips she said, 'Darling, we both know you want this, so don't let's keep fooling ourselves. Now relax. Let go of everything you've got going on up here,' she tapped the side of his head, 'then everything down here will take care of itself.'

He took a step back as she made to touch him, and felt more tense than ever as she laughed. 'I'm sorry,' he said in a strangled voice, 'it's not that I don't find you attractive – you know I do, but Nikki's here in the hotel, and it just doesn't seem right.'

Her eyebrows arched, but before she could speak his mobile started to ring.

'And now I suppose,' she drawled, 'you're going to answer that.'

Seeing it was Jessica and thinking immediately of Harry, he said, 'I have to.'

Her smile turned slightly glacial as she took the key from her purse and inserted it into her door.

'I'm sorry,' he said, but she didn't respond, and he was already clicking on to answer.

'Hi darling,' Jessica said sleepily. 'Is everything OK?'

'I think I'm the one who should be asking you that,' he replied, walking on down the corridor. 'Why are you calling so late?'

She yawned. 'Good question. Why am I? Oh yes, Nikki wants you to know that she and Freddy have sealed their relationship.'

'Sealed?'

Jessica's tone was sardonic as she said, 'That's the most tactful way I can put it.'

'Oh, I see,' he said stiffly. Then, letting himself into his own suite, 'So am I expected to go and congratulate them?'

She laughed. 'No, I don't think so.'

Belatedly realising how absurd his question had been, he laughed too. 'Are you OK?' he asked.

'Yes, I'm fine. Loving having Lilian here. I only wish she could stay longer, but don't tell her I said that or she'll get a fit of the guilts. She thinks we need a holiday, just us two.'

He hesitated, not quite sure how to respond to that. It wasn't that he didn't want it, he was just afraid of what a disaster it could be.

'Not grabbing you?' she said.

Though her tone had remained light, he knew she was hurt, so he quickly said, 'I was just thinking of somewhere we could go. The Maldives? Sri Lanka? What about Sicily? We had a wonderful time there on one of our anniversaries, do you remember?'

'It was our fifteenth – and of course I remember. Anyway, we can discuss it when you're back. Do you and Nikki need picking up from the airport? I guess I should offer a lift to Melissa too, as she's coming this way.'

'She's flying back to London first thing, and I think cars have been booked for the rest of us.'

'OK. Then I'll see you around eight tomorrow evening, but I'll probably speak to you in the morning. Sleep well.'

'You too.'

After ringing off he dropped the phone on the bed, then sat down next to it and covered his face with his hands. He was tired, hungry and so torn apart inside he barely even knew what he was thinking any more. If only he could heed the advice Melissa had given him a few minutes ago, and let go of the turmoil inside his head, then everything else might very well take care of itself. However, it seemed he had no control over the guilt that was consuming him, or the blame, or the sense of helplessness and shame, because as far as he was concerned his daughter was dead because of him, and no matter how hard he tried to tell himself there was nothing he could have done to prevent it, he knew that nothing was ever going to make him believe it.

Chapter Seven

'I'm off,' Jessica called up the stairs.

'Good luck,' Charlie shouted back. 'Call me when it's over, let me know how you got on.'

Experiencing a few gentle flutters of excitement, Jessica picked up the Prada briefcase Charlie had given her at Christmas, checked she had change for the tube, then closing the front door behind her, she started off down the street towards the underground station. It was a little breezy, though still wonderfully warm, and feeling the sun on her skin was as pleasing as the scent of jasmine that wafted to her as she passed the Kingsleys' house on the corner.

Nikki had chosen her outfit for today, and since they'd all acquired a bit of a tan at the weekend, it hadn't taken much to persuade Jessica to show off her legs a little in a dusky pink over-the-knee pleated skirt with matching short jacket and plain white boob tube, though she'd drawn the line at the stiletto sandals that went with it. They were OK for evening, but not for lunch in the middle of the day. So in the comfort of a pair of silver ballet pumps, she was soon descending the steps into Notting Hill station.

Though she'd intended to spend the entire weekend preparing her biography project for this lunch with Karina, it hadn't quite turned out that way, thanks to the celebrity cricket match which she'd forgotten Charlie was playing in on Sunday. There had been no getting out of it, even if she'd wanted to, for Harry was dead set on going, and since Freddy was on the team too, Nikki had made it very plain that she would never be forgiven if she tried to back out.

In fact, she'd really enjoyed it, relaxing in the sun, catching up with old friends who'd offered their condolences at the time so no need to go there again, and watching Nikki's eyes shine every time she looked at Freddy. In a way he reminded Jessica of a young Charlie, with his shock of shiny blond hair, light, humorous eyes and long gangly limbs. She suspected Charlie had noticed the likeness too, or maybe he just felt genuinely paternal towards the extremely likeable cub reporter.

When the match was over – which they'd lost – Charlie had invited everyone back to their place for drinks, though thankfully not everyone had accepted. As it turned out, they'd been an impromptu party of fifteen, until Harry became bored with the adult company and took himself off to his room with a friend, while Nikki and Freddy didn't hang about the garden for long either. Being in the first throes of romance, they preferred to go and watch DVDs in the den with no-one else around.

So all in all it had been an extremely pleasurable day, which had gone on until quite late in the evening, and in its way it had seemed to bring her and Charlie a little closer again. Not that anything had been said, or done, it was simply a feeling she had, and as she resurfaced at Green Park station she was aware of a great flood of affection for him sweeping through her. She might even have allowed herself to smile were she not alone in public, but not wanting to draw any more attention to herself than her small amount of fame and slender legs were already managing, she maintained a neutral expression and decided to go shopping as soon as this lunch was over to find something for him, just to let him know she'd been thinking about him.

'Hi, Charlie, it's Maggie,' his assistant said into the phone.

'Hi, Mags, how's everything your end?'

'Fine,' she replied. 'I've just sent you an email with details of the interviews you're doing next week . . .'

'For the Middle East series?'

'Yep. And I've attached the information you requested on nuclear energy. Ken Gordon's available to direct that documentary, by the way, which I expect will please you.'

'It does,' he confirmed, and scooted his chair away from the computer over to Jessica's desk to rummage around for the chequebook. 'I'm in the office tomorrow, aren't I?' he said. 'See if he's available to drop in for a chat.'

'Will do. Anyway, I thought you might like to know that I've just had a call from Melissa's new PA asking if we can send over the interview you did in Paris with Riad al-Turk, the Syrian Opposition Leader.'

Charlie's chair came to a stop halfway back to his desk. 'Really?' he said, his tone conveying how unimpressed he was to hear that, even though he wasn't entirely surprised. 'What answer did you give?'

'That it still isn't edited, because it isn't, and that I can't allow any of our material to go anywhere unless I've cleared it with you first.'

'And what was the response to that?'

'She said she'd get more details from Melissa and call me back. Incidentally, you're booked in to edit it at the weekend, just in case you want me to tell them it'll be ready by Monday.'

'No, if she calls again tell her I'll speak to Melissa about it myself. Anything else?'

'Nope. That's it for now.'

'OK, I'm due at the studios in a couple of hours, you can reach me there if you need to,' and ringing off he quickly wrote out a cheque for Harry's autumn term fees, then went out into the hall to collect the mail he'd just heard drop through the door.

As he returned to the study he could feel himself becoming increasingly angry about the way Melissa had checked up on him, as though he was lying about why he'd been in Paris at Easter, though God only knew why she thought he would. He felt so incensed by it that he set the mail aside and picked up the phone to call her. Not surprisingly her mobile was switched off, presumably because she was at lunch somewhere, so after the answer message had finished he said, tersely, 'Melissa, I'd like to see you in my dressing room at two thirty. I think you know what it's about,' and punching an end to the call, he dropped the phone back on the desk and returned to the mail.

It was a stack of bank statements, bills and insurance offers, along with a reminder from the *London Review of Books* that Jessica's subscription was about to run out. There was also a medium-sized white envelope addressed to him, written in a hand he didn't exactly recognise, though it seemed familiar, and realising whose it could be his insides turned to liquid.

His mouth was set in a tight, grim line as he tore the envelope open. Another, smaller one, fell out and he picked it up to find it unsealed and addressed to Jessica, while the pages he drew out after it were clearly for him.

Dearest Charlie,

I am writing to you now because the strangest thing has happened to me. Would you believe, darling, I was in London for my usual annual check-ups and a spot of shopping when the next thing I knew I was waking up in a rather glum little hospital bed. (Actually it wasn't so bad really, the people around me were very sweet and friendly, when they were awake, and the doctor was deliciously strict and even rather good-looking in a doctorly sort of way, but I wasn't sorry when Maurice popped in and had me moved to where I am now.)

Anyway, the reason I'm here is because it seems I had a little collapse in Bond Street as I was going into Fenwicks and in all the kerfuffle of getting the ambulance and carting me off to emergency some pesky little rascal stole my handbag, so no-one knew who I was, or who to be in touch with, until I came round.

Forgive me for not telling them about you and Jessica, darling, but I didn't want to be a bother to her, particularly after everything that's happened, and to be honest, I wasn't feeling quite up to dealing with her now she hates me so much. So, I called dear Maurice who came right away, and he's been such a sweetheart ever since with all his flowers and chocolates, and just sitting next to me so I don't feel too alone.

He's taking me home in the next couple of days, and then we're going off to his gorgeous villa in Italy for a while so I can have a bit of a rest. I don't want you to worry about me, darling, because I'm feeling very much better now, though I don't mind admitting the whole thing has given me a bit of a scare. I suppose it's because of that that I decided I had to write down everything that happened that day in France when we lost our dear little angel. You see, I don't really want to pop off with it all still on my conscience – not that I'm planning to go anywhere yet, you understand, but just in case something like it happens again and I don't manage to come bouncing back.

It is all in the letter I'm enclosing for Jessica, which I've left unsealed so you can read it first. It will then be for you to decide, dear Charlie, whether or not she should see it. I know how devastating it's going to be for her – for you all – so if you choose to keep the letter to yourself, or even destroy it, I will understand perfectly.

I'm truly sorry, Charlie, for the burden I'm putting on you now, and for the pain it's going to cause you. I know how hard you've found it to come to terms with the loss, and I don't suppose this is going to help at all. I only wish I didn't feel so compelled to do it, but I hope you will understand why I must.

Well, I guess that's about it. All being well I will have left here by the time you receive this letter, so you won't have to bother about coming to see me, or doing your duty in any other way. Rest assured, I'm very much better now, and I have every intention of staying that way.

Please give Nikki and Harry lots of huge hugs from me – Jessica too, of course, but you'd better just think of me when you do it, rather than tell her, because I don't think she'll want them. A big hug to you too, of course.

With love as ever,

Veronica

Charlie's face was chalk-white as he put his own letter aside, slid the one for Jessica from its envelope and started to read.

There were twelve pages in all, some apologising for the kind of mother Veronica had been, others relating a few more details about the 'little collapse' in Bond Street, but the essential part of the letter described what had happened at the grape-picker's cottage the day Natalie had died.

Even before he finished reading he knew he could never let Jessica see this. The damage it would do could hardly be measured, but nor could he bring himself to destroy it, at least not right now. So, with badly shaking hands and a heart ripping apart with horror, he tucked the letter into his pocket and tried to summon the strength to pick up the phone. He needed to call Rufus Keane to let him know he'd heard from Veronica. First, though, he must try to get hold of Veronica herself.

He wasn't surprised when her machine picked up, so he left a message asking her to get in touch as soon as possible so he could be sure that her 'little collapse' wasn't more serious than she was telling. He mentioned nothing about the contents of her letter to Jessica: Veronica clearly knew she wasn't to blame for what had happened so he had no reason to reassure her, and there were no other words he could bring himself to utter aloud.

For several minutes after the call he stayed where he was, seeing and hearing nothing, barely even thinking, until finally, rigid with pain, he dragged himself upstairs to sit on Natalie's bed. He didn't want to fall apart now, for Jessica's sake as well as his own, but with this letter in his pocket containing all the details of what had happened to his precious girl, the whole nightmare of it right there in black and white, he couldn't hold on any longer. Within seconds he was starting to gulp for air, as though suffocating under the dreadful weight of his torment.

'Well, Jessica, I think we've reached a very satisfactory agreement,' Karina Rutherford was saying with evident pleasure as she picked up their lunch bill. She was a small, kitten-faced woman with velvety brown eyes and an incisively quick intellect. It was no wonder, Jessica had always thought, that she'd made it so far at such a young age – she wasn't afraid of going after what she wanted, or of making a quick decision, even if it meant taking a gamble on an unproven biographer such as Jessica Moore.

After signalling to the waiter she looked at Jessica again. 'You do understand that the advance will not be more than ten thousand?' she said.

Jessica merely raised her eyebrows. It was a starting point, but she felt sure an agent would be able to push it higher. Not that the money was an issue, but she knew Karina enjoyed the bargaining as much as the publishing, so wasn't surprised that she'd started so low. 'I was thinking of asking Matthew Knox to represent me for this,' she said, naming a reputable, but quite unflashy literary agent for whom she'd always had an affection.

'Good choice,' Karina smiled. 'I'll look forward to his call.' Then after tapping her pin number into the machine presented by a waiter she said, 'If you were prepared to commit now about how you've coped with Natalie's death we could offer a two-book deal and a six-figure sum.'

'I'm sure,' Jessica responded smoothly, 'but I've only agreed to consider it, and I'm making no promises.'

'But you do feel you could be in a better frame of mind to tackle it after the biography?'

Jessica nodded. 'Possibly. More time will have passed, so by then I might have a better perspective.'

'Of course.' Karina smiled again. 'I don't want to be so crude as to put the condition in writing, but I'm afraid the lawyers might insist on it.'

'It's OK. I quite understand – you're willing to publish my biography on condition I give you first refusal on my own story, should I ever decide to write it.'

Karina's eyes twinkled warmly. 'But I'm sure the biography will do very well on its own,' she said, truthfully. 'The question is whether we publish it as fact or fiction, since you're going to have to create the parts of Jeanne Hébuterne's life that have gone unrecorded. Whatever, it could be a fascinating story – a great love story, in fact, that I feel will be very safe in your hands. I can hardly wait to read it.'

Jessica felt the kick of pleasure. 'I'll let you discuss deadlines with Matthew,' she said, 'but I'm delighted you're interested. I'm looking forward to getting started.'

As they stepped out onto Bond Street Karina hailed a cab, then turned to embrace Jessica. 'I've always had a lot of respect for you,' she said frankly. 'I know I'm going to enjoy working with you.'

'Thank you, the feeling's mutual,' Jessica assured her, and stood watching until the cab pulled away. She took out her mobile, hardly able to wait to call Charlie.

As she turned on her phone she realised she hadn't felt this good since she couldn't remember when. In fact, she might even call Melissa after to say thank you for not giving her a job, because if she had, she wouldn't be on the threshold of writing a book – just imagine, she was actually going to become an author, or at least she was going to try.

Realising there was a message waiting, she decided to check first to see who it was in case one of the children was trying to get hold of her. However, the voice that came down the line was Lilian's, asking how she was, and reminding her to let her know how the lunch with Karina Rutherford went.

'Oh, and any news on your mother yet?' Lilian added. 'Just wondering. I hope she's all right. Well, I'm sure she is, but I guess it would be nice to know. Anyway, I've got a big sale on this afternoon, so I'll try to catch up with you this evening. Love you madly. Toot, toot.'

As she rang off Jessica could sense her good mood starting to evaporate, for as angry and resentful as she felt towards her mother, she couldn't deny she was starting to worry now too. However, that didn't mean she was in any way prepared to forgive her, or even stop accusing her of lying, it only meant that deep in her heart – and much against her will – she still loved her, and cared about what might be happening to her. Since, however, it was a love and a care that had only ever brought her pain, she just couldn't bring herself to go there again.

As Charlie walked into his dressing room, his face was still ravaged and pale from the emotion he'd expended before leaving the house, while his body felt tense all over. He could really do without going on air today, since it was going to be hard concentrating on the news while he was still so distracted by the letter from Jessica's mother. However, he wasn't going to let anyone down at this late hour, so maybe a shower would help soothe some of the stiffness from his limbs, as well as cool him off a little after the sweltering humidity outside.

Not until he'd stripped off his shorts and polo shirt and was wearing only boxers and sports socks did he fully tune into the background noise he was hearing, which was sounding very like the shower in his private bathroom. No sooner had he registered it than it stopped.

He stood rooted to the spot, so many thoughts chasing through his mind that they barely had any order: one of the crew was sneaking a crafty hose-down on a hot day; a plumber had been called to rectify a fault; Nikki would obviously feel she had carte blanche . . . It didn't occur to him for a second that Melissa might be availing herself of his facilities, until she stepped out of the small alcove at the far end of the room, a towel in one hand and absolutely nothing else but tiny droplets of water on the rest of her.

Whatever he might have been about to say was lost in the sudden onslaught of lust – but even that was secondary to a rage that made him want to shove her out in the corridor just as she was, rather than even think about what was happening here.

'Charlie,' she drawled, sauntering towards him. 'I hope you don't mind. It's so hot out today, and I felt sure you wouldn't object if I cooled off a little first.'

For once in his life words continued to fail him. He'd totally forgotten he'd asked her to meet him here, and only now was he realising how his message might have sounded – or at least, how she'd chosen to make it sound.

Her smile was catlike and sultry as she began patting herself dry. 'So what did you want to talk to me about?' she asked, as though it were perfectly normal for them to hold meetings dressed – or undressed – like this.

At last he found his tongue. 'Melissa, you've completely misunderstood . . .'

Her eyebrows rose. 'Oh darling, do let's stop playing games now,' she drawled. 'I'm trying to make this as easy as I can for you . . .'

'It's not what I want,' he raged.

'But you asked me to come,' she said reasonably.

'Because you damned well checked up on me,' he growled. 'You sent for that interview . . .'

'And it clearly doesn't exist,' she interrupted with a smile. 'So shall we talk about what you were really doing in Paris that day, or would you like to . . .'

'Of course it exists!' he shouted.

'Then why not let me see it?'

'Because it's not edited yet, and I will not dance to your tune.'

She laughed softly. 'Really?' she said. Then, seeming to dismiss it, 'Now there's not much time before you're due in the studio, so how would you like me? Over the table . . .'

He couldn't be entirely sure exactly what happened next, whether he told her to stop where she was *before* the door opened, or after. All he knew was that someone was knocking, then Jessica was coming in saying, 'Darling, are you here? Ah, there you . . .' Then she froze, and so did he and so did Melissa.

How could he not see it through Jessica's eyes? Melissa was naked, he was in his shorts so what other conclusion was there to come to?

Feeling as though the world was dipping into some kind of horrendous slow motion, he heard himself starting to protest, uttering inanities like, 'It's not what it seems . . . I didn't know she was here . . . It was hot, she wanted to cool off . . .'

All the time Jessica was just staring at him, then at Melissa, who was casually wrapping herself in the towel, then back to him.

'So is this why . . .?' Jessica said, then her voice broke, making it hard to go on. 'I'm sorry, I . . .' A sob rose up from the pit of her stomach. She didn't know what to do, she had no idea what to say.

'Jessica, I swear this isn't what it looks like,' Charlie insisted.

She looked at him, but his words didn't seem to be making any sense. 'I came to tell you,' she began, as though her purpose was still valid.

'Melissa, for God's sake *go*,' he growled.

'No, don't,' Jessica said. 'I'm sorry I interrupted,' and turning on her heel she walked out and closed the door.

As she started along the corridor she barely knew what she was thinking. Somewhere, deep inside, she was aware of something terrible waiting to engulf her, but she had to keep it at bay. She needed to get out of here, to go home, or turn back the clock so that this had never happened. She couldn't let it be real, she wasn't going to allow it to be, because if it was there would be nothing to hold onto any more. Her life, her family was falling apart. First Natalie, now Charlie . . .

She was close to the door now. It was already open. She was blinded by the sunlight streaming through and made unsteady by the shock. Then strangely Natalie was there, coming towards her . . . But it wasn't Natalie, it was Nikki and she was saying, 'Hey Mum, what are you doing here? You'll never guess what, Freddy's asked me to go . . . Mum? Mum, are you OK?'

'I'm fine,' Jessica said, trying to walk on.

'No you're not. You're shaking like a leaf. What's happened?'

'Nothing. It's all right. I just need to go home.'

Nikki glanced down the corridor, then stepped in closer to her mother. 'Mum, what happened?' she said firmly. 'Tell me.'

And because her natural instinct was to try and spare her daughter, Jessica said, 'I chose a bad time. Dad and I . . . It doesn't matter. Nikki, no!' But Nikki was already racing down the corridor, and Jessica was unsteadied by the echo of her mother's voice shouting 'Natalie, no!'

As Nikki flung the dressing-room door open Jessica covered her face with her hands. She didn't want to listen, she didn't even want to think about Nikki catching her father like that. But there was nothing she could do to stop it. It was happening now. She could hear Nikki shouting, and when, seconds later, she felt her daughter's arms go round her, she held her closely, and could only feel glad she was there as they left the building together and searched for a cab to take them home.

Chapter Eight

Nikki was pacing up and down the kitchen, her lovely young face tight with anger as she raged about her father and did her best to comfort her mother. 'That woman is such a bitch!' she seethed. 'She's been trying to get her claws into him for weeks. Everyone could see it. The way she kept making eyes at him . . . They were a laughing stock. Some people even used to beg and pant like dogs behind his back, and he'd look up and laugh along with them, even though he didn't know what he was laughing at.'

Sickened by the mere thought of it, Jessica turned away. 'How could he?' she whispered brokenly. Her eyes closed as another wave of shock engulfed her heart. Even having seen it with her own eyes, she was still unable to make herself believe that he was cheating on her. The betrayal felt so enormous, even monstrous considering everything else they were going through, that she just couldn't connect it with the man she loved. 'Thank God none of it has got into the papers,' she murmured, with a shudder of revulsion.

'Yet,' Nikki added, and immediately regretted it as Jessica went even paler.

'What the hell am I going to do?' Jessica said, though more to herself than to Nikki.

'I don't know,' Nikki answered, 'but we'll think of something. Whatever, he has to stop seeing her. I mean, I know she lives right down the street, and he works with her, but it absolutely can't go on.'

Jessica inhaled deeply. 'Do you think . . .?' she began. 'He said it wasn't what it seemed . . .'

'For God's sake, Mum, the woman had no clothes on,' Nikki cried, not experienced enough to realise Jessica might need to allow her father the benefit of the doubt, at least for a while. 'Nor did he, or hardly.'

'You're right. It's just . . . Oh Nikki, it's so complicated between me and Dad at the moment, and . . .'

Nikki rushed to her side. 'But it's going to be all right,' she told her firmly. 'You'll get past this, Mum. I know it's going to be hard, and you're feeling really terrible right now, but it'll be all right. I promise.'

Jessica looked away. It would be unfair to make Nikki any more afraid than she already was, so she said no more.

'She doesn't mean anything to him,' Nikki said desperately. 'She just kept throwing herself at him . . . I mean that doesn't excuse what he did, I know, but he's a man and you know what they're like. Oh Mum, don't cry. Please. I swear it's going to be all right.'

'It's OK,' Jessica assured her, swallowing hard. 'I'm not crying any more. I think . . .' She looked into Nikki's eyes and attempted a smile. 'I just need to go and lie down for a while,' she said.

As Nikki made to come with her she started to protest, but then she put an arm around her so they could walk upstairs together. There would be time later for her to be alone so she could think and decide how she was going to handle this. Nikki's world had been shaken too, so she must now do what she could to reassure her.

When they reached the landing outside her and Charlie's room Jessica squeezed Nikki close and said, 'I don't think I want to go in there right now. Let's go and lie on Natalie's bed.'

A few minutes later they were side by side on the small double bed with its pink and lavender covers and scattering of frilly pillows. Jessica was gazing up at the colourful mobiles and star-covered ceiling and trying to feel Natalie's presence, wanting to wrap herself and Nikki in the gentle force of it, but Natalie wasn't there – the room was a shell full of her belongings, but it was as though her spirit had gone. For a moment Jessica felt a panic rising in her chest. Natalie had always been here before, absent, but somehow there, so where was she now? Why had she flown when she and Nikki needed her so much?

After a while Nikki began to talk about her, speaking softly with laughter and tears in her voice and so much love in her heart that Jessica could feel it spilling into her own. It was as though Nikki was coaxing her sister back, bringing her into the room through all the memories they shared, and the secrets they'd never spoken of to anyone but each other. Jessica smiled to hear them, and struggled to hold back the tears. Theirs had been a little world apart from her, she realised, one that only sisters shared. How precious they had been to one another, how loving and vital. And Harry, everyone's favourite, who had fought outrageously with Natalie and loved her with all his heart. As a family they had been so complete, so happy and involved with one another. Everything they did and everywhere they went, even if they weren't together, it was as though a part of each of them was always there with them. Natalie's death hadn't changed that, nor would it ever.

They lay together for a long time, still whispering and laughing, sometimes crying, and always holding each other's hands, until finally Nikki got up and Jessica closed her eyes. She could hear Nikki moving around, opening drawers, shutting cupboards, then she came to sit on the edge of the bed.

'Have you ever read any of these?' she asked Jessica.

Jessica opened her eyes and saw some of Natalie's diaries in Nikki's hands. She shook her head. 'No, have you?' she replied.

Nikki nodded. 'It's like I can hear her speaking, and it makes me feel close to her, so I decided she wouldn't mind.'

Jessica put out a hand and entwined her fingers round Nikki's. 'I don't think she would,' she whispered.

'Shall I read some to you?' Nikki offered.

Jessica thought about it. 'No. Not right now,' she said, then added, 'thank you,' in case Nikki was hurt.

Nikki sat gazing down at the diaries, then after a while she looked at Jessica. 'What are you thinking about?' she asked.

Jessica almost smiled. 'Dad, of course,' she answered, 'and what a difficult time he must be having trying to read the news.'

After a moment Nikki started to laugh, they both did, but

then Nikki turned away, and realising she was crying Jessica pulled her back down into her arms. 'You won't leave him, Mum, will you?' Nikki sobbed. 'I couldn't bear it if you two broke up. I know you must be angry, but . . . Harry needs you, and so do I so please don't make Dad go away . . . It's already horrible without Natalie, but if he went too . . .'

'Sssh,' Jessica soothed, smoothing a hand over her hair. 'Everything'll be all right, darling, I promise, but I do need to be alone with Dad when he comes home, OK?'

Nikki raised her head.

Smiling into her bloodshot eyes, Jessica used a thumb to wipe away her tears. 'I need you to take Harry to his guitar lesson, then on for a pizza,' she said. 'He'll like that. Can Freddy come with you?'

'I don't know,' Nikki sniffed, wiping her cheeks with the back of her hand. 'He doesn't know anything yet, I haven't had a chance to tell him.' Her eyes closed as her face crumpled again. 'But everyone else will have done it for me,' she wailed. 'He might end up feeling too embarrassed to go out with me any more . . . Oh Mum, what if he finishes with me?'

'I think you'll find he's made of stronger stuff than that,' Jessica assured her.

'Do you really think so?'

'Of course,' Jessica replied, tucking a strand of hair behind Nikki's ear.

'But anyway,' Nikki went on, 'Melissa's probably going to fire me after what I said to her.'

Though Jessica grimaced, she couldn't help relishing Melissa's discomfort at being confronted by Charlie's daughter, only seconds after his wife. But then she recalled Melissa's nudity and felt the sickening burn of betrayal again. She so desperately wanted to believe what Charlie had said, that he hadn't known Melissa was there, but the woman had been naked, for God's sake, and for all he'd been wearing he might as well have been too – and she could only conclude that they'd been so urgent for one another they hadn't even noticed the door wasn't locked.

'I keep thinking of how he's stopped even trying with me,'

she said to Lilian much later in the day, after Nikki had taken Harry off, and Lilian had finally managed to call back. 'I never dreamt it might be because he was having an affair. It never even entered my head.'

Concern resonated in Lilian's voice as she said, 'I must admit I feel as shocked as you do. Have you any idea how long it's been going on?'

Jessica's heart turned over. 'Not yet,' she answered, and found herself almost choking on the thought of it happening all through these past few months, possibly even longer.

'I'm sure it's not serious,' Lilian told her softly, as though reading her mind. 'And you never know, he might have been telling the truth today . . .'

'You mean that it wasn't what it seemed? You can't imagine how much I want to believe that, but honestly, Lily, how can you not know there's a naked woman in your room? It's farcical even to think it.'

'Maybe,' Lilian replied. 'But stranger things . . . What time's he due home?'

'Any minute now. He's on a shorter shift today, because he's filming early tomorrow.'

'Do you have any idea yet what you're going to say?'

'Not really.'

Lilian sighed. 'I suppose he's the one who has to do the talking,' she said.

As she thought of it, Jessica closed her eyes. 'I hardly know what's happening to us,' she said. 'As difficult as things have been lately, the way we haven't always found it easy to talk, as well as the physical thing, I've never doubted him, or thought he was lying . . . All our married life I've always trusted him completely. But now . . . It's as though everything's slipping away.'

'I know it must seem that way,' Lilian responded soothingly, 'but you're still in shock. It's going to be fine. I promise you. I just wish I could be there with you.'

'So do I,' Jessica said, though she wasn't entirely sure she meant it, for all she really wanted right now was to be on her own in a place where no-one could find her. Yet even as she thought it she felt a panic welling inside her.

'You never know, this might end up bringing you closer

together,' Lilian said, in a voice that didn't hold much conviction.

Jessica tried to answer, but couldn't. Then her head came up as the front door slammed in the hall, and she felt such a cruel twist of nerves that her words were faint as she said, 'He's just come in. I'll try to call you tomorrow.'

After putting the phone down she used her hands to wipe her eyes, then tore a sheet from the kitchen roll to blow her nose. She knew how ravaged her face must look, but there was nothing she could do about it now, nor would she try. She could hear him moving about upstairs and then her heart filled with dread as he started to come down. What was going to happen now? Where was this going to lead them? Suddenly she felt the need for his arms, to know that nothing was going to change, even though deep down inside she knew it already had, and then she was aware of the same desperate helplessness she'd experienced after Natalie died, when she'd tried to fight the horror of never being able to go back.

As he came into the kitchen his anguish was so plain and his remorse so deep that he barely needed any words. Though she might want to tell him it was all right, that they could forget all about it now, it would be foolish even to try, when it was far too big to be swept away as though it didn't matter. 'Where are the children?' he asked hoarsely.

'Nikki took Harry for a pizza. They'll be back later.'

Sighing, he pushed a hand through his hair. 'Is Nikki OK?' he said shakily.

'She's very upset.'

He nodded. 'I'll talk to her.' His eyes came to hers.

She waited, aware of how hard her heart was beating.

'I know how it must have looked today,' he began, 'but I swear . . .'

'Just tell me this,' she said, 'is your affair the reason you're not making love to me?'

For a moment he seemed shocked by the question. Then in a voice that rang with truth, he said, 'There isn't an affair. What you saw today . . .'

'Then why did she turn me down for a job?'

'Whatever the reason, it had nothing to do with an affair, because we aren't having one.'

'Yet she was comfortable enough to come into your dressing room and strip off all her clothes, and we both know if I were around the studios she wouldn't be able to do that.'

His eyes were dark with despair as he said, 'Jessica, you have to believe me – nothing is going on between me and Melissa. You know what a problem I'm having . . .'

'But maybe not with her. Maybe it's just with me.'

'You can't seriously think that. You mean everything to me . . .'

'She hasn't just lost a daughter. She won't remind you of your pain, so I can see she might provide you with an escape, the kind of release you need that you can't find with me.'

'It's not happening,' he told her forcefully. 'There is no affair. I admit I asked her to come to my dressing room today, but not for that – and I had no idea she was even in there until she came out of the shower. I know how hard that must be to believe, but I swear to God it's the truth.'

Jessica looked away, not knowing if it was fear that was making her want to deny her instincts, or whether it was simply that her instincts were all wrong.

'Would you like a drink?' he offered. 'I think we both need one.'

She nodded, then turned her mobile off as it started to ring. Nikki knew she was at home so she could use the landline, and there was no-one else she wanted to speak to tonight.

After handing her a vodka tonic he watched her take a sip, then when her eyes returned to his he said, 'The last thing in the world I ever want is to hurt you, and yet here I am, letting you down in ways I never even dreamt of. It's as though something crazy has come into our lives, or into mine . . .'

'Just tell me this,' she said quietly, 'even if it didn't happen today, either because I interrupted you, or because you're telling the truth . . .' She took a breath. 'I need to know, Charlie, have you ever had sex with Melissa Kingsley?'

He was about to deny it, but with her eyes fixed so intently on his, and the guilt so heavy in his heart, he knew his tone was going to lend the lie to his words. So in the end he said, 'It was a long time ago.'

Her mind started to reel as she stared back at him. Only now did she realise that it wasn't at all the answer she'd been expecting. 'How long ago?' she asked.

'At least six years. But it was never serious. It only happened a handful of times . . .'

She continued to stare at him as the shock went on rippling through her. 'But we were happy then,' she said. 'We were sleeping together regularly, so how could you have been having sex with her?'

Finally realising his mistake in not lying, his face turned grey. 'I don't know,' he answered lamely. 'It just happened.'

She took a breath, started to turn away, then turned back again. 'Is she the only woman you've been unfaithful with,' she asked, 'or have there been others?'

'She's the only one.'

She regarded him as though he were becoming a stranger. 'Do you know what's really frightening me now?' she said. 'It's that I don't know if I believe you.'

'You have to, Jessica, please. No-one's ever mattered to me more than you . . .'

'But if you can hide something like that, it makes me wonder what else you might be hiding.'

At that his face became more haggard than ever.

As she registered the change she felt suddenly sick with the dread of what she might have just stumbled into. 'There is more, isn't there?' she said.

'No. I told you, she's the only one and it was a long time ago.'

She started to shake her head. 'I don't believe you. Something else is going on with you . . .'

'There's nothing,' he cried. 'For heaven's sake, you're making much more of this than you need to . . .'

'No Charlie, I'm making of it exactly what it deserves, because you're lying about something and that's what you say to everything I do, right down to knowing that my own daughter was afraid the day she died. I'm making too much of it, you keep telling me. It's all in my head. Let it go, move on. Well, it's not going to happen. Do you hear me? I'm not letting it go, any more than I'm going to stomach your affair with Melissa.'

'How many times do I have to tell you . . .'

'I believe that's the children coming back,' she cut in, 'so I suggest you start preparing how you're going to explain yourself to Nikki, while I go and put Harry to bed.'

As she reached the bottom of the stairs he said, 'Jessica, what did you mean about not letting it go? What are you intending to do?'

'About Natalie?' she said, turning back. 'I don't know yet, but when I do, you can be sure I won't let you do anything to stop me,' and leaving him feeling heartsick with apprehension for what it could cost her if she ever found out the truth, she ran up the stairs to the children.

The following morning Jessica heard Charlie get up at five thirty and go downstairs. She was in one of the guest rooms, not because they'd fought again last night, but because she'd simply wanted to be left alone to try to think things through and decide where she should go from here.

She'd been awake most of the night, going over and over everything in her mind, trying not to torment herself with how many other women Charlie might have slept with, or what further lies he might have told, until finally she'd realised that this one betrayal, with its deceit stretching over at least six years, was enough on its own to tear her trust from the roots of their marriage. Whether they would be able to repair the damage was impossible to say, though she knew that at some stage she would want to try. For the time being, though, she merely felt the need to put some distance between them so she could think more clearly about everything they were going through, and what was really happening in her heart. As the hours had ticked on through the night her longing for Natalie had been growing all the time. In the face of this loss nothing else seemed to matter, nor could it until she found out the truth of what had really happened that day in France. She wasn't going to run away from it any more, instead she was going to do what she'd always wanted to do, and hadn't only because of Charlie's reluctance to accept her suspicions. It was a strange and sad irony that it should be his betrayal that was setting her free to follow her instincts now.

Hearing a muffled knock on the door, she turned onto her back and called for him to come in.

'Did I wake you?' he said, putting his head round.

'No,' she answered, sitting up against the pillows. 'How did you sleep?'

'Not too well.' He put a coffee on the nightstand and looked down at her. He was pale and drawn and his eyes showed how anxious he was. 'How about you?' he asked.

'Not much,' she replied, and patted the bed for him to sit down. 'Do you have time?'

'A few minutes. What are you going to do today?'

'Everything I'd planned to: take Harry to school, go to Tate Modern to see what books they have on Modigliani, pick up your dry-cleaning . . .'

'Do I take it from that Karina is interested in the biography?' he interrupted.

Almost wishing he hadn't asked, she said, 'That's what I was coming to tell you, yesterday. I was going to call, but then remembering you weren't due on air for a while, I decided to come over to the studios.'

Looking as tortured by the memory of what she'd walked into as he no doubt felt, he picked up her coffee and handed it to her. 'I really am sorry,' he said gruffly as she took it. 'I want you to believe that.'

'I do.'

He gazed helplessly into her eyes. 'Please tell me it's not too late,' he whispered brokenly.

Because she loved him she reached for his hand and held it tight. 'It's too hard to tell you anything right now,' she said. 'All I know is that I want to be on my own for a while, to think about us, and to find out if I'm right about Natalie. No, listen, please,' she said, as he started to interrupt. 'I'm going to call Lilian today to ask if I can go and stay in the grape-picker's cottage. I know you don't want me to, but this is something I feel I have to do, so please don't let's argue. I'll leave right after Harry goes to Devon and stay until he comes back.'

Nothing about his expression showed a willingness to

agree. 'I just don't understand what you think you're going to find,' he protested.

'I don't either,' she admitted. 'Nor will I until I go there.'

'Then let me come with you. I'll get some time off . . .'

'No. I told you, I want to be on my own. I need time to think about what we're going to do, how we go forward from here.'

As his eyes widened with concern she wondered if he'd ever looked more like Harry, and for that alone she couldn't help wanting to fold him in her arms. 'After all these years,' he said, 'with everything we've meant to one another . . . I know what I did was wrong, that it's hurt you deeply, but it was so long ago . . . Surely we can get past it?'

'I hope so,' she answered.

Looking down at their hands, he rolled his thumb over her wedding ring as he said, 'Will you be here when I get home tonight?'

'Of course. I told you, I won't leave until Harry goes to Devon – and only then if the cottage is free.'

His eyes came back to hers. 'You have to understand that any lies I've told, anything I've kept hidden from you, it's only to protect you . . .'

'It's also deceiving me,' she reminded him, 'but now isn't the time to get into it. You need to go, or you'll be late.'

After pressing his lips to her forehead, he left the room, closing the door quietly behind him, and a few minutes later she heard the sound of his car reversing out of the drive. In her mind she travelled with him to the end of the street, out onto Ladbroke Grove, and was almost able to feel the heaviness in his heart. But then she let him go and returned to her decision to go to France, and what she really hoped to achieve there. The obvious answer was to prove that her mother had been lying, though she knew already how difficult that was going to be unless she could persuade her mother to go with her – and even then there were no guarantees of getting her to change her story. So for now, at least, she was happy to go alone.

It wasn't until late morning that she finally got around to calling Lilian, and as usual she had to leave a message, since

Lilian was in the saleroom and not due out until one. A while later Charlie called, just to make sure she was all right, and no sooner had she put the phone down to him than it rang again.

'Jessica, it's Melissa.'

Jessica could only wonder why she hadn't expected this.

'I don't think either of us wants to get into a discussion about yesterday,' Melissa said, 'I'm just calling to ask if it's going to remain between us.'

Realising she was asking if Jessica had any intention of telling Paul, Jessica said, 'It's not something I anticipate coming up in conversation, but tell me, does your husband know about the affair you had with mine six years ago?'

Melissa took a moment to respond. 'No, he doesn't,' she replied evenly, 'but clearly you do.'

'Clearly. One more question, are you and Charlie having an affair now, or am I being painfully naive in asking, considering your state of undress when I walked in on you yesterday?'

'I was there at Charlie's invitation.'

'That's not really answering my question.'

'OK. Then let's just say I might have got my wires crossed.'

Willing to take that as a possibility Charlie might have been telling the truth, Jessica said, 'I'd appreciate it if, the next time you go into his dressing room, or anywhere else you might be alone with him, you'd endeavour to keep your clothes on.'

'Well, I guess I deserved that,' Melissa replied crisply. 'I'd like to say I hope this doesn't affect our friendship, but . . .'

'. . . it will,' Jessica finished for her.

When the call was over she decided to put it out of her mind by taking herself off to Tate Modern for a while. Once there she browsed through the bookshop searching out useful publications on Modigliani and his even more famous peers, before going upstairs to stroll around an uplifting exhibition of Pierre Huyghe's works. On the way home she made a stop at the London Library, where she spent some time photocopying and making notes about the great artist and early twentieth-century Paris, for if she did go to France, it could provide the perfect opportunity to make a start on her book, and even if she didn't, she still needed to gather as much research material as she could find.

'Hi, Jessica? Are you there?' Lilian's voice was coming from the answerphone as Jessica walked back in through the door.

'Yes, I'm here,' Jessica said, grabbing the phone.

'What's been happening?' Lilian asked. 'Did you and Charlie manage to talk last night?'

'Yes, we did. I can't say we've resolved anything particularly, but it's why I called you. I've decided I'd like to go back to the cottage – if it's free. Harry goes away with a friend at the end of next week . . .'

'Jessica, are you sure?' Lilian interrupted. 'I mean, you know how much I'd love you to come, but is it a good idea to stay there? Why don't you stay with us?'

'If I find I can't be in the cottage then I'll take you up on your offer,' Jessica replied, already feeling certain she wouldn't.

'What does Charlie say? Is he coming too?'

'No, and he's not keen on the idea, as you can probably imagine.' Then before Lilian could protest any further, 'Please don't fight me on this. I want to do it – no, I need to do it.'

Still sounding dubious Lilian said, 'OK, I'll call Luc to make sure it's still free. If it is I'll try to take some time off so I can be there with you.'

With a smile Jessica said, 'Thank you. I'd like that.'

Jessica was in Harry's room when the phone rang with what she hoped would be a call back from Lilian. It had been several hours since they'd spoken, but she guessed that was because Lilian had been busy with a sale, or maybe Luc hadn't been readily contactable. The reasons didn't matter, all that did was that the cottage should be free.

'Hello,' she said into the receiver. 'Jessica Moore speaking.'

'Jessica, it's Luc,' he said. 'Lilian tells me you'd like to stay at the cottage.'

For a moment she felt strangely unsteadied by his voice, as

once again it seemed to carry her into the very heart of the vineyard where Natalie had charged and yelped about like any normal ten-year-old girl. 'Yes, please,' she answered. 'If it's possible.'

'Mais bien sûr,' he responded. 'It is free for all of the summer, so you can have it for as long as you like. Will your family be joining you?'

'No. Well, not at first. Maybe later.' Then, remembering his father's tests, 'How is Fernand?'

With a note of irony he said, 'He is going to live, and already he's looking forward to seeing you.'

Jessica smiled as she realised she was looking forward to seeing the old man too.

'I will owe you a big favour,' Luc continued, 'because I believe Lilian is going to take some time off to be here too.'

'So she tells me. If she can.'

'Then we shall remain hopeful. Now, will you need one of us to pick you up at the airport, or will you drive?'

'I'll drive,' she told him, still feeling the pull of the link he provided to Natalie. She mustn't let it confuse her though, or embarrass him or his family, for she couldn't imagine any of them being comfortable in such a role. She just hoped that they really didn't mind her coming, for it was quite likely they were worried about how awkward it might be having her around, but were too polite to say so.

'Then let us know when to expect you,' he said, 'and if there's anything we can do for you in the meantime, just call.'

As she put the phone down Jessica could feel her senses swimming. Only now, after speaking to Luc, was she starting to realise what a big step she was about to take. Yet, in spite of the nerves, she felt a surprising calmness spreading deep inside her, a sense of purpose, even, that seemed to be telling her that she was making the right decision. She only needed to get through the next week with Charlie now, explain as much as she could to Nikki, then after seeing Harry off to Devon she would be on her way . . . she took a breath . . . to Natalie, for that was exactly how it was starting to feel.

Chapter Nine

The vine-covered valley of Valennes was basking quietly in the mid-afternoon sun as Jessica drove past the old farm gates that marked the start of the hamlet, to the staggered T-junction at its heart. On this top road, that came winding in from the nearest village, there were only a few squat cottages sitting like time-forgotten sentinels on the beautifully remote hillock, with a long-abandoned *boulangerie* whose faded sign was still visible on the crumbling side wall, and a single petrol pump with prices still displayed in francs. The rest of Valennes, which consisted of only four more cottages, a couple of derelict barns, the *manoir* and rows upon rows of abundantly fruiting vines, all lay in the magnificent *combe* below.

Before turning left to descend into the heart of it Jessica pulled over for a moment to absorb the seductive vista before her. At any time of year it was breathtaking, but now, at the height of summer, it was hazy and blurred, seeming almost to seep colour, as though it were aspiring to become a spectacular Pissarro or Monet. It was shaped like an amphitheatre, with the south-facing slopes comprising a vast cornucopia of heavily laden vines creating the tiers, and the lazy patchwork of fields that spread towards the horizon forming the stage. In the near distance was a shady wood of maples, yews and limes, and beyond that, though not visible from where she was, was a crystal-clear freshwater lake.

The road she was about to take was more gravel and potholes than tarmac, and dropped steeply away for several metres before easing its descent to a handful of small, closely shuttered dwellings that housed the workers during harvest, and the occasional tourists in summer. Further down, virtually in the bowl of the valley and nestling almost coquettishly in amongst the vines, was a bigger, sprawling cottage that was covered in jasmine and ivy and a liberal sprinkling of pale yellow roses. This was *la maison de vendangeur* – the grape-picker's cottage.

Still Jessica remained where she was, aware of how her breath had shortened as she allowed her eyes to follow the track on through the vineyard to where it ended in a roughly circular flourish in front of the *manoir*, which was halfway up the opposite hill. The *manoir* itself was a large eighteenth-century stone-built house with big sash windows in the upper levels framed by sky blue shutters, and a huge pergola right across the front, where morning glory, honeysuckle and jasmine intertwined with a ferocious ivy and big purple-blooming passion flowers. To one side of the *manoir* was a towering old *pigeonnier* – a dovecote – whose top two floors were used for storage, while the double arch at the bottom was the entrance to the wine *cave*. And to the other side of the *manoir* was a long, low structure that had once been a barn, but was now divided in two to make the office that Luc and Lilian shared when they were here, and the studio where Luc created his sculptures.

There was not a single person in sight, the only signs of life being the Charolais cows in one of the fields and the occasional soar or flutter of a bird. The trees were motionless, as were the vines and the cottages. She lowered her window to inhale the earthy perfume that filled the air, and feel the sun's heat stealing in like a burning cloak. It was strange how in spite of what had happened here she could still sense the silence and beauty settling around her like a balm, seeming to ease content into her heart and a kind of wonder into her soul. Then she found herself recalling the first time she and Charlie had arrived with the children and how she'd experienced a curious sense of returning, even though they'd never been here before.

'Déjà vu,' Natalie had immediately piped up, which had triggered a noisy and amusing ten minutes as she and Nikki explained the meaning to Harry, who ended up claiming he'd been everywhere in the whole wide world before, but he wouldn't tell them what it was like in any of the places because it was his secret and they had to find out for themselves.

On that occasion they'd come to meet the new man in Lilian's life and his family. It had been August, which would make it a year ago now, four months before the Christmas wedding, which was the second time they'd come.

Their third visit and all its horror would remain branded in her memory for ever, yet as she looked down at the glistening grey slate roof of the grape-picker's cottage and its walls of clamouring flowers, it might almost have been possible to persuade herself it was a dream, for the tragedy seemed to have changed nothing in its appearance, or in its spirit. It was still as sleepily benign as ever, and as welcoming in its calm and unobtrusive way.

Her eyes swept back out across the valley as she thought of how hard it was going to be to feel the same about the place if she discovered anything violent or sinister attached to Natalie's death. But was she really expecting to? Before she'd arrived she'd certainly been afraid of it, but now she was here she was starting to wonder why she'd felt so concerned, because there had never really been any suggestion of anything remotely untoward, no inconsistent injuries or suspicious evidence. In fact, looking down at the cottage now, it was almost impossible to imagine anything ominous or even curious happening there at all. So maybe, she thought with a lift of hope in her heart, she was going to find out that her instincts were wrong and everyone else was right.

Pressing her foot gently on the accelerator she let the car roll forward, then caught it with the brake as it picked up speed on the sharp descent. Seeing Lilian come out of the grape-picker's cottage she waved and quickened her speed, and as she turned onto the dry patch of land next to the cottage Lilian pulled open the car door to gather her into a loving embrace.

'You made it,' Lilian declared, her voice muffled by Jessica's shoulder. 'I'm so pleased to see you,' and after squeezing even harder she stood back to get a good look at Jessica's face. 'Are you OK?' she asked. 'It's such a long journey, you must be exhausted.'

Feeling only the pleasure of seeing Lilian, Jessica slid from the 4×4 and hugged her again. 'I'm fine,' she assured her. 'A bit spacey, maybe, but nothing a good leg stretch and glass of chilled Macon-Valennes won't sort out.'

'The leg bit I'll leave to you,' Lilian chuckled, linking her arm as they walked round to the back of the car, 'the wine is over to me – but first, there's someone else here to greet you.'

Expecting it to be Luc, or Fernand, Jessica's eyes widened with surprise when Daniella, Luc's sister, came out of the cottage and crossed the stone patio towards them.

'Sorry, I was up in the attic,' Daniella said, appearing every bit as pleased to see Jessica as Jessica was to see her. '*Ça me plâit très bien à vous voir*,' she said, kissing both Jessica's cheeks. 'We are all very happy you are here. My father is planning a very special dinner in your honour tonight, so I hope you are hungry.'

Jessica smiled into her rich brown eyes, and not for the first time found herself entranced by Daniella's amazing beauty, and the way she seemed so unaffected by it. She had the unmistakable elegance of many Frenchwomen, with exquisite poise and femininity and thick, dark hair which she wore in a single plait that fell almost to her waist. Her features were large and generous and, at times, almost wickedly humorous, while there was such grace to her movements that it was often difficult to stop watching her. Before becoming the wife of a prominent conductor and mother of three, she'd had a promising career as a mezzo-soprano, but apart from special occasions, such as the annual *vendange* celebrations, or the national *Fête de la Musique*, or at local fund-raising events, she rarely sang in public now.

'And I don't regret giving it up for a minute,' she had readily assured Jessica the first time they'd met. 'I love my life with Claude and the children, rolling around our ridiculous château like *petit* peas in a pot. Of course I miss him when he has to be in Paris, but it is good for him to be very important when he is away, because I am afraid he is not very important at home.'

Since Claude had been sitting right next to her when she'd said that, Jessica had seen the humorous light in his eyes that told how much he enjoyed their banter – and perhaps how much he missed her when he was away too.

'I must tell you,' Daniella said now, as they started to unload Jessica's car, 'that my father, *comme d'habitude,* is doing the cooking this evening, so you must prepare for a stew. I know it is very 'ot, and this is probably the very last thing you would like, but you 'ave only yourself to blame, because you and Charlie were so complimentary about it the last time he served you that he is determined to show off again.'

Laughing, Jessica swung her heavy suitcase down to the ground, while Lilian grabbed the laptop and a bag full of carefully chosen books, which included two Virginia Woolfs, an anthology of favourite poems, but most importantly of all *Suite Française,* the extraordinary novel Jessica had reviewed a year ago that had risen instantly to the top of her list of all-time favourites.

'We've cleaned the place top to bottom,' Lilian informed her as she led the way across the patio, where large pots of petunias and geraniums were starting to wilt in the sun. 'The attic bedroom was full of cobwebs, so I left that to Daniella. With a draughty old château, two boys and a girl who thinks she's a boy, she's much better at dealing with that sort of thing than I am.'

'The children are going to be most upset that I didn't keep some of the spiders for pets,' Daniella added, 'but I think we have enough right now, with our dogs and rabbits and mice and worms and goodness knows what else they have in their bedrooms. Always there is something new coming into the house, and always it has to have a name, so please be ready to think of some, because they will be sure to ask.'

'Where are the children?' Jessica asked, feeling a horrible mix of emotions as she thought of Daniella's twins alive and well, and how hard this was suddenly feeling as she approached the double French doors that opened into a spacious, old-fashioned kitchen. But now, she told herself firmly, wasn't the time to shrink from the place Natalie had died.

A moment later she was inside the kitchen and waiting for

her eyes to adjust to the sudden change of light. Already the musty smell of dry wood and centuries-old stone was reaching her, reminding her of how gracious she'd always felt this house to be. Its coolness was a welcome respite from the relentless sun outside, and it had a kind of composure to it that felt gently reassuring. She looked around, taking in the large centre table where various children had carved their initials over the years, and the huge recessed fireplace where an antiquated range was gleaming like new amongst its support cast of cookpots and ladles. Then there was the latched door at the top of two steps that opened into the sitting room, and next to that was the foot of the staircase that rose across the back wall of the kitchen. Straight away Jessica noticed the banister that had been put in since her last visit, and could only wish with all her heart that it had always been there.

'The twins are at a birthday party,' Daniella said, while tidying a broom and dustpan into one of the tall, creamy-coloured cupboards that only vaguely matched the rest of the kitchen, 'and Hugo is at home with his papa.'

'Claude's here?' Jessica said, surprised and pleased, for she liked Daniella's husband immensely.

'It is August,' Daniella reminded her, 'all of Paris takes their *vacances en août*, except,' she added, tapping Lilian's cheek with a finger, 'my workaholic sister-in-law who is off to Hong Kong in two days.'

Unable to hide her disappointment, Jessica turned to Lilian. 'So soon?' she said. 'When we spoke last night . . . I thought you were going to be here for at least ten days.'

'So did I,' Lilian groaned, 'but would you believe, Michel Racine, our current managing director, had a heart attack in the early hours of this morning. Not fatal, apparently he's likely to recover, but as yours truly is due to step into his shoes at the end of September, I was nominated to take his place at a major seminar in Kowloon.'

Jessica wanted to protest, in fact she was almost desperate to, but how could she without seeming absurdly needy or selfish?

'I shouldn't be much longer than a week,' Lilian assured her, 'so you'll still be here when I get back, and obviously

Daniella's going to be around . . . Now, what do you say we break out the wine.'

Being the closest to the cooler, Jessica pulled it open and passed a perfectly chilled bottle to Daniella to uncork. She was still unsettled by the prospect of being here without Lilian, not only because she took such comfort in her presence, but because she was afraid the family might consider her a burden. However, if Daniella's greeting was anything to go by, she probably didn't need to worry immediately, and after a few days of her being here they'd soon realise that she had no intention of disrupting their lives in any way, or indeed of putting them to any trouble at all.

'*Oh là là*, Papa will be most pleased that you have chosen this one,' Daniella informed her, holding up the wine. 'It is from last year, which was not too bad for us. He is saving his specials from Montrachet, or Montagny, or Chablis, I don't know where exactly yet, for dinner, naturally, but any time you would like to restock your cooler, you know you just have to pop into the *cave* and Jean-Marc or one of the *ouvriers* will carry it down for you. Now,' she said, looking at her watch, 'I will open this bottle, and then I am sorry, but I must leave. I have some things to do in Macon and then I have to pick up the twins.'

After she'd gone Lilian filled two glasses, then carried one to Jessica who was still standing at the French doors watching Daniella's car climb to the top road.

'Fernand is very tolerant of the way we English drink wine,' Lilian told her, going back for her own glass. 'He thinks we're mad of course, and very uncultured to take it without food, but luckily he isn't snobbish about it.'

Unable to imagine Fernand being snobbish about anything, Jessica smiled and turned back into the kitchen. 'It's too hot to sit outside,' she said, slipping into one of the rail-backed wooden chairs that surrounded the table.

'Which reminds me,' Lilian said, 'someone's supposed to be bringing a parasol down from the house to shade the table on the patio. The one that was here seems to have disappeared. Probably got taken by a tourist, or one of last season's pickers. Anyway, cheers and welcome back to *la maison de vendangeur.*' Her voice dropped a little as she added, 'How do you feel about being here?'

Though there was a tightness in Jessica's heart as she clinked glasses, she was able to say with reasonable honesty, 'Actually, not too bad. I thought it might be more difficult, but maybe I won't really know until I'm alone.'

Lilian was regarding her closely. 'Are you sure you won't stay up at the house?' she said. 'There's plenty of room and Fernand wouldn't mind a bit.'

'Thank you, but I really do want to stay here.' Then, after taking another sip, 'I don't suppose you found anything while you were cleaning up?'

Lilian's eyes were dark with feeling as she said, 'Nothing that isn't always here.' She took a breath, and sounding almost tentative, she said, 'I spoke to Charlie earlier. We're both hoping this visit will help you come to terms with what happened so you can stop tormenting yourself this way.'

Feeling annoyed both by their concern and their continued inability to believe in her instincts, even though they seemed to have deserted her now, Jessica said, 'How was he when you spoke to him?'

Lilian looked down at her drink and slowly shook her head. 'To be honest he sounded exhausted and very worried about you.'

Jessica sat back in her chair and rubbed her hands over her face. 'This past week hasn't been easy,' she confessed. 'He really didn't want me to come. He thinks I'll just end up even more confused than I already am.'

'I suppose there's always a danger of that,' Lilian said softly.

'Even if there is, I'm here now, and frankly I'm more relieved to be away than I expected. He's been so on edge since the thing with Melissa, snapping at everyone, especially me . . . It's strange, isn't it, the way we start to push away the very people we're afraid will reject us? I used to do it with my mother – maybe I still do.'

Lilian's eyes came up. 'Any news on her yet?' she asked.

Jessica shook her head. 'Actually, I was thinking about asking her to join me here, if we manage to find out where she is. I doubt she'll come though, and Charlie thinks it's a terrible idea. Well, he would when he saw how bad it got between us after Natalie died. He thinks I should just let it all go now, and focus on what's happening between me and him.'

The corners of Lilian's mouth went down. 'Maybe he has a point.'

Jessica sighed, and struggled for the words to explain what she barely understood herself. 'I had to get away from him for a while,' she said, 'not because I don't love him, but because I do and I'm afraid of how many more lies there might be – and if there are any, I don't want to cope with them before I've sorted out in my mind what really happened here.'

Though there was a light of understanding in Lilian's eyes as she looked at her she said nothing for a while, only picked up her wine and stared down into its depths as though there were some hidden mystery there. 'I know what I feel isn't relevant,' she said in the end, 'but it makes me so sad to think of you and Charlie having these problems. You were always so happy together.' She glanced at Jessica as though expecting a response, but Jessica didn't even look up. 'I used to envy you so much,' Lilian continued. 'You two had everything I ever dreamed of, a great marriage, close friendship, successful careers, lovely children . . . I'd virtually given up hope of any of it ever happening for me, and now it has, it seems so wrong to think it could be falling apart for you.'

Hearing it put like that, Jessica couldn't help but rise to her and Charlie's defence. 'Maybe it won't,' she said. 'I'm already missing him, and I only left this morning.' She had to wonder why she'd felt the need to add the lie. Was it to make Lilian feel better, or had she hoped that speaking the words aloud might make them true?

'He'll be waiting to hear from you,' Lilian prompted. 'He needs to know you arrived safely.'

'Yes, of course. I'll ring when I've finished my wine.' Putting on a smile, she said, 'Sorry, maybe I am a bit tired after the drive. I don't mean to sound so maudlin.'

'You don't. Just confused and perhaps a little strained. You've been through a lot lately.'

'Which is no reason to sit here feeling sorry for myself, or taking up all of your time.'

Lilian laughed in surprise. 'For you I have all the time in the world, you know that.'

'Except when you're in Hong Kong,' Jessica reminded her wryly.

Lilian grimaced. 'Do you mind?' she said. 'I could always try to get out of it, but . . .'

'Don't you dare, not on my account. I'll be fine here with Daniella and the children for company.'

'And Fernand,' Lilian reminded her. 'And Luc, when he gets back. He's at the foundry in Italy at the moment, checking on one of his sculptures.'

Jessica smiled, but her eyes were starting to lose focus, so Lilian said no more, simply let the next few minutes pass quietly, with only the drone of a wasp batting around the window and the steadying tick of a grandmother clock in the sitting room next door to break the silence.

'Shall we carry your things upstairs?' Lilian offered after a while. 'I prepared the big bedroom for you, and Daniella brought a mosquito net that's making it look very romantic up there.' Her eyes twinkled. 'Maybe after a couple of weeks away from Charlie, you'll be ready to invite him to join you.'

Jessica's expression became sardonic. 'You never know,' she responded, and getting to her feet she braced herself to approach the stairs.

Seeming to sense her hesitation, Lilian got up too and put an arm around her as they looked down at the spot on the flagstone floor where Jessica had been told Natalie had landed. To Jessica it felt odd that there should be no sign of the fall, no scratch or bloodstain or even the tiniest scrap of one of the newspapers that Natalie had apparently tripped over. It had been like this the day after it happened, everything cleaned up before she arrived, so that the place was looking perfectly normal, as though nothing tragic, or even remotely unusual, had happened here at all.

'I suppose it's like when someone is killed on the road,' she said. 'A hundred or more lives are changed for ever, while the road itself always stays the same. Probably that's why people take flowers to the spot, to make it different.'

Then turning to Lilian, she said, 'Not that I'm planning to set up a little shrine here on the floor, so please don't worry.'

Lilian squeezed her gently. 'Come on, let's get that monster suitcase up to your room,' she said, 'then I should leave you in peace to phone Charlie and the children.'

The upstairs landing was narrow and dark, with only a single window at each end, and three doors leading off, two to bedrooms, the third to a bathroom. The furthest bedroom was the one Natalie had used when she'd come with her grandmother at Easter, the closest was as large as the sitting room below it, and appeared every bit as romantic as Lilian had promised with copious folds of white muslin cascading over the bed, and nothing but crisp white linen sheets and a billowing explosion of pillows beneath it. The furniture itself was heavy and dark, with the same air of permanence as the cottage itself. The window was enormous, rising from just above the crooked floorboards almost to the beamed ceiling, and was swathed in more muslin that was fluttering gently in the breeze of a fan. From here there was a clear view of the vineyards and the *manoir* and the endless blue sky overhead.

'I'll close the hatch,' Lilian said, starting to climb the wall ladder that led up to the attic. It was where Natalie and Harry had slept when they'd come for the wedding, declaring it much more creepy and adventurous than just a boring old bedroom. In the height of summer it was hardly possible to go up there, but at Christmas they'd barely ventured down, they had been so engrossed in their make-believe worlds.

'OK,' Lilian said, jumping off the bottom rung, 'is there anything you need? There's soap, toothpaste, new toothbrush, towels, you name it, in the bathroom, and plenty of hot water, if you can stand it in this heat. The fridge has the essentials, butter, marmalade, eggs, cheese, well, you'll see when you go down. Jean-Marc, the wine-maker, tends to bring baguettes and croissants in the morning, so I hope you'll come over and breakfast with us, but if you prefer to stay here, he can always drop something off on his way.'

Jessica was regarding her fondly. 'Is there anything you haven't thought of?' she teased.

'If there is, be sure to tell me. Oh, if you need to access the Internet feel free to use my computer. You know where it is.'

'Won't Luc mind me crashing into the studio if he's working?' Jessica asked.

'Oh no. Anyway, his studio's separate to the office, remember? But don't worry, he's perfectly used to people crashing in on him, particularly little people who go by the names of Antoine, Elodie and Hugo. He tries growling at them, or threatening them with all manner of grisly deterrents, but it never seems to have an effect.'

Smiling at the spectacle of Luc trying to be menacing with his niece and nephews, Jessica said with some irony, 'Then I'll have to hope he doesn't growl at me.'

'As if he'd dare,' Lilian responded with a laugh. Then with a quick burst of affection she hugged her again. 'I'm so pleased you're here,' she said. 'I just wish this stupid Hong Kong thing hadn't come up, but I know Daniella will take great care of you while I'm away – or not, if you prefer to be left alone. Now, I'd better get back to the house. I have some calls I need to make before dinner, and I know you do too. Aperitifs at seven, is that OK for you?'

'Absolutely,' Jessica assured her. 'I'll look forward to it.'

'Oh, I can't remember,' Lilian said, turning back as she reached the door, 'did I already tell you that Luc's in . . . Yes, I did. So it'll be all of us, *sans mon mari*, this evening. He'd just better be back before I leave on Thursday, is all I can say,' and with a wink that told Jessica she had every confidence he would be, she started off on the five-minute walk back through the vineyard to home.

Left alone in the cottage, Jessica returned to the foot of the stairs and looked up to the landing above. For a while she saw only what was actually there, a steep wooden staircase with a new wooden banister, a shadowy archway above, and the hint of a curtain in its tie-back . . . until finally, in her mind's eye, she was able to see Natalie, clinging to her mobile phone and on the brink of running downstairs as she shouted, 'Mum! *Mum*!'

'Natalie, no!'

Jessica's heart froze as the echo of her mother's voice seemed to escape her imagination to cry out in reality.

She took a breath, then another. The spectral horror retreated and she was left feeling strangely alone, in a way she hadn't a few seconds ago.

She tried to imagine where Natalie might have been running from. Was it the large bedroom across the landing, or the one she'd been using further along? Maybe she'd come down from the attic. And where had her mother been at the time of the fall? Veronica had said she was in the large bedroom with the door open, which was how she'd been able to see Natalie at the top of the stairs, so provided Jessica believed her mother, that must mean Natalie had come from her own room, or even the bathroom. The problem was, Jessica didn't believe her mother. She wasn't even sure she believed in the walk they'd apparently taken just before the fall, for there had been no muddy boots that she knew of, or damp coats, and it had been raining that day.

Had the police checked for damp coats, or muddy boots? Had they questioned Veronica's story at all? Not in any great detail, Jessica was sure, because no-one had ever doubted her story. It was all just a terrible tragedy that the grandmother would probably never get over – and maybe the parents wouldn't either.

Feeling tears starting to well in her eyes, Jessica sat down on the bottom stair and covered her face with her hands. The frustration of not knowing why Natalie had called was almost as punishing as the loss itself. She felt constantly that she had let Natalie down, that she should have been there for her, should never have allowed her to go. If she hadn't Natalie would be with her now – the real Natalie, not the ghost that was impossible to hold, or see, or hear, nor the memory of a child who would never grow old, who had been as vital to her family as the air they breathed. A surge of longing rose up in her so forcefully that her arms started to reach out. She wanted her baby. She needed to feel the life in her tender little body, the pulse of blood beneath her skin, the softness of her hair. She wanted to feast her eyes on her face, watch her frown and smile, smell the freshness of her breath, taste the salt of her tears. She couldn't make herself accept that she'd never know Natalie as any older than ten. She would never be a teenager with tantrums and hormones, or a student with dreams and first loves, or a vet, which was what she'd always wanted to be, or a bride, or a young mother . . .

As the anguish intensified Jessica could hardly breathe. Natalie's life should never have been taken from her. It was wrong. There had been a terrible mistake. 'What happened, Nat?' she whispered brokenly. 'Why did you call me? What were you going to say?'

It wasn't as though she expected an answer, or even any kind of sign, but when her mobile started to ring she felt an absurd beat of hope in her heart. By the time she dug the phone from her bag the hope had gone, but seeing it was Nikki seemed to bolster her anyway.

'Hi, darling, how are you?' she asked, using her fingers to dry her cheeks.

'I'm good,' Nikki assured her. 'How about you? You sound as though you're crying.'

'Sneezing,' Jessica corrected. 'Probably a touch of hay fever.'

'So you're there now? How is it?'

'Very hot, and peaceful. Lilian and Daniella were here when I arrived. They've gone now.'

'So are you OK on your own? Is it hard?'

'A bit, but I'm glad I came. Where are you?'

'In Dad's dressing room. He's just popped along to the studio for something, but he wanted me to ring to make sure you'd arrived. Oh hang on, someone's just come in.'

As she waited, Jessica could hear Nikki informing whoever it was that Charlie should be back any minute, then the other person apparently leaving a message. She wondered how she'd feel if it were Melissa's voice she was hearing in the background, but then Nikki was back on the line saying, 'Sorry about that. Where were we?'

'You were saying that Dad wanted you to call, and I was wondering why he couldn't call me himself.'

'I think because he's like trying to give you some space. After all, it's what you wanted, isn't it?'

Jessica closed her eyes. Nikki's tartness she could do

without right now, but she had to remember that angry as Nikki might be with her father for what had happened with Melissa, she was still very close to him, and probably feeling overly protective now she could see he was hurting. 'What are you two planning this evening?' she asked, deciding to change the subject.

'Three,' Nikki responded. 'Dad's taking me and Freddy to Beach Blanket Babylon for dinner.'

Jessica felt the irony, for the contrast of their evenings could hardly be more striking – her under a flower-covered pergola in the middle of France enjoying the company of a family she felt more at ease with than most of the friends they'd known for years, and Charlie in a trendy eatery full of gaudy decor and famous faces. She knew where she'd rather be, but guessed that given the choice, Charlie would probably prefer to be here too.

'He's just come back,' Nikki said. 'I'll put him on. Oh, before I do, Freddy and I have been invited to join some of his friends in Norfolk for the last two weeks in August. I hope that's OK with you.'

'But it's your eighteenth . . .'

'I know, I know, but I really want to go Mum, so can't we do something when I get back? Dad says it's fine, so if he's OK about it . . .' She let the sentence hang in a way that was typical of her when she was playing her parents off one against the other.

'Then I suppose I am too,' Jessica responded, because she was clearly expected to, rather than because she meant it. Not that she blamed Nikki for wanting to spend her birthday with her boyfriend and in much younger company, it was simply that she'd hoped to do something special for her. 'Shall I speak to Dad now?' she said.

A moment later Charlie said, 'Hi, is everything all right?' No 'darling', she noticed, and his tone was clipped in a way that betrayed his nerves.

'It's fine,' she answered. 'I hear you're off to Babylon this evening.'

'I thought it was better than eating alone. Where are you?'

'At the grape-picker's cottage. I arrived about an hour ago.'

'So I take it you were going to call at some point to let us know you got there safely?'

Ignoring his terseness she said, 'Actually, Nikki beat me to it by seconds. Lilian's been here since I arrived, so this is the first chance . . .'

'You don't have to make excuses.'

'Dad, ease up,' she heard Nikki say in the background.

Jessica waited, and a moment later, sounding more strained than ever, Charlie said, 'Sorry. I guess I'm finding this all a bit strange, you going off without me.'

'It's not the first time we've been apart,' Jessica reminded him. 'Far from it . . .'

'It's the first time like this. Anyway, are you convinced yet that what happened to Natalie was an accident?'

She tried to bite her tongue, or at least take the asperity from her tone as she replied, but even as she spoke she knew she'd failed. 'Actually, I've hardly had a chance to unpack, never mind go into anything else, and I deeply resent the insinuation that I'm wasting my time. Besides, I didn't only come here for that, as you well know, so instead of doing your damnedest to get under my skin, maybe you might try asking how Lilian is.'

'I know how she is. I spoke to her earlier.'

'Oh yes, when you discussed my need to stop trying to make my daughter's death into something neither of you feel it is.'

'Not just me and Lilian, but the police, Fernand and his family . . .'

'All right, let's call a stop to this now,' she cut across him. 'I'm tired, I need to shower and change for dinner, and I don't want to spend the evening regretting saying things that would be better left unsaid. I take it you wouldn't enjoy that much either, so let's speak again in the morning, shall we?'

'OK,' he said. Then added, 'I'm sorry.'

Feeling her heart soften, she said, 'Me too.'

There was a moment's silence, then hearing him ring off she clicked off her own mobile, and taking her iPod from the computer case she carried it upstairs to the bedroom. Something soothing from Bach or Haydn should help calm her mind now, and blend her more fully into her surroundings, as she prepared for an evening she was actually looking forward to. She just hoped Fernand and his family were too.

Chapter Ten

By the time Jessica closed the doors of the cottage and started up through the vineyard the sun was spreading a soft rosy glow over the valley. The palette of colours would deepen and change as the evening advanced, until finally there would be a dazzling blaze on the horizon before this perfect summer day gave itself up to darkness.

As she walked, inhaling the warm, unsullied air as though it were an elixir, and admiring the fattening clusters of grapes that would soon be ready for harvest, she was thinking of Charlie and trying not to feel disloyal for being so glad she'd come alone. They really did need to be apart for a while, and now she was here the very ease of her movements and the lightness stealing into her heart as the tensions unfurled were telling her just how beneficial this time could be. Hopefully he would start to feel it too, and realise, now she wasn't around, just how much pressure they'd been putting one another under with all their grief and fears, as well as their needs and even their love. They'd been too close, expected too much of one another while neither of them really had it in them to give. Maybe she'd try saying that to him the next time they spoke, it might help him to stop feeling so angry and rejected.

As she approached the *manoir*, which appeared sleepily contented in the evening sun, she could already see Daniella and Claude beneath the nearside of the pergola, where a collection of cane and wicker furniture provided the setting for aperitifs, before everyone moved over to the large granite table at the other end to dine. The children were there too, as lively and noisy as ever, and though she was pleased to see them she couldn't help being painfully aware of the child that was missing.

As soon as they spotted her the nine-year-old twins – Antoine and Elodie – came zooming across the forecourt to greet her, reminding her of how Nikki had once commented, 'Those twins don't do shy.'

'*Bonsoir* Jessica,' they shouted, their beautiful young faces both eager and hesitant. '*Nous sommes très contents que vous soyez venue. Où est Harry? Il arrive bientôt?*' We're really happy you're here. Where is Harry? Is he coming soon?

She knew it wasn't that they'd forgotten Natalie, or no longer cared, it was simply that the world had moved on for them, as it should. It was also probable that Daniella had cautioned them not to mention their friend tonight, for which Jessica could only feel grateful. 'Harry *est en vacances en Angleterre*,' she said, stooping to embrace them. '*Mais il a envoyé un texto pour vous sur mon portable.*' And producing her mobile from the silver purse she was carrying, she called up the text message Harry had sent just for them and passed it over.

'*Mais c'est en anglais*,' Elodie protested, her stunning olive green eyes coming to Jessica's.

'You can read English very well,' Claude informed her as he strolled towards them.

Looking up Jessica felt her expression turn to one of genuine pleasure, for she truly liked this short, pot-bellied man with his balding head and soulful eyes. His smile was as roguishly captivating as his humour, and his gift for making people feel welcome was as exceptional as the skills that made him one of France's most celebrated conductors.

'Jessica,' he said warmly as he held out his arms. 'What a delight to see you. *Bienvenue ma chère.*'

As he kissed both her cheeks Jessica could see Daniella smiling at them fondly from the shade of the pergola, while four-year-old Hugo, unattended for a moment, plunged a fat little fist into a bowl of something creamy and green. Then Fernand was coming out of the house, a laden tray in his hands, and a big happy smile on his face.

'Aah, Jessica,' he said in his deeply guttural voice, 'you are here. Come, come. It is still very hot in the sun, you must be in the shade and we will give you *un petit verre*. This is a young Chardonnay from our *parcelle* at Nuit St Georges, which Luc tells me is a little too *corsé*, but he is wrong, *comme d'habitude*. It is a very excellent *cuvée*, which is why it wins an award.' Setting the tray down, he drew her into a pleasingly avuncular embrace. '*Ah ma petite*,' he sighed with obvious affection. 'I am very pleased that you come. Lilian, she is afraid you will not, after what happen, and it make her sad to think that her home cannot be yours any more.'

'*Papa! Papa!*' Elodie suddenly erupted, as she and Antoine finished deciphering Harry's text. '*Nous duvons envoyer un message à Harry. Tu as ton portable? Donnes-le, donnes-le.*' We must send Harry a text. Do you have your mobile? Give it to me.

'*Oh là là!*' Daniella cried, finally noticing Hugo's creamy green face and fingers. '*Hugo, tu n'est pas sage. Bon, tiens. Qu'est qu'on va faire de toi?*' Hugo, you naughty boy. What are we going to do with you?

'Give him to me,' Claude said. 'I will take him inside with the others to find my mobile so they can send a message, and then I'll wash him,' he added with a playful growl at his son.

After Claude and the children had gone Daniella greeted Jessica too, while Fernand poured no more than four centimetres of pale yellow wine into three plain tulip glasses.

'You see, we do not pour for the others until they arrive,' Daniella explained, as Fernand replaced the bottle in the cooler. 'This way the wine stays at the correct temperature in the bottle, and it will not become too warm in our glasses before we have time to finish.'

Smiling as she recalled Lilian telling her precisely that not long after joining the family, clearly thrilled to be learning about something that was so important to Luc, Jessica picked up her glass and imitated the way Fernand was swirling the wine around his.

'*Ah, c'est friand*,' Fernand declared after taking a generous sip and rolling it around his mouth.

'*Friand?*' Jessica queried.

'It means it is very good, delicious to drink,' Daniella explained.

Jessica was about to take a sip too when Fernand suddenly

said, 'Ah, here they are. I am thinking we must ring a bell to bring them.'

Curious, Jessica turned to follow the direction of his eyes, and in the glare of the setting sun she saw Lilian coming out of the studio. Then to her surprise she saw that Luc was with her.

'I tell them,' Fernand was saying to Daniella in French, 'that they work too hard. Always work, work, work, those two.'

As they drew closer it was evident to Jessica that they hadn't been working at all, for Lilian's cheeks were flushed and her eyes were shining, as a woman's eyes only shine after making love.

'Jessica, you're already here,' Lilian cried. 'I'm sorry if we kept you. Look who arrived about an hour ago without even telling me he was coming.'

Jessica was smiling as she looked at Luc. He was a tall man with thick, dark hair and deep-set eyes that were currently mirroring the warmth of her own, and just like every other time they'd met – or even spoken on the phone – she was aware of how drawn she felt to him. He was a man of many contrasts, one of which was in his muscular physique which seemed to show both the rugged maleness of the *vigneron,* and the sensitive elegance of the artist. She'd never really known whether she considered him handsome or not, though his heavy brows and irregular features certainly made him striking, and when he smiled, as he did now, the harshness of his mouth was utterly transformed.

'Jessica,' he said, kissing her on both cheeks. 'Welcome, it is very good to see you.'

She responded with equal sincerity, and was once again aware of the connection she felt to him because of the role he'd played at the time of Natalie's death. Since she and Charlie hadn't been there, it helped to know that Luc had been the one to carry her little body to the ambulance, rather than a stranger. She'd often wondered how they'd have got through it without him, for he'd been such a support to Charlie, taking care of all the complicated bureaucracy and even arranging the terrible flight home. Tonight was the first time she'd seen him since the little coffin had been loaded on board, which he would be aware of too, and she warmed to him all over again as his eyes seemed to tell her that he understood what she was thinking and that she didn't need to be embarrassed, or afraid.

She smiled and squeezed his hand, then hearing Lilian talking and laughing she turned to find out what was going on, while Luc dutifully greeted his sister. Fernand was fast becoming the object of much teasing and banter as Lilian and Daniella took him to task over the quality of the wine and choice of main dish, while Claude, having left the twins inside with his mobile, came to plonk Hugo into his mother's lap, before asking Lilian about her upcoming seminar.

When they eventually moved over to the table to eat Daniella drew Jessica into conversation, telling her what plans she had for the coming week, if Jessica wanted to join in. Then Daniella was intrigued to know more about the book Jessica was planning to write, which seemed to pique everyone's interest in a way that Jessica found not only flattering but inspiring.

Having yielded to his daughter's protests over his proposed stew, Fernand produced a delicious coq au vin, made, he told them with merrily gleaming eyes, to his very own secret recipe.

'He means he used one of *grand crus*,' Luc whispered to Jessica.

She chuckled and felt slightly light-headed as she reached for her glass. How was it possible to be so happy when this place contained the most painful memories of her life? She looked at Lilian and found at least one answer in her dear, familiar face, for her infectious good humour and unfailing support was as nourishing for her soul as it was for her heart. And this new family of hers – how could anyone feel anything but relaxed in their company, when they were so easy with one another and generous with their hospitality?

The sun sank over the horizon and candles were lit. The children were carried inside to continue sleeping, while Fernand sat back to savour the rest of the evening, his duties at an end. Jessica found herself remembering the dinner she'd planned for Charlie, which would never happen now. She couldn't regret it, she could only think of how different it was here where the talk flowed as freely and deliciously as the full-bodied Montrachet wine, from art to music to politics and literature, in a way that was never meant to impress, only to convey enjoyment or inform. In London the wits around the table would always dominate, never really engaging, or even listening, only ever performing. The self-importance and privilege were as rife as the need to excel, whereas here there seemed no need to prove anything at all.

The dessert had been prepared by Lilian, and Luc went into the kitchen with her to help carry everything out. They exuded such an air of romance that Jessica guessed they would steal a lingering kiss, and maybe even an intimate caress, and it made her feel a little sad as she thought of how often she and Charlie had stolen similar moments over the years.

When Lilian came back with a fresh fruit flan that she'd clearly picked up at the *pâtisserie* everyone booed and laughed, while Luc planted a kiss at the nape of her neck as she leaned forward to put the flan on the table before handing out the plates. Lilian's eyes came to Jessica's, and Jessica looked at her with all the affection that was in her heart. It meant so much to her to see Lilian as happy as she deserved to be, especially when she'd waited so long.

'Luc has to drive over to Geneva tomorrow,' Lilian informed her, 'so I'm all yours till he gets back. We thought we'd take you out to one of our favourite restaurants in the evening. Maybe you'd like to come too,' she said to Claude and Daniella.

'I think we would love to,' Daniella responded without hesitation. 'And you, Papa. Ah *mais non*, it is your evening for playing *boules*.'

'What takes you to Geneva?' Jessica asked Luc, as the others began to discuss a concert Claude and Daniella were planning in the garden of their château at the end of the month.

'One of our biggest clients,' he replied. 'It was my intention to stop there on the way back from Italy, but then I decided I would rather be here tonight.'

Jessica's eyes moved to Lilian, who seemed engrossed in something Fernand was saying. 'It's a shame you two don't see more of one another,' she commented with the hint of a sigh.

Luc looked at Lilian too. 'Yes,' he responded, 'but her work is important to her, as mine is to me. We understand this in one another, and I think it is safer to have these kinds of rivals than the other kind, *non*?'

Seeing the twinkle in his eyes Jessica realised Lilian couldn't have told him about Charlie, which was a relief. Picking up her fork to start on the flan, she said, 'When you say work, which work are you talking about? Your photojournalism? The winery? Your sculpture?'

'Ah,' he laughed, 'now I feel like a man who is unable to commit to one thing, and maybe this is true. Does that make me less of a person? Someone who is not worthy of respect in the eyes of the world?'

Jessica found herself laughing. 'I think that's going a little far,' she chided. 'If you're good at all three, it probably makes you worthy of more respect.'

'Ah, but modesty will not allow me to claim such a thing,' he replied. 'So I will say that photography is something I do. It comes very naturally, and is important to my sculpture so it is a part of that too. The winery is my father's passion, as you know. I'm not saying it's one I don't share, but for me the sculpture will always come first.'

'You must ask him to show you his works,' Fernand piped up.

Jessica turned to him, unaware he'd been listening.

'I know perhaps I am . . . *préjugé*?' Fernand continued.

'Biased,' Daniella provided.

'Biased,' Fernand repeated, finding the pronunciation hard, 'but he is very good. His expositions are receiving fine reviews and he even sells some of his pieces.'

'Because you buy them all,' Daniella reminded him.

'No, this is not true,' Fernand protested with a laugh. 'I buy some, I admit, but you and Claude buy the others.'

As Luc balled a napkin to throw at his father Jessica was wishing that she could capture the way she was feeling now, and go back to it every time she felt lonely, or afraid, or unable to cope. There seemed to be a calmness in her, and a quiet exhilaration that might be to do with the wine, but was also connected to the sense of freedom she was feeling at being no-one's wife, or mother, or someone who was recognised almost anywhere she went. Tonight she was merely an ordinary woman at a candlelit table in a secluded French valley who had found a place and a time to be happy, and who knew no desires beyond the next sip of full-bodied wine or taste of pungent *chevroton* cheese.

And that was how she continued to feel for the rest of the evening, tranquil, joyous and satisfyingly absorbed in the heady sensation of being somewhere she belonged, even though she didn't. And she was still feeling that way when Luc and Lilian walked her back through the vineyard to the cottage. Then, for the first time in months, she managed to fall asleep without the heaviness of guilt in her heart, because she was here with Natalie, doing what she should have done long before now, trying to find out why she had sounded so panicked when she'd called her in the seconds before she died.

The following morning when Jessica opened her eyes she was confused for a moment about where she was, until, remembering, she felt the pleasure of it unfolding gently inside her. She turned onto her back and lay quietly watching the iridescent rays of the sunrise reaching into the room, turning the gauzy nets around her into a pyramid of fiery mist. No more than a whisper of breeze was drifting in through the drapes at the open window, while the sounds of busy bird life chirped and warbled through the early morning hush.

She was barely even aware of what she was thinking as her mind, like the butterflies in the vines, pitched and flew, hovered, then soared on to somewhere new. Charlie, the children, Lilian and Luc, her mother, Jeanne Hébuterne and Amedeo Modigliani . . .

Natalie.

On the nightstand next to her the phone started to ring.

Guessing it would be Charlie, even though it was barely six o'clock with him, she reached over to pick it up.

'I hope I haven't woken you,' Luc said. 'If I have please blame Lilian.'

Jessica smiled. 'Consider her blamed,' she responded. 'But I wasn't asleep.'

'That is a relief, because she becomes very frightening when she is woken before she would like to be, and I wasn't sure if you might be the same.'

Jessica laughed. 'Where is she?' she asked.

'Would you believe, on the phone to Hong Kong? However, she is interested to know if you would like to walk with her to the village this morning to have breakfast in the café.'

Jessica couldn't think of anything she'd like more.

'Then she will come in an hour,' he told her. 'I will bring her as I leave.'

After he'd rung off Jessica got out of bed and walked down the stairs in her nightie. It was short and silky and clung to her slender body as the heat was already clinging to the air. She filled the kettle, lit the gas under it, then pulled the doors open and stepped out onto the patio. The sun's warmth felt as welcoming as a lover's arms, while the vines were as still as a painting, and the sky overhead was an immaculate expanse of blue. Seeing the pots were dry, she filled a watering can from a rusty tap, then walked about the patio slaking the thirst of the flowers that would soon burst back into life. In a way it was as though something similar was happening to her, for she was aware of a new fluidity in her movements, and an ease in her heart that hadn't been there twenty-four hours ago.

When she'd finished she stood looking around, and thought, if it weren't for her nightie, she could almost be Modigliani's *Standing Nude with Garden Background*. Smiling to herself she turned back inside, where she sat at the table waiting for the water to boil. For a while she became the *Seated Nude* (with nightie), then, enjoying having no demands on her at all, she began reading the carved initials on the table. She knew this cottage had once belonged to Luc's grandmother, and then his mother who'd died ten years ago from cancer. Jessica remembered how close to tears Lilian had been when she'd told her about it. This was typical of Lilian, to feel for someone else's pain just because she loved them, even if she didn't know the person they'd lost. It was one of the many things that made her so special.

The kettle began to whistle, and after making some tea with the lemon grass she'd found in a pot outside, she carried it upstairs where she set the cup down on the bathroom sink while she took a shower. Before she left she'd call Nikki and Harry, or at least send them a text. She should call Charlie too, but she didn't want him to snap at her, or tell her again that she was wasting her time, so maybe she'd speak to him later in the day, rather than let him spoil her mood now.

By the time Luc and Lilian pulled up in the car she was perched on the gatepost wearing shorts and a T-shirt, with her purse and phone clutched in one hand, and a small floppy hat in the other. As Lilian got out, Luc's door opened too and Jessica was touched to realise that he was coming round the car to say good morning to her.

'Did you sleep well?' he asked, kissing her on either cheek.

'Very,' Jessica assured him. 'I'm sorry you're not joining us for breakfast.'

His eyes were dancing as he said, 'But then my wife would not be able to talk about me.'

Lilian laughed, and tilted her head back onto his shoulder as he kissed her.

'I will see you later,' he said, to them both. 'Have a good day and try to spare a thought for those of us who must work.'

As he drove off they stood watching the car, waving and waiting for the small clouds of dust to settle as it disappeared from view. 'Well, I don't know about you,' Lilian declared with a gusty sigh, 'but making love in the morning gives me a hearty appetite. So, are you ready to head off to the hills?'

Chuckling, Jessica linked her arm, saying, 'I've been meaning to ask, has anyone rented the other cottages this summer? The place seems pretty deserted right now.'

'Funny, but I had an idea you might ask,' Lilian replied, 'so I can tell you that the German couple who rent the smallest cottage every August have taken it this year too, but they're touring the Loire at the moment and aren't due back for a week or more. And the others are booked for the odd two or three nights here and there, but no-one is English, so you can remain safely anonymous, which I think is the real reason for asking.'

Jessica smiled. 'You read me too well,' she responded, 'but I have to admit the very idea of someone turning up and recognising me . . .' She shuddered. 'It would feel like someone was walking into my sitting room, or even my bedroom, I feel so at home here.'

Lilian's eyes glowed with pleasure. 'I'm so relieved you still feel that way,' she said earnestly, 'because I want you to come whenever you like and for as long you like. Luc told me to be sure you understand that. He considers you my family, since I don't have one of my own, and so he should, because that's exactly how I think of you. The children too, of course, and Charlie.'

'And my mother?' Jessica prompted with an ironic arch of an eyebrow.

'Actually, believe it or not, her too. In a way.'

'Which wouldn't be maternal.'

'Not with your mother, no. But I've known her practically all my life, and you know how I always loved her glamour when we were growing up, her spirit of adventure. She always seemed so exciting and exotic.'

'Just what you want in a mother,' Jessica responded smoothly. 'Tell me,' she went on, as they walked past the old farm gates to start winding along the single-track road that led to the village, 'do you think Fernand would mind if I talked to him about the call she made, asking to come here?'

Lilian grimaced as she shook her head. 'I shouldn't think so,' she replied. 'He probably won't be able to tell you any more than he told me, though – that she wanted to come for a week at the beginning of June, if the cottage was free, which it was, but then she never called back again.'

'Or showed up.'

'Or showed up.'

Jessica gave a sigh and used her hat to bat away a wasp. 'I think she was intending to come here to collect something she'd left behind,' she said, 'or look for something she'd discovered was missing. I might even go as far as to say, something incriminating.'

Lilian seemed doubtful. 'I can't imagine what it would be,' she said, 'but if you're right, maybe she found it at home or somewhere else, so she didn't need to come here after all.'

Since it was the only explanation Jessica could come up with, at least for the moment, she let the subject drop and stood to one side as a yellow mail van came trundling along the road towards them.

After Lilian had exchanged a jolly *bonjour* with the sad-looking soul inside, and a few platitudes about the glorious weather, she said to Jessica, 'So are you worried about her?'

'You mean my mother?' Jessica replied. 'The truth is, more than I want to be, and certainly more than she deserves, especially when she's almost certainly hiding herself away to avoid facing me. I must remember to ask Charlie if the neighbour's had any luck contacting Maurice.'

Lilian's expression softened at the mention of Maurice. 'Dear old soul,' she said. 'He's adored her for ever, and she's always given him such a runaround. So that's where you think she might be?'

'Well, it's usually to him that she turns when she's in any kind of trouble, and since we lost Natalie she's been in plenty of that – at least with me.'

Lilian cast her a sympathetic glance, then walked on ahead as they wandered on to a narrow, stony footpath to take a short cut through a shady wood.

They were side by side and about to link arms again when Lilian's mobile started to ring.

'Sorry, it's the office,' she said, checking the number. 'I have to take it.'

As she began to speak in French Jessica gradually tuned her out, not because she didn't understand the language – she did – but so she could listen instead to the cheerful sound of the birds and faraway farm noises. She inhaled deeply, drawing in the musky scent of wood and dry earth mingled with the sweet tang of mayweed and wild garlic. As she looked around she could feel the beauty of the landscape as though it were moving through her, and found herself wondering how Lilian could remain so attached to her work when she had all this at her fingertips.

'Oh, I'll give it up soon enough,' Lilian assured her, when

she finally ended her call and they strolled into the picturesque fourteenth-century village. With its narrow cobbled streets, Romanesque church and bustling market square it was so quintessentially French that Jessica couldn't stop herself smiling with the sheer joy of being there, staring at the tricolour draped from its pole outside the centuries-old *mairie*. 'I'm even looking forward to it,' Lilian continued, 'but now isn't the right time.'

'So when will be?' Jessica pressed, as they stopped at a stall to test a home-made tapenade that was spread over a garlicky crouton.

'I suppose when Luc officially takes over the vineyard. Or when – *if* – I get pregnant.'

Jessica tucked an arm through hers as though to reassure her it would happen soon, then led her over to the *boulangerie* where they bought freshly baked croissants to eat now and a baguette to take back for lunch. The café terrace was shaded by a giant plane tree, and colourfully adorned with hanging baskets of geraniums and trailing fuchsias. When the owner came to take their order, he greeted Lilian with much warmth and interest in her family, and as Jessica looked at Lilian's happy face she felt her own breaking into a smile. Sometimes, she thought, being with Lilian was so soothing that she could almost believe if she just stayed with her then life would never be hurtful or complicated again – or if it was, she'd be able to deal with it much better than she'd managed these past three months.

When their coffee came they talked for a while about Lilian's upcoming trip, then about Claude and Daniella's concert and Fernand's troublesome heart. Soon, though, the subject returned to Luc, which made Jessica smile as she recalled what he'd said earlier. She was perfectly happy to talk about him, though, not only because she was interested, but because heaven knew, Lilian had spent enough time listening to her talking about Charlie over the years.

The day passed in a heat-induced torpor, through which they laughed and occasionally cried as they took trips down memory lane and relished this precious time together. After lunch, which was no more than a crispy baguette with a salty Maconnais cheese and a chilled Macon-Valennes, they took a siesta side by side on the bed in the cottage, where the mosquito nets were ruffled by the breeze of a fan and the downy pillows were scented with fresh country air.

The ring of Lilian's mobile finally roused them. Jessica stayed where she was, unwilling to move yet, or even open her eyes. Lilian barely stirred either, merely put out a hand to bring the phone to her ear. 'Lilian Véron speaking,' she mumbled. Then, 'Oh, darling, it's you. Mmm, I was asleep. Yes, we're having a lovely, lazy day, how about you?'

Jessica listened to the indecipherable sound of Luc's voice at the other end of the line, then to Lilian's groan of disappointment as she pushed aside the nets and swung her legs over the side of the bed. 'Are you sure?' she said. 'Oh, Luc, it's our last night before I go away.' Again there was silence, then she chuckled softly at something he'd said. 'OK, I love you too,' she said, and after putting the phone down, she glanced over her shoulder to see if Jessica was awake.

'Is there a problem?' Jessica asked, stretching and yawning.

'He can't make it back tonight,' Lilian answered, 'so it'll be just us with Claude and Daniella for dinner.'

'That's a shame,' Jessica said. 'What's keeping him in Geneva?'

'Oh, this client is notoriously difficult. He plays all the *vignerons* off, one against the other, and now he wants Luc to take him to dinner tonight. It'll be too late to drive back, so he's going to get up early in order to be here before I leave for Paris in the morning.' She cast another glance at Jessica. 'Do you think that means he loves me?' she said with a girlish twinkle.

Jessica laughed. 'I think that qualifies.'

Lilian spread out her arms in a luxurious stretch, then letting her head fall back she said, 'Sometimes I worry that he only married me because Fernand wants to see him settled with a family before he goes off to the great vineyard in the sky.'

Jessica looked at her in surprise. 'But you know that's nonsense,' she said.

Lilian shrugged. 'Maybe.'

Jessica was still baffled. 'If he was going to marry to suit his father surely he'd have done it with . . . Karin? Was that her name? The one he was with for fifteen years.'

'Mmm. Except he fell out of love with her, and sometimes I wonder if it was because she didn't want children.'

'People don't fall out of love for that reason. True, it might make them break up, but from what you've told me he didn't want them either, until he met you.'

'Which could prove my point,' Lilian countered. 'Fernand's getting older, time to think of the future . . .'

Jessica rolled her eyes. 'I think you're being typically you and worrying about nothing,' she told her bluntly.

Lilian chuckled. 'Whatever. I just hope I'm not going to continue having trouble carrying, because I'm starting to run out of time now, and I don't want him trading me in for a younger model.'

'It's going to be fine,' Jessica told her firmly. 'Plenty of women are having babies in their forties, and you're not even there yet. Besides, he doesn't strike me as the kind of man who'd leave you because you can't provide him with an heir.'

'He's French,' Lilian reminded her. 'Their machismo is very highly developed.'

Jessica had to laugh. 'You know him better than I do, but that certainly doesn't gel with how he seems to me. He's too intelligent for one thing, and too . . .' she searched for the word. 'Sensitive,' she decided. 'And in tune with himself.'

Lilian was laughing too. 'I must be sure to tell him what a big impression he's made on you,' she said. 'It'll go straight to his head of course, but I'm sure I can stand it. Now, what do you say to driving over to Claude and Daniella's for some tennis? It's about time I beat you, and I rather think I'm feeling on form.'

Chapter Eleven

Having stayed up talking to Charlie on the phone until the early hours, Jessica was still sleeping when Lilian left for Paris in the morning, so didn't get a chance to wish her bon voyage, as she'd intended. However, what really mattered was that Luc had clearly made it back before the taxi came to take her to the train – at least, Jessica presumed he had, for she was sure Lilian would have woken her otherwise. Since there were no messages or texts on her mobile, she didn't have much trouble guessing how they'd spent the time until Lilian's departure.

After calling Harry and Nikki, she showered and dressed in a thin pair of shorts and strappy top, before carrying her breakfast and the phone out onto the patio. This morning she was going to try making appointments to speak with the *gendarmes* and paramedics who'd responded to her mother's emergency call, just in case there was anything they could tell her she might not already know.

Experiencing much more nervousness than she'd expected as she dialled the *gendarmerie*'s number, she quickly cut the connection and allowed herself a few more moments to think. She'd felt certain she was ready for this, but now she was actually poised on the brink of opening it all up again, she was finding herself even more afraid of discovering any substance to her suspicions than she'd expected.

Her call was answered on the third ring, and a moment later she found herself on hold. After an interminable wait she was informed by the same curt voice that Monsieur Galeron was *en vacances*. Frustrated, and annoyed with herself for not considering this before, since everyone knew that virtually the whole of France was *en vacances* in August, she asked when he might be back and felt slightly cheered when the answer was, '*Lundi prochaine*.' Next Monday.

Not too long to wait, and in the meantime she could always speak to the paramedics.

However, the senior officer who'd completed the report was also *en vacances* and not due back until the following Friday, which left her wondering, somewhat pettishly, who was actually manning the emergency services right now.

Next she tried the office of the *Médecin Légiste*, France's version of the coroner. This was the call she'd been dreading the most, since she was terrified of learning that injuries had been found on the body that were inconsistent with the fall. The mere thought of it made her want to reel away from her questions and shut down her mind entirely rather than let her imagination go there, but surely, if there had been even the slightest hint of anything suspicious, there would have been a much more thorough investigation at the time. So, heartened by the logic of that, she pushed herself on, while thanking God that Charlie had no idea what she was doing, for it would probably send him right over the edge to know what horrible fears were lurking in her mind.

Eventually a kindly voice came down the line asking how they could help, but after Jessica had explained who she was and why she was calling, she was told that certain permissions would have to be sought before she could be allowed to see the report on her daughter's death.

Having expected as much, she swallowed her dismay and asked how to go about getting them.

'I will do it for you,' came the reply, 'then you must come in to sign the documentation, bringing with you some form of identity.'

'How long is it likely to take?'

'It is hard to say for certain, but if you call again next Tuesday or Wednesday we should have some news by then.'

After giving all the necessary details and taking the woman's name, Jessica thanked her, then clicked off the line and sat staring out at the vineyard. Felled at the first three hurdles, she was thinking glumly to herself. Except she hadn't been, it was simply that it wasn't going to happen as quickly as she might like, and actually, even if she could have the answers tomorrow they were never going to give her what she really wanted, which was Natalie back. So what was the point in feeling urgent or frustrated? No-one was saying they wouldn't speak to her, or help in any way, to the contrary, in fact, so maybe she should use this time now to try to focus on what she really wanted to discuss with the officials when the time came.

After finishing her tea, she took everything back inside, then drew a chair up to the kitchen table where she began to write down everything she knew about what had happened on that fateful day. It didn't take long, but once it was there in black and white, from the call Natalie had made to her, to the moment Luc had given her the life-shattering news, she realised that detached as she'd managed to make herself while doing it, now it was finished she couldn't bear to sit with it a moment longer. She needed to get some air, to put some distance between herself and the images coming from those words, so gathering up her hat and purse she started off on a walk in the hope it might soothe some of the angst from her heart.

She got no further than the top road before turning back again. She wanted to know where her mother and Natalie had walked the morning of Natalie's fall. It was all there in her notes, the fact that they'd – apparently – gone out in the rain that day, and Jessica would like to follow that route now. Since only her mother could tell her which of the many paths around here they'd taken, that was who she needed to call.

Letting herself back into the cottage, she quickly dialled Charlie's mobile. As far as she could remember he was at the production office today, so provided he wasn't out shooting she should be able to get hold of him to find out if there was any news yet on her mother's whereabouts.

'Actually, there is,' he replied, confounding her slightly. 'I've just received confirmation that she's with Maurice, in Italy.'

Jessica's insides tightened. 'Really?' she replied. Then added tartly, 'I should have known. And how typical of her to go off without telling her neighbours.'

'I don't think it happened quite like that. From what I can gather she hasn't been too well, so Maurice has taken her to his villa for some rest and recuperation,' Charlie said.

Jessica's tension increased. 'Why, what's wrong with her?' she demanded, wishing she didn't care.

'I don't think anything is now, but apparently she collapsed a couple of weeks ago while she was shopping in Bond Street.'

Jessica's expression changed to one of alarm. 'What do you mean, collapsed?'

'I don't have any details, only that she was in hospital for a week or so . . .'

'Are you serious? And we didn't know?'

'Frankly, darling, considering how things are between you, you can surely understand why you weren't the first person she called.'

'Yes, but if she's sick . . .'

'She's fine now.'

'How do you know? Have you spoken to her?'

'No, but . . .'

'We need to get hold of Maurice's number in Italy. She could be lying again, or for all I know she could be seriously ill, either way . . .'

'Jessica, if she has been unwell, and we've no reason to suppose she hasn't, it's not going to help if you start accusing her . . .'

'Then you speak to her. Find out exactly what happened when she collapsed and why they kept her in so long.'

'OK, but I can't do it now, I'm about to go out. I'll get onto it this evening, or first thing tomorrow.'

After ringing off Jessica remained standing where she was, looking around the kitchen, then up to the top of the stairs. Everything was exactly as it should be, perfectly still, apart from dust motes dancing in the hazy bands of sunlight and a spider scurrying towards a crack in the wall. She couldn't think why she might have expected anything to be different, but the longer she stood there the more unsettled she seemed to be feeling.

Not quite knowing why, she picked up the phone and

called Charlie again. 'Something's not right,' she said, when he answered.

'What?'

'Are you sure you're telling me everything? You're not holding anything back?'

'Darling, I'm just about to . . .'

'I know, you're going out. I'm sorry, but I . . .' She hesitated, not quite sure how to go on.

'You what?' he prompted.

'I just need to know – are you hiding anything from me?'

'You mean about your mother?'

'About anything. Maybe the *Médecin Légiste* told you something you don't want me to know.'

Sounding more exasperated than annoyed, Charlie said, 'Look, this really isn't the time, but the answer is I've told you everything the *Médecin Légiste* told me.'

'Did you actually read his report?'

'Yes, of course. Now, I'm sorry, darling, I really have to go.'

Jessica put her mobile back on the table and stood staring blankly at the notes she'd made earlier. Then with a horrible churning inside she went to stand at the door, needing to take in the calming spectacle of nature, as though it might disperse the doubts that were gathering like clouds inside her. She needed to believe what Charlie was telling her, because without trust they really were going to fall apart. So she must try to keep everything in perspective – just because he'd lied to her once, over an affair that had happened more than six years ago, didn't mean he was doing it again now. In fact, he couldn't be, not over this, because if he was hiding something then it would mean the French authorities must be too, and that, she realised with no little relief, really didn't make any sense at all.

'Jessica? It is Daniella. I hope I am not interrupting.'

'No, not at all,' Jessica assured her, closing the cover of her notepad as though not wanting anyone to see it, even though Daniella was at the other end of the phone. 'How are you? You can speak French if you prefer.'

'Thank you, but it is good for me to practise my English.

Are you OK? Do you have everything you need in the cottage?'

'I think so,' Jessica replied. 'It's kind of you to ask, but I don't want to be any trouble.'

'Ah, *mais non*, you are our welcome guest,' Daniella assured her. 'And really I am calling to find out if you would like to join Papa and me for lunch up at the house. I am here to help him with the little bit of exercise he must do, and he is grumbling so much that we thought you might help restore his smile. But of course, if you are busy with something else, we will understand . . .'

'No, I would love to join you,' Jessica interrupted. 'Can I bring anything, or help in any way?'

'No, no, we have everything under control. Lilian call me a few minutes ago, by the way. She was trying to reach you, but your line was busy. She wanted you to know that she and Luc have arrived in Paris now, and they will be there until she leave tomorrow, if you need to be in touch with her.'

'So Luc not only made it back, he went with her?' Jessica said, almost able to feel how much that would have pleased Lilian.

'I think they just decide this morning when he get here,' Daniella said. 'So you will come for lunch? We will have some terrine, and a little of Papa's delicious gazpacho. I have to say that because he can hear me, but truly it is very good.'

When Jessica arrived at the *manoir* half an hour later Daniella and Fernand were nowhere to be seen, but the table was already laid outside, and looking extremely inviting with its clear wine glasses sparkling in the sunlight, and vivid blue tablecloth arrayed with check napkins, shining cutlery and gleaming white plates. With the pergola and all its exuberant flowers around it, it was as exquisite a spectacle as she'd seen anywhere.

'Can I do anything?' she offered, stepping in through the open kitchen door.

'Ah Jessica,' Fernand exclaimed with pleasure. 'This is very good that you come to join us, because Daniella is very, how you say, *autoritaire* with me.'

'Bossy,' Jessica smiled, going to kiss him on both cheeks.

The kitchen was large and cool, with thick stone walls, and a big open fireplace that was filled with dried flowers now there was no need for a fire, and flanked by two capacious armchairs. In the middle of the room, beneath two pendant lights, was a long, wide table covered by a green check cloth that was almost the same shade as the dressers and cabinets that occupied the rest of the space. It was as homey as the warmth in Fernand's grey eyes, and as cluttered as every respectable farmhouse kitchen should be.

'Today,' Fernand informed her, 'we are going to drink some excellent rosé that is from the vineyard of my very good friend *dans le sud de la France*. You know that Provence has a very good reputation for rosé wine, and my friend, he is very highly respected *vigneron* in this region.'

Daniella was already opening the cooler. 'You see,' she said, holding up a bottle that was moulded into the elegant shape of a classical urn, 'the colour is a very pale pink, which tells us that Monsieur Simone has made his wine from the *jus de gouttes et le jus d'écoulage*, which are of the highest quality.'

Taking the bottle from her, Fernand said, 'In Provence they hold a glass of rosé to a very blue Provençal sky and if the colour mirror a blue that exist in an atoll in French Polynesia at midday they know they have a very good wine. *Mais, nous sommes en Bourgogne*,' he said with a twinkle. '*Quand même, c'est toujours un très bon vin*.'

Enjoying their expert knowledge as well as their evident passion for wine, Jessica encouraged Fernand to tell her more, but for the moment he was eager to explain his recipe for gazpacho, which he'd been given by the wife of a Spanish *vigneron* several years ago. As he talked Daniella laid a crispy baguette and *pain de compagne* on a wooden board ready to take outside, while Jessica arranged a platter of wild boar pâté and Maconnais cheeses. There was a bowl of roughly sliced avocado too, and cubes of icy green cucumber, with a plate of sun-ripened tomatoes that were oozing their juice all over a succulent bed of basil coated in a thick, yellowy olive oil with a splash of balsamic.

As they ate they talked about Daniella's children who were at a nearby water park with their father and other friends today, then about the kind of vintage they were expecting from this year's harvest, and on to Jessica's plans for the time she was here.

'Will you be making a start on your book?' Fernand wanted to know. 'I think it will be a very fascinating subject, and I have an excellent library about artists that belonged to my wife. You are welcome to take a look and if there is anything there about Modigliani you find helpful, please take it with you down to the cottage. But I must ask you to return it before you leave. They mean very much to me, these books.'

'Of course,' Jessica responded, knowing from Lilian how much he'd loved and still missed his wife. 'It's very kind of you to let me look through them at all, so I promise I'll take great care of anything I borrow.'

Apparently delighted to think he might be able to help, Fernand lifted the wine from the cooler and refilled their glasses as Daniella said, 'Will you be going to Paris to do some research? If you are, I'm sure Luc and Lilian will be happy for you to stay in their apartment, but you know that Claude and I have one too, which is on the floor below theirs. You will be welcome to use it, if you need to. I think our building is very close to where you will need to be.'

'It's exactly where I'd need to be,' Jessica agreed, 'and indeed I do intend to go at some point, but really, my visit here isn't only to make a start on my book, it's to try to get a clearer picture in my mind of what happened back at Easter.'

Fernand instantly looked mournful. 'Oh, such a tragedy,' he murmured. 'I blame myself for not putting a banister there before . . .'

'Shush now, Papa,' Daniella interrupted gently. 'It's not good for you to get upset.'

'I'm sorry,' Jessica said, full of remorse. Why had it never occurred to her that Fernand and his family might be suffering too, and blaming themselves, the way she and Charlie were? After all, it had happened on their land, and in one of their houses, and in a way that might have been prevented had the stairs been protected the way they were now. 'It really wasn't anyone's fault,' she told Fernand earnestly. 'It was an accident, and even if the banister had been there the outcome might well have been the same.'

Though she knew they all doubted that, she had to let him know that she bore him no resentment, or even held him responsible, for how could anyone have foreseen what would happen when the stairs had always been open and no-one had ever fallen before?

Daniella gave her a quick smile of thanks. 'This is what I try to tell him,' she said. 'It is very easy to know what to do with hindsight, but that is true of so many things in our lives.'

Jessica's eyes moved back to Fernand, and taking heart from the openness of his expression she said, 'I know you weren't actually here on the day it happened, but before that . . .'

'I was with Jean-Marc at the laboratories,' he told her gruffly. 'It was our day to meet with the oenologist.'

Jessica smiled, in an effort to keep him relaxed. 'Yes,' she said, 'but before that . . . In the days leading up to it . . . Did you see anyone else at the cottage? Or did anything happen that seemed, I don't know, unusual in any way?'

Fernand was starting to look slightly confused. 'I think everything was very normal,' he answered, glancing at Daniella as though seeking confirmation. 'The weather was not so good some of the time, and your mother has a very bad headache on one of the days, but this is not the kind of thing you are wanting to know?'

Jessica shook her head. 'Did you see either of them in the morning, before you and Jean-Marc left for the laboratories?' she asked.

'Not that I can remember. It was raining so the door was shut as we went by. Maybe they were still sleeping, because it was very early.'

'What about you?' Jessica asked Daniella. 'Did you see them that day?'

'We were supposed to,' Daniella answered. 'I was going to drive over and pick them up, but when Elodie called Natalie to find out what time we should come Natalie said she would call back because she had something important to do with her grandma.'

Jessica felt a small jolt in her heart. She hadn't heard that before. 'Did she say what?' she asked.

'I've asked Elodie,' Daniella replied, 'but apparently that was all Natalie said.'

Jessica thought it over for a moment, but since there was nothing she could deduce from it right now, she said, 'Did you speak to my mother at all that day, I mean before it happened?'

'Yes, I called a little after Elodie did to find out if your mother needs anything from the supermarket, because I was going. She says she does not because she thinks she and Natalie will go to the village café for lunch.'

Another surprise. 'In the rain and without a car?' Jessica said.

Daniella frowned, as though only just realising that it did seem a little odd. 'Perhaps they were going to ring for a taxi,' she said lamely.

Jessica sat back in her chair, knowing it wasn't just the heat and wine that were making her feel light-headed. Natalie and her mother had had something important to do. They were going to the café instead of seeing Elodie and Daniella. So were they supposed to be meeting someone at the café? Or maybe someone was coming to pick them up, so they wouldn't have to walk through the rain. But why not tell Elodie or Daniella that? And whatever their plans, they hadn't gone to the café because Natalie's fall had happened just before midday . . .

Suddenly noticing how tired Fernand was looking, she said, 'I'm sorry. I hope I haven't spoiled this lovely lunch with all my questions . . .'

'No, not at all,' he assured her. 'We are happy to answer as much as we can. I only wish we could be a little more helpful.'

'I think it is time you took your siesta, Papa,' Daniella said, patting his gnarled old hand. 'Jessica and I will do the clearing up.'

'You must take her to Luc's studio,' Fernand said, as he got to his feet. 'I think you will like his work, *ma chère*. But maybe you have seen it before?'

'Some pieces,' Jessica confirmed, 'but I'm sure there are some new ones by now, which I'd love to see.'

'They are very good. I think they are a little like Brancusi, *non*?' he said, looking at Daniella.

'Mm, *peut-être*,' she responded, apparently undecided.

'I am thinking of *La Muse endormie ou Le Baiser*,' he said. 'I think, when he is not doing abstracts, that Luc has some of this grace and . . . *comment on dit, caractère*?'

'Character,' Daniella replied, 'and of course, you are not biased.'

Chuckling, Fernand stooped to kiss her, then after embracing Jessica too he disappeared inside.

'I see you really do feel that the picture from that day is not complete,' Daniella said, picking up her glass. 'Lilian told us this was the way you were thinking.'

'She doesn't agree with me though,' Jessica admitted. 'Nor does Charlie, so don't worry, I'm not expecting you to either, but thank you for indulging my questions.'

'As Papa said, I only wish we could be more helpful, but you must feel free to ask whatever you like.'

Jessica's eyes were warm as she thanked her.

Smiling, Daniella said, 'So would you like to see the studio? You don't have to be polite, if you would rather not I do not mind at all, but Lilian asked me to show you where she had moved her computer, so you can use it if you have need.'

'I'd love to see the studio,' Jessica smiled, 'if you think Luc won't mind us going in while he's not here.'

'Oh, I am sure not. He is great exhibitionist with his work, and besides I would like to see how he is getting on with the sculpture he is making of the twins. They are very poor sitters, and he lose his temper often with them, but they refuse to be afraid of him.'

Amused by the image, Jessica finished her wine, and got up to follow Daniella the short distance to the converted barn.

'I think, since you last were here, Luc has the permit to put much more windows in the roof,' Daniella said, as she pushed against the heavy wooden door, 'but only over the part where he sculpts. At this end is where he and Lilian have their computers and other things, so it is a little more dark.'

As she switched on the lights, even if Jessica's eyes hadn't needed a few seconds to adjust she'd have known where she was the instant she stepped into the shady, cavernous space, for the smell of wet clay and turps and photographic chemicals was unmistakable. The air was thick with it, seeming to lend a heady, though acrid, texture to the coolness that emanated from the stone walls. She looked around at the posters and photographs clamped to various corkboards and surfaces, the cameras that stood on tripods or were tucked away in cases, the books and files strewn about the worktops, the large computer screen that was undoubtedly Luc's, the clay-spattered jeans that hung from the back of a door, the rough stone carvings that cluttered the shelves . . . Everything about the place seemed to speak of Luc.

'Here is Lilian's space,' Daniella said, closing the door.

It occupied a large, sheltered corner which had been given over to an L-shaped desk with a neat Sony laptop at its centre, four orderly shelves of art-reference books and a couple of exhibition posters, a few chosen sculptures, a pair of steel cabinets and a photograph of a blissfully happy couple on their wedding day.

Going to it, Jessica picked it up and gazed down into their faces. 'She looks so lovely, doesn't she?' she murmured as Daniella came to look too.

'I think this is the same one as Papa has in his sitting room,' Daniella responded.

Jessica glanced over to Luc's computer. 'Isn't that typical of a man,' she said in mock exasperation, 'no photo of his . . .' Then she saw the stunning black and white shot of Lilian that he must have taken himself. Her hair was tumbling wantonly around her naked shoulders, her eyes were heavy with desire, and her arms were crossed over her breasts, though one nipple was partly visible, which was obviously deliberate.

'Tell me,' Daniella said, gazing across at the photo too, 'do you think she is happy here?'

Jessica was startled by the question. 'Yes, of course,' she replied without hesitation. 'I'm amazed you ask.'

'Actually, it is because of something she have said once, and I wonder if she have say to you too.'

Frowning, Jessica turned to look at her.

'She tell me once,' Daniella said, 'that she think Luc only marries her because our father want to see him settled before he die.'

Though Jessica's frown relaxed, she couldn't help feeling concerned that Lilian had confided her fears in Daniella too.

'When Papa have his first problems with the heart,' Daniella went on, 'it is soon after this that Luc and Lilian meet. For her, she says, it was *un coup de foudre*, but for Luc she does not think the same thing happen.'

'What does Luc say?' Jessica asked.

'That it was, of course, *un coup de foudre* for him too.'

Jessica started to smile. 'I'm afraid it's very typical of Lilian to feel insecure when she has no need to,' she said. 'She was single for a long time, and has been hurt quite often in the past . . . In fact, she'd virtually given up hope of ever falling in love, so I think she still has to pinch herself to remind herself that it really is happening.'

'I am sure you are right,' Daniella said. 'And my brother, he is perhaps not always as attentive as he should be, but that is like most men, *non*?'

At that Jessica had to laugh, for Luc always seemed very attentive to her, and it was hard to imagine Claude as anything other when he clearly adored his beautiful wife. However, she had to concede that once in Paris with his music and musicians, Claude was most likely as single-minded as every other conductor she'd met. And as for Luc, it would surely be the same with him: once engrossed in his art he would be oblivious to the rest of the world, for that was always the case with creative people. In fact, Charlie was no different, for though his talents were perhaps not quite so esoteric, he was no less blessed with the male gift for closing down every other compartment of his mind to focus fully on the task at hand when required.

'The studio,' Daniella declared, reminding them why they'd come.

Jessica put the photograph down while Daniella went in search of a key.

'*Zut*, I cannot see it,' Daniella said, riffling about in a drawer. 'Normally he leaves it here, but maybe the door to his studio is open.'

Jessica watched her walk across the room.

'No, it is locked,' Daniella said, turning the handle. 'I think he must be worried the twins will come in while he is away. They will be very likely to add *un petit morceau* to his work, so he is wise to take a precaution. So,' she said, smiling brightly, 'I am sorry, we cannot go in there today, but I am sure Luc will be happy to take you in himself, when he returns.'

Thinking perhaps she'd prefer to go in when Luc was there to show her around, Jessica led the way back to the house and stayed to help Daniella clear up before strolling back down to the cottage.

Later that evening, as she walked through the lusciously overburdened rows of vines, touching the softening skins of the grapes and trailing her fingers lightly over the rugged leaves, she was wondering whether or not to tell Charlie about the conversation she'd had with Fernand and Daniella at lunch. To her mind Veronica and Natalie's proposed visit to the village café virtually confirmed that someone else had been at the cottage that day, since her mother was the last person to take a walk in the rain when she was likely to be seen at the end of it – it would spoil her hair, or streak her mascara. Yet apparently they had walked in the rain – or so her mother had claimed at the time – but not to the café for lunch, since it had been too early for that. So where might they have walked to that morning? And what had happened to change their plans to go to the château, since the call Elodie had made to Natalie suggested at least a casual arrangement to get together that day? Had her mother and Natalie met someone while out walking who'd they'd taken back to the cottage with them? Someone with a car who was then going to take them to the café for lunch?

It wasn't piecing together well, and with so much doubt and suspicion making her restless and anxious she decided not to mention anything to Charlie, at least for tonight. Instead, she would ring around the local taxi firms in the morning to find out if her mother had made a booking for that morning. If nothing transpired from that, she'd add this new information to her notes and wait to see if it merged or conflicted with anything else she managed to find out over the next couple of weeks.

'Hello? Mr Keane?' Charlie said into his mobile.

'Yes. Mr Moore. I recognise your voice. What can I do for you?'

'I was hoping you might have a number for my mother-in-law in Italy.'

'Capri,' Keane corrected. 'Yes, indeed I do. I'll get it for you.'

Appreciating the man's tact in not commenting on the fact that he had the number while Veronica's family didn't, Charlie waited for him to come back on the line, then after jotting the number down he said, 'I probably should have done this before, but thank you for getting in touch when she disappeared. We might not have known otherwise.'

'Oh, don't mention it,' Keane responded. 'What matters is that everything's fine now.'

'Yes indeed,' Charlie murmured, and after ringing off he sat for a moment wondering how much Veronica might have confided in her neighbour. In the end, accepting that it was impossible to tell without asking, he put it out of his mind and dialled the number in Capri.

To his surprise Veronica herself answered on the fourth ring.

'Charlie? Is that you, darling?' she cried, clearly surprised and delighted to hear him, though she sounded slightly sleepy, he thought, or maybe she'd been drinking. 'What a treat. How are you?'

'More to the point, how are you?' he countered.

'You got my letter? Yes, of course, or you wouldn't be calling. I expect my neighbour, Rufus, gave you the number here, did he? I said he could, if you asked for it.'

'We've been worried about you,' Charlie told her. 'First you disappear, then you send a letter telling us you're in hospital . . . You should have called, Veronica. You know we're here for you.'

'You might be, darling, but I don't think Jessica is or she'd be the one ringing me now. Did you give her my letter? No, of course not. I knew you wouldn't, and I'm sure it's the right decision, but you do understand why I had to write it?'

Not at all sure that he did, Charlie said, 'Jessica's in France. She's gone back to the cottage.'

Veronica fell silent.

'Are you still there?'

'Yes, I'm here. You have to tell her, Charlie. It was an accident . . .'

'But she won't see it like that.'

'She has to,' Veronica insisted. Then, sounding more troubled than ever, 'The doctor told me I should avoid any kind of stress, and now all this is catching up with me again . . .'

'I'm sorry, but I had to call. Jessica wants to be sure you're all right.'

'She cares?'

'Of course. She's still angry, I won't deny that, but you're her mother . . .'

'She's never put much store by that. She hates me, you know, and I hate myself now. I shouldn't have allowed myself . . .'

'If you're to avoid stress I think we should change the subject,' he broke in, unable to bear even the thought of her going into any kind of detail. 'How long are you staying on Capri?'

'We haven't decided yet. Maurice is being such a sweetie. We might stay the whole summer, if we can. It all rather depends on . . . Well, a number of things. Oh dear, I feel very upset to think of Jessica being back in France . . .'

'You still haven't told me why you collapsed,' he interrupted.

'Oh, it was nothing, really.'

'They don't keep people in hospital for a week or more for nothing.'

'They were running tests and that sort of thing. They'd have let me out sooner if there hadn't been a mix-up over some of the results, but it was all straightened out when Maurice got strict with them, and after that he was allowed to take me home.'

'Where is he now?'

'Poodling about on his boat somewhere. He'll be back soon.'

'Well make sure he has my number in case you decide to collapse on us again.'

'I will, but you're not to worry. I'm on top form now, or I will be after our little holiday. I should ring off now though, darling. You won't mind, will you?'

As he put the phone down Charlie felt such a weight in his chest that he was unable to move. He continued to sit at the wheel of his car, thinking of how neither of them had mentioned Natalie, or any of the details contained in the letter to Jessica. His eyes closed as though to block the images as they came crowding back in, but the darkness only made them seem more vivid and even more terrible than they actually were. Just thank God there was nothing at the cottage for Jessica to find, and no-one who could tell her what had happened either. Fernand's family clearly had no idea of the truth, or one of them at least would surely have spoken up by now.

Chapter Twelve

Over the weekend the valley became hotter and sultrier than ever, so that by Sunday afternoon even the thick stone walls of the cottage seemed to be sweltering in the heat, while in the distance the village clock chimed the hour so slowly and languidly it was as though it might not gather the momentum to reach five.

Jessica had spent much of the time either walking in the woods, or cycling through the sun-drenched countryside, or, when it became too hot to go outside, immersed in research for Jeanne and Modi's story. She'd never imagined she could be so contented spending so much time alone, though she knew in her heart it was the gentle connection she was feeling to Natalie that was really helping her to feel at peace. Being away from the others, not always having to put their grief first, or hide her own, she could speak to Natalie in her mind as often as she liked, telling her how sorry she was that she'd let this happen, and asking her over and over why she'd been afraid that day. What had happened to make her call in a panic? How had she really come to fall down the stairs? Was it true she'd tripped over a pile of newspapers, or was there more to it? Of course she never received any answers, nor did she expect to from that silent quarter, but her mother, she was certain now, had much more to tell.

Though she'd played tennis at Daniella's on Saturday evening, and stayed on for dinner, any hope she'd had of seeing Luc, who'd returned from Paris earlier in the day, came to nothing when Daniella told her he was taking Fernand to an informal gathering of the *Chevaliers de Tastevin* at a hotel near Pouilly-Fuissé. But there was no rush. They would catch up with one another soon enough, and if the truth were told she was more nervous about seeing him than anyone else, for in his way, he was her last link to Natalie.

Having spent most of Sunday immersed in the gaiety and romance of the belle époque in preparation for her book, she was still feeling enchanted by the images of saucy mistresses and struggling artists, as she rested her chin in her hand to stare out through the open French doors to the dazzling light around the vines. Apart from the copious notes she was making she had, as yet, to put pen to paper concerning Jeanne and Modi's tragic romance, but fortunately the book wasn't due to be delivered until the following July so she was free to indulge herself in as much reverie as she liked for now.

So she remained lost in the colourful surroundings of the Bateau-Lavoir where Matisse, Braque, Picasso and Modigliani had rented studios for meagre sums and created works that were now worth tens of millions. Finally, around six, she went to take a bottle of chilled Macon-Valennes from the cooler, and after pouring herself a glass she wandered outside. The sun was still blisteringly hot, and the air so thick and moist it wasn't easy to breathe. For a while she stood sipping her wine and watching tiny white butterflies skimming about on their gauzy wings, as she recalled cherished lines of French poems.

A summer night – a night whose wide-spread wings
Strike in the azure myriad sparkling things;

and

Sounds and perfumes are mingling on the evening air

The fact that she could still love it here so much after what had happened to Natalie both intrigued and confused her, but most of all it pleased her, for it would be unbearable to think that Lilian's home was no longer a place she could visit. To feel such a sense of tranquillity when her mind was hardly at rest must surely mean that nothing was as bad as she feared. Indeed, were it not for the anomalous walk in the rain, she might almost be ready to believe it was all as tragically simple as she'd been told.

Guessing Charlie would be finished in the studio by now, she wandered back inside, but his mobile was still off. After leaving a message she tried Nikki, and had no luck with her either. So she rang Harry, and as she listened to him chattering on she smiled and laughed and wanted nothing more than to squeeze him in her arms and smother him in kisses. However, it was hardly possible, so in the end she had to let him go and the next time she tried Charlie she got straight through.

'I just picked up your message,' he told her, sounding slightly sharp. 'Is everything all right?'

'Of course. Why wouldn't it be?'

'I don't know, you sounded . . . a bit vague, I suppose.'

'It's probably the heat – or the fact that I'm wondering if you're avoiding me.'

His tone was genuinely baffled as he said, 'Unless I'm imagining it we spoke at least twice yesterday, and again first thing this morning, so how is that avoiding you?'

'If you hadn't rushed off the line each time, it might not have been . . .'

'Some of us are still working.'

'OK. Sorry, it wasn't meant to be a criticism, it was just a roundabout way of saying I'm missing you, but clearly I've failed and now I've upset you . . .'

'I'm not upset,' he assured her, sounding much gentler. 'And I'm not avoiding you either.'

'Good, so you have time to tell me now what happened when you spoke to my mother?'

With a sigh he said, 'Nothing happened, as such. She sounded tired, but she might have been drinking . . .'

'Did you ask her where she and Natalie walked that morning – in the rain?'

'No, I didn't. She got quite upset when I told her you were in France, and since the doctor says she has to avoid becoming stressed . . .'

'Well, how convenient,' Jessica cut in sarcastically. 'It's perfectly obvious to me that she's lying and now she's hiding behind . . .'

'Darling, people go out in the rain all the time, even your mother . . .'

'How do you know they went out? Did anyone see them? Were there wet coats or muddy boots at the house?'

'As far as I'm aware, yes there were, but what the hell difference does it make now, if they went out or not?'

'If she was lying about that, then she could be lying about anything.'

'Jessica, for heaven's sake . . .'

Realising how close she was to losing her temper she said, abruptly, 'All right, let's drop it.'

There was a moment's difficult silence before he said, 'Have you spoken to Luc yet?'

'No. I haven't even seen him.'

'But he's back?'

'Yes, I told you yesterday.'

'And there was me thinking you could hardly wait to rush up there to ask him about this lunch your mother was planning at the café on a rainy day.'

Wishing now that she'd stuck to her decision not to mention it, she said, 'Why do you have to be so scathing? In anyone else's book it's a harmless question . . .'

'And it was a harmless intention.'

After a pause she said, 'Tell me, am I missing something here, because every time this comes up you behave as though I'm attacking you.'

'Now you're being absurd,' he retorted. 'I get *annoyed*, because you seem hell-bent on reading something sinister into just about everything that happened that day, when what you should really be doing is trying to let it go so we can move on with our lives. Better still, you should be here with me, so we can work through the trust issues you're having.'

Jessica's eyes moved to the door as she heard the sound of a car approaching. 'Would it make you feel any better if I told you I do trust you now?' she said, waving as Luc and Fernand drove past. She knew they were on their way to Daniella's, but she'd declined to join them since she'd been there the night before and didn't want to seem to take advantage of their hospitality.

Charlie was saying, 'Actually yes, it would, if you meant it, but it's hardly the impression you're giving.'

'Well, I'm trying,' she informed him, 'and I think it's helping to be away from London. In fact it would do you a lot of good to get away and relax for a while too.'

'You sound more on edge than relaxed to me,' he told her bluntly.

'Because we're talking about my mother. The rest of the time I'm totally chilled.'

He laughed at her use of Nikki's language, and as it seemed to diffuse the hostility she said, 'So, how about coming to join me?'

'Darling, please don't let's go there, or we'll end up falling out again.'

'But you need a holiday . . .'

'Not now, Jessica. I'm tired, it's been a long day . . .'

Sighing she said, 'OK, then what are you doing this evening?'

There was a moment's hesitation before he said, 'If I told you Melissa's invited me for dinner, would you hang up on me?'

Though she detested the very idea of Charlie going to Melissa's, she said, 'It depends whether or not Paul's going to be there.'

'He is – and the rest of the gang.'

'You know, I've always hated being thought of as part of a gang.'

'Oh, for Christ's sake, nothing I say is ever right,' he responded irritably. 'It's just a word.'

'Of course. I'm sorry. Give everyone my love,' she added, attempting to be friendly.

'I'm sure they'll send theirs too.'

'Just as long as I have yours, that's all that counts.'

'You know you do.'

'Even when you're annoyed with me?'

'Even then,' he said, and the smile in his voice made her smile too.

After assuring him she loved him just as much, she rang off and wandered back outside to watch the crimson glow of the sunset spreading like treacle over the vines. It was so exquisite and restful that once again she felt lines from Lamartine and Baudelaire gathering inside her, as though to soothe away her angst and bring her back into the beauty around her.

After a while she found herself thinking about her mother again, and the curious events of that fateful morning. She wished now that she'd asked Charlie for the number in Italy so she could challenge her mother herself, though she doubted he'd have given it, since he of all people knew how quickly any contact with Veronica could turn into a disaster. It didn't matter though, she'd speak to her sooner or later, while for the time being she'd continue along the path she was on, by talking to the officials who'd been involved that day, and of course to Luc.

When darkness finally began to fall she went back inside and settled down to indulge in a few chapters of *Suite Française.* It was the most entrancing escape she could think of, and if she were able to write anywhere near as beautifully she'd have no concerns at all for her own book. However, since she was never going to get near such a talent, she was happy simply to draw inspiration from Irène Némirovsky's wonderfully lyrical prose.

Much later, after taking a shower, she was gazing at her reflection in the mirror and thinking of how long it had been since she and Charlie had made love. She felt certain he must miss the physical release every bit as much as she did, so maybe she should tell him what an arousing effect the sun and good wine were having on her, because there must surely be a chance it would work the same magic for him. However, as she looked at the dark gleam in her eyes, and the soft light on her newly tanned skin, she could almost hear him telling her that if she thought being in the place Natalie had died was ever going to help him get over anything, she either didn't know him at all – or she was losing her mind.

The following morning, having called first thing and been told to try again at eleven, she was on the line to the *gendarmerie* when she heard footsteps on the patio outside. Turning to see who it was she felt her heart give a quick beat of unease, for a tall male figure was stepping into the doorway and the dazzling sun was making it impossible to distinguish his features. Then, realising it was Luc, she started to smile and beckoned him to come on in.

'Madame? Vous êtes toujours là?' a voice at the other end of the line demanded.

'Oui,' she replied. *'Oui, je vous écoute.'*

'Vous est il possible de venir demain à onze heures?' Can you come tomorrow at eleven?

'Oui, très bien,' she replied, making a note. *'Merci beaucoup. À demain,'* and she ended the call.

As she replaced her mobile on the table she was on the point of going to greet Luc in the traditional French way, when she found herself a little shy of attempting something that seemed rather intimate in such a small space, particularly when no-one else was around. Presumably he felt it too, for he stayed where he was, leaning against the sink with his arms folded as she said, 'It's good to see you. How was Paris? More to the point, how was Lilian when you left her?'

With a typically droll expression he said, 'Already half-way to Hong Kong, I'm afraid.' Then continued, 'She called last night to remind me to bring you a parasol, which I've left outside. I'll put it up before I leave. She also sends her love, and says you should call her mobile if you need to, any time day or night . . .' His head went to one side as he thought. 'I'm trying to remember if I have any more instructions.'

Laughing, Jessica said, 'Will a drink help refresh your memory?'

'I'm sure,' he replied with relief. Then, taking the bottle from her to uncork it, 'Do you have everything you need here?'

Her eyes were dancing as she said, 'Everything and more.'

Responding to her humour with an arch of his eyebrows, he filled the two glasses she put down in front of him. After saluting her with his he inhaled the bouquet, swivelled the wine around the bowl of the glass, smelled it again, then taking a sip he savoured the taste and aroma before finally swallowing. 'So, are you making good progress with your research?' he asked, glancing at the table where her books and notepads were strewn.

'I think so,' she replied, going to sit down and feeling

pleased when he pulled out a chair too. 'At some point I'll have to make a trip to Paris, to visit Montmartre, but it's not pressing. There's plenty for me to go through here.'

'Ah, *Suite Française*,' he remarked, picking up the novel she'd left open on the chair he was about to sit on. Then he added wryly, 'I think you'll learn a lot about the French character from this, and perhaps not all of it is flattering.'

She laughed. 'That must mean you've read it.'

'*Mais bien sûr*. The reviews were excellent, and deservedly so.' He frowned for a moment, then started to quote, ' "It's as though the rhythm of the words has wings that carry you right into the heart of their beauty and pain, their happiness and horror . . . " I think that is more or less accurate, *non*?'

Jessica was looking at him in amazement. 'You read my review?' she said.

'Of course. Lilian is one of your biggest fans, she reads everything you write for the magazines and passes it to me to make sure I do too.'

Jessica rolled her eyes. 'I'm sorry if it gets tedious.'

'It doesn't, but I admit in the case of *Suite Française* I was particularly interested to know what you'd written, because it is a book that fascinated me when the manuscript was first discovered here in France. Naturally I read it in the original when it was published, then Lilian gave me your review when the English translation came out, plus a copy of the book.'

'So you've read it in French and English?'

He nodded. 'Have you?'

'No, but I should. Is it a good translation?'

'Excellent.' He looked down at the copy he was holding. 'I know it is set at a different time to the belle époque, but it contains much about France that I imagine you are finding helpful for your story.'

'I'm finding it inspiring on just about every level,' she confirmed. 'I'm not sure I've ever read a book that I admire or love more.'

His eyebrows rose. 'A touching tribute to a woman who died so tragically,' he commented.

She smiled, then looked away as the resonance of his

words seemed to touch on the events that had taken place in the very room they were in.

Apparently following her thoughts, he said, 'Lilian tells me you are hoping to make things a little clearer in your mind while you are here.'

She continued to look down at her glass as she nodded. Then, bringing her eyes to his, she said, 'I suppose, like everyone else, you think I'm crazy, or at the very least in some kind of denial.'

'No,' he replied, seeming to wonder why she'd think that.

Surprised, she found herself momentarily lost for a response.

'You were her mother,' he continued, 'if you feel that something is not right, then I would not be the one to say you are wrong.'

His words were so unexpected, and so what she'd longed to hear these past months from Charlie or Lilian, that for a moment she felt herself swamped by emotion. 'But you were here,' she said. 'You came right after she fell, so if something wasn't right . . .'

'By the time I arrived the police and paramedics were everywhere, but I don't think you are so much worried about what happened then. It is what happened before that concerns you?'

Her eyes were fixed intently on his as her breath started to become shallow. 'Do you know if anything did happen?' she asked. 'I mean, apart from what my mother told us?'

His expression seemed paradoxically harsh and gentle as he said, 'All I can tell you is what I told Charlie and the *gendarmes*. I didn't see your mother or Natalie at all that morning. The first I knew that anything was wrong was when you called me.'

'So you didn't offer to drive them to the village for lunch?'

He was taken aback. 'No. Why? Does your mother say I did?'

'No. Apparently she told Daniella she was intending to take Natalie there, and I just don't believe she'd have walked in the rain. If I'm right, it can only mean someone was going to take them.' She sighed, then took a sip of her wine. 'Of course, they didn't go anyway . . .' Her eyes went to his. 'Did you speak to her at all that morning? Or see anyone here?'

He shook his head. 'As you must already know, the only unusual thing I saw was the car.'

Jessica's eyes opened wide.

Evidently surprised by her reaction, he said, 'I see you didn't know about the car?'

'No, I didn't.' Her heart was starting to pound. Her thoughts were coming too fast. 'Please tell me,' she said, almost breathlessly.

Clearly concerned about finding himself in a vacuum he hadn't even known existed, he said, 'I only noticed it because normally the space outside the cottage was empty, but that morning, when I happened to look this way, maybe at about eleven o'clock, or a little after, I saw that someone had parked outside. I knew your mother hadn't rented a car, so I presumed it was a visitor.'

Jessica rose to her feet, so thrown by this news that she couldn't fully take it in. 'So whose was it? What happened to it?' she asked.

'I believe it belonged to a tourist,' he replied. 'Someone who was lost and stopped to ask for directions.'

'That's what my mother said? Then she's a liar.' The words had escaped her before she could stop them. Realising he wasn't going to contradict her, she became more agitated than ever. 'Does Charlie know about this car?' she asked.

Though his eyes met the glittering challenge in hers, it was clear he didn't want to answer.

'He does, doesn't he?' she said quietly.

Unable to lie, he said, 'It was mentioned when we were talking to the *gendarmes*, but by then your mother had assured everyone that the car belonged to someone who was lost and had stopped to ask the way, so it was probably not considered to be important.'

Jessica turned sharply away. Important or not, Charlie had known about this car and never told her. Suddenly she turned back again. 'Does Lilian know?' she asked.

Appearing more uncomfortable than ever, he said, 'Yes, I believe so.'

Shock hit her heart hard. 'Then why has she never told me?'

'Probably for the same reason as Charlie, because she didn't want you to become upset about something that didn't matter.'

Jessica pushed a hand through her hair and tried again to make herself think. She'd had her suspicions for so long, and now to be told that both Charlie and Lilian were covering up for her mother was disorienting her badly. 'Do you believe it was a tourist?' she asked abruptly.

'I have no reason not to.'

She looked at him closely. 'But you're not convinced?'

Holding her eyes he said, 'No, not entirely.'

She took a breath, then quite suddenly she realised she felt afraid. 'I have to call the *Médecin Légiste* in the morning,' she told him, a ragged edge to her voice. 'And I've arranged to go and see the *gendarmes*. I think . . . I don't know . . .' She put her hands to her head, not sure what she was trying to say. 'This is changing what I need to ask and I can't . . .'

'Would you like me to come with you?' he said gently.

Startled, her eyes went to his. 'I could ask Daniella,' she said, 'but she has the children . . .'

'I'll take you,' he interrupted, and as her eyes filled with tears he got up from the table to go outside and put up the parasol, apparently realising she needed a moment to be alone.

He stayed for a long time that afternoon, listening as she talked about Natalie in a way she hadn't felt able to since she'd lost her. There was so much, too much, locked up in her heart, and though she'd never imagined she would unleash it all to him, as the words spilled from her she began to realise that maybe it could only ever have been him. After all, he was the one who'd been here that day, who'd seen Natalie at the end and carried her little body out to the ambulance when it was time to take her away. He'd even made sure he knew where they were taking her before they left; then he'd had the terrible ordeal of telling a mother her child was dead.

He mentioned nothing of his own role now, he merely listened as she spoke from her heart, never once showing any sign of discomfort, or saying anything to make her feel he would like to go.

She didn't cry then, that happened later, when she was alone, but during that long, hot afternoon she felt as though all the confusion and loneliness inside her was at last finding some small sense of relief.

'It's as though parts of me have been shut up in darkness since she died,' she told him, as she finally began to run out of words, 'and now you're allowing them to come into the light.'

His only answer was to look at her in a way that she couldn't quite fathom at first, until a kind of lambency came into his eyes that made her start to smile. This tragedy had forged a connection between them that needed no words, she realised, it was simply there, as gentle as the air and intangible as the understanding that was lifting her heart.

He got up to go and rinse their glasses, then refilled them from a fresh bottle of Macon-Valennes, and once again she watched the way he drank, appearing to savour every nuance of the flavour and perhaps each delicate part of the aroma before finally allowing himself to swallow.

'Tell me what you're doing,' she said.

He seemed confused.

Realising that to drink that way was second nature to him, she said, 'I'd like to know about the wine, what you're looking for when you're tasting, how it feels in your mouth.'

He stared down at his glass, then apparently understanding her need to talk about something else for a while, he brought his eyes back to hers and began to explain, as though it were the most natural thing in the world for her to want to know about wine, and for him to be telling her. 'With a white wine like this,' he said, 'I am checking for its acidity, because this is important to its freshness. What we have here is a *vin de table*, so the quality is not going to be the same as for the *premiers ou grands crus*. Nevertheless, we must establish the fruits or flowers of the taste, whether there is a residue of oak from the barrels . . . Maybe it will be easier to explain if we do a tasting at the *caves*, sometime.'

She was just saying she'd love to when they heard a car door slam outside and seconds later an enormous dog skidded into the kitchen, all glossy black fur and fat pink tongue, and launched itself straight into Luc's lap.

'Ah Rousseau,' he laughed, ruffling the dog playfully. *'Je pensais que tu nous avais quittés pour de bon.'* I thought you'd left home for good.

Jessica laughed as the dog insisted on giving Luc's face a thorough licking before rearranging its large, sleek body to plant two huge paws on his master's shoulders, as though preventing him from seeing anyone but his adoring beast.

'Tonton Luc. *Tonton* Luc. *Tu es là,'* Elodie cried as she and Antoine raced in after the dog. *'Maman, Tonton Luc est ici avec Jessica.'*

'So he is,' Daniella responded dryly as she came in with Hugo. Then she rolled her eyes as the twins circled a big embrace around both Luc and the dog. 'I hope we are not interrupting,' she said to Jessica, putting Hugo down so he could join in the hug.

'Not at all,' Jessica assured her, going for another glass. 'Luc was just telling me how to taste wine.' She laughed as Rousseau, having suddenly realised there was someone new to greet, whizzed round in front of her and sat very upright, tongue hanging out, tail wagging as he waited to be spoiled.

'You are too adorable for words,' she told him, catching his mischievous face between her hands and stooping to kiss him. 'I'm not sure if you remember me, but Harry hasn't forgotten you.'

'Maman, pouvons nous avoir une boisson?' Antoine cried, as Luc kissed his sister on both cheeks, then took over the pouring of her wine.

'You must ask Jessica,' she responded.

His big brown eyes turned to Jessica. *'Pouvons nous . . .'*

'In English,' Daniella interrupted.

Antoine looked anxiously at Elodie, who promptly drew him into a huddle so they could work out the translation. Not to be left out, Rousseau pushed his nose between them and began thumping a chair with his tail.

'I am bringing the twins for their next sitting,' Daniella reminded Luc, as he passed her a drink. 'And then I think we stay for dinner, because Claude is out for the evening. I hope you will join us, Jessica, I have bring plenty of food.'

Jessica was about to respond when Luc said, *'Brought* plenty of food – and of course she will join us.'

Jessica's eyes were shining as she looked at him, then Antoine cried, 'Jessica! Please can we 'ave a drunk?'

As the adults started to laugh his expression turned to one of confusion, then clearly offended he punched his sister who was laughing too, though it was doubtful she knew why. *'Tu m'a dis de dire ça!'* he protested.

'C'est toi, pas moi!' she shouted, thumping him back.

Before it could go any further, Luc caught them both by the arms and pulled them apart. 'I think it is better if I give you a *drink* at the studio,' he said, emphasising the word so Antoine would understand his mistake.

'Est-ce que l'on peut faire la course jusqu'à la maison?' Elodie cried, jumping up and down. Can we have a race up to the house?

'A race? In this heat?' Luc objected.

'Mais il fait moins chaud maintenant.' But it's not as hot now.

'Maman, puis-je y aller aussi?' Hugo asked. *'Je veux faire la course, moi aussi.'* Mummy, can I go too? I want to be in the race.

'You want to be in the race?' Daniella laughed. *'Non, chéri, tu es trop petit.'*

Hugo looked devastated. *'Mais ce n'est pas juste,'* he protested. *'Je veux faire la course avec Tonton Luc.'* But it's not fair. I want to be in the race with Uncle Luc.

'And so you shall,' Luc declared, scooping him up – and plonking him in Daniella's arms he turned round so she could put his chubby little nephew on his back. 'And what is more, Hugo, we shall win,' he informed him.

At that Elodie and Antoine erupted in protest and made for the door, hotly pursued by Rousseau.

Luc turned back to Jessica. 'Come for dinner,' he said, and a moment later he was going after the twins.

Amazed at how he could find the energy in so much heat, Jessica went to watch them charging through the vines in a race that appeared as full of cheating as it did shouting, thumping and stumbling about in the dirt. When finally she turned back inside, still laughing at what was developing into a very noisy dispute over who'd actually won, Daniella was perched on the edge of the table sipping her wine.

'Please tell me if you'd rather carry on working,' she said. 'I can always leave you in peace.'

'Oh, no, really, I'm enjoying having some company,' Jessica assured her. 'Would you like to sit outside? You might have noticed I have a parasol now.'

A few minutes later they were half-sitting, half-sprawling each side of an old wrought-iron table, with a large cream-coloured parasol shading them from the glare of the early evening sun. 'I think,' Daniella said with a smile, 'that you are beginning to feel quite at home here, *non*?'

'Very much,' Jessica agreed. 'Thanks to you and Fernand, and now Luc. Lilian's very lucky to have found herself such a lovely family. I always hoped she would, though I can't help wishing sometimes that she wasn't so far away.'

It was a while before Daniella spoke again, and when she did she seemed almost to be in tune with Jessica's thoughts as she said, 'I hope you don't mind, but Lilian told me that part of the reason you come here is because you are having some difficulties with Charlie.'

Jessica looked down at her glass, aware of how those difficulties had increased now that she knew about the car. 'No, I don't mind,' she answered. With a sigh she gazed out across the valley, to where the woods were turning into a fiery cluster on the horizon. 'Things haven't been right between us since Natalie died,' she said. 'At first it seemed to bring us even closer together, but then for some reason it started to change . . . I'm not sure if it was him or me . . . It was probably both of us . . . Did Lilian tell you about the other woman?'

Daniella nodded. 'But it was a long time ago, *non*?'

'Apparently. It still means he lied though, and now I've just found out he's been holding something else back from me.'

Daniella frowned.

'Luc told me there was a car here that morning.' Her eyes stayed on Daniella's. 'Did you know?' she asked.

Daniella seemed uncertain. 'Do you mean the one who belonged to someone who was lost?' she said.

Jessica nodded. 'Apparently that's the story my mother gave, but I don't believe it.'

'So who do you think it was?'

'I've no idea, but I have every intention of finding out.'

'Jessica, if you just listen to yourself you'll understand exactly why I didn't tell you,' Charlie cried when she challenged him later. 'I knew you'd read more into it, and end up in the very state you're in now.'

'If I'm in a state it's because you lied . . .'

'I didn't lie, I simply judged it better not to tell you something that meant nothing . . .'

'It amounts to the same thing, and you know it.'

'No, I don't. You've been twisting yourself up in knots ever since Natalie died, refusing to believe anything anyone tells you . . .'

'I'm not discussing it with you any more,' she said savagely. 'I want my mother's number.'

'You can't call her while you're in this kind of mood.'

'Give me the number, Charlie.'

'Jessica, you've got to stop this. I'll give it to you when you've calmed down . . .'

'Charlie! I don't want to argue about this . . .'

'I don't have it right now. I'm still at the office and it's at home.'

Since there was no arguing with that, except to accuse him of lying again, she forced herself to stop pacing and let her head fall forward. A moment or two later, managing to sound slightly less angry, she said, 'So you believe the car belonged to someone who was lost?'

Sounding incredulous he said, 'Why wouldn't I? It's happening all the time around there. It even happened to us, last Christmas. You must remember when someone knocked on the door . . .'

'Of course I remember, but doesn't it strike you as a bit too much of a coincidence that some tourist should bowl up in his car on the very morning my mother was planning to take Natalie into the village for lunch?'

'I hardly know what to say to that,' he responded. 'Whether or not you think it's stretching belief, it happened. You said yourself, Luc saw the car.'

'But not who was in it, so we only have my mother's word it was a tourist. My mother, Charlie! Someone who's never been reliable in her entire life, and who now, very conveniently, has to be protected from any kind of stress so we can't ask her any more questions. Surely to God you can see I might have a point.'

'If I thought so I'd pursue it myself,' he told her earnestly. 'But all you're doing is proving to me what I feared all along, that going back there is adding to your confusion and not helping at all.'

In the end, having to accept she was going to get no further tonight, she rang off and went upstairs to change for dinner. Just thank God she was spending the evening with people who didn't seem to think she was going off her head, or that she was an hysteric to be wary of, because the thought of sitting here alone tonight wasn't filling her with as much pleasure as it had before.

Once she managed to pull her thoughts from the quagmire of doubts that seemed to be getting deeper and murkier all the time, she realised how much she was looking forward to seeing Fernand, whom she hadn't seen for several days, and to talking to Luc about books and wine again, and to Daniella about opera. It would be a little oasis of sanity in what was starting to feel like an unnervingly alien world.

Immediately he'd finished talking to Jessica Charlie dialled the number in Capri, only for it to ring and ring, giving him no opportunity to leave a message. Having no choice but to ring off in the end, he repocketed his mobile and decided to try again as soon as he got home.

It wasn't so much that he didn't want Jessica to talk to her mother about the car, it was more that he considered it only fair to warn Veronica to expect the call.

However, when he tried again later there was still no reply from the villa, but at least there was some comfort in knowing that if he couldn't get through, Jessica wouldn't be able to either. So after leaving a message on Jessica's mobile with the number, he took himself off to bed, knowing already how unlikely it was he'd be able to sleep.

'Jessica? Is that you?' Lilian said drowsily. 'What time is it?'

'Sorry, I've woken you.'

'No, it's fine. I had a really late night. Is everything all right? It must be almost midnight there.'

'Yes, it is. I've just had dinner up at the *manoir*.'

Sounding much more awake now, Lilian said, 'You're calling about the car, aren't you? Luc said he'd told you.'

'So do you understand why I'm worried? Angry, even?'

'Yes, of course, but it wasn't that anyone was trying to hide anything from you, we were just hoping to avoid you turning it into something much bigger than it was. Have you spoken to Charlie yet?'

'Yes, and I'm sure you already know what he said, because you've probably worked this out between you . . .'

'Jessica. This is me you're talking to. You can't seriously imagine we'd ever do anything without your best interests at heart? We were just trying to stop you from putting yourself through any more torment . . . This poor guy, whoever he was, was lost, your mother didn't speak Danish, or Dutch – she never was sure of his nationality – and so he left. Luc happened to look down that way at the time the car was there. If he'd looked a little longer, he'd have seen him and his wife driving off again.'

It all sounded so reasonable the way Lilian was telling it that Jessica was starting to lose sight of why she was so suspicious. 'You have this from my mother,' she said, remembering.

'Of course. But there's no reason to disbelieve her . . .'

'Except she was planning to go to the café for lunch, and I think whoever was in that car had come to drive her.'

It was a long time before Lilian responded, in a voice that was imbued with feeling. 'It was a tourist, Jessica,' she said. 'Please try to accept that.'

'Why? What makes you so certain?'

'I just am. Darling, all this has been bad enough for you, so I don't understand why you seem so set on making it worse. There was no foul play involved in Natalie's death – even you accept it was an accident. There were no signs of anyone other than your mother and Natalie being at the cottage, and as far as everyone else is concerned, which includes everyone who was there that day, everything happened the way your mother told us.'

Jessica was tempted to tell her that Luc wasn't entirely convinced about the tourist either, but in the end she only said, 'No-one else has had a lifetime's experience of my mother. I know when she's not telling the truth, and I have to say this, Lily, I never dreamt you would take her side against me, especially over something like this.'

'But it's not about taking sides,' Lilian protested. 'It's about loving and protecting you at a time when you're at your most vulnerable.'

'Protecting me from what?'

'From yourself and any more pain. You've already been through enough, I just wish you'd stop trying to put yourself through even more.'

In the end, deciding it was pointless to go on trying to make Lilian see it her way when she was clearly determined not to, Jessica rang off and went to stand in the room Natalie had used. Maybe, in the days to come, she was thinking as she looked around at the moonlit shadows, she would manage to prove she was right and her mother was lying. Yet she had to admit it would be a truly pyrrhic victory if she did, for in her heart of hearts she wanted nothing more than the story of the lost tourist to be true.

Chapter Thirteen

When Luc pulled up outside the cottage the following morning Jessica was ready and waiting with a small attaché case containing the notes she'd made for her meeting with Monsieur Galeron at the *gendarmerie*.

'Good morning,' Luc said, as she got in beside him. 'Did you sleep well?'

'Actually much better than I expected,' she replied, fastening her seat belt. Then, easing her hemline back down towards her knees, 'Probably thanks to all the delicious wine Fernand treated us to last night.'

Appearing amused, he pressed his foot on the accelerator and the Mercedes began to glide up the hill. Once again the sun was blazing down on the landscape, baking the roads and scorching the vines, making her glad of the cool air that was filling the car.

'Have you spoken to Lilian this morning?' she asked, as they turned onto the top road. 'Did she tell you I called her last night? Or this morning, her time.'

'Yes, she did.' He pulled in for Jean-Marc to come past in the vineyard *camionette*. 'I think she's sorry now that she didn't tell you about the car before,' he said.

'She should have. Holding information back is never a good idea, because it'll always come out in the end, and then it acquires the very significance she – and Charlie – were trying to avoid.'

He glanced over at her, then picked up speed as they left the hamlet behind to begin heading towards the village. 'So do you believe it was a tourist now?' he asked.

'No. Do you?'

After a moment's thought he said, 'I think I'm probably

more prepared to give your mother the benefit of the doubt than you are.'

At that a light of humour showed in her eyes. 'Spoken like a true diplomat,' she commented.

He laughed, then after easing the car out to overtake a tractor he said, 'What news from the *Médecin Légiste*? Did you call this morning?'

'I did, only to be told that there is no news, so I have to call again tomorrow.'

'Bureaucracy moves slowly here in France, I'm afraid, particularly at this time of year.'

Knowing how true that was, she said, 'Do you think I'll get permission to see the report?'

'Probably. If not, I'll see what I can do.'

She gave him a quick look and wished she knew how to thank him without embarrassing them both.

Seeming to sense what she was thinking, he said, 'My family has lived around here for a very long time, so we know many people, and sometimes favours are the strongest currency.' Then, with a teasing look in his eyes, 'But I think you understand very well the key to a Frenchman's chivalry. You have only to say *s'il vous plaît, monsieur, j'ai un problème*, and we will all be knocking each other out of the way to try to please you.'

Loving the feel of the laughter inside her, she said, 'I'll be sure to remember that,' then as his phone rang she turned to look out at the passing countryside, unable to stop herself wishing that their purpose wasn't such a painful one when everything else seemed so simple and right.

Half an hour later Monsieur Galeron, a small wiry man with inky blue eyes and a curiously lopsided smile, was showing them into an interview room at the back of the *gendarmerie*. Apart from the language on the calendars and information sheets pinned to the walls, it was no different to any other police interview room with its battered table and plastic chairs, though she doubted British versions had quite so many overflowing ashtrays these days.

Since she'd guessed that Monsieur Galeron would feel more comfortable dealing with a French man, as opposed to an English woman – and Luc hadn't disagreed – Jessica sat quietly listening for a minute or two as Luc confirmed why they were there. Though Galeron's eyes came to her once or twice, on the whole they remained on Luc, until, giving her his whole attention, he said, in French, 'I don't think I can tell you anything that you do not already know.'

'Perhaps if you can just talk us through it again,' she prompted. 'From the time you arrived at the house.'

He nodded gravely, and folding his hands, he said, 'The paramedics were already there, of course, and by the time we arrived they had ascertained that your daughter was dead. One of them was taking care of your mother. She was in a very agitated state . . . Shaking, unable to stop crying . . . Of course she was in shock . . .'

'What was she saying?' Jessica asked.

His eyes narrowed as he tried to remember, then realising why he couldn't, he said, 'She was speaking in English, so I am afraid I could not understand. It was only when Monsieur Véron came into the house that we were able to communicate with your mother. That was when we understood that your daughter had fallen over some newspapers at the top of the stairs. They were still scattered on the stairs, and the floor. She had been on the telephone at the time, as you know, because I believe she was speaking to you, so she didn't see the papers.'

Jessica swallowed hard as she nodded. Her memory of those moments was still too vivid for her to bear without the horror of it making her shrink inside. 'Was anyone else there?' she asked.

Frowning with surprise he said, 'You mean besides the paramedics and ourselves? No, there was no-one else, until Monsieur Véron arrived, of course.'

'Did you check to see if anyone was upstairs?'

'Yes, of course. We would be negligent in our duty if we did not.'

'And no-one was?'

He shook his head.

'My mother claims that she and Natalie went for a walk that morning,' she went on. 'Did you find any evidence of that?'

'There were muddy boots outside the door, and damp

coats inside,' he replied, 'so it would appear that they did go out.'

'Did she say where they went?'

He consulted his notes. 'To the woods nearby, to find a bird's nest,' he replied.

Jessica blinked. 'My mother was looking for a bird's nest, in the rain?' she said incredulously.

He shrugged and looked at Luc as though he might be able to throw some light on it.

Jessica looked at Luc too. 'You did the translation,' she said in English. 'Does he have that right, about the bird's nest?'

Luc nodded. 'I confess I'd forgotten until now that it was the reason she gave for going out that morning, but certainly it's what she said.'

Still thrown by something that felt so unlike her mother, she turned back to Galeron. 'Did you believe her?' she asked.

He seemed surprised. 'You mean about the bird's nest? I had no reason not to,' he answered cautiously.

'Did you check for anyone else's footprints around the house that morning?'

This time he appeared amazed by the question, then a little perturbed. 'There were no suspicious circumstances to make that necessary,' he told her.

Not wanting to put him any further on the defensive, she softened her expression as she said, 'No, of course not. So what happened next? After Monsieur Véron arrived and he'd helped you to communicate with my mother? He told you about the car he had seen outside that morning.'

Galeron nodded. 'Your mother was a little confused by it at first, saying no-one had been there, but then she remembered some tourists who were lost.' He glanced down at his paperwork. 'She thinks they were Danish, or maybe Dutch.'

Jessica wanted to ask if he thought her mother had been telling the truth, but he evidently did or he'd have questioned her further, or even tried to trace the tourists. However, just in case, she said, 'Were you ever able to find these tourists?'

Galeron blinked. 'We didn't try, Madame. People are

getting lost all the time when they are travelling around this region.'

Not sure whether she was relieved or frustrated by his answer, she said, 'So after you finished talking to my mother . . .'

'Actually, before that,' he interrupted, 'the paramedics told us that they were ready to move your daughter, so Monsieur Véron went to lift her from the sofa to carry . . .'

'The sofa?' Jessica interrupted. 'I thought she was in the kitchen. Wasn't she on the floor, where she'd fallen?'

He looked puzzled as he shook his head.

Jessica turned to Luc. 'I thought she was on the floor, that you lifted her up from the bottom of the stairs.'

'No, she was on the sofa,' he said gently.

'But how did she get there?' She turned back to the *gendarme*. 'My mother couldn't have lifted her.'

Galeron looked at her blankly, then at Luc as he said, 'The paramedics were already there, so one of them must have carried her to the sofa.'

Immediately Jessica felt the tension lessening inside her. 'Of course,' she said, slightly breathlessly. 'I'm sorry. Please go on, Monsieur.'

'There really is not much more to tell you,' he said, apologetically. 'Monsieur Véron took your daughter to the ambulance and then we waited with your mother while Monsieur Véron called you in London.'

Feeling her chest starting to tighten as those terrible moments closed in on her again, Jessica rose to her feet. 'I'm sorry,' she said, 'it's just . . .'

'Please don't apologise,' Galeron broke in kindly. 'I understand this is very difficult for you.'

Jessica nodded, then attempted a smile. 'You've been very helpful,' she told him. 'Thank you for going over it again.' She turned to Luc. 'I think I need some air.'

Once they were outside, squinting in the dazzling brightness of the sun, she took several deep breaths, and pushed her hands through her hair. 'That was harder than I expected,' she confessed, realising she was shaking, 'but I'm glad I did it.' Her eyes went to his. 'Thank you for coming with me.'

Unlocking the car, he said, 'I have booked us into an *auberge* a few miles from here. I think it is time for you to relax a little and have some lunch.'

Though she wasn't at all sure she could eat, the mere idea of sitting somewhere peaceful with only him and strangers around her for a while was enough to put some warmth back into her veins. 'I don't know how often I can say thank you,' she told him as he held the door open for her to get in, 'but I'm beginning to think it won't ever be often enough.'

The eighteenth-century *auberge* with its yellow-rose-covered arbour and ancient stone walls was on the crest of a hill overlooking some of the famous Montrachet vineyards as well as the glistening black turrets of an ivory-coloured château, deep in the wooded heart of the *combe*. From the moment they arrived, entering through a crumbling stone arch, it was evident that Luc knew not only the owner, but several of the diners who were already tucking into their midday meal.

After some protracted and humorous greetings, as well as introductions, they were shown to a shady table at the edge of the terrace where a pristine white tablecloth was set with claret-coloured napkins and a triangular vase of wild flowers. Almost immediately the owner reappeared with a perfectly chilled Chablis, the bottle dripping condensation as he uncorked it, and the colour shimmering like pale amber in the sunlight as he poured a small amount into the bowl of Luc's glass.

After holding it up to the light, smelling, swivelling then tasting it, Luc declared it, *'Pas mal. Pas mal du tout. Comme d'habitude un bon vin de la maison de Jean-Paul et Benoît Droin.'* And continuing in French to Jessica, 'Crisp, light, slightly fruity with a hint of honey.' Then to the owner, whose expression glowed delight, *'Allez-y, Noel.'*

Jessica watched the wine going into her glass, while listening to Noel recommending the Coquilles St Jacques as an excellent accompaniment to the *premier cru*, then after wishing them *bon appétit*, he took himself off to greet another *vigneron* who was just arriving through the arch.

'So food is ordered according to the wine here, rather than

the other way round?' she remarked dryly, after she and Luc had taken their first sip.

His expression was droll. 'Of course. You are in Bourgogne. What do you expect? But you do not have to choose the Coquilles St Jacques, there is a very good menu . . .'

'No, I'm perfectly happy to follow expert advice,' she interrupted, glancing up as a waiter set down a filigree basket of delicious-looking breads. Then her eyes started to twinkle as, finding himself recognised again, Luc was forced to get up to greet the new arrival. The irony of it wasn't lost on him either, since he'd promised to bring her to a place where no English tourists were allowed, so it was unlikely she'd be recognised – what he hadn't warned her about was how well known he was himself.

'So why,' she asked as he sat down again, 'are no English tourists allowed here?'

His grimace was so comical it caused her to laugh even before he answered. 'I am afraid that Noel detests the English,' he admitted. 'So I have smuggled you in right under his nose, but from now we must speak only French.'

Delighted, she said, '*Enfin. Tout le monde veut parler anglais depuis je suis arrivée et moi, je meurs d'envie de parler français – et pas seulement aux gendarmes.*' Everyone has been wanting to speak English since I arrived, and me, I'm dying to speak French – and not just to the *gendarmes*.

So from there they continued in French, discussing what had transpired during their interview with Galeron, which they had to confess hadn't changed anything to any remarkable degree.

'But it seems they did go for a walk in the rain that morning,' Jessica said, putting down her glass. 'I'm still having a problem with the bird's nest story, but I suppose it does sound very Natalie, so maybe it is true. And obviously they've accepted my mother's story of some tourists being lost.'

'And what about you? Are you any closer to believing it?'

'No.' She sighed. 'I don't know. I'd like to ask her about it myself, because I can almost always tell when she's lying.'

'So why don't you?' he said, offering her the basket of bread.

She took a small piece, then watched his fingers as he broke apart a chunk of richly seasoned *pain d'olive.* It was reminding her of how he'd unwrapped a truffle last night after dinner, and passed it to her. For some reason the gesture had felt more intimate than it should have. 'I tried earlier,' she said, in answer to his question, 'but she's on Capri at the moment and the number's just ringing and ringing with no reply. Typical. Knowing her, she's jetted off somewhere else by now and not bothered to let anyone know.'

After putting a morsel of bread in his mouth, he chewed it thoughtfully, before saying, 'I think Lilian told you that your mother called to ask if she could come back to the cottage.'

'At the beginning of June, yes,' she replied, 'but she didn't show up. Do you know anything else about that?'

He shook his head. 'She spoke to my father, not me, so I can only repeat what he said.'

'Which was?' Jessica prompted, already half-afraid it was going to be more than Lilian had told her, not necessarily because of what it might be, but because she didn't want to find out that anything else was being held back from her. But she needn't have worried, for it turned out that Luc could only tell her what she already knew.

'I think,' she said, as the main dish arrived and their glasses were refilled, 'that you must have had enough of listening to me going round and round in circles by now, so why don't we talk about you?' Then suddenly worried about how flirtatious that might have sounded, she quickly added, 'And the vineyard. Has it always been in your family?'

The amusement in his eyes told her that he'd read her accurately enough, and though she blushed she slanted him a look that made him laugh.

Continuing to speak in French he said, 'I am sure Lilian has already told you this.'

'Even if she has, I'd like to hear it again.'

'OK,' he said slowly, still seeming to suspect that she was just being polite rather than genuinely interested. 'The vineyard has been in my family for four generations, but on my mother's side, not my father's. When my father married my mother, who was an only child, he was a financier in

Paris, and she was an artist who was enjoying a little success. They fell very deeply in love they tell me, and when she took him home to meet her parents, she says they liked him more than they liked her. So my father, after he married my mother – he had already made a lot of money by then – he took an early retirement, went back to university to study viticulture – how to make wine – and after my mother's father died, my parents left Paris to come and take over the vineyard. Since then my father has added several plots to our estate, which are scattered around Burgundy, Chablis, Clos-Vougeot, Côte de Beaune, Côte de Nuits and Côte Chalonnaise. Many of these are our *vins de garde*, naturally, while at Valennes we grow the grapes mainly for the *vins de table*. So there, I think, you have a potted history of our small winery.'

Aware that the Chablis, along with the perfect ambience of a hot sun and beautiful setting, were all adding to how entranced she was feeling, she said, 'Are all the paintings around the house your mother's?'

'Every one,' he confirmed. 'My father won't allow anyone else's.'

She blinked in surprise. 'But I've seen your sculptures and photographs.'

'They're not paintings.'

'Ah, I see.'

Seeming amused, though she wasn't entirely sure why, he watched her pick up her fork and dig it into a succulent scallop. Finding him still watching her as she looked up again, she put the scallop in her mouth and felt her appetite fade a little as his eyes dropped to her mouth. He was a man who seemed fascinated by almost anything, she was thinking, and whose scrutiny was almost as hypnotic as the ambience.

The subject changed then, several times, as he told her about his sculpture and the pleasure he got from using his bare hands to create art. Then she wanted to know about his work as a photojournalist which he was gradually winding down now, and soon they were discussing his love of other cultures, travel, film and opera. Then he coaxed her to tell him about where she'd grown up, the grandparents who'd cared for her, the time she'd spent in Canada, and why she'd chosen to read French at university. He listened so attentively that she became almost as carried away by his interest as she was by the wine. It was as though she wanted to open herself up to him, and hold nothing back . . . Then he was asking about her career, how she had come to be in TV, and if she regretted giving it up.

'Not at all,' she answered, feeling, as she sat there with the sun beating down on them and the landscape seeming almost to bleed colour it was so perfect, that her real life had been swallowed into another dimension. 'To quote my daughter,' she said, with a playful twinkle, 'I am so over it.'

He didn't smile in return, merely held her eyes, and as his intensity seemed to steal into her she felt her breathing slow almost to a stop. Needing to escape the moment she looked around, saying she hoped no-one had heard her drop back into English. It was only when she saw how unsuccessfully he was disguising his laughter that she said, 'I think you've spun me a line. Noel doesn't have a problem with English people at all, does he?'

'No,' he confessed, 'and yes. If you are local you always get a reservation first – and he prefers French to be spoken because we are in France. The real truth is, I wanted to make you speak my language because I have not heard you do it very much.'

Enjoying the way that made her feel, she said, in French, 'So now you know I'm not as bad as you thought, do I get a medal?'

'Not at all, because I speak much better English.'

Her eyes narrowed, but knowing he was teasing her she said, 'It's true your English is good, but I think your knowledge of wine is even better, and I'd like you to teach me.'

At first he only raised his eyebrows, then seeming to realise she was serious he lowered his eyes to her mouth again as he said, 'I would be happy to.'

The potency of his gaze made her gasp, very softly, but she knew he'd heard, and then it was as though all her senses became heightened: the sun felt hotter, the food smelled richer and the melodious sound of French being spoken merged with corks popping from bottles and wine gurgling into glasses.

As though at a distance she heard her mobile ringing, and reaching into her bag she took it out.

'Darling, is that you?' Charlie said loudly.

At the sound of his voice her mind seemed to go into a slow sort of spin. 'Yes, how are you?' she said. Her eyes went briefly to Luc as he continued to eat.

'I'm fine. Actually, missing you like crazy.'

He sounded drunk, she thought, and might have said so if Luc hadn't been there. 'Where are you?' she asked.

There was a moment's baffled silence before he said, 'Oh, I get it, you're not alone?'

'No.'

'So where are *you*?'

'At a restaurant. I went to see the . . .'

'I had a call from the Pettifers last night,' he interrupted. 'They're inviting us to spend the last two weeks in August with them, at their villa in Majorca. Harry too, obviously, he'll be company for their boy, Craig. I said we'd probably love to, but I needed to check with you. Remember how much we enjoyed it the last time we went? I think it could be just what we need, to get away together, relax, drink some wine . . .'

'Well, actually,' she said, 'I was thinking of staying on here for a while longer. The book's starting to take shape in my mind now . . .'

'Fuck the book!' he growled in a way that made her flinch. 'What about me and Harry? Don't we deserve some of your time too?'

'Of course, but you could always . . .'

'Jessica, I'm getting pretty sick of this now,' he told her heatedly.

'I went to see the *gendarmes* this morning . . .'

'Oh, for God's sake,' he snapped. 'When the hell are you going to let this go?'

Wishing Luc wasn't able to hear her, she said, 'You're doing it again, Charlie, getting angry . . .'

'What do you expect when you never stop to think how this is for me,' he cried. 'It's all about you and how you feel, never about anyone else . . .' His voice started to falter. 'I miss her too,' he said. 'I'd give anything in the world for our family to be whole again . . .'

'I know,' she said softly. 'I'm sorry.'

After a moment he said, 'No, I'm the one who should be sorry. I've had too much to drink. It's someone's birthday in the office.' He took a breath, then sounding more like himself he said, 'Did you get my message last night? Have you tried calling your mother yet?'

'Yes, but there's no reply.'

'I didn't get one either,' he said, 'but I'll keep trying.' Then after a pause, 'So what do I tell the Pettifers?'

Feeling her heart sink she said, 'It's up to you. If you want to go that's fine, but I'd rather stay here for the summer.'

'Don't be absurd. I'm not going without you.'

'Then I guess you say thanks, but no thanks.'

His tone was bitter again as he said, 'Which means you get a holiday, but Harry and I don't?'

'Harry's on holiday now.'

'Not with us – and please tell me, because I'm fascinated to know, who's supposed to be taking care of him when he comes back from Devon, if you're still going to be there?'

'He can come here too.'

There was no response, then realising how much she'd just hurt him by not including him, she said, 'You too, of course, but I know how you feel about it, so let's talk about this later, when you know if you can take any time off.'

As she put her mobile back on the table she looked at Luc intending to apologise, but as she started to speak her eyes suddenly filled with tears, and she looked away, hoping he wouldn't see. Everything felt too complicated and overwhelming . . . Charlie was upset, so was she and she didn't know how to make it any better. Aware of Luc signalling the waiter to bring the bill, she lifted her eyes to his.

'Tell me,' he said, before she could point out that they hadn't finished, 'how would you like to begin your first lesson in making wine?'

She looked surprised, then broke into a smile. 'You mean now, today?'

'Why not?'

Since there was no reason why not, she merely tilted her head to one side, and said, 'Actually, I'd love to.'

An hour later they were strolling between two soaring rows of almost fully ripened vines that rose up either side of them like huge glossy green walls, thick with rubbery leaves and cascading clusters of berries. There was no-one else in sight. It was as though the world was taking a pause, for nothing in the valley stirred except small colourful butterflies and sluggishly droning bees. Underfoot the ground was hard and stony and cracked with thirst, while overhead the sun was savage in its intensity, and the sky was as blue as it could ever be.

'How often do you water?' she asked, unable to detect any evidence of how it might be done.

'In France the *vignerons* must rely on nature to provide,' he told her.

She glanced up at him in surprise.

'Sometimes,' he said, stopping to test the *pinot noir* grapes with his fingers, 'we are forced to cheat, but that is our secret. Now, you will taste,' and after pulling a small bunch of fruit free from the vine, he broke off a single berry and put it into her mouth.

As she took it from him her lips touched his fingers.

'First you must suck at the pulp,' he told her, removing his hand. 'What you are looking for is a balance of sweetness and acidity. There will be an aroma too.'

As she crushed the grape with her tongue she felt the juice trickle into her mouth, and as the flavour began to awaken her taste buds she watched him take a grape into his own mouth and roll it slowly, almost lovingly, around his tongue, drawing out the pulp, then removing the pips to hold in his hand.

She did the same, and kept her eyes on his as he continued to chew. 'Now we have only the skin,' he said, 'and here we must try to detect the astringency of the tannins. The longer this takes the better the grape – and if you never find it, you have an excellent grape.'

'Is there any astringency in these?' she asked, having no idea how to taste for a tannin.

He nodded. 'Can you feel the dryness in your mouth?'

She tested it, then nodded.

'These grapes are for a *vin de table*,' he told her, 'so you would expect it. Now look at the colour of the seeds. If they are green this is bad, but these are a very pale brown, which is not too bad. Now we taste them. If they are bitter like grass, this is no good, but if you can find a little taste of nut it is starting to get better.'

As she chewed, crushing the seeds with her teeth, the taste of a mildly bitter grass began stealing across her tongue – then she became aware of him looking at her again, but in a slightly different way from before. It was as though his mind had moved away from what she was doing in order to see her in another, almost critical light that was putting an odd kind of distance between them, even as it drew them together.

She stood in the focus of his scrutiny, watching his eyes move over her face, following every contour and plane, probing each shadow and curve. They lingered searchingly around her eyes, moved gently down over her nose seeming to trace the flare of each nostril, before lowering to her juice-moistened lips. Then he reached out to put his fingers under her chin, and the feel of him touching her sent a small shock of sensation rippling through her.

Whether or not he noticed was impossible to tell, for he was still regarding her intently, objectively, tilting her face to the right, to the left, then up to the sky. She understood what was happening, and though she'd been waiting for it, she felt the pleasure of it starting to move through her.

'Can I sculpt you?' he said.

'Yes,' she answered, and knowing that there could be no more between them today, she turned to walk back through the vines.

Chapter Fourteen

At the sound of a car horn outside Jessica quickly grabbed her purse and phone and closing the door behind her, waved to Daniella as she went to join her. They were making an early morning trip to the market in a village a few miles away, which Jessica had never visited before but was keen to see, since Lilian had often waxed lyrical over it in a way that had almost got Jessica's mouth watering.

As they drove she called the children, the way she usually did first thing, then after ringing the office of the *Médecin Légiste* she found herself tempted to ask Luc to intervene, for there was still no news on the permission she needed. However, it hadn't even been a week since she'd made her request, so it was probably too early to bother him, and besides, it wouldn't be a good idea to start leaning too heavily on him. Not that he would mind, she felt sure, but she couldn't not be aware of how attracted she was to him. Emotionally fragile and needy as she was right now, it would be all too easy to start misinterpreting his kindness and understanding in a way that could end up causing intense embarrassment to them both.

When she and Daniella reached the riverside village, they parked in a field on the far bank, then strolled back across the humpback bridge into the bustling market square. After a while they split up, arranging to meet again in an hour, and as Jessica wandered amongst the stalls of fresh flowers and fruits, losing herself in the uniquely Gallic ambience of this centuries-old tradition, she could feel herself coming alive to a sense of freedom that she never had in London. It was making her almost recklessly happy, for she was able to move around unrecognised and unmolested here, to blend seamlessly into the background without even having to think about who might be watching or judging.

She stopped to talk to the vendors, loving the feel of the French words as they vibrated softly in her throat and rolled off her tongue. She feasted her eyes on the colours all around her, inhaled the freshness of melons and raspberries, and tasted honey, tapenade and pungent salamis. She bought fresh herbs and flavoured oils, thick wedges of cheese and the ripest tomatoes. The textures and sensuousness of everything she encountered seemed to pull her into a new world of sensations that she'd hardly been aware of before.

By the time she met up with Daniella again she'd become so entranced by it all that several of the tradesmen were recognising her now and smiling, while her basket was spilling over with all the produce Fernand had asked her to bring for lunch and so much more. Then she wandered over to a café to wait while Daniella went to buy a few last things for the children.

After ordering two coffees, Jessica clicked on her mobile to call Charlie, feeling sad that she didn't really want to, but knowing he'd be hurt if she didn't, and besides, nothing had yet been resolved – either about her staying on here, or whether or not he and Harry would join her.

'Hi, did I wake you?' she asked when his voice came sleepily down the line.

There was a moment of muffled movement before he said, 'It's half past nine in the morning, and I was in the studio till four, so what do you think?'

'I'm sorry,' she said. 'I'll call later.'

'No, no. You've woken me up now, so there's no point ringing off. Where are you?'

'In a café, waiting for Daniella. Have you called the Pettifers yet?'

'No. I was hoping you might have a change of heart.'

'I won't,' she told him. 'I'm staying on here. I'd really like you to come, though. If you can get the time off.'

'Well as it happens I can't, at least not until the last week of August, so I think you need to come home, whether you want to or not.'

'Why?'

'Have you forgotten you have a son?'

Ignoring the sarcasm, she said, 'I told you yesterday, he can join me here.'

'So are you suggesting he drive himself, or maybe he can qualify as a pilot?'

'I'm suggesting either Nikki and Freddy bring him before they go to Norfolk, or you can put him on a plane at Heathrow and I'll meet him at Lyon.'

'Well that might be fine for you . . .'

'Charlie, it won't be the first time he's flown alone, so please don't let's argue. Book a flight for when he returns from Devon, and another for when you can come yourself, if you can't make it at the same time.'

'Since when did you get to make all the decisions in this marriage?' he snapped angrily. 'In case you'd forgotten, there are two of us, and you know very well I don't want to go back to that cottage.'

'Why don't you at least think about it?'

'I don't have to.'

'I promise, it doesn't feel anywhere near as bad as you think. If anything it's making me feel closer to her.'

'I can't actually believe you're saying this . . .'

'OK, I'm doing a really bad job of putting it into words, but if you come, I'm sure you'll see what I mean. And if you end up finding it too hard, I promise, we'll leave. Now, instead of arguing any further, tell me, have you managed to get hold of my mother yet?'

'No.'

'She's running away,' Jessica stated. 'She knows I'm trying to track her down, so she's making herself scarce. Doesn't that prove she has something to hide?' Then before he could answer, 'OK, OK, only I would think that. So you go on giving her the benefit of the doubt, but I still want to speak to her.'

'You've already made yourself abundantly plain about that,' he informed her. 'So if there's nothing else, I need to use the bathroom.'

As she rang off she sighed heavily, then looked up as Daniella plonked herself down in one of the basket-weave chairs and gave an earthy murmur of delight as the waiter turned up with two frothy cappuccinos topped with powdery chocolate.

'Is everything OK, *chérie*?' she asked, as the waiter went away. 'You're frowning, and you seemed so happy just now.'

'It's Charlie,' Jessica confessed. 'He's woken up in a bad mood and now both of us are feeling bad.'

Daniella's exquisite sloe eyes regarded her sympathetically. 'I know I can't possibly fill Lilian's shoes,' she said gently, 'but I do have a good ear and strong shoulder.'

Jessica's expression softened as she looked at her. 'You're all being far too kind and patient with me,' she told her. 'And actually, the current issue between me and Charlie is nothing more than he wants us to go to Majorca with some friends for the second half of August, and I . . .' She took a breath. 'Well, I don't.'

'So what would you like to do?'

Jessica threw out her hands incredulously. 'Look at all this,' she said, meaning the bustling market square. 'I know you're used to it, you probably hardly even think about it because you live it, but for me it seems so vibrant and . . . *Real*.'

'So you'd like to stay here all summer?'

'Of course. Anyway I won't leave until I manage to see the *Médecin Légiste* and the paramedics, but if I stayed even longer it would mean I could spend more time with Lilian. And with you and your family.' Her eyes started to sparkle. 'Luc has offered to do a sculpture of me, which I have to admit I find very intriguing. I've never been a sitter before.'

Daniella's expression turned comical. 'Beware, he is not known for his patience when it comes to his muses.'

Jessica laughed. 'Thanks for the warning,' she said, and picking up her coffee she closed her eyes as she savoured its rich, creamy taste.

'Tell me,' Daniella said after a while, 'I know it is none of my business, and I have no right to ask, but what do you really think happened at the cottage that day? What are you hoping to find out?'

Jessica inhaled deeply and felt a chill inside as she put down her cup. 'What I'd really like,' she said, 'is to find out my mother is telling the truth, and there is nothing else to it. The trouble is, I know in my heart there's more. And now she's disappeared again, just when she knows I'm trying to get hold of her . . .' Her eyes returned to Daniella's. 'I can't let my mind go any further than that,' she said, 'because I'm too afraid of where it might end up, but I will tell you this, my mother hasn't always chosen wisely in the men she's become involved with.'

After a moment's confusion Daniella's eyes registered understanding, and seeming every bit as reluctant as Jessica to go any further down that road, she let the subject drop.

'Mr Moore? It's Rufus Keane here. I got your message, but I can't help you, I'm afraid. As far as I'm aware Veronica's still on Capri.'

'When did you last speak to her?' Charlie asked.

'It must have been three or four days ago.'

'And she didn't say she was going off anywhere else, or intending to come back to England?'

'No, but she and Maurice could have gone sailing. May I ask if there's a problem? Perhaps it's something I can help with.'

'Thank you, but no,' Charlie responded. 'My wife is keen to get hold of her, and we're probably overly anxious after learning about Veronica's collapse.'

'Understandable. But if anything like that had happened again, I'm sure Maurice would have let one of us know.'

'Of course,' Charlie said, relieved to have his own thoughts confirmed. 'But if you do hear anything . . .'

'I'll get in touch right away,' Keane assured him.

After ringing off Charlie tried the number in Capri again, but there was still no reply, and feeling irrationally furious with both Veronica and Jessica he slammed the phone down and went off to tackle Nikki about the appalling mess she'd left in the kitchen last night.

Jessica was laughing so hard it hurt. The absurd thing was, she couldn't even remember what had started her off now, apart from the hilarious dance Luc had performed a few minutes ago whilst trying to prevent a stack of empty boxes from falling. Ever since, his struggle to keep a straight face, added to his efforts to be serious again, were only making matters worse.

'If you remember anything of this tour of the *cave*,' he told her, trying to sound stern, 'I think it will be my excellent juggling, rather than the way we make wine.'

Though she tried to answer, the word juggling set her off again, and as she bent double, holding herself about the waist, he put his hands on his hips and tapped his foot waiting for her to finish.

'I'm sorry,' she gasped, wiping the tears from her eyes. 'It's just . . . Oh God, don't look at me like that.'

'Like what?' he cried, throwing out his hands, though his eyes were brimful of laughter.

'That!'

His head fell back in despair, then a menacing gleam came into his eye as he began advancing on her.

With a shriek she took off along the row of vats, looked around quickly for somewhere to hide, then slipped into a shadowy niche just outside a storeroom. As he came into view she gurgled with laughter again, and was just about to run off in another direction when his mobile started to ring.

Though clearly exasperated, he took it from his shirt pocket and clicked on. *'Ah oui, François,'* he answered. *'Si, je t'entends, mais très mal, je sors avec le téléphone,'* and shooting a look at Jessica that told her he hadn't finished with her yet, he started back through the *cave* towards the daylight.

As he went Jessica stood watching him, still smiling all over her face and breathless from so much hilarity. She couldn't remember when she'd last laughed like this, though guessed it would have been with one of the children. It would very probably have been with Natalie, since she'd had a genuine gift for making her mother laugh. Thinking of how much her daughter would have enjoyed this larking about with Luc sobered her a little, but she continued to smile, because right now she felt so happy that her heart simply wasn't ready to let it go.

Luc had been waiting when she and Daniella had returned from the market, pacing up and down outside the *cave*, looking at his watch and reminding her that they had made a rendezvous for ten thirty to begin her first lesson in wine-making.

'Mais non!' she'd cried, astounded that she could have forgotten.

'OK, *non*,' he'd agreed. 'It was in my head, but I think I might not have remembered to tell you.'

Grinning, Daniella had waltzed off into the house at that point, taking the groceries with her, while Luc whisked Jessica into the *cave*, informing her as they went that new pupils who were late usually had to pay a forfeit and he'd let her know later if there was one.

Finding him in such a playful mood had been exactly what Jessica had needed to lift her spirits after her call to Charlie. Now, enjoying the cool mustiness of the *cave*, she wandered idly around the giant vats – or *fûts* as they were called here in Burgundy – wondering if naked men really did climb in to trample and hack at the *chapeau* – the debris of skins and pips – or if it was something Luc had made up to tease her. Actually, she'd heard that it did still happen, so she was at least half-willing to believe him, and now what she wanted to know was whether he was one of the naked men. The idea of him sloshing about in the wine with not a stitch on started her laughing again, though it was an image she didn't allow to linger for fear of it taking her off in a wrong direction.

As she walked on past giant pyramids of empty bottles and a row of settling tanks she could hear him talking in the distance, so eventually she turned round to wander back towards the mouth of the *cave*. He was standing beside the tasting counter, noting down whatever the person at the other end was telling him.

'Oui, j'ai l'information,' he said to the caller, looking up as she approached, *'dès que tu as une date fais moi signé. D'accord. À bientôt.'* As he rang off he continued to look at her, then as she started to turn away he said, 'I wish I had my camera now. With the light coming in on you like this, you could be Meditrina herself.'

Her eyebrows lifted. 'The Roman goddess of wine?'

He nodded.

She started to smile, flattered even though she knew he was teasing her, then becoming aware of the misty shafts of sunlight she was standing in, she stepped aside. 'Have we reached the tasting bit now?' she asked, looking at the bottles lined up on the counter.

'I would think so,' he replied. 'Red or white?'

'Red.'

As he picked up an unlabelled bottle and uncorked it she watched how deftly his hands moved, and thought how their masculine elegance was so true of an artist. Then she looked at his face. His eyes were lowered, showing her the fullness of his lashes, and heavy lines of his brows. The whiteness of his shirt made his skin seem darker, and because it was open almost to the waist she could see the coarse hair on his chest.

He passed her a glass, and began to explain the process of tasting, first holding his glass to the light to check the wine's transparency, then assessing the surface for the liquid's brilliance.

'At the side of the glass,' he told her, his voice sounding low and deliberate, 'you will see the robe. In a young wine, it is purple.'

She listened and learned that inhaling the fragrance was called the *premier nez*, and should be done without unsettling the wine. Then she swivelled her glass to allow the elements to evaporate into the air. Now the scent was stronger. She looked for the *jambes* around the bowl of the glass, understanding that the more traces she found the more alcohol there was. Then finally she was allowed to take the wine into her mouth.

As the flavours began to unfold across her tongue, liquorice, cherries, a hint of wood, she was watching him as he watched her, then without thinking about what she was doing she swallowed the wine. Instead of smiling as she'd expected him to, his eyes remained on hers, and for one strange moment it was as though she could feel him touching her . . . She understood that it was the potency of the wine moving through her, but then it seemed more than that, as though there was a will, a wish for it to be real, and feeling a heat come into her cheeks, she lowered her head.

The next moment Jean-Marc was in the *cave* and the strangeness had passed almost as though it hadn't occurred, for they were soon laughing at her descriptions of taste, and how overly eager she was to try again.

'After lunch,' Luc said, when they finally walked back to the house, 'will you be free to sit for me? I will only ask you to pose for an hour, so that will leave you some time for your own work.'

'I'd love to,' she responded, then as Fernand came out to greet them her smile became one of genuine affection.

'Ah, *chérie*,' he said, taking both her hands as he embraced her. 'I hear you are becoming an expert on wine.'

Jessica laughed. 'Not even close,' she assured him, 'but I have a good teacher so there's hope for me yet.'

'Pah,' he replied dismissively, 'he knows only what I have taught him, but I have to admit that probably makes him good.'

As Jessica laughed, he put an arm around her and steered her into the kitchen, where she was assailed by the delicious aroma of grilling goat's cheese and garlic.

'I had a call from François,' Luc said, going to wash his hands, 'he tells me we're supplying some of the white wine for the *vignerons'* ball.'

'Ah yes, I forgot to mention this,' Fernand responded, slapping a hand to his forehead. 'But it is OK, *non*?'

'Mais bien sûr.'

'I believe Lilian has offered to be on the committee to organise the ball,' Fernand continued, as he shuffled to the stove to check the cheese. 'Have you spoken to her today? She called very early while you were in the studio.'

'Yes, she caught up with me there,' Luc replied, reaching for a towel.

'How is she?' Jessica wanted to know. 'I tried calling her myself first thing, but had to leave a message.'

'She was being very mysterious when I spoke to her,' Luc answered. 'She tells me she has something big in the offing, but will not say what it is until she knows for certain.'

'Just as long as you remember to be suitably impressed,' Jessica advised him. 'Except when is she ever not impressive? She's so good at what she does, it's no wonder they're promoting her.'

'There is no-one who admires my daughter-in-law more

than I,' Fernand told her, 'but at the moment the tomatoes are here and she is not. So please will you slice them and put them onto this plate.'

Obediently Jessica took the knife he was offering, saying, 'Tell me more about the *vignerons'* ball. When is it, and what happens?'

'It is after the harvest, *naturellement*,' Fernand replied. 'And because we never know for certain when that will be, we hold it at the beginning of November. *Au fait*, I think it is an event you and Charlie would enjoy. The children too, of course.'

Smiling, Jessica said, 'We'd love to, if it fits in with the school holidays, and Charlie's able to get the time off.'

'What's this?' Luc demanded, holding up an open bottle of red wine that was one of four resting on the dresser.

Addressing himself to Jessica, Fernand said, 'This is one of our Vougeot *premier crus*. It must be opened six hours before drinking in order for the flavours to take the air, and two hours before we drink it, it is to be put into a decanter. So,' he continued, turning to Luc, 'it is for dinner this evening.'

'Four bottles?' Luc exclaimed, laughing.

'Because Jules and Babette are joining us,' Fernand explained. 'They are friends of Daniella and Claude who are on their way to the French Riviera,' he told Jessica, 'so they are staying overnight at the château. Daniella and Claude are bringing the children too. I hope you will join us, *chérie*.'

'Oh, no, really,' Jessica protested. 'You've already been too kind . . .'

'*Mais non*. It is not kind to feed your family, it is normal, and this is how we think of you now. *C'est vrai*, Luc?'

Seeing the laughter in Luc's eyes, Jessica found herself responding with a warning look, but when he reached round her to help himself to a slice of tomato, she was careful to step clear and then refused the half he offered to her.

'*Voilà*, I believe our lunch is now ready,' Fernand declared, carrying the crusty white *crotins* from the grill to the table. 'You have made an excellent selection at the market, *chérie*. This cheese will make a very happy companion to our *crémant*. You have drunk a *crémant de Bourgogne* before?'

'No, never,' she replied. 'What is it?'

'It is our pink champagne,' he replied, with a prideful twinkle. 'We make it with the *pinot noir* to the *méthode champanoise*. It is very fresh and delicious on a day that is so hot like this. It is in the cooler, Luc, and over there, *chérie*, you will find fresh basil – in the pot by the window.'

A few minutes later they were seated under the pergola, the chill, fruity wine sparkling in their glasses, napkins draped across their laps and the succulent cheeses oozing over beds of crisp green radicchio and sweet red tomatoes. As they ate Fernand took much delight in describing the menu he was planning for the evening, having decided to centre it around a *lapin forestière*. Jessica was astonished to hear how much preparation was involved and tried to offer some help, but Fernand was adamant about working alone in the kitchen.

After a while she noticed how quiet Luc had become. In fact he hardly seemed aware of anything that was being said. She kept glancing at him, trying to get a sense of what might be distracting him, but his eyes were focused away from her, to a place only he could see.

'Do not be offended,' Fernand told her, clearly registering her concern, 'he must be planning to spend time in his studio, because always he goes inside his head before he starts with the sculpture.'

'In English they would say I'm psyching myself up,' Luc informed him, apparently having heard. 'Jessica has agreed to sit for me,' he added.

Fernand's eyebrows rose. 'You feel safe to put your beauty in his hands?' he enquired.

Jessica gave a splutter of laughter. 'I am relying on him to turn me into a veritable goddess,' she declared.

The light in Luc's eyes showed that her reminder wasn't lost on him.

'It is more likely he will turn you into an electric plug or a carrot,' Fernand informed her. 'He has created some very lovely things in the past, but lately he sees things in very strange ways. Not at all as they are – I think this is because he no longer knows how to create the realism.'

Luc was laughing. 'When have I ever turned a person into

something abstract?' he challenged. 'Unless they have asked me to.'

'You made Rousseau look like a *cornichon*,' Fernand retorted, with a wink at Jessica. 'How can you make a dog look like a *cornichon*?'

'A gherkin!' Jessica cried.

'That wasn't Rousseau, it was you,' Luc responded, taking a mouthful of food.

Fernand's eyes widened, then realising he was being baited he started to chuckle.

'Which reminds me,' Luc went on, 'where is my dog? No, don't tell me, he's decamped to the chateau again. Are they bringing him back tonight?'

'Oh, I am sure they will. The children do not like to leave him at home on his own. How is their sculpture coming along, by the way? *Oh là là*,' he suddenly exclaimed. 'I am very sorry, but I take a message from the foundry earlier. I think there is no big problem, but they would like you to call them back.'

Luc checked his watch. 'They're still at lunch in Italy,' he said, 'so I'll call in an hour. Will you take some more wine?' he said to Jessica, reaching for the bottle.

She gave it a moment's thought. 'Well, I guess that depends on the pose you want me to strike,' she replied. 'If I have to lie down, any more wine will send me to sleep. If I'm to stand I'll probably sway . . .' She started to laugh as he poured. 'So are you intending to send me to sleep or to watch me roll around like a drunk?' she wanted to know.

'You will have to wait to find out,' he told her, and saluting her with his glass he drank.

An hour later he led her into his studio, a vast, airy space with cool stone walls, a dusty concrete floor and high vaulted ceilings. Though it wasn't the first time she'd been in here, much about it had changed in the past few months, such as the skylights in the roof, and the new mezzanine and staircase constructed from bare pine boards at the far end of the room. Most of all, though, the sculptures themselves were different, for he'd long finished those he'd been working on the last time Lilian had showed her around. Now there were abstracts both large and small, grand-looking armatures, some of only bare wire, another half-covered in clay. A number of moulds labelled in black ink were stacked haphazardly in a corner, while all manner of tools, terracotta slabs, plaster sacks, lumps of marble and granite, as well as a small crane and an air compressor, were lying all about the place.

'So,' she said, turning to find him setting up ready to work, 'I'm bracing myself for instruction.'

Though he laughed at her choice of words, his attention was clearly more focused on the armature of bunched newspaper and wire that he was positioning on the sculptor's horse – a turntable atop a tripod – as he said, 'The way I see you . . . the impression you're always giving me, is that you are in transition – moving from one phase of your life to another.'

She felt surprised and even slightly unsettled by how easily he'd put her feelings into words. And then she was fascinated to know how he was going to capture it.

'There is a bench there,' he said, nodding towards it. 'If you set it lengthways to me, and sit astride it . . .'

She did as she was told, glad she was wearing shorts and not a skirt, then awaited further instruction.

'*C'est bon*,' he said, though whether he was referring to her position or the armature was hard to tell. 'Now, if you put your hands in front of you,' he said, 'pressing them into the bench as though you are about to get up . . . *Oui, c'est ça. Très bien*, but only lift yourself a little, and raise your chin so that your neck is stretched. *Oui, oui. C'est impeccable.* Now turn your head very slightly to the left, because I think your best profile is the right one. Mm,' he responded. '*Si.* This is the image I will create.'

She looked at him in astonishment. 'You want me to hold this position for an *hour*?' she demanded. 'I'm struggling already.'

He started to laugh.

Her eyes narrowed.

'I accept it is a difficult position to hold,' he said, 'so I will take some photographs, very quickly, then you can relax. But that doesn't mean you can leave. You must stay sitting there, so that I can measure you and look at you as I begin to work.'

After retrieving a camera from the next room he began shooting her from all angles, many of which she'd probably prefer no-one ever to see, especially him. He clearly had no intention of looking at them now, however, for when he'd finished he set the camera aside, and began laying several large plain sheets of paper on the workbench next to him. 'Now I will measure you,' he told her.

Knowing how vital this was to the process she sat very still on the bench, looking up to the light as he took first the length, then the width of her face, to create the all-important T. After a while she found herself inhaling the warm, masculine scent of him each time he came close, and almost straining towards the calipers in anticipation of their touch. She loved the tingling sensation of them grazing her skin, and felt deprived when they didn't quite connect. Her breath became shallow and her eyes fluttered closed as they gently pricked the corners of her mouth, then her eyelids, then the length of her brows.

She watched him going back and forth, eyeing her critically, making his notes, and then returning to measure some more. He seemed almost oblivious to her as a woman, and completely unaware of how, every time the calipers touched her, she responded somewhere deep inside to the tiny showers of sensation.

Finally he began moulding the clay, standing in front of it, swivelling the platform from time to time, frequently glancing at her, while using his thumbs and his fingers to start recreating her.

She wasn't entirely sure when his frown turned from one of concentration to something much darker, it was just there, and growing blacker all the time, until finally he threw out his hands in frustration.

'*C'est une perte de temps*,' he growled, glowering at his efforts so far. '*Ce n'est pas ici. Que se passe-t-il? Mes mains ressemblent à des choux-fleurs*.' What is happening? My hands are like cauliflowers.

Unable to stop herself, she started to laugh.

His eyes came to hers. 'You think this is funny?' he challenged, clearly trying not to laugh himself.

'No, not at all,' she assured him, but the quivering of

her lips was giving her away. 'I'm sorry, it's just . . .'

'Yes, it is just what?' he demanded, his eyes belying the harshness of his tone, but underneath it all he was angry, she could tell, though presumably with himself, not with her.

'Nothing,' she said, knowing she couldn't even begin to explain her happiness when it had no real logic.

'OK, I think maybe that is enough for today,' he said, picking up a rag to wipe his hands. 'I hope I have not scared you with my temper and you will come again tomorrow at the same time.'

'I'm terrified of your temper,' she told him, 'and I will see you before that, at dinner.'

He seemed baffled for a moment, then remembering he said, 'Ah yes. You will enjoy the wine – and Daniella's friends are very interesting people.'

Their eyes met as they smiled, then she turned away, glad to be leaving now, because it just seemed right that she should.

Chapter Fifteen

By the time she returned to the cottage Jessica was struggling to hold onto her good mood, but it was hard, for even as she dialled Charlie's number she was aware of how afraid she was of falling out with him again. However, if it was going to happen it luckily wouldn't be right away, as her call was diverted straight to his voicemail.

'Hi, darling,' she said affectionately, 'just wondering how you are, and if you've managed . . .' Realising any mention of her mother was likely to annoy him, she quickly altered what she'd been about to say, and continued with, 'to speak to Harry today. He seemed a bit homesick when I called him this morning, so I wondered if he sounded the same to you. Anyway, give me a call when you can – and sorry about waking you this morning. Love you.'

Not sure how she felt about having to tread so carefully around him for fear of being snapped at or told she was insensitive to his feelings, she rang off and gave a deep, shuddering sigh. She guessed the important thing was that they didn't keep arguing over nothing, and maybe it would help if she stopped telling him about her meetings with the officials. After all, he'd gone through the horror of it once before, and to a far greater degree than she had. Maybe she should accept that this was her quest for answers, not his, since he clearly believed he already knew them.

With that thought still in her mind, she began dialling her mother's number in Capri, and to her amazement there was an answer after the fifth ring. 'Hello?' she said, sounding as uneasy as she felt. She'd been so certain of finding no-one at home that she couldn't quite remember what she intended to say now. 'Is that Maurice?'

'Yes,' a male voice replied. 'Who am I speaking to?'

'Jessica.'

'Ah, Jessica.' He sounded genuinely pleased to hear her, and he had no reason not to be, she thought, for unlike most of her mother's conquests she'd always got along very well with Maurice. 'How are you, my dear?' he asked. 'I hear you're in France. Is it as hot there as it is here?'

'Probably,' she answered, grateful to him for not mentioning the reason she was here. 'I've been trying to get hold of my mother. Is she still with you?'

'She most certainly is. She's in the pool at the moment, but I'll go and get her.'

'Before you do that,' Jessica said, 'tell me, is she all right? I mean, what was the collapse all about?'

'Oh, she's on fine form,' he assured her warmly. 'Never looking better, if you ask me. Ronnie, darling, here's Jessica to speak to you.'

Jessica heard the splash of water as her mother climbed out of the pool, then after a muffled exchange with Maurice, Veronica's voice came down the line saying, 'Darling, how are you? Charlie said you were trying to get hold of me, but we've been sailing for a few days . . .'

'You've spoken to Charlie? When?'

'Maurice, when did Charlie call? It can only have been about an hour ago, can't it? Yes, Maurice is nodding, so about an hour ago.'

'Did he tell you why I want to speak to you?' Jessica asked, sounding more terse than she'd intended.

'Yes, I'm afraid he did, but you're not to go shouting at me again, darling. I can't help it if a tourist got lost and stopped to ask the way . . . Of course, I understand that someone should have told you before now, but it was nothing, darling. Really. Nothing at all.'

'I don't believe you. It's too much of a coincidence. So who was here that day, Mother?'

'Nobody,' Veronica protested. 'It was a tourist. Everyone else believes this, the police, Charlie, so why won't you?'

'Because I know what you're like, and I know the kind of people you mix with.'

'Oh, Jessica, don't say those things,' Veronica cried. 'I only ever knew one man like that and he was put in prison for the things he did.'

'So is he out now? Have you started finding girls for him again?'

Veronica gasped. 'Jessica, I never in my life did anything like that and you know it. I might have my faults, but . . .'

'Then tell me who carried Natalie to the sofa.'

Veronica fell silent.

'Who carried her?' Jessica shouted. 'You couldn't have done it . . .'

'I'm trying to think,' Veronica wailed. 'It was all so terrible, and . . . It must have been the paramedic person . . . It can only have been him, but I don't remember it happening . . .'

'How can you not remember someone picking her up? It doesn't make any sense.'

'I'm sorry. I'm trying my best . . . We were all so upset . . .'

'We?' Jessica exclaimed, pouncing on it. 'Who's we?'

'Oh you're twisting everything I'm saying. I mean all of us who were there. Me, the paramedics, and the police . . .' She broke off and a moment later Maurice's voice came gently down the line.

'Jessica, I'm sorry,' he said, 'but I can't allow you to go on upsetting your mother like this. I understand – we both do – how difficult this has been for you, but it hasn't been easy for her either. She was Natalie's grandmother, she loved her very much, so you can't believe she would let any harm come to her.'

'But it did,' Jessica cried, her voice shrill with pain.

'It was an accident,' Maurice replied quietly. 'A terrible one, that should never have happened, it's true, but it did, and to keep going back over it like this is helping no-one, least of all you. Now, your mother's told you everything that happened, I believe she's even written it in a letter . . .'

'What letter? I haven't received a letter.'

'Ronnie, did you send the letter?' Maurice asked.

Jessica could hear her mother replying, but was unable to make out what she was saying.

'Apparently I misunderstood,' Maurice told her, coming back on the line. 'But that doesn't change the fact that your mother can't keep going through this. You know she hasn't been well, so please, for both your sakes, try to accept what she's told you . . .'

'I wish I could, Maurice,' Jessica cut in, 'but I only have to stand here in the place my daughter died, to know there's more to it. And I will find out what it is. I swear on her little grave that I will get to the bottom of what really happened here that day.'

After she'd rung off Jessica stood beside the table trembling, as much with shock at what she'd said to her mother, as with anger that it still hadn't got her anywhere. Then feeling a near overwhelming sense of exhaustion and even defeat crawling through her limbs, she took herself upstairs to lie down. She almost wished she hadn't made the call now, but what she'd told Maurice was true. There were times when she did only have to be in this house to know she was right, and it wasn't simply her instincts that were telling her, because it was as though Natalie herself was telling her too. She couldn't confide that to anyone, of course, or she really would be written off as deranged by grief. But whatever anyone else might think, she knew what was happening inside her, and there was no question in her mind that she could sometimes feel a connection to her daughter that seemed almost as real as the pain in her heart.

'Are you there, Nat?' she whispered brokenly. 'Are you trying to find me? I'm here, darling. Come and lie down with me.'

Almost as though it were happening, she turned on her side and wrapped an arm around a pillow. 'They're keeping their secrets from us,' she said, her voice thick with tears, 'but we have ours too, don't we? We know we're together, and I won't ever really let you go, sweetheart, you know that, don't you? You'll always be my baby and nothing, no lies or secrets or anything else is going to change that. I just have to know what happened to you, why you were so upset when you rang me, and if there was anything I could have done to save you.'

She must have fallen asleep for a while then, because the next thing she knew the phone was ringing and the sun was in the very early throes of its evening glory. For a moment she simply continued to lie where she was, wishing herself back in Luc's studio where she'd felt happy, or even still in oblivion. Then making herself get up, she ran downstairs to find her mobile, hoping it would be Nikki or Harry, while suspecting it was probably Charlie. However, the readout was saying private number, so she had no idea who it was until she heard Lilian saying, 'Jessica? It's me. How are you? I'm sorry I haven't called back before now, it's been absolutely manic here.'

'Don't worry,' Jessica told her, loving just the sound of Lilian's voice, for it was like slipping into a sanctuary after a bruising go-round with her demons. 'I'm fine. Hot, but fine.'

'Good. Luc tells me you're considering staying on a while longer. I'm so pleased. It means you'll still be there when I get back.'

'I was always going to be,' Jessica reminded her.

'Yes, if I were returning on schedule, but you know the big problem with networking, you will find great contacts and they just have to be followed up.'

In spite of her disappointment Jessica started to smile. 'So what's happened?' she prompted. 'Are you about to take over the world?'

Lilian laughed. 'Not yet, that's on next month's agenda. On this month's it's just a small but rather exclusive sale-room in Mumbai. I've been in discussions with the owners virtually since I arrived, and now they want me to stop off on my way back to France to have a look round. I've had them in my sights for ages now, so I can't pass up this opportunity, especially with my promotion in the offing.'

'So when will you be back?'

'Only two or three days later than planned. Meaning next Friday or Saturday instead of Wednesday, by which time you would have gone. So that's why it's so great that you're staying. I couldn't bear it if I missed you altogether.'

'No, nor could I,' Jessica responded, wishing Lilian was there right now.

'And I believe Luc's doing a sculpture of you,' Lilian chattered on. 'I know he'll do a wonderful job . . . Of course I'm biased, but I guarantee Charlie will be thrilled. It's a lovely idea, let's just hope it's ready in time for his birthday. Tell me, is he any happier about you being there now?'

So Luc had told Lilian the sculpture was for Charlie, and Jessica couldn't help wondering if he'd said it to make the time she spent in his studio appear innocent and above board, when maybe he too was finding it . . . 'No, not really,' she answered, cutting the thought off. 'Things are still quite strained between us, but I've asked him to join me here as soon as he can get some time off.'

'Do you think he will?' Lilian said doubtfully. 'I know it probably won't be easy at first, but I'm sure once he gets there he'll find it's not as hard as he thought . . . And it'll be wonderful for us all to spend some time together. Will he bring Harry?'

As the call ran on with all the usual back and forth Jessica found herself returning to the conversation she'd had with her mother, and how guilty she was feeling now for having accused her the way she had. She didn't really think her mother would commit such a terrible crime. She never had thought this, but nor did she have any clear idea what she did think. She only knew that Charlie would never conspire with anyone to protect someone who'd hurt his daughter, so no matter what her suspicions might be concerning men from her mother's past, they had to be wrong.

'Oh listen to me yawning,' Lilian said eventually. 'I'm sorry, it's one in the morning here, but before I go, have you managed to talk to the *Médecin Légiste* yet?'

'Not in person,' Jessica answered, 'but they've told me I can call back tomorrow.' Thinking of what she might discover turned her cold inside. 'Lily, if I find out there were any other injuries on her body . . .'

'You won't,' Lilian said firmly. 'Remember Charlie's seen the autopsy report. And for heaven's sake, France is a civilised country – they wouldn't cover up anything like that, so you have to stop tormenting yourself.'

'I know. But I have to be sure. Please try to understand.'

'I do, just don't lose sight of how hard this is for Charlie, because he probably senses the way your mind's working, even if you never discuss it.'

'You could be right, and I've already decided to try and

ease off him a little now. I just wish he could let go of some of his grief. Not that I blame him for keeping it bottled up, God knows it's hard to face, and he loved her so much so of course he wouldn't want to know if someone had hurt her . . . I don't either, but I owe it to Natalie to find out if someone should be paying for what happened to her, particularly when I feel so strongly that someone should.'

After a moment Lilian said, 'I'm not going to argue with you. You were her mother so, as Luc says, your feelings should be respected. I just wish you could see it from a more objective point of view . . . No, that's the wrong thing to say. All I want is that you don't go on suffering the way you are.'

'I won't if I can prove myself wrong, or even right . . . The head of the paramedic team is due back from holiday tomorrow, so hopefully I'll manage to fix a time to see him next week. Then all the official business will be over and done with before Charlie gets here – if I can persuade him to come.'

'Tell you what, if I get a moment I'll give Charlie a call and add my voice to yours. Or I'll ask Luc to do it. It might help if Charlie feels we all want to see him. Now I really do have to go. I'm exhausted and I have to be up at six. So have a lovely evening, all of you. You're going to adore Claude and Daniella's friends. I just wish I was there with you.'

'So do I,' Jessica said.

A few minutes later she was standing at the door, gazing out at the exquisite evening light as it spread like liquid honey over the vines, while trying to make some sense of what was happening inside her. She didn't seem able to contain either her thoughts or her feelings in a way she could fully understand, for they were elliptical and strange, alighting on one thing, then, as though burned or afraid, flitting on to another. At first she felt anxious about hurting the people she loved, Charlie, her mother, even Nikki and Harry, then she was uneasy about her suspicions, and the route they were taking. A moment later she was confronting the attraction she felt towards Luc, though she barely stayed with that for a second, because it simply wasn't real. It was only his kindness that was drawing her to him, and the way he was making her laugh, allowing her to forget for a while.

It was hardly surprising that she wanted to spend time with him, rather than be left alone here with the burden of her pain.

Hearing her phone ring twice then fall silent again, she took her cue to go and call Harry back, and to her relief, just a few minutes of listening to his excitement about coming to France was enough to start untying some of the knots inside her. So it seemed Charlie had booked him a flight, which pleased her even more than she'd imagined it would. Then wondering if Charlie was intending to book one for himself, she tried calling him again to find out.

'I can't make any promises,' he told her, 'but I am trying to get the time off. It might only be for the last week, but if I can make it any sooner . . .'

'So you really are considering coming?' she said, hardly able to contain her joy.

'Since it seems to be the only way I'm going to get to see my wife, yes, I'm considering it.'

'I wonder if you know how much that means to me,' she said softly. 'I'm missing you, and I need you to be here.'

'I'm missing you too,' he said. Then after a pause, 'I have to go now, but next time we speak, let's try to make it more like this, shall we?'

'It's a deal,' she responded.

Later she was upstairs getting ready for dinner, when it occurred to her that neither of them had mentioned speaking to her mother. She could only feel glad of it, however, since it would inevitably have changed the tone of the conversation, and right now she was enjoying the reassurance of how much better just a few tender moments with Charlie could make her feel.

'Bloody hell!' Jessica seethed, throwing her mobile back on the table in a rage.

'Ah ha. Something tells me I've chosen a bad time.'

She spun round to see Luc standing in the doorway. 'Sorry,' she said, starting to laugh in spite of her frustration. 'It's just that sometimes I wonder how I'm ever going to get anywhere when life itself is squaring up against me . . . But you didn't come here to listen to me complaining. What can

I do for you? And please don't tell me I outstayed my welcome last night, because I know I did, and my only excuse is I was having such a good time that I had no idea it was so late until I rolled into bed at two a.m.'

Leaning against the door frame, he said, 'You were welcome to stay as long as you liked, and I would have been happy to walk you back through the vineyard . . .'

'But it made much more sense for me to leave with Claude and Daniella,' she jumped in. 'You were right about their friends, by the way, they were wonderful company.' Then remembering her duties as a hostess, 'Can I get you a drink? I've just made some tea, which I believe I was about to hurl against the wall, and actually I still might.'

Apparently undaunted, he came into the kitchen, put a large brown envelope on the table and unhooked two small cups from a rack over the window. 'Please tell me it's not lemon-grass-flavoured,' he said, lifting the lid from the pot.

'It is.'

Drawing back from the smell, he said, 'Then maybe I will hurl it against the wall instead.'

'No, please don't, I feel in need now,' and whisking the pot from his grasp, she said, 'I can always make coffee for you, if you prefer.'

'English people don't know how to make coffee, and anyway, I don't have time. I just stopped by to bring this. It arrived for you this morning, but now I'd like to know what was making you swear.'

Remembering the phone call, her spirits started to sink again. 'Would you believe,' she said, 'the paramedic I need to speak to has broken his flaming leg in two places, so he's still in the Auvergne and not due back until Monday week at the earliest. I mean, I'm sorry about his leg, obviously – though frankly I want to kick it – but I'm starting to feel as though the fates are conspiring against me, because they'll only let me speak to *him*, since he was in charge that day, and therefore responsible for filling out the report. Grrrr,' she added, in another fit of impatience. 'And what's more,' she suddenly ranted on, 'the clerk at the *Médecin Légiste*'s office left a message while I was on the line to cancel an appointment I'd only just made for Monday. So now I have to call back to make another.'

Going to the table, he picked up the envelope and handed it to her. 'This is the reason she cancelled your appointment,' he told her. 'It's a copy of the autopsy report which came by fax about half an hour ago.'

Jessica blinked, felt her heart turn over, then looked at him in confusion.

'Monsieur Clavier, the *Médecin Légiste,* is a *Chevalier de Tastevin,*' he said, as though it was explanation enough. And perhaps it was.

'So you spoke to him on my behalf?'

'My father did. They are old friends, and you could spend a long time trying to get through the *fonctionnaires* at the Institute. I hope you don't mind that we . . .'

'No, no, of course not,' she interrupted. 'I mean, thank you. I just . . . Well . . .' Now she was holding the report in her hand, she was feeling more nervous than ever about reading it. 'Have you . . .? Is there . . .?' She couldn't bring herself to form the words, or even to open the envelope.

'It's all right,' he told her. 'You don't have anything to be afraid of.'

Even though relief rushed into her heart, her eyes were still so anxious as they came to his that his smile filled with affection. 'It's fine. I promise,' he reassured her.

She swallowed, then nodded and looked down at the envelope again.

'I'll leave you to read it . . .'

'No,' she said quickly. 'Please stay. I mean, if you don't mind.'

Stepping back, he perched on the edge of the table and watched her slide the report from the envelope. 'The information you're looking for is on page three,' he said.

She turned to it shakily, then searched for the words that would tell her what she needed to know.

As she read, even though she understood most of it, she was finding it hard to connect it to Natalie. Maybe this was because she didn't want to, or because the words so coldly charted the medical condition of a body, with nothing at all about its personality or vibrancy or beauty, that they almost seemed meaningless.

What it all amounted to in the end, however, was that Natalie had died of a massive blow to the head, which had shattered her skull and broken her neck, and all the other wounds on her body were sustained in the fall. There was no evidence of any old injuries, apart from the usual bruises and grazes on the limbs of a child that age. Most importantly of all, though, there *had* been an internal examination, and the results showed she had died *virgo intacta* with nothing abnormal about the vaginal region at all.

When she had finished reading she continued to stare down at the words. She still couldn't seem to connect them to Natalie, or even to make herself feel the way she probably ought – but something deep within her was responding, because tears were beginning to roll down her cheeks, and her chest was becoming too tight to let in air. 'I'm sorry,' she choked. 'I didn't expect . . .'

Pulling her to him, he wrapped her in his arms, and she didn't resist. There was so much relief flooding into her heart, and so much fear relaxing its grip, that she might have found it hard to stand alone.

He held her for a long time, letting her tears soak into his shirt, while her body shuddered against him, until finally she lifted her head and looked up into his eyes. 'You knew what I was thinking,' she said, her voice husky with emotion. 'You understood what I was afraid of?'

He nodded.

'Was I alone in thinking that way?'

'I believe so, but when there doesn't seem to be any rhyme or reason to what's happened, it's natural to make your own – and more often than not it can take you to places that are very much worse than reality. So you had to find out for yourself.'

'Yes,' she said, and her eyes moved off to the distance as she wished Charlie had understood that, or perhaps that she'd been more able to explain it. She turned around then and looked at the stairs, trying to get a sense of what she was feeling. 'Do you think it was just the fact that she was about to fall that frightened her?' she said, unsure of where her instincts were now. 'Is that what I heard in her voice?'

'It seems probable,' he replied.

Her gaze moved up to the top of the stairs. 'So everyone else was right?'

When he didn't answer she turned to look at him.

'I want them to be,' she said. 'I just couldn't help feeling . . .' A lingering sob shook her breath. 'Maybe I was too afraid to accept it was as simple as everyone was telling me. I needed to make it more, to blame someone, so I allowed all the years of bitterness and frustration I've felt towards my mother to cloud my judgement . . . That's what everyone's been saying, and now . . . Now, I think I'm much closer to believing they were right.'

'So do you still want to speak to the paramedic?'

She thought about it, and started to shake her head, but then she decided she probably did. 'I know it must have been him who carried her to the sofa,' she said, 'but I need to hear him say it, and then I can thank him, because it could only have been kindness that would have made him move her. Officially he wouldn't have been allowed to.'

Luc's eyes were tender as he looked down at her, and she found herself smiling as she looked back.

'I must go now,' he said. 'I have a rendezvous at the labs. Will you be OK?'

She nodded and swallowed. 'Thank you,' she whispered.

His fingers moved under her chin, tilting her face upwards. 'Let yourself relax for a while now,' he said softly.

'Yes, I will,' she responded.

For several minutes after he'd gone she remained standing where she was, still feeling his fingers on her neck, and seeing the expression in his eyes as he looked at her. Then turning to pick up the report again, she read the vital words once more and this time, when she cried, her tears didn't feel so fraught with the agony she'd known since that terrible day.

It was almost midday before Charlie rang back, by which time she was experiencing so many new feelings that she could almost sense the pain unravelling inside her. Of course, there still remained a profound and immutable sadness at her core, which she knew would never leave her – but now her fears were being cleansed away by relief, it was almost as though she could feel herself breathing more freely.

'I've seen the report from the *Médecin Légiste*,' she told him, almost immediately.

There was a momentary pause, before he said, 'And?' The stiffness in his voice might have irked her, were she not so concerned now about his inability to deal with his grief.

'And everything happened the way they said. There were no other injuries, nothing to say she might have . . .'

'You're telling me something I already know,' he cut in. 'I just wish you hadn't found it so hard to believe me.'

'It wasn't that I didn't believe you, I was just afraid you weren't telling me everything, and if you weren't, the only thing I could imagine you hiding was that she'd been abused in some way.'

'Well now you know she wasn't.'

She blinked at the harshness of his tone. 'Why are you still so angry?'

With a sigh that was both lengthy and tired he said, 'I'm sorry. I guess I'm just finding it hard to come to terms with how you were thinking . . . I mean, I knew it, on one level . . . Anyway, the important thing is, do you feel able to move on now?'

'More or less. I still think there's a chance someone else might have been here, obviously not in the way . . .'

'For heaven's sake, Jessica, what is it going to take?'

'I just need to talk to the paramedic,' she said, 'which should be done long before you or Harry arrive, so you don't even have to think about it. Please understand, it's something I have to do, then I will be able to let go completely, I'm sure of it.'

Sighing again, he replied, 'OK, have it your way, but whatever else you do, I think you should apologise to your mother for what you said.'

'She told you about that?'

'Maurice did. She was in a terrible state after you called, apparently. She couldn't believe you'd think her capable of something like that, and frankly nor can I.'

'I didn't mean it, at least not in the way I said it. I just thought that she might have invited someone to stay and things got out of her control . . .'

'Do you seriously think I'd have been defending her all this time if I'd had even the slightest indication there was anything like that?' he demanded. 'I saw the reports, every one of them, police, paramedics, autopsy . . . I told you what the results were, and there was never any mention of anyone else being there. It was all in your head . . .'

'OK, let's drop the subject now, because I don't want us to fall out over this again. In fact, besides owing my mother an apology, I owe you one too, so I'm sorry, darling, for everything I've put you through.'

There was a gentle gruffness in his voice as he said, 'Apology accepted. And I'm sorry too, for not being more understanding.'

Smiling, she carried the phone to the door and hugged it closer to her as she gazed out at the view. 'So is it too soon to ask if you might be feeling a bit better about coming here now?'

With a note of irony, he said, 'Considering the way I'm being ganged up on . . . First you, then Harry, now Lilian . . .'

'Lilian's already called?' She laughed. 'You see how wanted you are.'

'Mm,' he responded sceptically, but she could tell Lilian's call had helped. 'She told me Luc's making a sculpture of you for my birthday.'

'Well there goes the surprise,' she replied humorously. 'Maybe he can make one of you too and we can put them on the gateposts of our country mansion, when we get one.'

With a laugh, he said, 'Anything to please you, but I'm afraid I'm wanted in the studio now, so I'll have to go. Nikki's here though, and she wants a word.'

'OK, ring me later, when you come off air.'

'I will. And think about calling your mother.'

Knowing the conversation with Nikki was likely to be a long one, Jessica went to take a Macon-Valennes from the cooler to accompany her lunch, and was just deciding what she might eat to go with it, when Nikki came on the line.

'Hi Mum. Can't stay long, but sorry I didn't get back to

you earlier this morning. Is everything all right with you? From the things Dad was saying, you sound pretty chilled. Everything is like totally cool here, but I've got a spot on my boob that is like so humungous you wouldn't believe it. On my boob! Can you believe it? Did you ever get them there? Anyway, Dad and Freddy are playing cricket this weekend, did Dad tell you? It's like this celeb thing, for charity, and I'm kind of on the committee. Don't ask me what that means, because no-one's told me yet, but I guess I'll find out. Oh yes, in answer to your question, I speak to Harry nearly every day, boring little twerp that he is, but you've got to love him. Actually, I really miss him, but I am so in love, Mum. It's like better than anything. I miss you, though. The house isn't the same without you, and Mrs Lentil is so crap when it comes to laundry. And I so hate not having you to go shopping with. You always know the best places to go. Anyway, they're counting down to the headlines now, so I have to go. Love you Mum. Love you, love you, love you.'

'Love you too,' Jessica responded, but the line might already have gone dead.

Well, she thought wryly to herself, as she took her books and wine out to the table, at least her family seemed to be coping without her, in spite of Mrs Lendle's shortcomings with the laundry – not to mention her own with the credit card. However, Charlie was right, she should call her mother to apologise, and she would, just as soon as she was one hundred per cent certain that it was the paramedic who had carried Natalie to the sofa.

'So what do you think Charlie and Harry would like to do when they get here?' Luc was asking later that afternoon, as he gave a critical eye to the sculpture he'd clearly done more work on since the day before.

'Oh, I don't know,' she answered, with a dreamy sort of sigh. 'I've hardly given it any thought yet, but it's still over a week away, so plenty of time. For now, I'm just relieved Charlie's agreeing to come.' She fell to wondering if he'd got round to booking a flight yet, and how things might be between them when they saw one another again. Then, finding herself drawn into the music that was filling up the room, she let go of her thoughts so that her spirits could cascade and flow with the exquisite sound of a solo piano. 'Is this Ravel's *Jeux d'eau*?' she asked, glancing at him. 'Yes, I believe it is.'

For a moment he seemed not to have heard, but then, with his attention still fixed on his work, he said, 'It's Yves, Claude's brother, playing.' He moved around the sculpture, narrowing his eyes as he looked her way. 'Turn your face to the light a little more,' he said. 'Yes, that's it. Did you have wine with your lunch?'

Curious, she said, 'Yes. Why do you ask?'

'Your eyelids are drooping. I think you are about to fall asleep.'

She gave a splutter of laughter. 'Actually, I was trying to look appealing in a seductive sort of way.'

With a droll lift of one eyebrow he said, 'You're better at it when you don't try.'

Her eyes moved quickly to his, but he was focusing on the neck of the sculpture now, giving it tension and grace, drawing its length with the tender strokes of his fingers, and pressing down gently to create the flare of her shoulders. As she watched him she became aware of the strange thrill of being touched, and yet not, and felt her chin rise up a little, almost as though allowing him more access to the tendons and muscles beneath her skin.

Realising he was becoming lost in his work again she drifted back into the music, loving the way it seemed to carry her along in its soothing and rushing waves, while the sun shone down through the skylights in white misty bands to pool all around her. Her shorts had ridden high over her thighs, and her neck and shoulders were bare, giving her the sensation of bathing in light. Her eyes closed as she savoured the feeling, until eventually she began looking around at the exhibition posters of Luc's dramatic abstracts. There was a powerful elegance to their shapes, she thought, a kind of beauty that was both bold and bashful, not unlike the man himself. She knew she wasn't alone in considering his work exceptional, because much of it was in galleries or museums now, or in some cases a few rich people's gardens. She wanted to ask him how difficult it was to let his pieces go after spending so long creating them, but now wasn't the time to interrupt, so she let her eyes wander on around the room, while her heart continued to float in the lightness she'd been feeling since reading the report that morning.

'You need to turn to your left,' Luc said.

She did as she was told, and once he was satisfied she was at the right angle, she found her thoughts returning to Charlie and how it would be when she saw him again. She'd missed him in so many ways that she had no doubt she'd be pleased to see him, but for now she was perfectly happy to be spending another week alone. Already she was sensing how much it was going to nourish her simply to feel the pleasure of her surroundings now she was free of the dark thoughts she'd had before, and that would benefit them both. She also wanted to work on her book some more, take long walks in the countryside, read, explore and listen to music, so many small things that she could do for herself before allowing him and Harry to return to the centre of her world.

Sighing gently to herself as the prospect of more solitude coasted warmly through her, she then fell to wondering if, when the time came, she and Charlie would celebrate their reunion by making love. She hoped they would, because sitting here now, basking in the fierce scrutiny of an attractive man, with the sun streaming down on her, and the music swirling and eddying through her, she was sensing her body in a way she hadn't in so long. She could feel the arch of her back, the smoothness of her arms, the slender length of her legs, the angle of her shoulders . . .

'Mmm,' Luc murmured, standing back to inspect his work.

She looked at him, and felt a small spread of heat in her cheeks. Had her inner pleasure somehow found its way into her expression?

He continued to regard the sculpture. 'There is something I am not capturing,' he said, glancing her way.

She only watched and waited as he tried to fathom out what it might be.

'Perhaps that is enough for today,' he said in the end.

Feeling oddly let down, she was almost tempted to remain

where she was, but understanding she couldn't, she picked up her phone and started towards the door. 'Shall I come again tomorrow?' she asked, turning round.

He was still looking at the sculpture. 'Yes,' he said distractedly. 'Maybe in the morning. It is not so hot.'

She nodded and started to walk on, then as she reached the door he said, 'Are you doing anything this evening?'

She paused for a moment, then turned back. 'I was planning to do more research for my book,' she replied. 'Notes. Not actual writing. I'm not at that stage yet.'

His back was still to her. 'I have the French version of *Suite Française*,' he reminded her. 'Would you consider reading some chapters for my father after dinner? I think he'd like to hear you, instead of me. We both would.'

She started to smile. 'I'd love to,' she told him, and picking up the straw hat she'd hung by the door, she put it on her head and left.

As she walked back to the cottage she felt the urge to reach out her arms as though she could embrace the beauty of the pristine blue sky, along with the succulence of the fruits and stillness of the leaves. The sibilance of crickets was a continual, rhythmic sound, while jasmine and dust were elusive scents in the air.

She rested a hand against her chest, and felt the swell of a nipple, pressing into her palm. Then keeping her hand there she inhaled gently, as though to take in the potency that was like a hypnotic essence all around her.

When she got back to the cottage she spread a towel on the patio, then slipped into her briefest bikini. As she lay down she gazed up at the big empty sky, and the sense of freedom she felt was so exhilarating it was almost like wine. She closed her eyes as the merest whisper of air turned itself into a caress. She thought of nothing and nobody – for once not even of Natalie – all she knew was the exquisiteness of melting away from fear and blending with nature this way.

That night she sat under the pergola with Fernand and Luc, a lamp glowing on the book she was holding, while all around them the vines seemed to shimmer in silvery moonlight. As she read the chapters Luc had selected she thought her voice seemed lower, as though the meaning of the words was going to another depth now she was speaking them in French.

The portrait of forbidden love between a middle-class Frenchwoman and a German officer had always resonated with her, for the words the author had used to describe it seemed to float as gently as dandelion clocks in the air, conveying all its fragility and ephemerality. Sitting here now, on this perfect summer's night, not so far from where the story was set, it was as though its beauty and power might take her over completely.

At first Lucile and her German barely even knew there was an attraction between them. It was as though their feelings were just another part of the strangeness that had come into their lives. They almost never touched, and yet they became aware of one another in ways that often made it feel as though they had, or perhaps it was in ways that were even more potent than touch. They knew no-one would ever understand, or accept how they felt. Maybe they didn't either. They only knew that life was allowing them this brief, bittersweet spell to feel love at a depth most never reached, and perhaps to find out if they really had the will to resist it.

The next morning when Jessica arrived at the studio Luc was already there. Neither of them mentioned her reading of the night before, or her refusal to let him walk her back through the vines afterwards. It was almost as though the evening hadn't happened at all, for they merely picked up their conversation of yesterday, as though hardly any time had passed.

'There is something about your face that I am not understanding,' he told her, as she came to join him in front of the sculpture. 'It is not the obvious features, because I think I have them. It's something else.'

As Jessica studied the clay replica of herself, the barely discernible slant of her eyes, the wide flare of her nostrils, and the full bow of her long upper lip, she could only feel awed by the way his hands had taken her beauty and turned it into something that was both her, yet not her, for there was a quality about this sculpture that was almost disturbingly transcendent.

'Right now you're escaping me,' he told her. 'You are moving away, going towards what is to come, or perhaps back to what was, while I need to feel that you are here, with me, the viewer, in this time, this place. Do you understand what I am saying?'

'Yes, I think so,' she replied pensively. Then looking at him, 'I don't know what to tell you.'

'It isn't for you to tell, it is for me to find,' he responded. 'And I will. Perhaps today.'

But by the time the village clock chimed midday in the distance his frustration was clearly building, and finally conceding that he could be trying too hard, he suggested they take a break.

'I was wondering,' he said, as she got up to leave, 'if you would be interested in taking a drive to Issy-l'Evêque.'

Her eyes widened with delight, for it was the village where Irène Némirovsky had begun writing *Suite Française*. 'I'd love to,' she replied, 'but are you sure it's not too far?'

'It'll take perhaps less than an hour,' he assured her. 'I think my father will expect us for lunch first, but I've already asked him not to tempt us with wine. I hope that wasn't presumptuous,' he added with a drollness that made her smile, 'but I felt sure, if you had nothing else arranged, that it was a place you would like to visit.'

An hour later, after a meal of smoked salmon with creamy herbed cheese, and garlic-dressed salad, Jessica slipped into the Mercedes next to Luc and tried to scowl at the look he gave her, because, unlike him, she'd been unable to resist the wine.

'But I only had one glass,' she protested, as he started down the hill.

He gave her a look of dismay.

'OK, maybe it was two.'

'I stopped counting at three.'

She started to object, then laughing she simply let her head fall back against the seat until he brought the car to a stop outside the cottage.

'I am hoping you won't snore when you fall asleep,' he said as she started to get out.

She turned back. 'I would never do anything so inelegant, but my mouth might fall open, so please feel free to lift up my chin. Now, I shall be less than two minutes, so please don't go without me.'

True to her word she was back a moment later with a hat, a belt purse and a tube of sunblock that she began rubbing into her neck and shoulders as he steered the car out of the *combe* onto the top road.

Soon they were passing through undulating countryside with sunbaked acres of vines and shady forests all around them, and constant reminders of the past, so she coaxed him to tell her what he knew of the region's colourful history, from the great Dukes of Burgundy and their ties to the French throne, to the bloody massacres of the French Revolution, right through to the ignominy of German Occupation. As he talked, particularly about the Second World War, she felt herself transported back to last night's reading for a while, thinking of Lucile and her young officer, but then he was describing the resurgence of the great wine estates, followed by their slow, inexorable dissolution due to the French Inheritance laws and competition from New World blends.

By the time they arrived at Issy-l'Evêque the topic had moved on to Alphonse de Lamartine, the celebrated poet and politician who was born in Macon. They were still trying to recite various extracts of *Jocelyn* as they parked close to the *mairie,* where an abundance of vivid flowers tumbled from the window sills and the ubiquitous tricolour hung limply from its pole. She stood looking at it for a moment, imagining the German swastika in its place, then with an imperceptible shudder she turned away.

As they set out along a sleepy cobbled street, with no particular goal in mind, they absorbed the feeling of timelessness that seemed to seep from buckled stone walls and closely shuttered windows. Though *Dolce* – the second part of *Suite Française* – was set in another village, they agreed that this one must have provided its share of inspiration, for it was there to be seen in the church, the war memorial and a beautiful golden house with a blue front door. They imagined the sound of German boots on the cobblestones, and the shadows of suspicious old women who'd lost husbands and fathers in the First World War, then sons in the Second, as they peered out of their darkened windows. Then there were the young girls who sashayed along the streets, flirting with the smartly uniformed officers while the local traders took pleasure in fleecing them. And lastly, there were the broken, embittered men who'd limped back from the front to find their homes inhabited by the enemy and their women not always pleased to see them.

They'd fallen quiet for a while, when Luc said, 'You read very well last night.'

'Thank you,' she replied, pleased by the compliment. They were crossing a small shady square towards a fountain, where the afternoon sun was making the single trickle of water sparkle like crystal beads on a harsh bedrock of stone. 'It's the most beautiful part of the book, so I'm not surprised you chose it.'

His voice was droll as he said, 'I had a feeling it might be the section you enjoyed most. I find Lucile a very subtle and courageous woman, do you?'

She thought about that. 'Subtle, certainly. But do you say courageous because she was able to resist her desire for Bruno, the German officer, or because she was willing to indulge it for a while?'

He started to smile. 'Both, I suppose – except she never indulged it in the ultimate sense.'

'You mean they never made love?'

He nodded.

'Do you think they should have? Would it have made the story more believable? Or perhaps more poignant?'

'No, I think its greatest power is probably in the fact that they did resist one another.'

She put her head to one side as she considered that, then slowly started to nod. 'I agree,' she said, and stopped to put a hand in the cool, clear water of the fountain. 'I think,' she continued after a while, 'that I especially love the scene where he plays the piano for her, then stops when he realises that the beauty of his music is touching her loneliness and making her cry.'

Perching on the wall he looked thoughtfully back across the square towards a *pâtisserie*, where a scattering of tables and chairs on the cobbles outside appeared both restful and abandoned. Then quoting the German officer he said, '*"Come, let's go away together. I'll show you many different countries. I'll be a famous composer, of course, and you'll be as beautiful as you are at this very moment . . ."*'

Jessica was on the point of picking up Lucile's response, when she realised she couldn't – not because she was unable to remember the words, but because of what they were. *And your wife, and my husband, what will we do about them?* Her eyes went briefly to his, but he was still staring across the square, so looking down at her hand swirling about in the water, she said, 'You know what I find extraordinary about that part of the book is that they hadn't yet admitted to their feelings for one another. They might not even have recognised them.'

'I think he had,' he said.

Her heart contracted, and knowing they couldn't go any further with this she removed her hand from the water and walked away from him, towards a narrow archway the other side of the square.

When he eventually caught up with her the lane they had followed was yielding to a footpath around the edge of a wheatfield where ploughs had left deep gouges in the earth, and the occasional hare could be seen scurrying its way towards a farm in the distance. 'Do you think the German was serious?' she asked, snapping off a blade of grass, and twisting it around her fingers.

'About them going away together? He probably wanted to be,' he replied, after considering it, 'but it's my belief he was giving them both a dream, a reality apart from the one they were in, because it was the only way they could be together.'

'To step outside their world?'

When she glanced up at him he nodded.

'So what if she'd said she'd go with him?'

'I think he knew she wouldn't.'

Focusing her attention on the small copse they were

approaching, she said, 'I can almost see Irène Némirovsky walking this path, can't you? Going to find herself a secluded spot in which to write.'

'And all those terrible and tragic characters would be with her,' he added, 'with their real and imagined sins and secrets, their pettiness and futile squabbles. And of course their passions and dreams. I wonder how many of them were based on people she knew, or came across?'

'If she'd been allowed to complete her symphony, as she called it, then there would be five parts to the book, instead of two, and we might have more of an idea. Everything changed so dramatically after the spring and summer she wrote about. No-one could have remained the same.' As she spoke, it was as though the horror of the Gestapo had started to permeate the air, a haunting presence, a malign slip of time. They'd come to take Irène from her sanctuary, removing her from her beloved husband and children as though . . . Well, as though she were a person of no consequence, and no rights. Terrifying as it must have been, none of them could have even begun to guess just how terrifying it really was, because none of them had ever heard of Auschwitz then.

Feeling a lump in her throat, she swallowed hard and looked down at the mossy undergrowth and trodden leaves. She wondered if Luc was thinking of Irène now, or if his mind had moved on to less painful and safer ground. She didn't ask, nor did she turn round when she sensed he was no longer behind her, she merely walked on, skirting the edge of the copse, then moving into its heart, inhaling the woody scent of the trees and absorbing their stillness as the shade cooled her skin. The ghosts of Irène's characters moved silently, almost comfortingly around her, perhaps accompanied by Irène herself.

Eventually she found another lane that twisted and turned through the back streets to connect with the main square. There were more people around now, and shops were opening, so she went to sit outside the café to wait for Luc. By the time she saw him strolling her way, deep in conversation with an ancient-looking woman, she was talking to Charlie on the phone, and trying not to think of how discordant his English voice sounded when everything around her was so inescapably and harmoniously French.

'If I'd realised I could get off that soon I'd have delayed Harry's flight till Wednesday,' he was saying, 'and we could have flown down together.'

'Ah, but this way I get him all to myself for two days,' Jessica responded, waving to show Luc where she was, 'though with Antoine and Elodie around I'll probably have some competition. I was wondering if you might like to go off somewhere for a few days towards the end of the month, just the two of us, unless Harry wants to come too, of course.'

'If there's a chance of him staying at the château, I've no doubt he'll jump at it,' Charlie said wryly. 'Where did you have in mind?'

'Oh, I don't know. How about somewhere secluded and romantic?' Her eyes were on Luc's as he sat down. 'Maybe we could go into Switzerland, or over to the Loire.'

As Charlie replied a motorbike roared up, so she had to ask him to repeat it, but it was still no good, because for some reason the connection seemed to have failed. She tried his number again, but went straight through to voicemail, so she left him a message saying she'd call back later this evening, and turned the phone off.

'So you found a friend,' she said to Luc as he signalled to the waiter.

He laughed. 'I was trying to find out what she might remember of the war, but it turned out not to be much, and she was in the south anyway, not here. Was that Charlie you were speaking to? Has he managed to get some time off?'

'It would seem so. He's arriving two days after Harry, which gives me just over a week to relax and maybe make a start on chapter one of my book. You know, I wish, in some ways, I'd suggested doing a biography of Irène, but I'm sure, once I get into the characters of Jeanne and Modi, and the time and places they lived in, I'll find them every bit as inspiring.'

'I have no doubt of it,' he replied, and turning to the waiter he ordered two pastis.

They drank mostly in silence, watching the comings and

goings around them, until finally they strolled over to the car to start the journey home.

It was close to seven o'clock by the time they pulled up outside the cottage. So far neither of them had mentioned spending the evening together, even though they knew that Fernand had gone to play *boules* in the village, while Claude and Daniella had taken the children to friends near Chalon. But Jessica felt the need to be alone now, to talk to Harry and Nikki, and perhaps to read for a while before going to bed.

'Thank you for today,' she said, as she opened the car door.

'I'm glad you came,' he responded.

'Sleep well.'

'You too.'

As he drove away she watched the car, its silvery colour glinting like glass amongst the vines, then she let herself into the cottage, and went straight upstairs.

As she started to undress for a shower she was thinking of how much she had enjoyed the day, being an artist's model, a guest for lunch, a tourist listening to Luc, and a romantic losing herself in the history of her surroundings. However, as stimulating and satisfying as she found her friendship with Luc, she felt certain it was their shared love for Lilian that was their greatest connection. It was there at the root of everything, making the chemistry between them seem almost as natural as the air they breathed, or the subjects they discussed.

After taking off the rest of her clothes, she slipped into a robe and was on her way to the bathroom when she noticed that the photograph of Natalie she kept on the chest had fallen over. Going to pick it up she gazed down into her daughter's beautiful young face, and felt her smile starting to waver. Always it was there, underlying everything, the longing and loss that dug so deeply into her heart she almost didn't want to breathe for fear of bringing in more pain. Would it ever stop, she wondered. Would a time ever come when her life might feel whole again? She wasn't even sure she wanted it to, for it would mean she'd left Natalie behind, and merely to think of that caused a wave of panicked resistance inside her.

'Mum. *Mum.*'

She turned towards the top of the stairs. She knew the voice wasn't real, that it was the ghost of her imagination, but how could it not disturb her?

She looked out of the window towards the sky. It was awash with a rose-coloured hue, clear and gentle, impenetrable and sublime. *Why did you scream?* she whispered. *Was it really that you were about to fall? Could you see what was going to happen? Was that it? Or is there more?*

There was no answer, but to her relief the chilling sense she'd had before seemed to be fading. She looked around the room, as though searching for something, but there was only the bed with its gauzy drapes, the old-fashioned chests and armoire, the door to the landing – and the wall ladder that led up to the attic.

Chapter Sixteen

The following morning Luc called early to tell her he was going to a second-hand book fair in a neighbouring village.

'I will understand, of course, if you have had enough of me by now,' he said, with the drollery that never failed to make her smile, 'but Lilian informs me that it would be very remiss of me not to invite you to come along to something that is – to quote her – so you.'

Loving the idea, Jessica said, 'As usual Lilian is right, but please feel free to dump me as soon as we get there, just as long as you promise not to leave without me.'

'No promises and no dumping,' he responded dryly. 'I will pick you up in fifteen minutes. Will you be ready?'

'Do I have a choice?'

'We could make it ten.'

Laughing, she put the phone down and, thankful she'd already showered, she threw off her towel and went to the armoire to decide what to wear. Since the heat wasn't abating at all, she rejected shorts as being too hot, and chose a floaty lime-coloured dress with thin plaited straps, and a pair of flat silver sandals that were easy to walk in. Satisfied that her tan had done away with the need for make-up, she ruffled her wet hair with her fingers, coated her lips in a translucent gloss, then grabbing her purse and phone, ran down the stairs.

Luc was already waiting outside in the car and as she got in, almost simultaneously both their mobiles started to ring.

'Only Nikki would call me at this hour,' she declared, looking down at her own phone, and seeing she was right.

'And mine is from an old colleague in Paris,' he told her, reading his incoming number. 'So do we take these calls like a caring parent and interested friend, or do we pretend we're not sad enough to be available at nine o'clock on a Sunday morning?'

Bursting into laughter, she said, 'I'm afraid a mother's conscience never allows her to be off duty, so I should warn you, this call could go on for a while.'

'Then just for the company I shall answer mine too,' he said decisively.

She must still have been laughing as she clicked on her mobile, because Nikki said, 'Well, listen to you, anyone would think you're having a good time.'

'Would they? Is it not allowed?'

'No, it's totally cool, but at eight o'clock on a Sunday morning?'

'We're an hour ahead here,' Jessica reminded her. Then, breezing on past it, 'So how's the hangover?'

'What hangover?'

'It's Sunday morning, and I know you were going out last night . . .'

'Yeah, well, that's just it, isn't it? Dad grounded me last night.'

'No!' Jessica said, genuinely shocked. 'What for?'

'Because I swore at him.'

Jessica wanted to laugh, but managed not to. 'I suppose you must have had a reason,' she said, 'so what did he do?'

'Oh nothing except tell me I looked tarty in my dress, and that my make-up made a Goth look lively, and that it was time I had an early night – *on a Saturday* – because *he'd* had enough of me coming in at all hours. So I'm sorry, Mum, I ended up using the F word, but he like so deserved it. I'm not eight, I'm eighteen, or nearly, and it's just not right to treat me like that. I mean, you never do, so he's got to wise up and realise I'm an adult too, and it like really hurts when he's being insulting, which there's no need of, is there?'

'None at all,' Jessica assured her, still wanting to laugh. 'So why are you only calling me now?' she asked, curious that she hadn't been brought into this sooner.

'Because,' Nikki said, managing to sound both defiant and sheepish, 'I did the obvious thing, didn't I, and escaped . . . Well, Mum, honestly, I had to. Freddy and I were going to this really cool club in Vauxhall – I mean we went in the end, and it was with the friends we're going to Norfolk with, so I could hardly call up and say sorry, can't come, been grounded . . . I mean, it's like just too juvenile, so I've got to tell you Mum, Dad really needs to grow up . . .'

'If I'm reading this correctly,' Jessica interrupted, 'you're calling to ask me to smooth the way for you to go home again.'

'Oh, Mum, you are like so brilliant. I knew you would. You see, I have to go back there now because Freddy and I have been invited to a barbecue in Islington, and by the time I get home and get ready . . . You know what I'm saying, and like, I just can't cope with Dad going off on one like he did last night, so you've got to tell him how to behave like a real person.'

'First,' Jessica said, still sounding amused, 'Dad's always been much more lenient than I have, so don't you forget it. And second, does he actually know you crept out last night? If he doesn't, you can always creep back in . . .'

'Yeah, like I know that, but I need you to find out if the coast is clear.'

'Darling, we love him, so don't let's gang up on him.'

'I thought you were going to help me with this!'

'I am, but only because I happen to know that if you wait another half an hour he'll have left for the studio. So if he doesn't know you crept out, and he didn't mention it to me when we spoke last night . . .'

'He didn't tell you we had a row?'

'No, actually.'

'Oh that is like so typical! Have a go at me, ruin my night, then just forget . . .'

'Nikki. Think before you speak, darling, even when it's me. Now, I'll find out if he knows you disobeyed him . . .'

'You don't have to put it like that . . .'

'Darling, get over yourself, and wait for me to call back.'

Glad to see Luc was still engaged in his call, while feeling pleasingly unrattled by her own, Jessica dialled Charlie, spoke to him affectionately for a few minutes, then curious, but nonetheless relieved, that he didn't mention anything about his blow-up with Nikki, she called Nikki back.

By the time she'd given the all clear, then listened to an explicit, sleep-inducing account of last night's rave in Vauxhall, Luc was holding the door open for her to get out of the car and join him at the book fair.

'Is sorry going to do it?' she asked, as they strolled across the grassy car park to mount some steps into the village. 'There just seems to be no escaping family crises of one size or another . . . I hope your call was less . . .' Turning to look at him, she said, 'Let's just forget the journey here, shall we, unless of course your call was of such profound fascination that we need to share it.'

With a laugh he said, 'If having to go to Paris on Tuesday is profoundly fascinating, then by all means let's share. If not, I think there's something of interest to you right here.'

To her delight he was pointing her towards a stand full of art books, and within minutes she'd uncovered two treasures – one documenting life in the Bateau-Lavoir published in 1933, and the other containing some high-quality photographs of Modigliani's nudes.

'You know, it's never been established whether or not he slept with his models,' she said, flicking through the slightly dog-eared but still glossy pages, 'apart from Jeanne and Béatrice of course, whom they say he never painted nude anyway.'

'But would it be possible for a woman to imitate that expression,' he wanted to know, stopping her at *Reclining Nude with Loose Hair*, 'if she hadn't just been made love to?'

Jessica frowned as she considered it. 'To me she looks more as though it hasn't happened yet, but she knows it will. Do you see where her hand is? Resting between her legs. I think it's unlikely she'd strike that pose with such a saucy expression if she was already sated.'

Nodding, he said, 'I guess that makes sense. Now this one,' he said, stopping her at *Nude with Necklace*, 'is one that's always inspired me in an odd sort of way. Is she meant to be a prostitute, or a goddess?'

'Mm, I don't know, what do you think?'

'I'm not sure either, but there's something about it that makes me want to complete the beauty that he's only captured in part.' His eyes started to twinkle. 'Am I getting above myself?'

'In thinking you could improve on a master?' she said. 'Mm, yes, that could qualify if it were one of his best, but as it's not . . .' She pondered it for a moment. 'I can see why it makes you feel that way, because her beauty is very apparent on the left side of her face, and there's a shapeliness to her body that's almost sexual, but not quite. I wonder who she was.'

'If you're writing part-fact, part-fiction, you could be at liberty to give her an identity,' he said. 'Perhaps she's a rival of Jeanne's that he was deliberately trying to make less appealing.'

'Or a woman who was resisting him, so he took his revenge by sending her off to eternity looking gorgeously grotesque. Or, at the very least, he was paying her back by making her lie in a very uncomfortable position.'

He appeared amused by that, and laughing too, she closed the book, paid the stallholder, then strolled on to the next stall where Luc was already leafing through a collection of nineteenth-century poems. 'Here is a complete version of de Lamartine's *Jocelyn*,' he told her, as she joined him. 'From this we can find out how accurate we were in our recitals yesterday.'

'Are any of his other poems there?' she asked, looking over his shoulder.

'Only *Le Lac*, which is actually one of my favourites. It also contains Baudelaire's *Black Venus* – another great work inspired by a woman called Jeanne.'

'Both the poem, and Manet's portrait *La Maîtresse du Baudelaire*,' she reminded him, as he continued to turn the pages. 'You're an admirer of Baudelaire?'

'I certainly find some of his arguments interesting.'

'Do you mean the one in which he holds that vice is natural, while virtue is artificial because it calls for us to restrain our natural impulses?'

'Precisely. An intriguing viewpoint on human nature. I'd also like to read again some of his poems that were inspired by Goya's etchings, but it doesn't appear that any of them are here. Nevertheless, I think I will take this book.'

After paying for it, he took her parcel, slipped his own inside and carried all three books around the fair, adding to them here and there as she bought gifts for Charlie and Fernand, and he found a highly prized – and priced – history of Mogul miniatures for Lilian.

By the time they returned to Valennes they were in deep discussion about Modigliani's caryatids, which might have continued had his mobile not rung as they drew up outside the cottage.

'My father,' he told her. *'Oui?'* he said, clicking on. He listened for a moment, then said, *'Oui, tu as raison, j'avais oublié. Je lui dirai.'* After ringing off he said, 'I had forgotten my father was playing in the tournament again today, but he tells me he has prepared a lunch for us anyway. Would you like to come?'

Jessica's eyes were dancing. 'Of course,' she replied, and relaxing back in her seat, she gazed happily out at the vines as he drove them up to the house.

'I was thinking,' he said, as they got out of the car, 'perhaps we could take our meal over to the lake. It'll be cool there, beneath the trees, and if you are willing, you can continue to tell me about your book.'

'The lake and the trees sound irresistible,' she responded, 'but I'm sure you've had enough of my book by now.'

With a wry smile, he said, 'I'll go and fetch the picnic box from my studio. Maybe we can take some towels too, in case we decide to swim.'

Half an hour later Jessica was standing barefoot on the pebbly shore of the lake, gazing out across the shimmering, silvery-green surface with its undulating reflections of sun-sparkled leaves and rich blue sky. It seemed as though the world had forgotten this sleepy vale where the reeds grew tall and the fields on the far bank sloped gently up to the horizon. Everything was quiet and still, even the crickets sounded sluggish, and though larks and blue tits twittered about in the trees, and jays soared through the empty skies, the sense of tranquillity was unbroken.

Luc was spreading out a blanket in the shade of a horse chestnut behind her. He then set up the picnic box as a table, and opened a bottle of Pouilly-Fuissé ready to pour. After a while she sensed, rather than heard him coming to stand beside her, and as she continued to absorb the beauty around them she began to recite the opening verse of de Lamartine's *Le Lac*.

Ainsi, toujours poussés vers de nouveaux rivages,
Dans la nuit éternelle emportés sans retour,

His voice came in to speak the next lines with her,

Ne pourrons-nous jamais sur l'océan des âges
Jeter l'ancre un seul jour?

So, always driven to new shores,
In the eternal darkness swept away
Will we ever be able to throw anchor
Into the ocean of time for one sole day?

She turned to look at him, wondering if the words were creating the same resonance within him, and feeling almost afraid that they were. Then, trying to overcome the tremors in her heart, she said, 'Do you think it's possible de Lamartine might have had this lake in mind when he wrote the poem?'

'It could be,' he replied, though they both knew he hadn't.

She smiled and might have turned away then, but his eyes seemed to hold her to him and as she continued to look at him she could feel herself becoming strangely light-headed, almost as though she was floating. There was no escaping the attraction between them now, it was there like an entangling force refusing to let either of them go.

'Would you like to swim?' he asked.

She took a breath that was a small gasp, then said, very softly, 'Yes. Yes, I would.'

He moved behind her and as he began to lower the zip of her dress the shock she felt didn't seem to connect to the reality of what he was doing, only to the sensation it was creating. It rippled from her centre to the very extremes of her. She felt slightly dazed, even disoriented, for she knew this shouldn't be happening, yet she could find no will to resist it. It was as though her mind and conscience had turned away through the trees, taking their judgements and fears with them, leaving her exposed – and free to move shakily, yet inexorably into this dream.

She was barely thinking, or even breathing, as he eased the straps from her shoulders. The softness of the chiffon was like the whisper of a breeze as it cascaded down over her body to pool at her feet. She was naked now, apart from a silvery-blue thong.

She waited for him to touch her, but he didn't. The only sensation on her skin was the sun burning it fiercely, and the air embracing it. She was aware of no dread of what was happening and where it might lead, for she knew she had nothing to fear.

Feeling his eyes on her back, she stepped away from him and waded into the water. As it lapped around her ankles, then her thighs, she could feel its silky coolness like milk on her skin. When it reached her waist she gave herself to it entirely and started to swim. It was as though she was moving through a lake of glistening sunlight, for all around her the surface sparkled and rippled in an ethereal white glow.

After a while she turned onto her back and let her arms rise up. As she floated she thought only of how wonderfully restful this felt, as though time had taken a pause, and the world beyond this vale was simply fading away. The only reality was the moment she was in, so perfect and still, so gentle and pure. She wanted to stay here for ever, feeling as liberated and unburdened as she did now.

Eventually she began to swim slowly back to the shore. He was standing beneath the horse chestnut now, watching her. Still she knew no concern, nor even a sense of wrong, yet she could almost feel the presence of those they loved, as though they were ghosts on the other side of the horizon. They were there, but unreachable, indefinable.

As she stood up and waded onto the shore, she felt tiny droplets of water running over her body like pearls. His eyes stayed with her as she came closer, and it was as though she was moving through an oasis, suspended in a dream that was more beautiful than she'd ever known, more elusive, and yet so very real.

When she reached him he passed her a drink and looked deeply into her eyes. Her lips parted slightly as she looked back, for she could read his desire as deeply as she could feel her own, yet strangely it seemed to need no physical contact or even expression. It was simply there between them, powerful and invisible, both pulling them together and keeping them apart.

They tasted the wine at the same time, savouring the coldness and flavours, allowing them to roll over their tongues before trickling into their throats.

'Honey, cherries and orange,' she said huskily.

'Perhaps a hint of lime?'

She waited a moment, then felt the after-tang and nodded.

They sipped again, then putting his glass on the small table he'd set up at one end of the blanket, he took off his own clothes and started towards the lake.

She turned to watch the litheness of his limbs as he walked, the width of his shoulders, the slenderness of his hips. His masculine power seemed as intransigent as the hills around them. It was as though he was a part of the landscape, as rugged, as beautiful and almost divine.

As he entered the water, she picked up a towel and dabbed it over her arms and face. He'd hung her dress from the branch of a tree, a lime green wisp like ivy, or moss. She walked over to it and resisting the urge to remove her thong so she was as naked as him, she put the dress on. Then she went back to the blanket and sat down with her wine.

She was trying to make some sense of what was happening inside her, to give some substance to the emotions, but there was only the movement of his arms as they carved a path through the glittering lake, and the perfection of being here.

When he walked back she took in every part of him, registering his desire and feeling it too, and even when he stood over her to dry himself she didn't look away. Then her eyes went up to his, but with the sun behind him she wasn't able to see his expression.

'Are you hungry?' he finally asked, wrapping the towel about his waist.

'I'm not sure,' she replied.

Kneeling beside the hamper he started to unpack, handing small packages to her to unwrap and set out on the makeshift table between them. When everything was ready he refilled their glasses, then leant on his side in a way that made her smile.

'You look like a Roman centurion,' she told him.

He laughed, and saluted her with his glass.

They ate mostly in silence, spreading thick wedges of terrine onto small chunks of bread, savouring each mouthful, before preparing some more. He offered her a small cherry tomato and as she bit into it, the juice dropped onto the upper slope of her breasts. She felt him watching her as she wiped it away with a finger that she then lifted to her mouth to lick clean. When her eyes came to his he held them in a way that sent more waves of desire rippling softly through her.

After a while he offered her grapes and goat's cheese, which she ate from his fingers before feeding him apricots and Brie. All the time she was conscious of the magnetising tension between them, feeling it in ways that was sometimes making it difficult to breathe.

'Do you think Jeanne Hébuterne might have picnicked with Modigliani somewhere like this?' he asked, when they'd finished eating and were simply gazing out at the lake.

'They might have,' she replied.

'So will you add it to your book?'

'Why not?'

He turned to pick up the wine and poured the last of it into their glasses. Then lying down on his back, he said, 'She must have loved him very much.'

'You mean to have killed herself when he died?'

'Could you imagine yourself doing that, if you were nine months pregnant?'

'No, but I can imagine loving someone enough to want to die with him rather than go on living without him.'

When he said no more, she turned to look at him, but his

eyes were closed, so she lay down too, stretching her legs into the dappled shade of the tree and inhaling the sweetness of the grass.

Some time later she raised one knee and felt her dress slip down over her thigh to expose her legs. She was thinking of Modigliani and the nudes he had painted in necklaces and hats, some standing, others kneeling or reclining. She wondered what the women themselves had really meant to him, with their soft curves and sumptuous flesh. Were they simply objects of sensuality and shape for him to capture with his eye and his gift? Or was he joining with them completely before, after, even during his process of creation? She tried to imagine how it might feel to be one of those women. Was it possible to be naked with a man that way and not feel the need to make love with him?

'Do you ever paint?' she asked, keeping her eyes closed.

It was a while before he said, 'Not really. Only sketching. And of course sculpting.'

She allowed a few moments to pass, feeling strangely uncertain, yet knowing what she wanted to say. 'Would you draw me?' she asked softly.

He turned to look at her.

Opening her eyes, she turned to look at him.

'Yes of course,' he said.

She felt a faint tremble of her lips as the promise of the experience stole through her. Closing her eyes again, she lay quietly, feeling every part of her body as though it were coming alive to the softest, most intimate caress. She let her knee fall slightly to one side so that the coolness of the shade met the essential heat of her. It was so exquisite that she stretched her arms out behind her head, and moaned softly.

For a long time neither of them spoke again, or opened their eyes. When finally she did she turned to find him lying on his side, his head propped on one hand as he watched her. She smiled almost sleepily, and continued to gaze into his eyes.

'Are you ready to go?' he asked.

'Mm,' she responded. 'I think so.'

As they began packing everything away they fell to talking of Baudelaire's novel *La Fanfario*. It suggested, she thought, that their minds had been travelling similar roads during their sleepless siesta, just as their lives had seemed to move into a parallel existence.

When they were ready they carried everything back through the woods, no longer talking, only listening to the birds and feeling the resonance of de Lamartine's beautiful poem as though it were following them like a gentle tide through the trees. But there really was no throwing an anchor into time, because eventually the tide began to ebb, taking this precious afternoon into the past – and even as they stepped out into the vineyard to begin walking towards the *manoir*, she could feel the unforgiving masters of the world and her conscience waiting to escort her home.

Chapter Seventeen

By the time she reached the cottage it was as though the world had changed completely. While everything had seemed so beautiful and right when she was with Luc, so exquisite in its unstated expression of how they felt and understanding of how it must be between them, now she could hardly believe herself capable of such self-delusion.

Going into the kitchen, she stood beside the table with her hands over her face. To think she had allowed him to take off her dress, to see her virtually naked . . . Yet even as the guilt seemed to crush her, there was no escaping the truth, because it was there too, refusing to be silenced. They desired one another in every way it was possible for a man and woman to desire one another, intellectually, physically and emotionally. And she knew already that if he wanted to see her that way again . . .

Sitting down at the table she tried to take a breath, but her chest was too tight. She thought of Charlie and how he'd betrayed her, and felt more wretched than ever for what she'd now done to him. In its way it was worse, because she knew how shattered his life already was . . . And then there was Lilian – *oh dear God, Lilian.* Her eyes closed as the horror of it descended through her. How could she be doing this to her best friend, who would rather die than ever do anything to hurt her?

Her mobile started to ring, but seeing it was Charlie she let it go through to messages. She couldn't speak to him yet, she could only think of how she was going to stop herself feeling this way about Luc. She wondered what was going through his mind now, if he was as tormented by guilt, as covered in shame. Was he seeing her in his mind as she'd been at the lake, as she was still seeing him? She couldn't get away from the image, or the consuming need that was still there, even now, despite everything. She'd asked him to draw her, and she still wanted him to, more than anything, but she must stop it from happening. Perhaps by now he had come to the same conclusion. She hoped he had, because if he hadn't she was afraid she might not find the will to resist him.

In the end, unable to bear the confines of the cottage any longer, she went outside in the hope of calming herself with the tranquillity of the evening air. She tried not to look towards the *manoir*, but it was impossible to keep her eyes from straying, or her mind from travelling in directions she wanted desperately to avoid. She thought of Lilian and tears fell onto her cheeks. If Lilian were ever to find out about the way she felt, she knew it would be an end to their friendship and break both their hearts. So maybe she should leave now, pack everything into the car and return to the safety of her marriage and her home. But what excuse could she give that either Charlie or Lilian would understand, and even if she could find one, she knew she wouldn't go.

By the time she went to bed that night the whole truth of her feelings was finally starting to surface from the place she'd kept it buried all this time. Like tiny seeds searching for light, memories were now showing themselves in the fullness of an attraction she'd clearly felt right from the start. She'd seen no danger in it then, though, had even put it down to a natural liking for anyone who cared for Lilian as much as Luc plainly did. And she had to admit a part of her really did love him for that, so somehow she had to stand back from the rest of her feelings and think only of that when she was with him. But how was it ever going to be possible when even her conscience seemed incapable of protecting her?

She passed a restless night, full of dreams that made no sense and seemed only to scare her. She kept seeing him, feeling his tenderness, and hearing his voice, but she could never reach him. No matter how close she got he just kept moving away until she finally caught him, only to find when he turned round that it was Charlie. And then Charlie was so broken apart about Natalie that she had to hold his full weight in her arms to keep him together. She kept trying and trying, but Charlie's grief was so heavy that she had to let go or they were both going to drown.

Not until dawn did she finally fall into a deep and dreamless slumber that she didn't come out of until after nine. By then the sun was high in a pristine sky and the birds were chirping loudly in the trees. For a while she simply lay where she was, letting everything come slowly back to her, the lake, her dress hanging from a tree, his naked body, the terrible struggle between her emotions and her conscience.

To her relief she found she was calmer this morning. Though none of it could be forgiven, she seemed less afraid of herself now, and of what was happening between them. She felt certain that no matter how strong their feelings might be, neither of them would ever take that final step to betray those they loved. They could continue to spend time together – in many ways it was going to be impossible to avoid – but they must never talk about how they felt, or touch, not even to shake hands or formally kiss, for she was afraid if they did they'd be unable to stop.

Going downstairs she pulled open the French doors and a faint breeze, warm and consoling, sighed into the kitchen. It was auspicious, she thought, and glad to be feeling more in control, she looked up towards the *manoir* where she saw Madame Fortuny's car parked outside. Knowing the old lady would come to the cottage later, for the laundry, she went back up to the bedroom to take off the sheets.

It was as she was carrying them out onto the landing that she felt a strangeness starting to come over her. At first she couldn't think what it was, but then she found herself looking down at the stairs and becoming aware of their steepness, in a way she hadn't before. Then a kind of vertigo began making her dizzy, and she drew back, almost as though she were about to go over. Dropping the sheets she pressed her hands to her cheeks as her heart began pounding unsteadily.

With her senses still swimming, she turned to look towards the room Natalie had slept in. There was nothing there, just a crumpled, threadbare rug on the wooden boards of the landing, and a half-open door. Going to it, she pushed it open and stood staring down at the bed. She wasn't really seeing it, nor was she fully conscious of where she was, she only knew the fear that had come into her heart a moment ago.

It was a while before she left the room and took the sheets downstairs. She dropped them next to the door, then put some water on to boil and stood waiting, knowing it was crazy to think that the fear she'd experienced at the top of the stairs had been Natalie's, but that was how it had felt. She glanced up to the landing, and realised that while her mind had been occupied elsewhere, it was as though her instincts had found the space, the oxygen to start working again.

After making some tea she carried it outside and sat for a long time gazing absently out at the vines. She wanted to recapture the feeling she'd had, or at least try to understand it, but as the minutes ticked on it became more and more elusive, until finally she began to wonder if it had happened at all.

It was close to midday when Madame Fortuny came to pick up the sheets. By then Jessica was sitting at the table inside surrounded by the books she'd found at yesterday's fair, her notepad in front of her, her laptop open, as yet untouched. Her concentration was poor and she knew why, but she was trying to work anyway. He would come, she felt sure of it, even though it might be better if he didn't – and when a shadow appeared in the doorway she was so certain it was him that the disappointment she felt when she recognised the small, portly figure in front of her would have appeared offensive, if Madame Fortuny had been paying attention.

'Ah, Madame,' Jessica said, having to clear her throat. *'Comment ça va?'*

'Pas mal. Pas mal du tout,' Madame Fortuny replied busily, coming to bestow the requisite embrace. *'Et toi?'*

'Oui, très bien.' She watched the old lady scoop up the sheets and stuff them into the laundry bag she'd brought with her. Then almost without thinking she said, *'Est-ce que Monsieur Veron est à la maison?'*

'Père ou fils?' Madame Fortuny responded. Then without waiting, *'Le père est dans son bureau en ce moment, et le fils est*

parti assez tôt ce matin.' The father is in his office at the moment, and the son left early this morning.

It was as though Jessica's heart stopped beating. He'd left? But to go where? 'Is he coming back?' she heard herself ask. Then realising the old lady hadn't understood, she repeated it in French.

Madame Fortuny merely shrugged. *'Mais oui,'* she replied, as if it had been a silly question. *'Mais je ne sais pas quand.'* Of course, but I don't know when.

Aware of how dry her throat had become, Jessica stood up and went to pour herself some water. Then she blinked, because he was there, walking across the patio towards her, and the relief she felt was so overwhelming that she found herself starting to laugh.

Apparently amused by her response, he stood aside for Madame Fortuny to come out, then after carrying the laundry bag to the vineyard *camionette* she'd driven down in, he waited for her to pull away before turning back to Jessica. She was standing in the doorway now, watching him as he came towards her.

'How are you?' he asked, his tone and his eyes telling her that he'd spent as much time thinking about her since their parting, as she had about him.

'I'm fine,' she said, knowing she was now. 'How are you?'

He merely nodded, keeping his gaze on hers. For a moment he looked as though he might step forward and kiss her, but he didn't, nor did she go to him.

'Would you like a drink?' she said. 'I can offer you an excellent Macon-Valennes. Or perhaps something a little more full-bodied?'

Irony came into his eyes as she blushed at the innuendo, then noticing a large, flat parcel leaning against the wall she glanced at him curiously.

'Bring the wine, and a hat,' he told her, and tucking the parcel under one arm, he started back across the patio.

Intrigued, she went to put a Macon-Valennes into an ice bag, along with a corkscrew and glasses, then patting a small floppy straw hat on her head she followed him across the lane and up into the vines.

When they were deep inside the foliage, exposed only to

the sky above and tumbling clusters of succulent Chardonnay grapes, he set down the parcel and tore off the brown paper wrapping. Inside were two pale blue deckchairs, and something else that seemed to be in a parcel of its own.

Not quite sure why, she started to laugh.

He set up the deckchairs facing one another, but several feet apart, then after uncorking the wine he filled the glasses and handed one to her.

As she took it she looked up into his eyes, and seeing the expression in his she felt her smile starting to fade. For one fleeting moment her conscience seemed to graze across the silence, but then it was gone, leaving only the profound connection between them and a scorching sun.

He sipped his drink, and so did she, then handing her his glass he turned to the other parcel and tore it open.

The moment she saw what was inside a quiver of excitement ran through her. She took another sip of her drink and felt the headiness of anticipation blend with the wine. He was holding a large sketch pad and several pencils.

Taking the glasses away from her, his eyes came to hers as he said, very softly, 'Take off your clothes.'

Her breath seemed to catch on the words. Neither of them had mentioned she'd be nude for the drawing, but she couldn't deny it was what she had meant, and clearly he'd known it.

A few minutes later, feeling the unsteadying pleasure of being naked while he was dressed, she looked into his face as he began his artist's scrutiny of the model he was about to sketch. She stood very still, feeling the stiffness of her nipples as his eyes took in their fullness and even seemed to measure their length. Then he was regarding the smoothness of her tummy where fine, silvery scars shimmered against her tan. For some reason she started to lift a hand, almost modestly, then she let it drop again, as his gaze moved down to her closely cropped pubic hair. She knew, because she was able to feel the air around it, that he was able to see her clitoris, moist and pink and hard with desire.

It was a while before he allowed his eyes to travel on down her legs. By then she had such a powerful sense of having been probed by his eyes that small shivers of release were starting to pulse inside her. He picked up her hat and told her to put it on.

'Now sit down,' he said, holding the back of one of the chairs, 'and show me the position you would like to take.'

When she was seated she arranged the hat so it wasn't covering too much of her face, and glanced up at him to seek his approval. He gave it, then stood watching as she stretched out her legs and rested a hand on her upper thigh. From the darkness that came into his eyes she knew that he was remembering what she'd said about Modigliani's *Nude with Loose Hair*, and why her hand was positioned where it was. Putting her other arm behind her head, she looked up at him again.

'I think you will find it difficult to keep your arm there,' he told her. 'It is easier when you are lying down, but when you are sitting . . .' He narrowed his eyes thoughtfully. 'Perhaps you can just let your hand fall to the floor, as though you have interest only in what the other hand is doing. Yes, yes, that is good,' he decided.

She stayed as she was while he turned to pick up her wine, then after handing it to her, he settled himself into the other chair and opened his pad.

To her amusement it didn't seem to take long before he became every bit as absorbed in his work as when he'd sculpted her. She listened to his hand and pencil moving over the page in a soft, whispering sound, and watched his eyes as they came to her, unseeing of the woman, only of the texture and shape, light and shadow.

Since he was fulfilling her desire to model nude for an artist, the way so many had for Modi, she began paying attention to how she was feeling, what was passing through her mind, and how she was responding in her body.

After a while she found her thoughts travelling back through time, seeking the colourful squalor of the Bateau-Lavoir where chaotic, sunlit studios were filled with future masters at work, and sumptuous girls at play. From there it became easy to hear the cries of artistic frustration mingling with the groans of sexual release and shrieks of raucous hilarity. She saw oil paints splashing onto canvas, fingers digging into clay and flesh moving against flesh. There was the cancan, men in silk capes, and gaily painted whores. And on the periphery of all the concupiscence and wealth was starvation, disease, alcoholism and the kind of decadence that made the period so appallingly frayed.

'What are you thinking?' Luc said.

Opening her eyes she looked at him, and smiled at the furrow of his brow. 'I was getting into the mood for my book,' she told him.

His eyebrows rose. 'Why don't you tell me about it?' he said. 'How do you think you will begin?'

Inhaling deeply as she thought, she let her eyes drift to the leaves beside her, made richer in colour, or translucent, by the sun, then she lifted a hand to the grapes, wanting to feel their plumpness, while her other hand remained still on her thigh. Eventually she began trying to put her various ideas into words, at first hesitantly, exploratively, seeming to test their worth as she took them down avenues that she either quickly abandoned, or occasionally continued. He listened attentively while continuing to draw, though sometimes he questioned her, needing something clarified, or at other times making suggestions of his own. She took them willingly, as though they were fruits to be tasted and assessed, and gradually she became aware of a pleasing lilt inside as a tentative confidence began to take root.

Then they were laughing as they fleshed out the characters – moody artists and their models, flamboyant mentors and their mistresses, shark landlords, violent police and despairing priests. They wove all kinds of fiction into the facts, bringing the period and the people to life in ways that made everything seem dazzling and fraught. It was full of cruel and outrageous passions, jealousies and rivalry, murderous rages and suicidal declines, all clashing with the tender poetry of the times, not to mention the opera, orgies, opium – and the approaching eve of a war to end all wars.

'Never forgetting,' he said, still sketching, 'that Picasso was in the next room to Modi creating *Les Demoiselles d'Avignon* – or, put another way, giving birth to Cubism.'

How exciting that felt, she thought, imagining it. 'You know, it's going to be interesting recreating scenes between those two,' she said, 'particularly during the time Modi was painting Picasso's portrait. Tell me what you think might have passed between them.'

He considered it for a while, then started to smile, and soon he was making her laugh again with a hilariously irreverent description of how two inebriated masters might discuss their work. 'Of course it must lead to a magnificent brawl,' he informed her decisively, 'which I think we can imagine the heavily pregnant Jeanne walking into – was she pregnant at that time, we'll have to check – and perhaps she separates them with a bucket of slop water, or violent squirts of paint.'

'Or,' she suggested mischievously, 'the threat of a knife to the portrait.'

'Oh là là,' he murmured, clearly in pain at the mere suggestion. 'Certainly, that would have the desired effect. No artist, no matter how high on drugs or drink, could bear to see his work destroyed – unless of course he was to do it himself. And now,' he said, sitting forward, 'may I present to you *La Déesse des Vignes.*'

As she took the sketch pad she felt a moment's surprise to see herself, for she'd become so relaxed amongst the vines and involved in the story that she'd all but forgotten she was nude. Then, gazing down at the image he'd created, she began to feel the extraordinary pleasure of her own sensuousness coming from the page. Even to her own eyes she looked wanton and voluptuous, yet somehow shy beneath her hat, and even demure. She'd forgotten about the tiny platinum chain she was wearing, but he'd drawn it in over her collarbone, adding yet another touch to the femininity that seemed to float up from the sketch.

Just as in life her breasts were small, while her nipples were large and dark and hugely distended. Unthinkingly she put a hand to one of them, almost as though his pencil might still be there. Then she was looking at the hand he'd drawn on her thigh, her fingers semi-crooked, nails with crescent tips touching the very edge of her pubic hair.

Her eyes went to his as he came to kneel beside her, then they moved with his pencil back to the page. As he placed the point gently between her legs she felt a searing sensation go through her, as though he was touching her flesh instead of the sketch.

She looked at him again, the heaviness of desire showing in her eyes. She so badly wanted to feel his lips on hers, his tongue, his hands . . .

'You're making this very difficult,' he said softly, and with an expression that was both rueful and accepting, he took the pencil away and stood up.

She felt oddly shaken and abandoned, slightly breathless and so very, very close to pulling him back, but she didn't, because she was making herself think of Lilian and Charlie. God knew it was bad enough that she and Luc were here like this – they couldn't go any further, they just couldn't.

When she was dressed they walked quietly back through the vines, carrying the wine they hadn't drunk, the chairs and the sketch pad. She wondered what he would do with the drawing, if he'd offer it to her, or decide to keep it. She didn't ask because for the moment she didn't want there to be any words.

When they reached the road he said, 'We're going to Daniella's for dinner this evening.'

She nodded.

'My father and I will pick you up at seven.'

Again she nodded, then as he turned towards the *manoir*, she started back down to the cottage, her eyes fixed sightlessly on the dusty road in front of her. For long minutes she barely knew what she was thinking, or even feeling, all she knew was how hard she was finding this. Then suddenly there was so much emotion gathering inside her that she could only wonder how it was possible to feel such happiness when she was so riddled with guilt and despair.

'Jessica,' Fernand said, pronouncing her name in low, warm tones as he stepped out of the car to greet her. 'Please forgive me for being a bad host, it would seem it is my time for *les tournois en ce moment. Les boules. Les échecs. Mais, je suis là maintenant, et tu es très belle ce soir.*'

Jessica closed the French doors of the cottage behind her, and went to embrace him, her eyes soft with affection as she thanked him for the compliment. Then slipping into the back seat of the Mercedes she started to say *bonsoir* to Luc, who was driving, but catching his eye in the rear-view mirror she only looked at him as a current of desire passed between them.

As they drove on up the hill to leave the valley Fernand half-turned in the front passenger seat, saying, 'Luc has shown me the sculpture he has created of you, *chérie*. It is *formidable. Vraiment formidable. Le plus belle qu'il ait crée, je crois.*' The most beautiful he has created, I believe.

'Jessica hasn't seen the finished version yet,' Luc told him. 'I completed it last night, and this afternoon,' he added, glancing at her in the mirror.

She let her eyes meet his for a second, loving how dark his were, then turning back to Fernand she gave a mischievous twinkle, as she said, 'If mine is *la plus belle*, then I think yours is *le plus beau*.'

Fernand chortled with amusement, and was about to embark on a modest protest, when his expression changed as something else came into his mind. *'Oh, là là,'* he murmured, tapping a hand to his head, 'I am forgetting that I have *des bonnes nouvelles pour toi*. Is it good news? Maybe. Well, it is news. Today I play chess with the brother of *le Chef des Pompiers* for this region. *Le Chef* himself, like all the world at the moment, is *en vacances*, but his brother is going to call him at his house in Italy to ask for his help. Maybe he can give the order for someone else to show you the report of the paramedic since the poor man, *lui-même*, cannot yet return from the Auvergne.'

'What about speaking to the paramedic on the phone?' Luc suggested. 'Maybe we can get a number.'

Jessica nodded. 'I'm sure it'll only be to thank him for his kindness,' she said, feeling almost certain she was right, but not quite, particularly since the strange moment at the top of the stairs when she'd thought her instincts were trying to tell her something again.

In French Luc explained to his father how the paramedic had probably carried Natalie to the sofa, rather than leave her crumpled on the floor.

'Ah oui,' Fernand said gravely, 'there are some very good people in this world and this young man who has broken his

leg, I know him a little by reputation, because he win an award once for bravery. So I think, without doubt, that he would be very kind to Natalie.'

Jessica swallowed as she smiled.

'My friend,' Fernand continued, 'the brother of *le Chef de Pompiers*, says he will call me as soon as he has some news, but he thinks it will be by Friday, or perhaps even Thursday.'

Though Jessica could have wished it would be even sooner, it was a relief to know that her mind could be completely at rest before Harry and Charlie arrived.

Letting her head fall back against the seat she turned to stare out of the window for a while, watching the passing trees and hedgerows and wondering when her heart had ever felt so full. Her eyes moved to Luc and she felt a surge of gratitude, mixed with longing and so much else, rise up in her. She had no idea if it was his intention, but it was as though he was helping to heal her, lending her his strength and support, not only by listening and believing, or by opening doors she couldn't open alone, but by encouraging her to work on her book, to take part in life again and to remember that she was a woman with passions and desires that went beyond those of a mother.

She looked out at the countryside again and sighed silently to herself. What did it all mean, she wondered. Why had they been brought together like this, given this time and these feelings, when surely no good could come of them in the end?

By the time Luc finally steered the car through the gates of the château to start following the twisting, leafy drive to the house, Fernand was entertaining them with stories from that weekend's chess tournament, which had clearly been far less sedate, or even sportsmanlike, than the game, on the surface at least, might appear.

Jessica and Luc were still laughing as they got out of the car, but as Jessica made to link Fernand's arm to start across the lawn towards the arbour where they could see Daniella sitting, Luc said to his father, *'Vas-y. Je voudrais dire un mot à Jessica.'* You go ahead, I want a quick word with Jessica.

As Fernand ambled off, already preparing to catch the

twins who were hurtling towards him, Jessica turned questioningly to Luc, and seeing how troubled he looked she felt a pang of unease.

'I'm leaving for Paris in the morning,' he said. 'I'll be back on Wednesday.'

Knowing she couldn't ask him not to go, even though she wanted to, she let her eyes fall away for a moment.

'I want you to come with me,' he said.

She looked at him again, and almost started to protest, but how could she when her heart wasn't in it? Already he was saying, 'Claude and Daniella's apartment is below mine. You can stay there.'

Her gaze remained on his until finally she nodded, then turning together they began walking across the lawn, saying no more until Daniella came to greet them, and the twins pulled Luc into a rowdy game of football.

'Is that Yves?' Jessica said, referring to Claude's brother as she and Daniella embraced.

'If you mean is that him playing the *Gymnopédies* you can hear,' Daniella replied, 'then the answer is yes, but it is a recording, because, as you can see, the man himself is currently in goal.'

Catching them looking his way, Yves set off a storm of protest as he started towards them, leaving the goal clear for Luc to score.

Greeting Jessica with a twinkle that was very like Claude's, he said, 'It is a great pleasure to meet you again. The last time must have been at the wedding, not so very long ago, of course, but I must be getting old, because I cannot quite remember when it was.'

Jessica barely had time to respond before Antoine and Elodie came bounding up to her, hotly pursued by Rousseau, the dog.

'Jessica! Jessica!' Antoine was shouting. *'Maman dit qu'Harry arrive. C'est vrai?'* Mummy says Harry is coming. Is it true?

'Quand est-ce qu'il arrive? Quand est-ce qu'il arrive?' Elodie pressed excitedly. When's he coming?

'A week from today,' Jessica answered, touched by how eager they were to see her son.

'Est-ce qu'il peut dormir chez nous?' Antoine wanted to know. *'Il peut dormir dans ma chambre.'* Can he sleep here with us? He can sleep in my room.

'I'm sure he'd love to,' she told them, smiling at Luc as he came to join them.

'I see the game is abandoned as soon as I start to win,' he objected.

'No! No!' the twins shouted, and grabbing both him and Yves they dragged them back to the pitch.

Daniella rolled her eyes, and linking Jessica's arm she walked her to the table under a vine-covered arbour where Fernand was already pouring two glasses of what he declared to be a very fruity and slightly oaky Côte de Beaune.

'Where is Claude?' Jessica asked, as Daniella offered her a dish of Tunisian olives.

'On the phone,' Daniella replied. 'He'll be out in a minute.'

'Papi, you must be in goal now,' Elodie shouted. 'I want Tonton Yves to be on my team.'

With a helpless shrug, Fernand put down his glass and went off to join in, while with a sigh of contentment Jessica gazed up at the dark green leaves and vibrant flowers that climbed the chateau's silvery-white walls. Then she started to laugh as Luc broke into an argument with his nephew about one or other of them being offside, though she couldn't quite tell which of them it was supposed to be.

It was a moment before she realised Daniella was watching her, and as she turned to meet her eyes she felt her cheeks grow warm with colour.

'I know this is none of my business,' Daniella said softly, 'but Luc spoke to Claude about the apartment . . . Of course it is not a problem for you to stay there, but just now, when I see you coming across the garden together . . .'

Jessica's heart turned over in alarm. If Daniella had picked up on it so quickly, then how on earth were they ever going to hide it from anyone else?

'I am not judging you,' Daniella assured her gently, 'I know how much you both love Lilian, so of course you didn't mean this to happen . . .'

'Nothing's happening,' Jessica told her.

'Then I'm sorry. It is just the way you look at one another. I saw it in his eyes a moment ago, and I can see it in you now, but if I am wrong . . .'

'We're not making love,' Jessica said. 'It hasn't gone that far. We haven't even kissed.'

Daniella sighed quietly. 'Maybe it would be better if you did,' she said.

Jessica shook her head. 'No.'

'But why? Please don't think I'm saying you should, because I love Lilian too, and I don't want to see her hurt any more than you do, but sometimes, when these things are bottled up . . .' She didn't finish, she didn't have to, her meaning was plain enough.

'We both know – and accept – that nothing can ever come of the way we feel,' Jessica told her. 'We're just going to spend this time together and then . . .' What then? She didn't know, and right now she wasn't even sure she wanted to.

'What about when you're in Paris?' Daniella said. 'Do you really think you will be able to resist one another then?'

As her heart caught on the thought of it, Jessica said, 'We have to,' while privately she was thinking that she must never undress for him again. They couldn't tease and torment one another that way any more, it was too difficult now. It was asking too much of themselves to make it stop there.

Much later that night, after returning to the cottage, Jessica found herself crying so hard down the line to Charlie that he could barely make any sense of what she was saying.

'But darling, what's happened?' he kept asking. 'Why are you so upset?'

'I don't know,' she sobbed. 'I guess it's all just catching up with me. Oh Charlie, I'm so sorry.'

Almost laughing, he said, 'But you don't have anything to be sorry for. OK, you've had some strange thoughts, and we haven't been getting along quite as well lately, but we've been under a lot of pressure . . .'

'I love you,' she told him.

'Is that what you're apologising for?'

'No. Oh I don't know what I'm saying. I just wish you were here. Or I was there. I don't ever want to lose you.'

'Darling, what on earth . . .'

'No, don't listen to me. Please don't take any notice. I'm fine really. Perhaps I've had a little too much to drink.'

'Well you're in the right place for it. Where have you been this evening?'

'To Daniella's.' She started to tell him about the dinner, but stopped when she realised she had to mention Luc. 'I should let you get some sleep now. You've got an early start in the morning.'

'You remember my schedule better than I do,' he said wryly. 'Are you sure you're all right?'

'Yes. I promise. I love you.'

'I love you too.'

She waited for him to ring off, but he didn't.

'Jessica, do you want me to see if I can come sooner?'

'No,' she answered. 'I mean, yes, but you need to be there when Harry gets home, and honestly, I'm fine.'

'I wish you sounded it. When's Lilian back?'

Closing her eyes at the mere thought of it, she said, 'On Friday or Saturday.'

'Then not long to go. You know she always makes you feel better.'

'Yes, yes she does,' she agreed, but she was so close to breaking down again that this time she had to end the call.

'Oh Lily,' she sobbed into her hands, 'I'm sorry, I'm so sorry. If I could make myself feel another way, I swear I would. But it will be over after Paris, I give you my word. And nothing will happen while we're there, I promise. I just have to be with him. That's all. Nothing more – and please, *please* God you and Charlie will never even know.'

Chapter Eighteen

It was extraordinary, Jessica was thinking to herself as she and Luc joined the autoroute the following morning, how different everything felt when she was with him. While alone her conscience was merciless in the way it tore her apart, but now, sitting here beside him, it was as though all her guilt and anxieties were simply melting away.

She wondered how it was for him, if he suffered the same inner turmoil when alone, or even now, as they were driving. If he did he showed no sign of it.

She smiled as he glanced her way, and realised that her concerns about what would happen when they got to Paris had vanished too, because the arrangements had been made: he'd drop her and the car at the apartment block before going on to a retirement lunch for an old colleague from *Libération*. She had plenty of ideas for how to fill the time until they met up again, though he'd asked her to save some of her research so he could share it. Then this evening they would go for dinner at a restaurant he knew, before returning to their separate apartments – and tomorrow they'd drive back to Valennes.

'Tell me what you're thinking,' he said, as they tore down an open stretch of the fast lane, leaving most other vehicles to quake in the slipstream.

'That you drive like a true Frenchman,' she told him wryly.

He glanced at her with humorous eyes. 'Would you prefer I slow down?'

She shrugged. 'If you feel safe, then I do too.'

He laughed. 'Such confidence,' but he eased off the

accelerator as he said, 'Is that all you were thinking, that I am a crazy driver?'

She smiled, loving the way he seemed so genuinely interested to know what was in her mind, but this time her eyes went down as she said, 'You don't really want to know.'

'If it was about me, maybe I do.'

She threw him a look.

'You mean it wasn't about me?'

She shook her head, then realising there was nothing wrong in telling him the truth, she said, 'Actually, I was thinking about Lilian, and wondering . . . You do love her, don't you?'

He seemed puzzled by the question. 'Of course,' he said. 'I thought you knew . . .'

'I did. I do. I just had to ask. I mean, it makes everything easier, doesn't it, if we know that you love Lilian and I love Charlie?'

He almost laughed. 'I don't know about easier, but I suppose it makes it clearer.' Then, turning to look at her for a moment, 'We're not going to hurt anyone,' he said, 'maybe apart from one another, and we're going to try very hard not to do that.'

Her eyes closed at the way she was already hurting, but after a while she found herself starting to smile. 'What is it about you,' she asked, trying to sound humorous, 'that makes me think I can say anything?'

Though he laughed, his reply was more serious than she'd expected. 'Probably because you don't have to tread so carefully around me. Everyone else in your life is suffering over what happened, so you're always trying to protect them, not wanting to say anything that will make it worse, or leave them thinking you blame them in some way, or feel they've let you down . . .'

'But I'm doing it all the time,' she came in despondently, 'especially with Charlie. Do you know, we hardly ever mention Natalie's name unless we're talking about what happened, and even then he tries not to. He's taken it so hard he can't even look at photographs or home videos or anything else to do with her, and sometimes I find that really difficult to deal with. It's not that I don't understand, because obviously I do – losing a child is like having part of yourself amputated with no anaesthetic, and nothing to hold onto . . .' She stopped, embarrassed in case she'd run on too long.

'I saw what Natalie's death did to him during those early days,' he told her. 'You'll remember I was with him through most of it. He gave me the impression that if he had a favourite amongst your children it might have been her.'

Jessica nodded as her heart contracted. 'It was,' she said. 'Maybe because we waited so long for our second, or because she just had that special twinkle for her daddy . . .' She swallowed hard and turned to look at him. 'Did he talk to you about her during that time?'

He shook his head. 'Not really. It was mostly official business we were having to deal with, and his French, as you know, is as good as yours, so he didn't need me too much for that. I think it was more as a driver, and some moral support.'

She reflected sombrely about that time, then almost without thinking she said, 'So while Lilian took care of me, you took care of Charlie . . .' She gave a sigh of confusion . . . 'and now look where we are.'

As she looked at him she saw he was smiling.

'I guess the world is just a very strange place, with a highly capricious master,' he commented.

'You mean fate?'

He nodded.

She started to respond, but found her feelings too close to the surface, so trying to focus her mind elsewhere she said, 'Can I choose some music?'

'Of course,' he replied, as she opened the glove compartment. 'There is a very good recording of Claude conducting *Il Trovatore* at La Scala a couple of years ago. If you don't already know it, I think you will like it.'

'I do know it,' she told him, 'and I remember how well received it was at the time. Did you go to Milan, to see it?'

'*Mais bien sûr*,' he replied. 'It was before I met Lilian, of course. I went with my father and Daniella – and Karin.'

Since he'd never mentioned his ex to her before, she was unprepared for the jolt it gave her. She wondered if it was jealousy or curiosity, and decided it was probably both. She wanted to know everything about him, yet it was hard having to accept that unlike Karin – or Lilian – she would never be a real, or acknowledged part of his life.

Slotting the CD into the player, she closed the glove compartment and sat back to let the captivating sounds of the overture fill the car. 'Are you ever in touch with Karin?' she asked after a while.

Seeming surprised by the question, he said, 'Rarely. She moved to Rome soon after we broke up. I think she and Daniella contact one another from time to time, though.'

'Why did you break up?' she asked. 'Did you just stop loving her? Is that what happened?'

He glanced at her curiously. 'I suppose so. I still cared for her though, very deeply, which was why it took me so long to tell her.'

She was thinking of Charlie now, and all the years they'd been together, how much they'd shared, everything they'd meant to one another – and how devastated either one of them would be if they suddenly woke up one day to discover they no longer felt the same way. 'It's frightening to think you can be in love with someone for so long, and then suddenly find that maybe you aren't any more,' she said, not really wanting to believe it could happen. 'Was it gradual? Or did you suddenly look at her one day and realise it was all over for you?'

He took a moment to consider it before saying, 'I think it had been happening for a while without me knowing, but then yes, I suppose I did look at her one day and think, "This is wrong. I don't love her the way she loves me." It was a terrible moment, and I tried very hard to tell myself it was just a phase, but in the end I couldn't get away from it.' He shrugged, not unkindly, more helplessly. 'Your feelings are what they are, whether you like them or not, and ultimately you seem to have very little control.'

Knowing how true that was, particularly at this moment, she said, 'When you met Lilian, did you know right away that she was the one?'

He nodded. 'More or less. Yes, I think I did.'

At that she smiled. 'It's how she felt about you. *Un coup de foudre.*' She turned to look at him. 'Do you still feel that way about her?' she asked. Then, before he could answer, 'I'm sorry, I shouldn't have said that. Please forget I even mentioned it.'

His eyebrows rose. 'Mentioned what?' he said by way of a tease.

She swallowed hard and turned to look out of the window. Had she really wanted him to doubt his love for Lilian? Surely to God not, for what purpose would that serve, other than to break Lilian's heart, and that was something she could never want. Nevertheless she couldn't help wondering how she might have felt if he had admitted to being less certain now. Would it change anything for her? Maybe things were already changing, because she wasn't sure it was possible to feel as strongly for him as she did and still love Charlie the way she always had. Yet she did love Charlie. She couldn't imagine ever not loving him. So why was she here? What was it about this man that was making her long to be the most important and cherished part of his life, as though neither of them had anyone else in the world to consider but themselves?

For a while she was foolish – and selfish – enough to let herself imagine how it might be if she were able to give herself to him completely the way she so desperately wanted to, even become a part of his life in Valennes . . . But then she forced herself to let it go, knowing that she was only going to make this time together so very much harder if she kept allowing her thoughts to run this way.

It was after midday when they finally arrived in Paris, by which time the intensity inside her had abated, enabling her to laugh and tease him for taking a wrong turn in a city he knew so well. It meant that as soon as they arrived at the apartment block he had to give her the keys to Claude and Daniella's flat so she could let herself in, while he left the car in its private space to go and hail a cab.

Not wanting to stay indoors any longer than necessary on such a beautiful day, Jessica left the shutters closed in the apartment, quickly freshened up, then taking her notebook, camera and phone set off ready to explore. As she'd expected, Montmartre was swarming with tourists, and because of the hour all the bistros and cafés were packed. However, in spite of the crush, she managed to make a leisurely browse along the many rows of colourful street art, either parked on easels, propped against walls, or hanging from stalls, finding much that she liked and plenty she didn't. Then she climbed and descended some of the steep stone staircases that zigzagged through the narrow, pale grey buildings, and all the while she tried to imagine a young Jeanne Hébuterne taking the same steps. It was hard with so many people around, and so many bad copies of Picassos and van Goghs and even Modiglianis on just about every corner, but if she looked up to where small delicately carved balconies embraced the fading slats of old brown or blue shutters, it was much easier to get a feel of how it might have been almost a century ago.

Soon she was lost in a reverie of Jeanne exchanging what few coins she had for fruit and bread before climbing back to the studio where her tempestuous and often sick Modi was working. She could see her watching him with anxious eyes, or gazing from a window, lost in thought. She even felt Jeanne's happiness at sitting for the man she loved, watching him work and sharing his frustrations as well as his poverty and pride.

She wasn't sure when she first started to find the crowds claustrophobic, she only knew that everything around her was suddenly seeming blurred and discordant and disturbingly oppressive. She needed to find some shade to escape the heat, and fresh air so she could breathe again, but she appeared to have lost her way. She pushed on through the bustle, heading towards the Basilica, thinking of its cavernous, shadowy interior as a sanctuary, but just like in a dream, no matter how fast she walked towards it, it seemed to get further away.

Finally realising that a strong cocktail of sun and hunger was making her delirious she sat down on an empty chair outside a café, and ordered a glass of water with a tuna-filled baguette. By the time she'd eaten and drunk she was feeling much steadier, and even faintly embarrassed by how close she'd come to fainting, but now she was ready to set off again. A few minutes later she was slipping quietly into the hallowed environs of one of the most beautiful churches in the world, the *Basilique du Sacré-Coeur*. For a while she merely stood gazing up at the dazzling colours of the stained-glass windows and magnificent cupola, then she went to admire the mosaic that she'd seen many times over the years – something that never failed to move her. She went to confront the statue of Christ with his arms outstretched, and as her eyes rose up to his she felt her heart contract, partly with anger, partly with shame, for since losing Natalie she'd lost any faith she might have had. However, before leaving, she found herself lighting a candle for Natalie's soul and saying a quiet prayer.

Once outside again she waited for her eyes to adjust to the new glare of the sunlight, then walking to the top of the wide marble steps in front of the Basilica, she gazed down at the spectacular view of Paris, unfolding out to the horizon. Such a haphazard arrangement of streets and boulevards, tree-lined avenues and lush green parks. She thought of the thousands of people going about their daily business down there, all strangers and yet somehow connected, if only because they were in the same city. She wondered where Luc was amongst it all, then she smiled warmly as her mobile rang and she saw it was him.

'Hi, are you OK?' he asked.

'I'm already here, waiting for you,' she told him.

'I'm going to be about ten minutes late. Don't leave without me.'

Laughing, she said, 'Where are you now?'

'Close to the Place Vendôme, trying to get a taxi. Have you bought me a Modigliani?'

'How did you guess?'

'I have something for you.'

'Oh?' she said, pleased and intrigued.

'It's a surprise. Here's a taxi. I should be there very soon.'

After she'd rung off she wandered over to a nearby wall to sit and watch the world go by, but almost as soon as she got there her mobile rang again.

Seeing it was Nikki she felt a pang of guilt for where she was, mixed with relief that Nikki didn't know, and clicking on she said warmly, 'Hi darling, how are you? Did you get my message? I tried to call you earlier . . .'

'Oh Mum, I'm terrible,' Nikki wailed, 'I've just had a really, really big row with Freddy and I think it's over.'

'No, I'm sure you're wrong,' Jessica told her gently. 'What was it about?'

'I don't know. I mean I do, but it was really stupid, because he said I should grow up and stop clinging onto you and Dad all the time, and I'm not! Am I? I mean, you're not even here, so how can I be clinging onto you? And Dad's hardly ever here either, because he's working all the time . . . Oh Mum, I said some really horrible things to him too, but I was really mad, and now I don't know what to do. If he finishes with me I'll just want to *die*.'

'Don't say that,' Jessica responded, more sharply than she'd intended, but Nikki should have known better.

'I'm sorry, but I mean it, Mum. I really, really love him, and I just couldn't bear it if he doesn't want to see me any more.'

'I'm sure it won't come to that. He was probably just in a bad mood and took it out on you.'

'Yeah, like Dad does. Everyone's doing it to me lately, and I hate it. I feel so miserable, and I miss you so much. Please come home, Mum. *Please*.'

'Nikki, you're going to Norfolk next Monday . . .'

'Yeah, but what if I don't?'

'Then you can come here with Harry.'

'I don't want to come *there*. It's where Natalie died so I don't know why you want to be there either. It's sick.'

'Darling, how I deal with my grief is my business, and if it happens not to fit in with your ideas then I'm sorry, but . . .'

'Don't be nasty to me!' Nikki cried. 'I can't stand everyone being mean to me all the time. I told you I just had a row with Freddy and now you're making me feel even worse.'

'Well, you're not making me feel very good either,' Jessica told her. 'It's time you understood that I'm a person too, Nikki. I have feelings and they can be hurt just as easily as yours.'

'Oh Mum,' Nikki sobbed. 'I'm sorry. I didn't mean to hurt you. Everything I do is wrong. I'm just a waste of space . . .'

'Now you're feeling sorry for yourself, and though you might have cause it'll be more helpful if you stop crying and go and try to sort things out with Freddy.'

'I would if you were here, because you'd be able to tell me what to say.'

'I can do that on the phone, but I won't, because Freddy might have a point. Maybe you are too close to me and Dad, which I know is only to be expected after what we've been through, but you're going to be eighteen in ten days, darling. You have to start thinking for yourself . . .'

'Oh, like, so you don't ever ask Lilian for advice,' Nikki broke in hotly. 'Any time anything happens to you, you're straight on the phone to her, but when it comes to me needing a friend, you don't want to know.'

Wondering if it was the sun or her conscience that was making her feel light-headed now, Jessica said, 'That is absolutely not true, Nikki, and you know it. I love you in a way you won't even begin to understand until you have children yourself . . .'

'Then come home, Mum. *Please.*'

'No, darling. I'm sorry, but we both know that by the time I get there you'll very probably have made up with Freddy, and you won't need me any more. So I'm staying right where I am, and if you need to come here next week I'll ask Dad to book you a flight.'

'Well, thanks for nothing,' Nikki snapped, and the line went dead.

Clicking off her own phone Jessica put her hands to her flaming cheeks, still feeling shaken and angry, and unsure whether she'd been too harsh with Nikki. She knew it was the mention of Lilian that had made her lose touch with what she was saying, so maybe she should call Nikki back and try again. However, as she started to dial the number, she asked herself if it really wouldn't be better to let Nikki deal with this alone. After all, she couldn't keep stepping in to sort things out for her, whether it was with Freddy, or Charlie, or anyone else.

Having made the decision to step back she promptly continued to struggle with her conscience, hoping Nikki might ring again, whilst resisting the urge to call Charlie, which she knew Nikki would probably find unforgivable. It wasn't until she saw Luc coming up the steps towards her that she felt the tension starting to unravel at last, and by the time he was looking down into her eyes her own were soft with pleasure.

The afternoon passed in a haze of heat and laughter as they sauntered about Montmartre, looking at the art, talking to the oldest people they could find, and then finally visiting what used to be the Bateau-Lavoir. She hadn't really expected to find anything dramatic, or even very inspiring, for she knew the building where Picasso had given birth to Cubism, and where Jeanne and Modi had lived and worked for a while, had long ago been destroyed by fire. It disheartened her anyway to see that a small and unprepossessing plaque was all that now marked such an auspicious past. It left her with such a dispiriting sense of impermanence and irrelevance that Luc started to despair of breaking her out of it, until finally he suggested ice cream.

'If I'd known you were going to eat it like this,' he said, as she licked the spoon so suggestively, 'I would have booked an orchestra and sold tickets.'

She burst out laughing, and taking the spoon from him, she began to feed him, watching his mouth and wanting to kiss it so very, very much.

Next stop should have been across the river at Montparnasse, where Jeanne and Modigliani had lived until their tragic and untimely deaths, but since Luc wasn't prepared to risk another tumble into the bleakness of mortality, or to be cast as a poor, starving artist who suffered with typhoid, pleurisy and – on a good day – alcoholism, he insisted they return to the apartments because he hadn't showered since that morning, and in this heat and street grime he was feeling sorely in need.

'Besides which,' he added, as they started back, 'there should be something there for you by now, if the same-day delivery system is working.'

An hour later Jessica was perched on the sofa in Daniella's sitting room, a blaze of afternoon sunlight streaming in through the wide-open shutters along with the distant growl of traffic and chattering of passers-by three floors below. Luc had gone into his own apartment, leaving her alone to open the parcel they'd found with the concierge downstairs.

'Won't you come in while I open it?' she'd asked him at the front door.

'If I do it's doubtful I'll leave,' he told her sardonically.

It had been on the tip of her tongue to say, 'Maybe I don't want you to,' but somehow she hadn't.

Now, as she broke apart the shiny silver paper of the parcel and saw what was inside, she felt tears come to her eyes as she started to smile. It was a French edition of *Suite Française.* She lifted it to her cheek and felt the cool softness of the cover on her skin, then opening it she turned to the title page and saw that he'd written: *To Jessica, from Luc.* Underneath there was the date, followed by another number that didn't seem to have any relevance at first, until she realised it must relate to a page.

As she turned to it she was expecting to find the exchange between Lucile and her German that she and Luc had recited whilst in Issy-l'Evêque, but she soon discovered she was wrong. In fact there seemed to be nothing there at all that made any sense – until she noticed the very faintest pencil line under a small group of words near the bottom of the page. As she read them her heart seemed to fold in two, for she knew what she was reading was a misquote of Keats that might not have conveyed his message so well had Irène Némirovsky remembered the line correctly. What she had written was, *This thing of Beauty is a guilt for ever.*

She was just absorbing the words and their meaning, when she noticed a small card lodged inside the wrapping. Breaking open the envelope, she saw that he had written out the correct verse from Keats:

A thing of beauty is a joy for ever:
Its loveliness increases; it will never
Pass into nothingness; but still will keep
A bower quiet for us, and a sleep
Full of sweet dreams . . .

*

Later, instead of going to the restaurant he'd booked they strolled in the opposite direction to the crowds until they found a small, friendly-looking brasserie with old-fashioned coach lamps outside, and snug, private booths inside. Since there was no English translation of the menu and nothing but good wines on the *carte* they felt they'd chosen well, and when they were presented with a tasty selection of *amuse-bouches* they were convinced.

When the waiter finally went off with their order she looked across the table and said, 'Thank you for the book, and the poem.'

He held her gaze as he said, 'You know there's much more I want to say.'

She nodded, and looked down at her hands. Then, bringing her head up again, 'Would it be so very wrong for us to have one night together?'

He only continued to look at her, searching her eyes, until finally he said in a voice that sent tremors all the way through her, 'I want to make love to you like I've never wanted to make love to another woman in my life, but it goes much deeper than that and we both know it.'

Feeling the resonance, and truth, of his words she looked away. 'That's why we can't be together,' she said, her voice faltering. 'It'll mean too much.' She looked at him again. 'It'll be a guilt for ever.'

He nodded. 'If you didn't love Charlie . . .'

'And you didn't love Lilian . . . They don't deserve to be hurt, but do we deserve this? Neither of us asked for it to happen. It's not what we wanted . . .' At the note of anger that had crept into her voice they both started to smile.

'If you want me to take you home now, I will,' he said. 'I'll make love to you all night long, and all day tomorrow, but we both know it still won't be enough.'

'But if it's all we're going to have . . .' She stopped, so torn she barely knew what she was saying, except she wanted him so badly it seemed beyond her control.

His expression darkened as he watched her. 'The decision has to be yours,' he said in the end.

She knew he was right, because hers would be the greater

betrayal – her husband, her best friend, and even her children. 'If I thought it would be just one night,' she said, 'but it can't, can it? It's already more than that. Even sitting here now, having this conversation . . . Isn't this the greatest betrayal of all? Feeling the way we do?'

He didn't deny it, only said, 'I don't want to lie to you, or about you, to anyone.'

Understanding what he meant, she said, 'It's not what I want either. So maybe it has to be enough for us to know that if things were different . . . If there weren't other people to consider . . .'

'Then I promise you,' he said, a light of irony coming into his eyes, 'we really wouldn't be sitting here now.'

Charlie was checking his mobile for messages as he walked into the kitchen to find Nikki sending a text on hers.

'I thought you were making breakfast,' he said, sounding more irritable than he might have had Jessica bothered to return any of his calls in the past twenty-four hours.

'I am,' Nikki informed him chirpily, 'I just needed to let Freddy know that I definitely forgive him.'

'I thought you did that last night. You were out late enough.'

'Oh don't be such a grump, and pour yourself some coffee. It's already made.'

After filling a cup, Charlie cut two slices of bread and stuck them in the toaster. 'Have you spoken to Mum this morning?' he asked.

'No, not yet. She was in a bit of a weird mood when I spoke to her yesterday though, but I texted her later to tell her I forgive her too.'

'If you ask me she's always in a weird mood these days,' he grumbled, then he brightened a little as the landline started to ring. There was a good chance this would be her, since she often called early in the morning.

'Dad, it's me,' Harry sobbed. 'I want to come home and I can't find Mum. She's not answering her phone.'

'What's up, son?' Charlie said, moving Nikki aside so he could get to the fridge. 'I thought you were having a great time down there.'

'I was, but I had a fight with Kieran just now, and he made my nose bleed, and if he comes near me again I'm going to smash his face in.'

'What did you fight about?' Charlie asked.

'He said I was dumb trying to speak French just because I'm going there, and then he said I might end up dead too, like Natalie.'

Charlie took a breath. 'That wasn't a good thing for him to say,' he responded quietly. 'I think I'd better have a word with his mum.'

'She knows, and she's made him go to his room and he can't come out till he apologises, and she wants to speak to Mum to apologise too, but Mum's not answering her phone, so can she speak to you?'

'Of course. Put her on.'

After dealing with Esther Grant and agreeing that it would probably all be forgotten by lunchtime, Charlie spoke to Harry again, told him he'd come to collect him if he and Kieran hadn't made up by the end of the day, then after promising to get Jessica to call him, he rang off just as his mobile started to ring.

'Blimey, we're in demand this morning,' Nikki commented. 'I expect that'll be Mum.'

'It had better be,' Charlie said, going to pick it up, but seeing it wasn't her number his spirits sank again. 'Charlie Moore,' he said wearily.

'Are you near your computer?' his assistant asked. 'I need you to OK some emails I've drafted . . .'

'Mags, what are you doing at the office, it's not even half past eight . . .'

'I know, but I'm off to Spain this afternoon, *remember*, so I need to get everything done before I go.'

Sighing, he said, 'Yes, of course. Give me a moment, I'll go up to my study.'

Ten minutes later, having finished with Maggie he was sitting at his desk staring at nothing, thinking of Jessica, when he heard Nikki coming in behind him.

'Are you OK, Dad?' she asked.

'Yes, yes I'm fine,' he assured her, turning round.

'Your breakfast was going cold,' she told him, putting a

plate of sparsely buttered toast and a lukewarm coffee on his desk. 'I've just spoken to Mum. Apparently her phone ran out of battery. Anyway, she's going to call Harry straight away, but she'll call you later in the day, she said.'

Rubbing his hands over his face, he said, 'OK. Did she sound all right?'

'Yeah, fine. You know, normal.'

He picked up the coffee, then putting it down without drinking he said, 'So what did you mean when you said she sounded weird yesterday?'

Nikki shrugged. 'I don't know. I suppose she was like, just not her usual self . . . Well, I mean she was, but then she got a bit cross with me, which I probably deserved, but I was like really upset about Freddy, so I didn't need her having a go at me, which actually she didn't, really. She just said I had to try to sort things out for myself, so I did. You know, I think I probably do take her a bit for granted sometimes, but then she's my mother, so I would, wouldn't I?'

With a smile of exasperation Charlie pulled her into his arms. 'We probably all do,' he said, hugging her close, 'which is why it'll be good for her to have this time to herself. I miss her though, don't you?'

'Are you kidding? It's like really strange not having her around. I'm so glad I'm going to uni in London – I mean, if I get the right grades . . . You do think I will, don't you, Dad? Oh God, it'll be too awful if I don't.'

'I'm sure you will,' he told her gently, 'and we're going to find out very soon now . . .'

'But what if I don't?'

'We'll sort it out. Everyone knows what you were going through when you sat your exams . . .'

Nikki's head came up to look at him, and seeing her eyes were full of tears he smoothed a hand over her face.

'I miss Nat so much, Dad,' she said shakily.

'I know,' he whispered.

'Do you think she's safe, wherever she is?'

'Of course. In fact, she's probably watching us right now, thinking what chumps we're making of ourselves for worrying about her.'

Nikki smiled through her tears. 'Mum worries about her all the time,' she said. Then her face crumpled again. 'Oh Dad, I said a really terrible thing to Mum yesterday. I told her she was sick for being over there, in the place where Natalie died. I know I really hurt her feelings when I said that, and I didn't mean it, but honestly, Dad, I don't know if it's normal, do you, for her to want to be there? I mean, I know she wanted space after that thing between you two, and it's Lilian's home and those two have always been close, but Lilian isn't there . . .'

'Darling, you're as bad as she is,' he scolded lovingly. 'You think too much, tie yourself up in knots and never really come up with an answer – but don't tell her I said that.'

Nikki gave a snort of laughter, then looked at the phone as it started to ring.

'This'll be her,' Charlie said decisively, and scooping up the receiver he used his warmest voice to answer in a way he knew made Jessica smile. 'The Moore residence, number one slave speaking.'

'Charlie,' Veronica slurred. 'Charlie. I want to speak to you.'

'Veronica? Are you all right?'

'Yes. I need to know . . . Have you shown Jessica my letter? I want you to show her my letter.'

Gently letting Nikki go, Charlie said, 'Not yet, I . . .'

'But you must. Please, she has to see it . . .'

'Veronica, are you sure you're all right? Is Maurice there?'

'Yes. He's right next to me. He said I could call. Charlie, please . . .'

'Can you put Maurice on?'

A moment later Maurice's voice came down the line saying, 'Charlie?'

'Yes, I'm here. Is she drunk? It's so early in the morning . . .'

'She's not drunk,' Maurice cut in, his voice low and firm. 'We're leaving Capri today to come back to England . . .'

Charlie started to ask why, but Maurice was still speaking.

'I'm not going to beat about the bush any longer,' he said. 'We need to talk, so we can either do it now, on the phone, or we can meet. I'll let you choose.'

Charlie's face had turned very pale. 'I'll be at my office in just over an hour,' he said, turning away from Nikki. 'I'll call you then to set up a time for us to meet.'

Chapter Nineteen

It was late on Wednesday afternoon when Luc and Jessica drove into Valennes. He'd spoken to his father during the drive, so the clouds gathering overhead and undecided wind stirring the vines came as no surprise. Nor, for the moment, was anyone unduly worried about the grapes, as the forecast had mentioned nothing about hail, or even prolonged rain.

'We sprayed at the end of July,' Luc told her, pausing at the top of the hill to allow a lorry to come through, 'so provided the *météo* is correct, there will be no threat to the harvest, and tomorrow, so they say, the sun will return.'

Jessica was about to respond when the lorry driver pulled alongside them and wound down his window. Since he spoke in Italian she couldn't understand what he was saying, until Luc thanked him and closing his own window, said, 'He's just made a delivery from the foundry.'

Jessica turned to him in surprise. 'Does that mean a new sculpture has arrived?' she asked.

He shot her a glance, then steering the car into the vineyard he said, 'It's of Lilian.'

At the mention of Lilian's name the light in her eyes dimmed – with guilt, and with a jealousy that made her feel more wretched than ever. She tried to shut it from her mind, to pretend it wasn't real, and thought instead of last night, and how hard it had been to say goodbye to him at the door of Daniella's apartment. They had come so close, so very close to kissing, but somehow she'd made herself turn away, all the time wanting him to pull her back, to persuade her that just one night would be acceptable, as long as no-one ever found out. It hadn't happened though, he'd let her go, which had made her realise how very much he loved Lilian, for he had the will power to stop himself betraying her. She could only feel ashamed of how willing she would have been, had he given her just one sign.

Bringing the car to a stop outside the cottage, he kept the engine running and sat staring straight ahead.

Several seconds ticked by. There was too much to say, and yet no amount of words was going to change the fact that Lilian would be back on Friday, and then this affair – how could she even call it that? – would be over.

'I should go in,' she said. 'I have to ring the children, and I expect you have things to do too.'

'Yes,' he answered.

But still neither of them moved.

'I'm sure my father will be expecting us for dinner,' he said in the end. 'Why don't you come early and I'll show you your sculpture? You still haven't seen it.'

She nodded, then getting out of the car, she took her overnight bag from the back seat and walked across the patio to the door. Not until she was inside did she hear him drive away, and as her head fell forward into her hands she could only feel confounded by the sheer futility and frustration of what was happening between them. Why couldn't she be like the millions of others who were able to take what they wanted and still find it possible to live with themselves? God knew, she wanted it badly enough . . .

After unpacking the few things she'd taken with her, she showered and dressed for dinner, then went downstairs to ring Charlie. It was the strangest thing, she reflected as she picked up her mobile, to find herself so full of love for him now, when in her heart she was betraying him. Suddenly she wished he would come now, tonight, or tomorrow, and make her realise how foolish she was being, show her what really mattered in her life, which was him and Nikki and Harry.

She had barely begun dialling when her phone started to ring. Seeing it was the *manoir* she clicked on and said a quiet hello.

'Jessica. It's Fernand. I hope I am not interrupting.'

'No, not at all,' she assured him, feeling suddenly anxious

that he was going to talk to her about Lilian and friendship and loyalty, and all the things he must be so worried about, for he was far from stupid, he must know she'd been in Paris with Luc.

'That is good,' he was saying. 'I believe you will join us for dinner, but Luc thought you would want this number that I have been given by my friend, the brother of the *Chef des Pompiers*. It is for the paramedic who has broken his leg. He is still in the hospital, but you can call him tomorrow morning between eleven and twelve. Also, I have received a fax copy of his report, which I will give to you when you come to the house.'

Jessica's heart was contracting as she reached for a pen. 'Thank you,' she said. 'Can you tell me, is there anything in the report that . . .? Does he say that he carried Natalie to the sofa?'

'No, but that might be because officially he should not have done it, so he wouldn't want his superiors to know.'

'Of course. OK, I'll take down the number.'

A few minutes later she was still staring at the ten digits she'd noted, trying to imagine what had happened here that morning, how desperate it must all have been, when her mobile rang again.

'Jessica! It's me. How are you?'

At the sound of Lilian's cheery voice she felt such a conflict of emotions that it was hard to keep her voice normal as she said, 'I'm fine. How are you? *Where* are you?'

'In Mumbai – my God, it's a zoo here! But so exciting. We'll have to come together one of these days. Anyway, I should be back in Paris around midday tomorrow. Unfortunately I'll have to go to the office, so I'll overnight at the apartment, then on Friday I'll be *home*. I can hardly wait, and knowing you're going to be there too . . . Is the weather still good?'

'There's going to be some rain tonight, apparently, but it's been so hot.'

There was a note of concern in Lilian's voice as she said, 'You sound tired. Are you all right? Or is it just the heat?'

Wondering how on earth she was ever going to hide anything from Lilian, when even over the phone she was able to detect her moods, she said, 'Fernand's just given me a number for the paramedic, which is making me feel a bit shaky again. I'm going to speak to him tomorrow.'

Lilian's silence was very brief, but it was long enough for Jessica to feel the disappointment, and to think of how much easier she found it to discuss this with Luc. He never seemed to disapprove, or even sound doubtful, in fact he appeared to have a far greater understanding than those closest to her of why she had to see this through.

'I'm sorry you still haven't resolved this in your mind yet,' Lilian said gently, 'but you will, I'm sure.'

Needing to change the subject Jessica said, 'Tell me more about Mumbai. How's the takeover going?'

Lilian's laugh sounded slightly forced, but she answered the question lightly enough as she said, 'Actually, I've been in meetings almost since the moment I got off the plane, and I'm ever-hopeful that something will be signed before I leave. I have to tell you that Vasu, the owner of the saleroom in question, is such a charmer I could fall madly in love with him, were I not a happily married woman, and he was twenty, or maybe even ten years younger. Anyway, as gorgeous and accommodating as he appears, he's definitely no pushover, but I'm pretty sure it'll come off, and we're already planning a sale for September . . . Oh hang on a sec.' She went off the line leaving Jessica with her senses swimming, and her heart trying to cope with all the emotions crowding into it. Seconds later Lilian was back saying, 'So tell me, have you managed to persuade Charlie to join us at Valennes? Luc says Harry's coming on Monday, which is great, but it would be wonderful if Charlie came too.'

'He's booked a flight for Wednesday.'

'Oh, that's fantastic. We're going to have such a wonderful time, all of us. I feel so in need of a break, and I think Luc does too. Which reminds me, Fernand told me your sculpture's finished and it's *ravissante*.'

Jessica took a breath. 'Did Luc tell you that yours arrived from the foundry today?' she asked.

'Yes, but he hasn't opened it yet. He says he wants to wait until we can do it together.' She laughed happily. 'He's such a romantic at times. I just hope it continues when I finally chuck in my job and become a full-time wife.'

'Do you have any plans to do that soon?' Jessica asked, the words seeming to echo in her head.

Lilian laughed again. 'Maybe,' she replied. 'Oh hang on, someone's just come in again.'

As Jessica waited she could only thank God that things hadn't gone as far as they might have with Luc, for she felt certain now that she'd never have been able to face Lilian again if they had.

'Hi, are you still there?' Lilian said.

'Yes.'

'Listen, I'm bound to be interrupted again, so I should probably go. I just wanted to catch up with you before I leave here in case there's anything you'd like me to bring back. The jewellery is fantastic and I can easily send one of the staff out to get some. In fact, I'll make time to go myself and choose something for you . . .'

Jessica started to protest.

'. . . and now I'm loving you and leaving you,' Lilian said over her. 'With any luck I'll see you in time for lunch on Friday.'

After she'd rung off Jessica stood staring at the swirling clouds outside, feeling almost as though she was being carried along with them as she imagined Lilian over there in Mumbai, Luc up at the house and Charlie preparing to go into the studio. On the grand scale of things, what was happening to them was so unimportant, irrelevant even, for the truth was, no matter whether she slept with Luc and Lilian found out, or even if Charlie decided to leave her because of it, the world would continue to turn. Nothing would change – she'd learned that when Natalie died. It made no difference to the world. It simply continued to go on in the same impervious way, and even if she discovered the paramedic hadn't carried Natalie to the sofa, and someone else had been here that day, it still wouldn't bring Natalie back. And in her heart that was all she wanted. For that she'd give up everything, anything, but that was something else she'd learned when Natalie went, there were no bargains to be made, or discussions to be had. There was only a cruel reality followed by an emptiness that nothing would ever be able to fill, no amount of love, or happiness, self-sacrifice or even pain. It would always be there, because Natalie no longer was.

So was there really any point in continuing to deny her feelings for Luc, in trying to pretend that she hadn't fallen in love with him when she knew she had? No matter what she did, or didn't do, the world would keep turning, life would go on and one day, not so very distant from now, they'd all be gone and forgotten anyway.

'Do you have anything at all to say?' Luc prompted, breaking the silence. He was standing against a workbench, arms folded, one leg crossed over the other as he watched Jessica looking at the sculpture.

Her gaze remained where it was, taking in her own features in a way that felt almost surreal. Though it was unquestionably her, there seemed to be another dimension to her features now. Her eyes, in fact her whole expression seemed more haunting, even ethereal, yet alluring and perhaps even seductive. She shook her head. 'What have you done?' she asked. 'It's different. It's . . . It's . . .' She glanced at him, and seeing the laughter in his eyes she began smiling too. It was extraordinary the way everything seemed to be all right now she was with him, when less than an hour ago she'd felt so bleak.

'You're making this impossible,' she chided. 'If I tell you how beautiful it is, it's like saying it about myself, but it is, and I don't think it's down to me . . . It's down to you. So what have you done?'

His expression was droll as he said, 'I saw a look in your eyes while we were at the lake, and again while we were in the vines, that I think, I hope, is what you are seeing now. A woman who is radiant in her beauty, brazenly seductive in her charm, and fully trusting of the man who is watching her. It was an epiphany for me.'

She couldn't help but laugh. 'Not only trusting,' she murmured, looking at the sculpture again. Those moments at the lake and amongst the vines felt almost like a dream now, or a game, where they'd teased one another, showing their attraction, even their desire, with no real understanding yet of what it was going to mean. She couldn't help thinking of how different it would be if she were naked with him now, right here in his studio, with rain pattering on the skylights and the scent of damp earth seasoning the air . . .

'I have something to say to you,' he told her.

She turned to look at him, a nervousness breaking through inside her. His gaze was so intense it almost seemed to take hold of her, and she wondered if it was his eyes that made her feel the way she did. But as magnetic as they were, she knew it was only one small part of what drew her to him.

'Luc, tu es là? Ton portable n'arrête pas de sonner,' Fernand told him, coming into the studio. 'Ah, Jessica, *tu es là aussi.'*

Taking the phone from him, Luc turned it off and watched as his father went to Jessica, arms open wide. 'The sculpture is *magnifique, non*?' he declared, embracing her. *'Elle est vraiment superbe.'*

Jessica's eyes were shining. 'It's beautiful,' she agreed, smiling up into his face. If he knew, or sensed, what was happening between her and Luc he was hiding it well, and appeared neither disapproving nor censorious, for which she could only feel thankful.

'I think it is one of his very best,' Fernand decided, standing back to admire the sculpture again. 'And once it is in bronze, it will be truly *exceptionel.'*

Jessica looked at Luc and wondered if the sculpture, once cast, was still intended for Charlie. Neither of them had ever mentioned it, but of course Lilian would remember, so it would have to be Charlie's. It didn't feel right, when it had been created by a man who had captured so much more of her than her likeness, but it would be impossible to explain why it should stay here, so perhaps Luc would keep the drawing for himself. It was what she wanted, and felt certain he did too.

'I must return to the kitchen,' Fernand informed them. 'Yves, Claude's brother, has some friends staying at the chateau – I think one of them is a young lady of much interest to him,' he added with a romantic twinkle, 'so they are all coming over to eat. It will be much different under the pergola this evening with all the rain, *non*? Ah, but it is beautiful to see.'

After Fernand had gone, Luc and Jessica looked at one another again, and seeing his expression she felt another tremor of unease.

'Tomorrow my father has a *Chevaliers* dinner at Vougeot,' he told her. 'He won't return until Friday morning. It will be our last opportunity to spend a night together. You know how much I want to be with you, but if you would like to take some time to think, I will . . .'

'I don't need any time,' she said.

His eyes darkened, and for a moment it seemed he might come to her then, but in the end he stayed where he was and they both smiled with relief to know that at last they had accepted the inevitable.

Chapter Twenty

The next morning, following torrential downpours through the night, everything looked as fresh and vivid as a newly painted Gauguin. The sun sparkled on the vines, while the damp earth seemed to breathe a gentle sigh of relief. Overhead there were only a few lingering clouds floating around like small clusters of foam on a sea of blue, while the air was perfumed with the scent of the vines and their soil, mixed with the wet stone of the cottage and all the clinging flowers on their trestles and wires.

As Jessica walked over to her car she was feeling both exhilarated and anxious, thinking of Luc and their plans for later, and of the call she needed to make to the paramedic this morning. She would deal with each event as it came – for now she was only going to concern herself with the market and what she wanted to buy when she got there.

She'd just put her basket on the back seat when she heard the sound of a vehicle coming down from the house, and turning saw the vineyard *camionette* bumping over the potholes towards her. Presuming it was Jean-Marc, she was about to wave when to her surprise she saw Luc at the wheel, with Jean-Marc beside him.

She waited as he brought the van to a stop, and started to smile as he got out.

'Ça va?' he asked as he came to her.

'Oui. Et toi?'

He nodded, and knowing what he was thinking as he continued to look at her, she felt tiny frissons of desire moving all the way through her.

'I was just off to the market,' she told him. 'I thought I'd make dinner for us this evening. Where are you going?'

'The rain was much harder in other parts of the region, so we need to make a check on the *parcelles.* I should be back around . . .' He was about to look at his watch when they both noticed a car turning from the top road into the valley.

She glanced back at him in surprise as he muttered under his breath.

'It is the German couple who have rented one of the other cottages,' he explained. 'Clearly they have returned from the Loire.'

Hearing that made her heart turn over. 'Does that mean we . . .? Will that make it impossible tonight?' she said.

'No, of course not,' he replied, and with a wryness to his tone he added, 'I have to admit, however, it might have been better if they'd waited another day to come back, *mais, c'est la vie.*' He waved as the Germans pulled into the space reserved for the other cottages, then turning back to Jessica he said, 'My father will be leaving around three. I hope to be back by then.'

'OK. Is there anything in particular you'd like to eat?'

'Whatever you choose will be fine for me.' Then after a brief moment, 'I should go now.'

As she watched him walk back to the *camionette,* she was remembering him at the lake, how beautiful he was naked, and how powerful his desire had been when he'd come back towards her. Knowing she would see him like that again later, and feel him in every way possible, started such a turmoil of longing inside her that it was only as he turned and cocked a humorous eyebrow in her direction, as though knowing what she was thinking, that she was able to let the intensity go with a laugh.

By ten o'clock she was back from the market with a basket full of fresh fish, locally grown salad and fruit, baguettes still warm from the oven, and two bottles of Bâtard-Montrachet *grand cru* that had cost almost a hundred euros each. She'd bought candles too, and pink, starburst lilies which she arranged in a vase to set down on the kitchen table, not only so their wonderful scent could start filling the house, but as a centrepiece. Now the Germans were back it wouldn't be possible for them to eat outside.

After preparing the fish, she began to wash the salad, then noticing a small grey dove pecking around on the wall outside she went to watch it. A moment later it fluttered over to perch on the flower box in front of the kitchen window. Not wanting to scare it, she remained very still watching it inspect the earth and geraniums, then to her surprise it raised its head and seemed to look right at her. She looked back and for a while neither of them moved. Then, very gingerly, she reached for a baguette, broke off a few crumbs and putting them on her palm she held them out. Almost immediately the dove flew away, but after a minute or two it returned to the wall and watched, hesitantly, as she dropped the crumbs into the window box. A few seconds later it came to gather them up.

Delighted, she was about to feed it some more when her phone started to ring. Immediately fearing it would be Charlie or Lilian she was tempted not to answer, since she knew her conscience would put an end to everything if she spoke to either of them today. However, to her relief, she saw it was Luc and quickly clicked on.

'Am I interrupting?' he asked.

'Well, as a matter of fact,' she replied, 'I was busy making friends with a dove. Would you believe, it's almost eating out of my hand.'

He laughed. 'Yes, I would believe,' he told her, 'because it's probably Solange. The twins – and Natalie – found her at Easter. She was injured so we took her to the vet, and she stayed at the cottage with your mother and Natalie until the twins took her to the chateau. She's been there ever since, but every now and again she comes back to Valennes.'

Jessica was smiling. 'Well, she chose a good day for her return,' she declared, watching the dove flit back over to the wall. 'She's very pretty. You say her name's Solange?'

'You know how the twins love to name everything.'

She did indeed, but realising he hadn't called to discuss that, she said, 'Is everything all right with you? No problems at the other plots, I hope.'

'None so far. I was just thinking about you, and wanted to hear your voice.'

Feeling her heart swell, she said, 'Funny because I wanted to hear yours too.'

'No second thoughts about tonight?'

'None at all.'

'That's good.' Then after a pause, 'It's almost time for you to call the paramedic.'

As anxiety returned to her heart, she said, 'Yes. I know.'

With a reassuring warmth, he said, 'It'll be all right. I'm sure no-one else was there. As my father told you, the paramedic probably wouldn't have put the truth in his report if it could get him into trouble.'

'But I have to be certain. You do understand that, don't you?'

'Of course. Call me after you've spoken to him?'

She smiled, loving his concern, and after assuring him she would, she rang off.

At ten past eleven she sat down at the table and holding the paramedic's number in one hand, she began dialling with the other. Her insides were in a tumult of dread and hope and no little fear, because if the paramedic hadn't been the one to carry Natalie to the sofa . . . But of course he had. It could only have been him, so she must stop putting herself through this unnecessary strain and remember that her instincts hadn't served her correctly over the autopsy report, so there was every chance they were about to let her down again.

A muffled voice answered after the third ring, saying, *'Oui? Qui est là?'*

In French Jessica said, 'This is Madame Moore, Natalie Moore's mother. Is that Monsieur Lemoine?'

'Vous voulez mon frère,' the voice told her.

A moment later another, slightly clearer voice said, in French, 'Stefan Lemoine speaking. I was told to expect your call.'

'I hope you don't mind, when you're . . .'

'No, no, not at all,' he assured her. 'I am happy to be of help in any way I can. Did you see my report? I think someone was going to fax you a copy.'

'Yes, I have it,' she said. 'Thank you. It's very clear, but I was wondering . . .' She took a breath. 'What I'd really like to know, when you arrived at the cottage . . . You were the first here?'

'With my colleagues, yes.'

'And was my daughter . . . Did you find her . . . I know you say she was on the sofa, but I need to know, was it you who carried her there?'

There was a moment's hesitation before, sounding slightly baffled, he said, 'No, Madame. It was as I say in my report. She was lying on the sofa when we arrived.'

Jessica swallowed hard as her heart turned over. 'I understand that it might be against regulations if you were to move her,' she said, 'but if you did, I only want to thank you for your kindness in not leaving her on the floor.'

She heard him inhale, then in a gentle but firm voice he said, 'It is true, Madame, I might have broken the rules and moved her if I had found her on the floor and realised there was no more we could do, but my report is accurate. She was on the sofa when we arrived.'

Jessica's eyes closed as she took a moment to collect herself. 'Do you have any idea how she might have got there?' she asked. 'Did you see anyone else, besides my mother?'

'No, only your mother,' he answered. 'I assumed she had moved your daughter, but I think from what you are saying, that maybe she did not?'

'No, she didn't. Apart from anything else she wouldn't have had the strength.'

There was a brief silence at the end of the line before he said, 'I'm afraid that wasn't something I considered at the time. She was the only one there, so I came to my own conclusions. Are you sure it wasn't her?'

'Yes,' she replied, and pressing a hand to her head she tried to think what to say next. 'Monsieur Lemoine, you've been very kind speaking to me like this, but would you mind if we went over it again? It's very important I get it right.'

'But of course. I have plenty of time.'

He was every bit as patient and polite the second time around as he'd been the first, answering everything she put to him as clearly and accurately as he could, so that by the time they'd finished there really could be no doubt in her mind – he was telling the truth.

After thanking him and wishing him a speedy recovery, she clicked off the line and sat for a long time staring at nothing. Oddly she felt none of the anger, or even outrage, she might have expected, only a profound sense of having finally come within sight of a truth she'd always known was there. Of course she still had to find out what it was, and for that she needed to speak to her mother again, but first, because she'd said she would, she rang Luc.

He listened quietly as she told him about the call, not interrupting at all, until finally he said, 'You're absolutely certain your mother said the paramedic carried her there?'

'Yes,' she replied. 'I admit she was flustered at the time, but one thing was clear, she hadn't taken Natalie there herself. How could she? You've seen how tiny she is.'

'This isn't at all what we expected,' he murmured. 'Would you like me to come back? I could be there in an hour.'

'No, it's fine,' she assured him. 'You need to finish what you're doing, and I don't know yet whether I'll be able to get hold of my mother. As you must have gathered by now, she can be very elusive when it suits her.'

'*D'accord*. Call if you need me.'

After ringing off she searched for Maurice's number in Capri, then pressed it into her mobile. Her hands were slightly shaky, but she was still experiencing no rage, or recriminations, only a steely determination now to get to the truth.

Though it was a disappointment when the phone rang and rang at the other end, it was no real surprise, nor was it when the machine picked up at her mother's Oxfordshire home. Feeling certain a sixth sense was warning Veronica, she decided not to leave a message, instead she called Charlie. Since he was on air now, she went through to his voicemail, told him she needed to speak to him urgently, and after ringing off she went to sit at the bottom of the stairs, where she always seemed to go when she needed to feel closer to Natalie. And right now, it was the only place she wanted to be.

*

Charlie received Jessica's message when he returned to his dressing room during a break in transmission. The instant he heard the tone of her voice he knew, without being told, that the first part of the truth was finally starting to emerge through the cracks in its cover.

Accepting there was no point putting it off, he turned the key to stop anyone popping in, then going to stand at the window he dialled Jessica's number.

She answered almost straight away.

'What is it?' he asked, watching the traffic stop and start below. 'You sounded upset.'

'Yes, I suppose I am,' she responded, 'though I wasn't aware I'd sounded it, but right now I'm much more interested in getting hold of my mother. I've tried the number in Capri. Once again, no reply. Do you know if she's still there?'

'Actually, I believe they left yesterday, so they're probably at Maurice's by now, in Kent. Why? What's happened?'

'What's happened,' she said, 'is that I've just spoken to the paramedic who was first here the day Natalie died. He says she was already on the sofa when he arrived. He didn't carry her there, and nor, apparently, did my mother, so I want to know who did.'

Charlie could feel the blood leaving his face. 'Jessica,' he said, in a voice that was so strangled he could hardly get the word out.

'I'm sorry, darling,' she said gently, 'I know how difficult this is for you. You never wanted to believe there was anything else . . . Nor did I, but please accept, we owe it to Natalie to find out the truth. Surely you agree with that now.'

Taking a breath, Charlie pressed his fingers into the sockets of his eyes as he tried to think. 'Maurice has asked to see me,' he told her. 'We've arranged to meet on Tuesday, but I can call again now to see if he can make it any sooner.'

'It's my mother we need to speak to,' she reminded him.

'I realise that, but let me speak to him. I think, well . . . I'll get onto him now and call you straight back.'

A few minutes later, after receiving no reply from Maurice's number in Kent, he rang Jessica again. 'There's no-one there,' he told her. 'I'll have to try tomorrow, it'll be too late by the time I come off air.'

'Why? You're due to finish at six.'

'I'm doing an extra shift. Holiday cover.'

'Oh, I see, but I want some answers, Charlie . . .'

'No-one's home, what am I supposed to do?'

'I'm just saying, someone around here is lying, and I don't think it's the paramedic. Do you?'

'How do I know, I didn't speak to him.'

He flinched as she said, 'Charlie! You accuse me of being in denial, but just listen to yourself. Why on earth do you think a paramedic, who's never met my mother before, would lie?'

'To save his job, why else?' he countered.

'Then please take it from me, that's not the case. Someone carried Natalie to that sofa and I want to know who it was.'

'I wonder if it's even occurred to you that there might be a perfectly reasonable explanation.'

'If there is, then please tell me what it might be, because right now I can't think of a single one.'

Realising they were already far too close to dangerous territory, he said, 'I'm sorry, I can't have this conversation now. I'm due back in the studio any minute, so I'll ring them again tomorrow, OK? And as soon as I have anything to report, I'll call you.'

With a sigh of acceptance, she said, 'OK.' Then, after a moment, 'I guess there's no rush, because nothing's going to bring her back, is it?'

'Oh, Jessica, please don't get emotional on me now. It's really not a good time . . .'

'Goodbye,' she said, cutting him off. 'I'll talk to you tomorrow.'

Before he could respond the line went dead, leaving him regretting just about everything he'd said throughout the entire call. Since he had no time to deal with any of it now, he used a towel to wipe the sweat from his face before heading to make-up, to have at least some of his colour restored.

After putting the phone down to Charlie, Jessica blinked back the tears that had come to her eyes, and went to make herself some tea. She wasn't feeling angry, exactly, just let down and resentful that Charlie had responded the way he had, for she'd truly expected him to give her more support once he knew what the paramedic had said. To her mind his irritability showed that he was still trying to avoid being pushed headlong into the pain of Natalie's death – and as for there being any kind of mystery or complications attached to it, clearly that was something he couldn't deal with at all.

Shuddering to think of how he was going to be once he finally did confront his loss – which would obviously be never if he could help it – she decided to try and put it out of her mind for now, since there was very little she could do without speaking to her mother. Or until Charlie had met up with Maurice.

Thinking of Maurice she wondered, not for the first time, if he might have been here that morning, but as usual she almost instantly dismissed the idea. The man they'd always euphemistically called her mother's lawyer – though indeed he had been a very prominent solicitor before his retirement – had been in Veronica's life for so many years now – though on and off, as most things were with her mother – that Jessica simply couldn't see him as anything other than the devoted, gentle and extremely caring man she'd always known. He'd never married, because he'd never been able to persuade the elusive Veronica to become his wife, but he'd always been there, loving her anyway quietly and undemandingly, and try as she might, Jessica couldn't think of a single reason for them to hide the fact that he'd been here that day – if he had. If anything, it would have been much more in his character to step forward right away to make clear what had happened, and even take charge in his understated, lawyerly way.

So no, she couldn't suspect Maurice of anything underhand, though she had to admit he did appear to be shielding her mother now, which must surely mean Veronica had told him the truth of what had happened.

'Yes, that does seem to make sense,' Fernand agreed, when she wandered up to the *manoir* to join him for lunch. 'And you say Charlie has arranged to see him?'

'Apparently they're meeting on Tuesday, but Charlie's

going to try to make it sooner – once he manages to get hold of him. I'm afraid Maurice and my mother have never been ones for mobile phones.'

'Now that I understand, because I have no fondness for them either,' Fernand confessed, while helping himself to a forkful of tasty grilled sardines. 'Luc and Daniella insist I have one, of course, but I'm afraid they're very bossy when it comes to their father.'

Jessica smiled at him fondly. 'I'm sure if I had a father like you I'd be equally as protective,' she told him.

Seeming to like the compliment he saluted her with his glass and said, 'Is your father still alive?'

Jessica's expression became wry as she said, 'I'm afraid I've no idea. My mother's never told me who he is, and I gave up asking a long time ago.'

'Oh là là,' he murmured regretfully, 'that is a very great pity.'

She shrugged. 'It doesn't really matter any more. Actually, I always used to hope it was Maurice, but apparently he didn't meet my mother until I was almost three. I think he might have financed a few things along the way for me though, like my education and helping my grandparents out – I can't imagine where else my mother might have got the money.'

'From the little your mother told me while she was here, I believe you could be right. He's obviously been a very good friend to her over the years.'

'Mm, perhaps too good if he's helping her to cover something up now.'

Fernand nodded pensively and sipped his wine. 'I am sure the answers are going to come out very soon,' he told her, staring down at his glass. 'I think they must.'

She looked at him curiously, experiencing a small beat of unease, for there had been something about his tone that was making her wonder if he might actually know more than he'd ever told.

When she asked him he shook his head for a long time, as though no more certain about his suspicions than he was about sharing them. 'I have never lied to you, *ma chère,*' he said in the end. 'I truly don't know what happened down at the cottage that morning – as you know, I wasn't even here – but I will tell you this, I am glad you have come to find the truth, because like you, I have often thought there was more. It is why I have helped you as much as I can. Like Luc, I believe in your instincts. Perhaps his reasons for helping you go a little deeper than mine, but that is a subject we will leave alone.'

Jessica swallowed and looked down at his old hand, lying on the table between them. Without really thinking about it she covered it with her own and gave it a gentle squeeze. 'Thank you,' she whispered, 'for believing in me, and for not judging me, at least not as harshly as I deserve to be judged, or as I've been judging myself.'

His watery old eyes came up to hers. 'I wouldn't have chosen this for you, or my son,' he told her, 'but nor would you have chosen it for yourselves. All I can tell you is that it will pass. It will take time, and I don't think it will be easy, but in the end I know you will both do the right thing, by those you love, and by one another.'

Relieved he didn't know about their plans for tonight, Jessica nodded, but her voice was constricted as she said, 'Yes, we will. That much I can promise you.'

He smiled and turned his hand to hold hers. 'It is almost time for me to leave,' he said. 'It is a long drive, and I am instructed by Luc and Daniella that I must go very slowly these days. Not very French, huh?'

She twinkled. 'Not very,' she agreed.

As they got to their feet a phone inside the house started to ring. 'Maybe one of these days we'll talk again,' he said, embracing her, 'but for now, I think that is probably my son or my daughter trying to reach my mobile.'

It was just after three when Fernand went by in the Mercedes, giving a jaunty little hoot on the horn. Jessica waved from where she was sitting beneath the parasol on the patio, with her laptop open as she worked on the first few pages of her book.

She wasn't really expecting to make much headway, but she was trying anyway, for she needed to focus her mind away from the call to the paramedic, and from her conscience, which she could sense, like a growing shadow in the wings, ready to burst into the centre of the stage. Until now she'd felt convinced she'd be able to go through with tonight, but as the minutes and hours ticked by, she was becoming more and more concerned about how difficult it could be in the days to come. Lilian would be back as soon as midday tomorrow, only hours after her best friend and husband had emerged from the same bed. Even to think it burned her with shame, yet, a moment later, the thought of never knowing what it would be like to hold him, to feel his kiss on her mouth and his body claiming hers, was more than she could bear.

Becoming exasperated with her own agitation she took herself inside, hoping the cooler air might help to clear her mind.

By four she was fully controlled by her conscience, so had no more doubts about what she was going to do. She'd serve dinner outside, where the Germans could see them, then she'd explain why she'd changed her mind about making love. She knew he'd be as disappointed as she was, but perhaps, in his heart, he'd be relieved. They'd come this far without committing the ultimate betrayal, so it would surely be madness to make it so much more difficult for themselves now.

The next time she looked at her watch it was almost five. He should have been back by now, but there was still no sign of him, and nor had he called. Suddenly certain something had happened to him, she grabbed her phone and pressed in his number.

His mobile was out of action.

'Oh my God,' she murmured, clasping a hand to her head. She was seeing so many horrifying images now, dreading that fate had gone to these lengths just to keep them apart, that it was a while before she realised the *camionette* had pulled up outside. Even when she saw him coming across the patio she still couldn't quite believe it.

'I thought you'd had an accident,' she cried, meeting him at the door. Had they not been in full view of Jean-Marc she'd have flung her arms around him, but they were, so she stood aside for him to come in. 'Are you all right?' she asked. 'Why weren't you answering your phone?'

'The battery ran out,' he replied, taking it from his pocket and tossing it on the table. 'Of course there wouldn't have been a problem if I'd remembered to take a charger, or Jean-Marc hadn't forgotten his . . . Then we had a flat tyre, then we were surrounded by *cows*. I thought I was never going to get here.'

She started to laugh, as much with relief as at the image of him surrounded by cattle. 'You look very cross,' she told him. 'I hope you didn't scare the cows.'

His smile was only fleeting and didn't quite reach his eyes.

'Luc?' she said, taking a step back to look at him. 'You're really angry.'

As he turned away she walked round in front of him, and fear gripped her as she saw so much anguish in his eyes. 'Tell me what happened,' she insisted. 'Something obviously did.'

'Nothing's happened,' he said, 'except this! Us! The craziness of what we're doing.'

Her heart seemed to stop. 'Are you saying . . .? Do you mean . . .?' She couldn't bring herself to utter the words. After so much soul-searching and wrangling with her conscience, to be faced with the prospect of him not wanting to go through with it was now making her desire him more than ever.

'What I'm saying,' he growled, 'is that tonight should be a beginning for us, not an end. But it can't be, and we're fooling ourselves if we think one night is going to be enough, because the way I feel about you . . .' He stopped abruptly. 'I'm sorry, I can't do this.' Turning away, he started for the door.

'Luc, wait,' she cried, going after him.

'I'll be back for dinner,' he said, 'but I need to calm down before I start saying things we'll both regret.'

As he strode across the patio towards the van she watched him helplessly, understanding his frustration, even sharing it, but there was nothing she could do with Jean-Marc there, so she turned back inside. Seeing his phone on the table, she almost threw it across the room in despair. She couldn't make this any better. God knew, she wanted to, but how could she change the fact that they were both married to other people, or somehow magic their guilt away so they could at least have this one night in peace? There seemed little point to it if they were going to tear themselves apart like this, so when the phone rang a few minutes later and his voice came down the line she heard herself saying, 'You're right, this is crazy, so I think it would be better if you didn't come for dinner . . .'

'Jessica, listen,' he interrupted.

'No, it'll be easier this way. Please don't . . .'

'Jessica, listen to me,' he said forcefully. 'I'm sorry about just now. I shouldn't have taken my anger out on you . . .'

'But you were right . . .'

'No, I was wrong, and it wouldn't have happened if it weren't for the cows.'

She drew breath, then blinked, not sure she'd heard right.

There was irony in his voice as he said, 'As I sat there, surrounded by cows, unable to get to you, even by phone, I found myself wanting to ram the van into every one of them, bulldoze them out of the way, even kill them if I had to, and then I realised it was what I wanted to do to everything that is standing between us.'

'And you think I don't feel the same way?'

'No, I think you do, which is what's making this so hard. It shouldn't be so intense, but we've made it that way by holding back when all the time we've wanted to be together.'

'So what do we do?'

There was a moment's silence before he said, very softly, 'Do you want me to come?'

'Yes,' she whispered. 'I mean, if you want to.'

'Don't ever doubt it. I want to make love to you so badly I feel I might go insane if I don't.'

Turning weak with desire she said, 'It's the same for me.'

'Then we'll have this night,' he said. 'I need to finish here with Jean-Marc, then I'll shower and come straight to you.'

It was almost half an hour later that Jessica heard a car going past, and looked down from the bedroom window to see Jean-Marc leaving. Immediately the nerves in her stomach began churning again, making her wonder when she'd last felt so gripped by excitement and apprehension.

Though she'd already showered and washed her hair, as yet she still hadn't decided what to wear. Part of her wanted to greet him the way she'd been amongst the vines, completely naked apart from her hat, while another part longed for him to undress her, as he had at the lake. Recalling the exquisite feel of the chiffon sliding down over her body sent such a wave of desire coasting through her that she opened her robe and let it fall to the floor, as though trying to recreate it. Without him there, it wasn't the same at all.

Turning to the mirror she gazed at her reflection. Her skin was the colour of honey, glistening softly in the evening sunlight, while her sun-bleached hair shone like ivory, making her dark eyes seem larger, and almost blurred by their inner glow. She could feel the rhythmic beat of her heart as her gaze dropped to the small swell of her breasts. Her nipples were large and thickly taut, and as she touched her fingers gently to them she gasped at the sensation that shot between her legs. She imagined him coming to stand behind her, pressing himself against her as he watched her reflection, and her eyes closed with the joy of knowing it would be soon.

She went to the armoire and began going through the clothes she'd brought with her. Nothing seemed quite right, which made her feel more certain about not dressing at all. She looked at her shoes and jewellery, then at the hat hanging from a post at the end of the bed. She was just reaching for it when she heard a car pulling up outside, and smiled to herself as she realised he hadn't wanted to waste time walking. So she would greet him as she was, for she really didn't want to eat, or even drink any wine, she only wanted to be with him.

She waited, wondering if he would come upstairs to find her, or if he'd call out to let her know he was there. If he called out, she'd walk down as she was, letting him look at her the way he had amongst the vines, knowing that this time she would be his. If he came upstairs, she would undress him and look at him the way she had at the lake.

Hearing footsteps in the kitchen her heart fluttered with

anticipation. Then, to her confusion, she realised the engine was still running outside.

'Jessica! Are you up there? *Surprise*!'

Jessica's heart stopped. Then grabbing for her robe she put it on, shouting, 'Lily, is that you?' She stuffed her feet into a pair of flip-flops. 'I'm just coming,' she called, and feeling dizzied by shock she forced herself out to the top of the stairs.

'Oh my God, look at you!' Lilian cried, gazing up at her in rapt admiration. 'Such a tan. And your hair is so blonde. My darling, I don't think I've ever seen you looking so lovely.'

Jessica tried to laugh. 'What are you doing here?' she asked shakily as she started down the stairs. 'I thought you weren't coming until tomorrow.'

Lilian was watching her with gentle affection. 'I managed to get through everything by lunchtime today,' she replied, pulling Jessica straight into an embrace, 'and it seemed crazy to stay in Paris when I could be here with Luc. And you!' she added. 'Oh God, I'm so pleased you stayed on.' Standing back, she looked searchingly into Jessica's face, showing how concerned she'd been, and how genuinely happy she was to see her.

Vaguely noticing how pale and tired she looked, Jessica said, 'Does Luc know you're here?'

Lilian laughed light-heartedly. 'You're going to think I'm mad, I know, but I thought I'd surprise him, only I couldn't go by without coming in to see you.'

Still too thrown to cope with this well, Jessica waved a hand towards the cooler. 'Will you have a drink?' she offered.

'No thanks, I've kept the taxi waiting, and I'm just dying to see Luc . . . Are you entertaining?' she asked, looking at the table set for two, complete with flowers and candles.

'No,' Jessica answered. 'I mean, yes,' she added hastily, since she obviously was. 'Daniella's coming over.'

Lilian's delight showed. 'Oh I'm so glad you two have become friends,' she declared. 'Isn't she wonderful? The three of us must get together over the weekend. I've brought loads of jewellery back with me, so you can take your pick.' Then her eyes started to twinkle. 'I don't suppose your dinner would stretch to three? I'm thinking of Fernand. If you could invite him, Luc and I could have the evening to ourselves.'

Jessica almost felt as though she was drowning. 'It's OK,' she said, her voice ringing hollow in her ears, 'Fernand's away for the night at a *Chevaliers* dinner.'

'Oh, excellent,' Lilian cried, leaning forward to help herself to a raspberry. 'Do you know if Luc's at home? Mm, delicious,' she said.

As Jessica watched her she could only think of how she'd imagined sharing those berries with him later, then dismissing it quickly from her mind, she was about to respond when Lilian frowned.

'Is that Luc's phone?'

'Uh, yes,' Jessica replied. 'He dropped in earlier – with the raspberries – and forgot to take it with him.' Why had she lied about the raspberries? It seemed so absurd and unnecessary.

'Then I'll take it for him,' Lilian said, going to pick it up. 'Do you mind if I rush off now? We'll have loads of time to chat over the next few days, before Charlie gets here, and I don't want to wait any longer to see Luc.'

'No, of course not,' Jessica said, returning yet another embrace.

'My goodness, you're shaking,' Lilian said, pulling back. 'Are you OK?'

'Yes, of course,' Jessica responded, with a laugh. 'You just made me jump when you came in.'

Lilian peered at her closely. 'Are you sure that's all it is?' she asked, concern showing through the tease in her eyes.

'Yes. No. I mean . . .'

Lilian's head went to one side.

'It's nothing,' Jessica said. Then, grabbing her by the arm, 'Go and see Luc. He's really missed you, you know.'

Lilian's smile showed her appreciation. 'We'll get together in the morning,' she promised. Then added with a laugh, 'Or maybe it'll be closer to midday.'

As she got back into the taxi Jessica stood at the door, managing to smile and wave, though not really knowing whether she was more horrified by how close she and Luc had come to being discovered, or crushed that they would now never make love.

Turning back inside she looked at the table, all laid out for dinner, then became aware of her nakedness beneath the robe and felt her head starting to spin. She wondered how Luc would react when Lilian walked in the door. She could easily imagine his shock, God knew she'd felt it herself, but after that . . . Would he be pleased to see her? She wondered if she should call to let him know Lilian was on her way, but when she picked up the phone she asked herself what right she had to ruin Lilian's surprise. None at all, and besides, she wasn't sure she could speak to him now. So instead she called Daniella, feeling utterly wretched about embroiling her in a lie, but if she was going to avoid any awkward, or even impossible situations later she didn't seem to have a choice.

'I see,' Daniella said, after Jessica had finished explaining. 'Well, I think the best thing is for me to come and share your dinner. That way neither of us is lying, and you won't be alone tonight feeling completely terrible.'

'No, really, you don't need to do that,' Jessica assured her, even though she was already dreading the evening ahead.

'Yes I do,' Daniella responded. 'I will have to explain things to Claude, because as you know we have guests . . .'

'Then you absolutely cannot come . . .'

'But it is only his brother and the friends you met last night, and we're all thoroughly bored with one another really . . . No, please don't argue any more, *chérie*. Lilian will be sure to ask if we had a nice time, and I cannot lie to her so *ouvertement*, and I don't think you can either. But I will warn you, I am hungry, and though I doubt you can eat, I will certainly need to.'

By the time Daniella arrived Jessica had dressed and put the fish in to bake, but she was hardly aware of what she was doing. She had so many terrible emotions roiling around inside her that she might not even be the same person she'd been an hour ago, for there was nothing good, or even defensible about the way she was feeling. Her thoughts were inextricably entangled in images of what might have been, and what was really happening . . . She could see them together, Lilian's beloved face so happy as she looked at her husband, her eyes closing as he kissed her, her body melding into his as his arms went round her . . .

'I think I'm losing my mind,' she confessed to Daniella. 'I can't believe this is happening. It's like I'm in the middle of a nightmare, but I keep reminding myself it could have been so much worse. If Lilian had come back any later . . .' Her eyes closed at the very thought of it. 'She looked so thrilled to see me,' she said brokenly, 'and so excited about being with Luc. Oh God, how could I have done this to her? What's happening to me?'

'Here, drink some wine,' Daniella said, passing her a glass, 'it might help to relax you.'

Though Jessica put it to her lips, she didn't take a sip. 'I'd give almost anything not to be feeling the way I do,' she said, putting it down again. 'I'm so ashamed . . . I . . . Oh Daniella, how on earth is it possible to be so jealous of someone you love? No, I can't go there. I just can't. He's her husband. They love one another, and what happened between us . . .' She broke off as her heart seemed to fold in two. 'Please tell me how we can feel the way we do, and still love other people? It doesn't make any sense.'

'Maybe not, but it is a reality,' Daniella responded. 'So perhaps it would help if you ask yourself this . . . If you were able to take him away from her, would you?'

Jessica almost gasped at the jolt she felt inside. 'No! Of course not,' she cried. 'But it doesn't mean I don't want to, and that's what's so wrong. Oh God, I wish Charlie was coming tomorrow. If nothing else, it would remind me how much he means to me, because right now I seem to have lost sight of everything.'

Daniella's smile was full of sympathy as she sat down. 'Believe it or not, you're probably still in a state of shock,' she told her gently. 'Lilian turning up like that . . . I'm sure it won't seem quite so bad in the morning.'

Knowing it would, Jessica's hands went to her face. 'What if she finds out?' she said. 'What if somehow . . .'

'From what you tell me there's nothing to find out,' Daniella reminded her.

Jessica lifted her head. 'It's true, we've never made love,

but tonight we were going to. And there have been other things . . . So much . . . For heaven's sake, you know we went to Paris. How do you think Lilian would feel if she knew that?'

'But you stayed at my apartment, while Luc was in his?'

'Yes, but all the time we were there we were fighting our feelings for one another.' Her eyes went to Daniella's, and there was a look of such utter helplessness in them that Daniella reached for her hand.

'It'll be all right,' Daniella told her.

Jessica shook her head. 'It won't. It can't. Oh God, I feel so afraid . . .'

'But there is nothing to be afraid of. As long as Lilian and Charlie never find out . . .'

'You don't understand. I keep trying to tell myself that it's just a passing attraction, or an infatuation . . . Maybe it is for him, but for me . . .'

'Ssh,' Daniella chided. 'Your feelings are very tender right now, which is only to be expected, but what is important is how much you love Lilian. You're not going to do anything to hurt her. No-one is. And you're not going to hurt Charlie either.'

'No, no, of course not. He's already hurting so much over Natalie . . .'

Daniella turned round as Jessica's mobile started to ring behind her. Reaching for it, she looked at the number and said, 'It's someone up at the house.' Her eyes came to Jessica's. 'That means it's either Luc or Lilian.'

Jessica pressed her hands to her head, unable to think what to do.

'Let me answer,' Daniella said, and without waiting for permission she clicked on.

Jessica's heart was beating hard as she watched her, then she felt almost faint as Daniella said, '*Oui, elle est là. Je te la passe*,' and she held the receiver out to Jessica. 'Luc,' she said.

Feeling almost stifled by her emotions, Jessica took the phone and put it to her ear. '*C'est moi*,' she whispered.

'You know that Lilian's here,' he said.

'Yes.'

She heard him inhale, and could almost feel the turmoil inside him, and even see the strain in his eyes.

'Just tell me . . .' She took a breath. 'Just tell me you were pleased to see her.'

'Jessica . . .'

'I need to hear you say it. She loves you, Luc . . .' Her voice faltered and she didn't try again.

'I admit the timing could . . .'

'Please just say it,' she whispered.

Several terrible moments ticked by. Eventually he said, 'Yes, I was pleased to see her.'

Knowing he meant it, she fought down all her other feelings, and smiled past the tears in her eyes as she looked at Daniella and said, 'Then that's all that matters.'

Chapter Twenty-One

That night Jessica had a dream about Natalie. In it, Natalie was beckoning her to follow, as though she had something to show her, something that was hidden in a place Jessica didn't want to go. Natalie pleaded and begged, all the time laughing and skipping around, as though they were playing some kind of a game. Jessica was laughing too, but she was afraid. She didn't know what of, but she thought there was something wrong with what was happening. Then her mother was there and Jessica kept asking her, 'Where's Natalie? I have to find her.'

'I'm here, Mum,' Natalie called out, but Jessica couldn't see her. 'I'm here,' Natalie shouted again.

Jessica turned round and round, looking at the ceiling, the walls, the windows. She had no idea where she was, she only knew that Natalie was nearby and she had to find her before she fell.

'Mum! *Mum*!' Natalie cried.

'Natalie, no!'

Jessica came awake with a start. Her heart was pounding and her skin was chill with sweat. The dream had felt so real, as though everything had happened right here in this room just seconds ago. Even the screams still seemed to resonate in the clammy air.

Finding it hard to breathe, she sat up and swung her legs over the edge of the bed. The nightmare still wouldn't leave her, so in the end she went downstairs to make some tea.

After a while she started to feel calmer, but as her mind finally relinquished its hold on Natalie, she was left facing the other nightmare in her life – how close she'd come to betraying Lilian.

But nothing had happened between her and Luc, she kept reminding herself. No promises had been made, and she had no right to be feeling cheated now. Nor could she allow herself to go on regretting all the times she could have given herself to him and hadn't, because if she had she'd be feeling even worse now than she already was. So somehow she needed to accept that they weren't meant to be together, not even for a night, which was why fate had stepped in to save them from themselves.

However, telling herself these things and believing them was one thing, putting an end to the feelings was another altogether. She kept going over and over all the times they'd spent together, wishing she'd behaved differently, while knowing how much she'd detest herself now if she had. She loved Lilian so much. How could she even begin to regret not betraying her, as if her feelings weren't already a betrayal enough? The truth was, she really didn't want to hurt her, so she must only think now of how fortunate it was that Luc hadn't fallen for her in the same way she had for him, because if he had . . . But no, she couldn't let her mind go there, she just couldn't, it would serve no purpose other than to deepen her guilt and intensify her shame.

It was almost dawn by the time she went back to bed, but she only tossed and turned, until finally, knowing how distorted the world could become through lack of sleep, she decided to put some distance between herself and Valennes, even if only for a while. It might help to clear her mind, or at least instil some rational thoughts into the chaos that was milling around inside her.

She took only her purse and car keys, deliberately leaving her mobile behind, for she really didn't want to speak to anyone right now. Nor was she going to look up at the *manoir* as she reversed her car out, because she didn't want to imagine him sleeping, or making love, or even lying in the same bed as someone else. It hurt too much, and she simply didn't have the right to feel that pain.

As she drove towards the village she had no clear idea of where she was going to go, or how long she would be, but it hardly mattered. All that did was that she should stop listening to the madness inside her that was telling her she couldn't give him up, because it wasn't true. He'd never been hers in the first place, nor would he ever be, so she must make herself understand that somehow she'd allowed her feelings to run out of control, and now, for her own sake, as well as everyone else's, she had to get a grip.

In the end she pulled into a lay-by somewhere close to Macon and turned off the engine. She was reminding herself now of why she'd come to Valennes in the first place, which was to follow her instincts about Natalie. Just please God don't let the truth of what had happened make things any worse than they already were. It was simply her mother hiding a lover. No-one had done anything to Natalie, she knew that already. So it was all just a terrible accident . . . But why would her mother lie? Why? Why? Why?

Putting her hands to her head she pressed them in hard, as though to stop her mind going round and round. She must make herself think of something else, something less painful that would not wring her heart and conscience. Almost immediately her thoughts went to Nikki and Harry, but they provided no release. Picturing their faces brought such a deluge of love into her heart that she felt utterly wretched for not being in London now, when Harry was on his way back from Devon, and Nikki was packing for Norfolk. She should be there to sweep her boy into her arms as he bowled in through the door, and to tell Nikki that she could borrow whatever clothes and make-up she needed. Why hadn't she thought about this sooner? She could have flown back for the weekend to be with them, then returned with Harry on Monday. The answer, of course, was that she'd been too distracted by other things, things that shouldn't matter, and didn't, but dear God they felt as though they did, and right now she didn't know how she was ever going to make them stop.

It was past one o'clock when she returned to the cottage. She knew it would have been naive to hope she might return feeling less confusion, but at least she seemed calmer inside than when she'd left. She looked around, but there was no sign of anyone. Everything was perfectly still and hot and as beautifully benign as it had ever been.

Once inside she checked her phone, knowing there would

be no message from Luc, but unable to stop herself hoping anyway. When there wasn't the disappointment was terrible, so in an effort to get past it and focus her mind on where it should be, she rang Charlie.

'Hi, is Harry back yet?' she said when he answered.

'Apparently they're just past Reading, so not long now.'

'You must be looking forward to seeing him. I know I am.'

'Of course. It's been pretty quiet around here without him. Without you both.'

She smiled and felt her heart fill with affection. 'I miss you too,' she said. 'I'll be glad when Wednesday's here.'

'Will you pick me up at the airport?' Then before she had a chance to reply he put a hand over the receiver and shouted, 'Yes, I'm speaking to her now. Nikki's been trying to get hold of you,' he told her. 'I think she wants to raid your wardrobe. Correction, I think she's already doing it, and is getting herself worked up because you've taken things with you that she wants to take with her.'

Jessica had to laugh. 'I'll talk to her in a minute,' she said. 'Have you managed to get hold of Maurice or my mother yet?'

The brief pause before he answered was enough to tell her the question had annoyed him. 'I haven't had a lot of time,' he said, 'but I'll try later.'

'Why don't you give me the number, and I'll try?'

'You can have it, but what are you going to do? Yell at her down the phone again? It's never got you anywhere yet.'

Sighing, she said, 'No, you're right, it hasn't. I just need to know . . .'

'Darling, I'm aware of what you want to know, so I'll try to find out. OK?'

'OK. I just wish you weren't being so hostile about it. I mean, you surely want to know too.'

'Of course, but I've got other things on my mind right now.'

'More important than Natalie?'

'Don't be absurd. It's not a contest. It's simply that life goes on. For you too, if you'd let it.'

Feeling her throat tightening, she said, 'I'm not in the mood to fight, so let's leave it there. Just promise me you'll try to call them later, and if you can't get anything out of my mother, you'll at least arrange to see Maurice before Tuesday.'

'I'll do my best,' he assured her. 'Now, do you want to talk to Nikki?'

'Yes.'

As she waited Jessica found herself staring down at the copy of *Suite Française* Luc had given her, and began idly turning the pages. There hadn't been a happy end for Lucile and her German, she was thinking, nor for Modi and Jeanne. It made her realise that there was never a happy end to anything, because the only real end was death . . .

'Are you still there?' Charlie said. 'She's on the phone to Sophie, or Camilla or whoever the heck it is, then she has to go and meet Freddy, so she'll call you later.'

'OK. She's all right about me not being there, is she?'

'She seems to be. I'm sure she'll let you know if she's not.'

Sure of it too, Jessica told him she loved him and rang off. Then, feeling weighted by tiredness, she took herself upstairs to lie down on the bed Natalie had used.

As she inhaled the scent of fresh sheets and dried lavender flowers she turned her face to the pillow, wanting to hug everything to her, squeeze it and love it, as though it were Natalie herself. She thought of the dream last night, and then of Harry, and felt tears burning her eyes. She could hardly wait to see him. Her son, her boy, the most precious little soul in the world, who was arriving on Monday. When he came she would give him the time of his life, spend as many hours with him as he wanted, and be as close to him as she'd ever been.

She was sobbing almost without realising it. She longed for her precious girl so much that she just couldn't bear it. Her silky hair, her little white teeth, her impish eyes and those lovely gangly limbs that wrapped themselves around her mother as though they might never let go. Why did God have to take her away? Why couldn't she have fallen and been injured, instead of having to die? It just didn't seem right. She'd been so full of life, and had so much to look forward to.

'Oh Natalie, my darling,' she choked. 'Where are you

now? Are you here? Can you see me?' She turned onto her back and looked up at the beams overhead, knowing she should try to sleep, but feeling almost afraid to, because all the pain and heartache would only be waiting when she woke up.

Hearing her mobile ringing in the kitchen below, she pulled herself up from the bed and went down to answer it. It was Nikki, full of excitement about her approaching holiday, and determined to spare Jessica no detail of all she had planned, particularly for her eighteenth. Jessica knew Charlie was going to give her a cheque so she could afford a party – then suddenly wanting to be there to share it, she started to cry.

'I'm sorry, darling,' she said, trying to pull herself together. 'I shouldn't get emotional like this. It's just that I miss you and I feel Dad and I should be throwing a party for you.'

'But I'm really cool with it being like this,' Nikki assured her. 'Freddy's going to be there and all our friends, so you don't have to be upset. We can go out for dinner when you come back. It'll be much more your thing than having all us lot traipsing through the house.'

'Are you sure you don't mind? It seems so wrong to me . . .'

'Hello! I just told you, Freddy's going to be there, and as much as I love you guys, he's the one I really want to be with. Can you understand that without being hurt?'

Jessica smiled. 'Yes,' she said. 'Yes, of course.'

'I'll call you on the day, obviously,' Nikki assured her. 'Well, I'll call you every day, the way I always do. And Dad'll be with you by then, so you can drink a glass of champagne together and try to get over being the parents of an *eighteen*-year-old daughter.'

Though Jessica laughed, the reality of Nikki's age was more sobering than she cared to admit. It was a sign of how time was passing, carrying her along at a speed she really didn't want to go, taking her away from Natalie, and the dreams that hadn't come true, with no chance now of ever realising them.

'You're not still crying, are you?' Nikki demanded.

'No.'

'Good, because I have to go. I wanted to be here when Harry got back, but I'll have to see him later. Oh God, look at the time. Love you, Mum. Love you, love you.'

'Love you too,' Jessica said, and found herself swallowing another lump in her throat as she rang off.

She was much too emotional today, far too close to the edge, so she must at least try to get some sleep. However, she got no further than the foot of the stairs before her phone rang again.

This time it was Lilian, sounding happy, breezy and full of laughter. 'I'm sorry I haven't rung all morning,' she said, 'but I don't expect you have much of a problem guessing why. Anyway, I've just spoken to Daniella and she's invited us over there for lunch on Sunday, so I'll bring the jewellery and the two of you can take your pick. And you'll be here for the party tonight, of course. Fernand's invited the Schmidts who are staying in the other cottage, and the whole family, naturally, and there's another couple due to arrive from Brittany later today. If they get here in time, they'll be included too.'

Jessica desperately wanted to say she couldn't make it, but how could she when a part of the reason she'd come was to spend time with Lilian? Besides, what excuse could she give that wouldn't worry Lilian, and that the others wouldn't see straight through? So all she could say was, 'Yes, of course I'll be there.'

Lilian sounded delighted, then regretful as she said, 'I was hoping we could get together this afternoon, but Luc's about to take me to the studio to see my sculpture, then we're going into town to pick up a few things Fernand needs for tonight. Actually, there's no reason you can't come with us, if you'd like to.'

'No, it's fine,' Jessica responded, probably far too quickly. 'I have a few things to do before Harry arrives.'

'OK, but we'll be around for another hour if you change your mind. Otherwise, Fernand wants everyone here about seven.'

'I'll look forward to it,' Jessica replied. As she put the phone down she found herself so close to tears again that this time she turned off her mobile, before going upstairs in the hope that she'd finally manage to fall asleep. If she didn't, she really couldn't see how she'd be able to cope with this evening.

Lilian's gentle blue eyes were bright with excitement as she watched Luc breaking open the wooden crate containing her bronze. All around them his other works were covered by white sheets to keep off the dust, apart from the one of Jessica, which Lilian had insisted on seeing, and was now sitting on a workbench nearby.

The initial impact of Jessica's likeness had almost made Lilian gasp, for it was clear that Luc had captured an inner radiance in her that even Lilian wasn't sure she'd seen before. However, now the shock had worn off, she was feeling only pride in her husband's talent, in place of the moment's jealousy she'd experienced of such exceptional beauty. Jessica always had been the more attractive of the two of them, so there was nothing new there, it was probably just the fact that Luc must have noticed it that had unsettled her.

'I can hardly wait for Charlie to see it,' she commented, looking at Jessica's sculpture again. 'She looks so lovely I think he's going to fall in love with her all over again.'

Luc's eyebrows rose. 'Actually, I've arranged to send it to the mould-maker on Wednesday,' he said, letting the crate panels drop to the floor, 'so it'll be gone before he gets here. I guess I could always delay it, though.'

Lilian gave it some thought. 'You know, maybe it's better for him to see it in bronze first. That would be really special, particularly if we can get it back in time for his birthday.'

'Which is when?'

'At the end of September.'

'It shouldn't be a problem.' Plunging his hands into the polystyrene pieces, he made sure she was looking, then said, 'OK, are you ready?'

Her eyes shining again, she watched him starting to lift the bronze from its packing.

'Et voilà,' he declared, pulling it free and placing it on a stand.

Small flecks of white foam still remained on the sculpture, but even before he brushed them away she could feel her heart sinking. It wasn't that it was bad – on the contrary, it was outstanding if one were only judging the likeness and skill – but there was no doubt that beside Jessica's exquisite features her own seemed almost lifeless and plain.

'You don't like it?' he said.

'No, I do,' she assured him quickly. 'I love it. It's just a bit of a shock, I suppose, seeing myself so immobile, cast in one expression that doesn't . . . Well, it doesn't seem an especially happy one, which I don't think I noticed when it was in clay.'

Putting an arm around her, he said, 'If you remember, you'd just lost a baby when we did this.'

Feeling her heart turn over, she leaned into him, and felt the strength of him wrapping itself around her.

'We can do another,' he told her, tilting her face up to his. 'If you don't like this one . . .'

'No, I do, but . . .' She hesitated, really not wanting to offend him. 'I would like to do another,' she said. 'Do you mind?'

'Why would I mind? At least it'll keep you in the same room as me for a day.'

'Oh don't,' she groaned, 'you know I want to be with you all the time, but . . .'

Interrupting her with a kiss, he said, 'It's not a complaint. It's just a way of letting you know that I'm glad you're back.'

Her eyes narrowed playfully. 'Are you sure?' she said. 'You looked so shocked when I walked in last night . . .'

'Maybe because I was,' he said, with no little irony.

Laughing, she looked at her sculpture again, then with a sultry gleam in her eyes, she said, 'I wonder if the next one should be a nude.'

'There's no reason why not,' he said, appearing to like the idea.

'And who knows,' she continued, looking up at him, 'I might be pregnant by then. Wouldn't that be wonderful, to have a sculpture of me carrying your child?'

'Yes,' he whispered, gazing into her face. 'Yes it would,' and pulling her against him he let his eyes rest briefly on the sculpture of Jessica before they moved back to the one of his wife, and then to his wife herself as he started to kiss her.

By the time Jessica walked up through the vineyard for dinner that evening she was feeling much more together than she had earlier, mainly thanks to having slept for most of the afternoon. Nevertheless, it was impossible not to feel nervous about seeing Luc, and concerned in case Lilian sensed she wasn't quite herself. However, she could always put that down to another difficult call with Charlie, who, only ten minutes ago, had told her to stop nagging him about getting in touch with her mother – he'd tried again, there was still no reply, but as soon as there was he'd let her know. If ever there was a stuck record, that had to be it.

Now, as she approached the *manoir*, wearing a cream silk dress that showed the slender outline of her figure, and revealed the whole of her back, she could hear the hypnotic voice of Mirella Freni singing Desdemona in *Otello* floating from inside, while the vibrant colours of the flowers seemed to be seeping into the air. Everyone was already gathered under the nearside of the pergola sipping *crémant* and helping themselves to a succulent assortment of canapés, and she felt sure, as she greeted them, that her lingering tension didn't show.

Smiling and teasing Fernand, who was looking very dapper in a pair of loud red braces and a black bow tie, she was just taking a sip of her champagne when she spotted Luc at the far end of the terrace, talking to Claude. The jolt in her heart was so harsh that she felt the smile falter on her lips, but since he hadn't seen her she turned quickly away, not wanting their eyes to meet for fear of what might pass between them. Then Lilian was coming towards her, smiling with affection and holding out her hands.

'Where did you get that dress?' Lilian demanded, kissing her on both cheeks. 'It's heavenly. Doesn't she look gorgeous?' she said to Daniella, who was just coming out of the kitchen.

'Absolutely beautiful,' Daniella agreed, handing a tray of hors d'oeuvres to one of the helpers.

'And have you seen her sculpture?' Lilian asked. 'It's so

lovely I swear it takes your breath away.'

Jessica only smiled, more embarrassed by the compliments than pleased, particularly with Daniella there – then she noticed Luc was coming towards them and fought the urge to excuse herself. It would be ludicrous to start trying to avoid him, even though she had no idea how natural she could be.

'In fact I told Luc,' Lilian was saying to Daniella, 'that once Charlie sees it he'll probably fall in love with her all over again.'

Knowing Luc was listening now, and feeling terrible that Lilian was on the outside when the rest of them knew, Jessica attempted a change of subject as she said, 'Lily, tell us about your sculpture. What's it like, and when do we get to see it?'

Lilian pulled a face, and tilted her head back briefly as she felt Luc come up behind her. 'I have to admit I wasn't thrilled,' she replied, 'but we've already decided to do another, haven't we darling?'

Jessica's eyes remained on Lilian as Luc said, 'Indeed we have. I'm afraid my wife is my harshest critic.'

'Don't say that,' Lilian laughed, leaning in to him. 'There's nothing wrong with your skill, it's my expression I don't like, but there was a reason for it which we don't need to go into. The important thing is, I have my own personal artist who can create me another.'

Jessica's eyes went only briefly to Luc as he and Daniella laughed. This was proving even harder than she'd expected, for just seeing his arm around Lilian was causing all kinds of problems inside her.

'Have you shown everyone the jewellery?' Luc asked, glancing down at Lilian.

'No, we're doing that tomorrow, after lunch,' she answered. 'Have you and Claude worked out what you're going to do about seating for the concert yet?'

'We're getting there.'

'You know, I could always talk to Madame Bouvier about borrowing, or hiring, some chairs,' she suggested, falling into the domestic trivia common to wives and husbands. 'I'll see her on Tuesday at the meeting for the *vignerons*' ball. She knows anyone and everyone, so she's sure to have some ideas.' Then, turning excitedly back to Jessica, 'You and Charlie should try to get over when it's happening. It's great fun. You'll love it, and you can always stay with us if someone's in the cottage, can't they darling?'

'Of course,' Luc responded, 'and I believe my father's already made the suggestion.'

Whether or not he was looking at her Jessica didn't know, for she'd felt it wiser to turn her eyes vaguely towards Fernand. She really couldn't look at Luc while Lilian was there, because Lilian always saw too much, and feeling the way she did she was afraid of how much there was to see. Then to her relief he was waving to Yves, Claude's brother, who'd just strolled over from his car.

'Darling, before you go,' Lilian said, catching his arm, 'is it OK if I take our visitors to see the sculptures? The Schmidts were asking, so were – what's the name of the French couple?'

'Coursan. Félice and Gilles,' Luc reminded her. 'The studio's not locked, so go ahead.'

'Perhaps I can come and see the one of you?' Jessica suggested.

Lilian laughed and grimaced. 'Next to yours, I'm afraid you'll see just how sadly mine pales,' she said, linking Jessica's arm to start across the terrace. 'But I was probably expecting too much. Maybe next time, he won't be so honest.'

Since she was supposed to laugh, Jessica did, but she had to add, 'Honestly, Lily, you really shouldn't put yourself down. You're gorgeous, and not only on the outside, because if the rest of us were even half as beautiful as you on the inside we could count ourselves truly blessed.'

Lilian gave a hoot of laughter. 'Believe me,' she stated dryly, 'I'm no less terrible inside than anyone else, but I have to admit I'm finding it hard to pull any bad feelings out of the hat right now. Oh Jessica, I'm so happy to be back and to have you here . . . And we still have plenty of time to be just us before Charlie comes, because Harry's bound to be all tied up with Antoine and Elodie, and Luc's always in his studio or somewhere. I'm absolutely dying for a chat. I've got so much to tell you, but we'd best go and gather up the

Schmidts and the Coursans now. Have you been introduced to any of them yet?'

'I met the Schmidts earlier, as they came back from a walk,' Jessica replied, already smiling to greet them again, and a few minutes later, having shaken hands with the Coursans too, they were all on their way to look at the sculptures.

Virtually the instant she stepped into the studio Jessica wished she hadn't come, not only because of the memories that swept over her in a wave of guilt, but because the contrast between her likeness and Lilian's was so startling that everyone fell silent. A beat later they were all talking at once, admiring both sculptures, but paying such effusive compliments to Lilian about hers that it only seemed to make matters worse. In the end, realising the best way to help Lilian out of her embarrassment was to leave, Jessica excused herself and went to rejoin the party.

To her relief she found herself seated between Claude and Fernand at the table, while Luc was at the other end next to Lilian – the only couple seated together. And as Fernand's helpers for the evening began serving the first course of watercress soup with an artistic swirl of whipped crème fraiche and jaunty sprigs of mint, she focused her attention on Claude, who was extolling the virtues of a very fine Montrachet – fruity, not too much body and with a delicious aftertaste of almonds. She tested the wine too, enjoying the little knowledge she'd gained from Luc, then after a while the subject moved to the following weekend's concert. This was causing Claude some concern, since the line-up so far consisted only of Daniella, who was singing three of her favourite Puccini arias, and Yves, who was arranging a musical transition from Satie, to Debussy, to Schubert. Since those two, between them, could easily fill a concert hall twice over, Jessica had to laugh at Claude's grimace of helplessness.

'A mere two acts,' he complained, 'but what am I to do? She won't be upstaged, and he won't appear with anyone else.'

'What about the orchestra I hear is making the trip down from Paris?' Jessica enquired. 'Isn't that another act in itself?'

'Orchestra?' he cried, throwing out his hands. 'They will

be only ten in number. I don't understand why we French have to take such long holidays in the summer. Is it not a great pleasure to play music all of the time?'

As Jessica laughed, her eyes, as if they had a will of their own, moved to Luc, and as if he'd realised it his flicked towards her. She looked away quickly and tried to engage herself in one of Andrea Schmidt's stories, while listening to the tragic aria of *Madama Butterfly*. She sipped more wine, ate more food, then laughed as Fernand refilled her glass and Claude and Daniella fell into one of their wonderfully entertaining disputes. The fact that they were still deeply in love in spite of – or maybe because of – three children and twelve years of marriage, was so evident that no-one ever took their bickering seriously. It made Jessica think of how she used to be with Charlie, so easy and relaxed, teasing him, as he teased her, while always knowing how close they would be when they got home. Then she saw Lilian whisper something in Luc's ear that made him laugh, and as he looked into his wife's eyes before pressing a kiss gently to her lips Jessica felt as though a light was going out inside her.

The salt-baked sea bass with sorrel and chilli was served, but she ate very little before her plate was taken away. Then the cheese was put in front of her, followed by the dessert of flambéed cherries with ice cream, though she was unable to eat that either. She wanted to apologise to Fernand, but his kindly eyes showed she didn't have to, which made her feel worse. She didn't want anyone's sympathy or understanding, she just wanted everyone to realise that no matter how she felt about Luc, no-one mattered more than Lilian, or Charlie, who, Lilian was just informing everyone, was about to join them at Valennes.

In the end, waiting only for coffee to be over, Jessica managed to excuse herself, saying she was tired after too much sun and wine. Lilian immediately suggested she and Luc should walk her back through the vineyard, but to Jessica's relief the Schmidts decided to leave with her.

Just after she let herself into the cottage her mobile started to ring, and though she desperately wanted it to be Luc, she knew from the ringtone that it was a message.

'Darling, it's me,' Charlie said. 'I'm just saying goodnight, because I know you're up at the *manoir* this evening, and Harry and I are off to bed early – in case you'd forgotten I have to leave at six in the morning. Nikki's going to be here for Harry, so don't worry about that, then he's coming to the studio with me later. Also, I wanted to say that I'm sorry for being short with you earlier. I promise I'll try to get hold of your mother, or Maurice, again tomorrow, but if I don't have any luck, I still have an arrangement to see him on Tuesday. He hasn't cancelled, and obviously I won't either. Anyway, hope you and Lilian are having a great time now she's back. Say hi from me. Love you,' and a moment later the line went dead.

Wishing it weren't too late to call back, Jessica went upstairs and lay down on the bed. This would get easier, she told herself. She would stop wanting Luc, and it would stop hurting, just as long as she kept reminding herself that it really wasn't as serious as she'd feared. She hadn't fallen in love with him, it only felt that way because attractions, or infatuations always did at first. So she really would get past this, and it wouldn't take long provided she could stop herself imagining how powerfully he would make love, how exquisitely he would move into her body, and how right it would feel to be with him that way, when in reality it would be so very, very wrong.

Chapter Twenty-Two

'Mum! You'll never guess where I am,' Harry cried excitedly down the line.

'Um, let me see,' Jessica replied gamely. 'Up a tree?'

'No.'

'On a camel?'

Harry giggled. 'No, I'm sitting in Dad's chair in the studio where he reads the news, and there's a camera looking at me.'

'No! So what are the headlines today?'

'I don't know. Um, a bus fell off a bridge and floated in the river and everyone got swept out to sea, but they could swim so now they're in America, all wet and worn out.'

Jessica laughed. 'Where *do* you get your imagination?' she wanted to know.

'Dad says it's from you.'

She was still smiling as she lay back in her deckchair and gazed out across the front lawn of the chateau to where Lilian and Luc were playing badminton with Antoine and Elodie. Everyone else was relaxing in the shade, replete from a delicious lunch, sleepy with wine, and wanting nothing more than to soak up this perfect Sunday afternoon, but as always, children had other ideas. 'Has Dad finished now?' she asked Harry.

'Yes, I think so. He's here talking to some people. Shall I put him on?'

'Not if he's busy.'

Harry didn't answer straight away, but she could hear voices in the background, then Charlie came on the line saying, 'Hi, how are you?'

'I'm OK,' she answered. 'Harry sounds as though he's enjoying himself.'

'I think he is. We should be out of here soon, though. It's just some things are due to come up at the UN about Syria this week, so they want to talk about the interview I shot with the Opposition Leader while I was in Paris.'

Remembering it was what he'd been doing at the time Natalie died, she felt a jarring in her heart, but she didn't mention it, and nor did he.

'Where are you now?' he asked.

'At Claude and Daniella's, having a very lazy day.'

'Sounds good. How's Lilian? Over the jet lag?'

'She seems to be, but we haven't had a chance to spend much time together yet. I think she and Luc are enjoying a bit of a second honeymoon.'

There was a wry note in Charlie's voice as he said, 'Well, let's hope that spending some time apart has the same effect on us.'

'I'm sure it will,' she said, wishing she could believe it. 'So what do you and Harry have planned for the rest of the day?'

'Before we get into that, have you spoken to Nikki since she left for Norfolk?'

'I had a text about an hour ago letting me know they'd arrived safely. Are you missing her?'

'I haven't had a chance yet, but I'm sure I will, especially when Harry leaves tomorrow. The house is going to seem very empty for the next couple of days.'

'Speaking of empty houses, have you managed to get hold of anyone at Maurice's yet? Or don't tell me, you haven't had the time to try.'

'Actually, I did earlier, but there was still no reply from either number, Maurice's or your mother's, so I rang the next-door neighbour, what's-his-name Keane. Apparently they called Keane yesterday to check on things there, but he didn't ask where they were, and the only number he has is the same as the one I have.'

'Does she know I've spoken to the paramedic?'

'I can't think how, when neither of us has been in touch with her since then. Have you mentioned it to Lilian, by the way? What does she say about it?'

'We haven't had a chance to go into it, but there's not very much she can say. It's my mother who has the answers.'

'Of course, I just wondered if it might have prompted someone over there into remembering something.'

'Luc was the only one around at the time,' she reminded him, 'and all he saw was the so-called tourist's car. Anyway, it's looking as though we'll have to wait until Tuesday now, when you're due to see Maurice.'

'I think so. Listen, I have to go, they're calling me into the meeting. I'll talk to you later.'

Relieved that he hadn't become irritable while talking about her mother, Jessica rang off and let the phone drop into her lap. A few minutes later she found herself becoming aware of the heat in a way she hadn't before. It felt fierce and biting, as though it were trying to scorch her limbs, while the air seemed languid and thick, like a storm might be brewing. She closed her eyes and after a while the sounds of the game seemed to come and go as a relaxing heaviness descended over her. Then a shout of triumph from the makeshift badminton court made her look up.

Elodie was bouncing up and down with her arms in the air, while Luc was rolling on the ground with Antoine in some kind of dispute about who was to blame for their defeat.

Smiling, Jessica watched them, then her eyes followed Lilian as she left them to it and wandered over to a nearby lounger. As she flopped into it she was still panting slightly from the effort of the game, then the fight lost momentum and everything went quiet again as Luc and the children lay spreadeagled in the grass in the shade of a giant cedar tree.

Long minutes ticked by with just the rasping of crickets and the occasional bird to break the silence. A phone started to ring inside the chateau, and groaning, Claude got up to answer it. He was back a few minutes later, and once again the stillness resumed, only to be broken by the wonderfully dreamy sound of a jazz piano that Yves put on the CD player before coming out to join them.

From behind her sunglasses Jessica looked at Luc, prone on the grass, and possibly sleeping. Then she turned away, trying not to think of how much she'd like to go and lie there with him. What for a while had been the sweet torment of holding back and waiting was now becoming an agony of longing. Though she tried to stop her mind going in directions that would only make it worse, she all too often found herself in a world where there was no Lilian, or Charlie, there was only the beauty of what they'd known, and the passion that still needed to be shared.

Close by, Fernand gave a snore, and then a bee started to buzz noisily around the lavender bed. Her eyes drifted closed again, then she was aware of Luc getting up and going into the house.

'Jessica?' a voice beside her said.

She turned to see Antoine looking down at her. 'Yes?' she answered, smiling up at him.

'Can I come to the airport when you pick up Harry tomorrow?'

'Of course,' she murmured, lifting a hand to smooth his cheek. 'Provided Maman says it's OK.'

'I'll go and ask her,' he said.

When he'd gone she watched Lilian get up from her lounger and come to sit on the grass beside her.

'It's so perfect here, isn't it?' Lilian sighed, leaning back on her hands and gazing around.

'Mm,' Jessica responded sleepily.

After a pause Lilian said, 'What time are you collecting Harry tomorrow? I thought we could have lunch, or breakfast, or at least a couple of hours together before he arrives.'

'Just after two, so breakfast would work, if you two lovebirds can drag yourselves out of bed.'

Lilian laughed, but there was a ring to it that made Jessica open her eyes.

Lilian's face was tilted up to the sun, making her expression difficult to see.

'Is everything all right?' Jessica asked.

Lilian seemed surprised. 'Yes, perfectly,' she answered. Then after a pause, 'And with you?'

'Absolutely,' Jessica replied.

A few more seconds went by. 'Actually, you've seemed a little . . .' Lilian began. 'I'm not sure, maybe distant, since I got back.'

Feeling a beat of alarm, Jessica said, 'I'm fine, honestly,

except my mother's done a vanishing act again, which seems highly convenient when I now know that the paramedic didn't carry Natalie to the sofa.'

Lilian's head came round. 'You didn't tell me that,' she said. 'When did you find out?'

'On Friday. You've had other things on your mind . . .'

'But that's important,' Lilian interrupted. She seemed genuinely upset not to have been told, and angry with herself for not asking. 'I knew you were talking to the paramedic, of course,' she said, 'but I hadn't realised . . . Actually, I should have, but I was so full of myself on Friday . . .'

'It doesn't matter,' Jessica said gently. 'We'll get to the bottom of it as soon as we speak to my mother.'

Lilian was about to respond when Antoine returned to inform Jessica that he had permission to come to the airport. Then Daniella was calling over to Lilian, 'When do we get to see the jewels you've brought from India? I've promised to deck myself out in them for Claude later, to try and put some rev back into his ageing little Renault.'

Everyone laughed as Claude chuckled from under the newspaper that was folded over his face.

'It's all inside,' Lilian said, getting to her feet. 'Shall I bring it out? Or perhaps it's better indoors, where it's cooler.'

Jessica held out a hand for Lilian to pull her up, then arm in arm they strolled across the lawn towards the house.

As they entered the kitchen Luc turned round from where he was washing his hands. He looked at Lilian, but as she went over to the centre table where she'd set out the jewellery, his eyes moved to Jessica and their intensity caught fiercely at her heart. He looked away again quickly, but just that one glance had left her in no doubt he was spending as much time thinking about her as she was about him.

Then Daniella was saying, 'This is a strictly female affair, Luc, so I'm afraid you have to go.'

With a humorous lift of his eyebrows he planted a kiss on his sister's cheek, and wandered back outside.

Lilian had brought necklaces, bracelets, earrings and even toe rings, all set with onyx, amethyst, turquoise and amber. Daniella chose several pieces, while Jessica held back, unable to accept gifts from Lilian when she was already taking so much more than Lilian would ever want to give.

In the end Lilian laughed and threw out her hands. 'Please choose something,' she cried, 'even if it's only earrings or a bracelet.'

'This necklace is beautiful,' Daniella suggested, holding up a strand of pearls mixed with aquamarines.

Lilian eyed it critically. 'Maybe it's a little garish,' she said. 'Jessica usually prefers something more understated, like this,' and picking up a delicate silver bracelet with tiny crystals sparkling between the links she let it drape over her hand. 'I had you in mind when I chose it,' she told Jessica. 'Do you like it?'

'It's beautiful,' Jessica said, because it was, and since she could give no reason to refuse it, she watched as Lilian fastened it around her wrist.

'It looks even lovelier with your tan,' Lilian said, as they all admired it.

'But Lily, I can't . . .'

'Yes, you can.'

'Oh là là,' Daniella murmured as a heavy thud, followed by running footsteps, came from upstairs. 'Sounds as though Hugo is awake.'

After she'd gone to fetch him Jessica began helping Lilian to pack the jewellery away, and for the first time in all the years they'd known one another they seemed lost for something to say.

'What is it?' Lilian asked after a while. 'Have I done something to upset you?'

'Oh God no,' Jessica cried, pulling her into her arms. 'How can you even think it?'

'I don't . . . I mean . . .' Lilian tried to laugh, but too many tears had come into her eyes. 'I'm sorry. I seem to be very emotional at the moment . . . Jet lag and overwork . . .'

Feeling her heartbeat starting to slow, Jessica looked into her face. The paleness of her skin, how tired she seemed . . . 'Lily, are you . . .'

Lilian's eyes came to hers, then her mouth trembled as she began to nod. 'Yes, I am,' she whispered, 'but please don't say anything. I haven't even told Luc yet.'

Trying to push aside everything else she was feeling, Jessica hugged her again. 'But why?' she said. 'He's going to be thrilled.'

'I'm just so afraid of losing it,' Lilian confessed. 'I thought maybe I should get the amnio over with, make sure everything's all right, then tell him.'

'But whatever happens he'll want to go through it with you.'

Lilian's eyes filled with tears again. 'You're probably right,' she said. 'I just . . . I don't know . . . You don't really think straight at a time like this, do you? You imagine all kinds of things . . .'

Hoping it was only her conscience that was making her read Lilian's anxiety the way she was, Jessica squeezed her hands, saying, 'There's often nothing as unstable as a pregnant woman, and with your history it's understandable you'd be worried. How far along are you?'

'Almost three months.'

Jessica tried to smile. 'It's wonderful news, Lily,' she said, her voice sounding strangely normal. 'It really is.'

Lilian's eyes started to dance. 'It is, isn't it?' she said. Then putting a finger to her lips, 'Ssh, Daniella's coming.'

'I was thinking perhaps everyone would like some tea and *pâtisserie* now,' Daniella suggested as she carried a sleepy-eyed Hugo into the kitchen.

'Sounds a wonderful idea, if anyone's got any room after that delicious lunch,' Lilian responded, going to put some water on.

'I don't think I have,' Jessica said, 'but I'll go and ask the others.'

Wishing it was as easy to escape her feelings as it was the kitchen, she wandered back into the garden where the children had coaxed their father and Yves into another game of badminton, and Fernand was still sleeping. For the moment there was no sign of Luc, but then she saw him coming out of the music room, and because it would have appeared odd, even rude, to turn away she waited for him to join her.

'We have to talk,' he said quietly.

'No . . .'

'I have to see you.'

'You don't understand . . .'

'No, it's you who doesn't . . .'

'Luc, please don't say any more,' she interrupted, and forcing a smile in case anyone was watching, she said, 'OK, one slice of apple tart for you,' and turning away she went to take orders from the others, knowing that no matter what, she had to avoid being alone with him again.

It was after midnight when Lilian woke up to find the bed empty beside her. For a moment she lay where she was, listening for the sound of Luc in the bathroom, or perhaps on the balcony outside, but beneath the occasional chirruping of night birds and rasp of crickets there was only the incessant, immutable silence.

Swinging her legs over the side of the bed she sat for a moment, still naked after their lovemaking earlier, then she reached for a robe.

He would be in his studio, of course. It was where he always went when artistic urges came over him in the night, or if he had difficulty sleeping.

She moved quietly down the two flights of stairs and along the hall into the kitchen. Then, looking through the window over to the studio, she felt her heartbeat slow. There were no lights. Everything was in darkness. He wasn't there.

Trying to push away the fear she looked down through the vineyard, searching for lights in the grape-picker's cottage. There were none. Then she saw him, leaning against a pillar on the terrace, his back to the house as he stared out at the night.

For a long time she stood watching him, knowing if she went to him he would gather her against him and kiss her, and probably say sorry for waking her. Then they would go back to bed and maybe even make love again. It could be as easy as that. She didn't need to ask him why he was there, or what he was thinking, and even if she did, she could pretend to believe whatever he told her.

In the end, fearing the truth too much, she turned around and went back to bed alone.

*

Jessica was sitting on the low, cushioned window ledge, her arms wrapped around her knees, the diaphanous mesh of the drapes falling about her in silvery moonlit folds. She couldn't sleep, she couldn't stop her mind working or her conscience tearing her apart. Even knowing about the baby hadn't stopped her wanting him, or imagining a world in which they could be together.

Putting her head back she closed her eyes and felt a cool draught of night air come in from the vines. When her phone started to ring she wasn't sure if she'd been expecting it to, she only knew it would be him, and that she was going to answer in spite of knowing she shouldn't.

'I have to see you,' he said gruffly. 'I want to hold you so badly.'

Though it was how she felt too, she said, 'We have to try to forget these past two weeks. If we're going to stand any chance of keeping a friendship, and you know we need to, we have to pretend they didn't happen.'

'And you can do that?'

Her eyes closed, because she knew she couldn't, but it would do no good to admit it.

'I keep thinking about you,' he said. 'I should have made love to you that first time, at the lake.'

'I wish you had.'

'Let me come to you now.'

'No. You know you can't . . . There are things you don't know, Luc, but you will, and then you'll understand why we have to end this conversation now.'

'Jessica . . .'

'I have to go.'

'Wait.'

But she didn't. She pressed her thumb to disconnect, then after turning off the phone completely she remained sitting where she was, letting tears roll down her cheeks while promising herself that they would be the only ones she would shed, for she simply didn't have the right to any more.

The rising sun was burnishing the overhead beams in a soft rosy glow as Lilian lay on her back, staring up at the ceiling.

Luc was beside her now, facing away, towards the door that he'd left slightly ajar when he'd finally returned to bed a few hours ago.

She turned to look at the familiar breadth of his back, the darkness of his skin and hair, and felt such an edge of panic to her love that she was barely able to fight it. Once again she tried to push herself past the wall of denial she'd constructed, to make herself admit when she'd first started to suspect them. With a painful churning inside she recalled the moment she'd first seen Jessica's sculpture, and decided it was probably then. If she was right, the suspicion must have buried itself in her subconscious, for she hadn't really been aware of it at the time.

It was there now though, along with all the curious incidents and small memories it was awakening . . . Such as the shock they'd both experienced when she'd turned up on Friday, that seemed so out of proportion. And the raspberries Luc hadn't remembered dropping off at the cottage, when he could only have done so less than an hour before. Then there was the table set so romantically for two, and the way Jessica had claimed she wasn't entertaining, then quickly said she was. But what was lending her suspicion the most conviction of all wasn't really the sculpture, or the dinner, or even the way they were treating her, it was the way they seemed to be avoiding one another. She couldn't even recall them saying hello or goodbye since she'd got back, which wasn't normal for two people who'd just spent so much time together – unless they'd fallen out, or unless they had something to hide.

Finding herself unable to lie still any longer, she got quietly up from the bed and pulled on a pair of shorts and a T-shirt. As she started towards the door Luc stirred and turned onto his back. She looked down at him, waiting for him to wake up, but he didn't. She wondered if he'd gone to Jessica in the night, if that was why he'd taken so long to come back to bed, but quickly she pushed the thought away. This was all in her head, she was being paranoid, falling victim to her conscience, for she'd always been afraid of the price she might one day pay for concealing what had happened just before Natalie's death. And Luc would be the ultimate price. So there was still a chance she was wrong, that she was making up an affair to punish herself for a crime that couldn't be forgiven. But it had only been done to protect Jessica. They'd only lied to spare her any more suffering . . .

Going down to the kitchen she put some water on to boil, then stood gazing out at the vineyard, seeing nothing but images of them together, her best friend and her husband, and in ways that were so painful to imagine that she truly didn't know how she'd cope if they turned out to be true.

Tears began falling onto her cheeks. To keep trying to tell herself it wasn't happening was delusional to the point of stupidity. Somehow she had to confront this, and then she must find a way to keep him.

Though she'd half-intended to make coffee, instead she let herself out of the kitchen and went over to the barn. In all her life she'd never wanted to do anything less, but something was carrying her forward, telling her that if any proof existed of a relationship between them then this was where she would find it.

Pulling the cover from Jessica's sculpture she gazed down at the exquisite features, so serene and aesthetically perfect, and so lovingly carved by Luc's own hands. She could imagine them in here together, the light pooling around them, in their own special world. Anything beyond this room would have ceased to exist, because all that mattered was this beautiful work they were creating together.

As a sob escaped her she put a hand to her mouth to stifle it. Could life really be so cruel? Had the two people she cared most about in the world really betrayed her? If they had, neither of them would have done it lightly, so that could only mean they loved one another more than they loved her. She put her hands to her face, wanting to scream with the need to deny it, but she fought it down, forcing herself to remain calm. This was no proof, it was merely a sculpture. There was still a chance she was wrong.

A few minutes later she was sitting in front of Luke's computer, scrolling through his files, but the only shots she could find of Jessica were the usual ones he took of subjects he was sculpting, the head from all angles, top, bottom, sides, full on . . . Oh please God let this be all there was. Please let it be her conscience playing her tricks.

Not entirely sure what she was looking for now, she began searching through the drawers in his desk. The top one was a chaos of pens and tools and small scraps of paper that bore only scribbled notes to himself. The next contained photo cards for the computer, a diary with no recent entries, chequebooks and cash. It was in the bottom drawer that she discovered the sketch pad, and it was on the first page that she finally found the proof.

As she stared down at Jessica's naked body, so brazen and beautiful, and so obviously aroused, she could see, in her misery, why he would love her more.

'No!' she cried brokenly. 'No! No! No!' And ripping the drawing from the pad she began tearing it to shreds. As the pieces fell to the floor she looked down at them, breathless and confused. Then running back into the studio she grabbed a chisel and began stabbing it into Jessica's face, destroying the most beautiful piece Luc had ever created.

When it was no more than a pile of mangled clay she dropped the chisel, and stood staring in horror at what she had done. How would she ever explain this? Now her insanity was spent, what reason was she going to give for such an act of savagery other than to admit she knew the truth? But she didn't want it to be true. She wanted to be wrong, she had to be wrong, and clasping her hands to her face she sank down to her knees as she started to sob.

Chapter Twenty-Three

Having slept only fitfully, Jessica was dressed and downstairs when she heard a gentle grating at the window, and looking round saw that Solange, the dove, was back. She smiled. It was amazing how much pleasure such a little creature could give, she thought, as she searched for some crumbs. Hoping it would stay at least for today, because Harry was going to love having a wild bird almost eating out of his hand, she opened the window.

The dove immediately flew off, but was soon back when the crumbs were in the box, pecking away, giving a little flutter to her wings, and throwing a beady eye Jessica's way. Jessica watched her, smiling, then to her surprise she spotted someone coming down through the vineyard. When she realised it was Lilian she glanced at the clock. They hadn't arranged to meet until ten and it was still barely eight.

Pulling open the French doors, she was about to ask to what she owed the honour at such an early hour, when the look on Lilian's face dried the words on her lips. 'What is it?' she said, trying to swallow her unease as Lilian came towards her. 'What's happened?'

'I think you know,' Lilian said brokenly. 'So please don't let's pretend.'

'Lily, I don't . . .'

'I've seen the drawing,' Lilian told her. 'So just tell me, how serious is it?' Her face was so ravaged that Jessica had to fight the urge to lie rather than cause her any more pain, but knowing it wouldn't help in the end, she turned back into the kitchen and waited for Lilian to come in after her.

'How serious is it?' Lilian repeated. 'I need to know.'

Jessica swallowed and shook her head. 'It's not what you think . . .'

'How can you say that? You were naked. Out there, in the vineyard, with my husband . . . Oh God, Jessica, how could you?' she choked. 'You know how much I love him, how long I've waited for this . . .'

'Lily, nothing's happened between us, I swear,' Jessica cried, tears starting in her own eyes. 'I know how it must look, but we haven't slept together. We've never even touched one another.'

Lilian was shaking her head.

'I swear it's true. He loves you. It's why nothing happened between us. He didn't want to betray you. Neither of us did.'

'And you think being with him like that isn't a betrayal? '

Knowing it was, Jessica could only look at her helplessly.

'And now you're trying to tell me he didn't lay a finger on you . . .'

'I won't deny we were attracted to one another . . .'

'Of course you were. Look at the pair of you. People don't come much more attractive.' As her face started to crumple, Jessica said, 'Lily, I'm sorry. I'd give anything to spare you this pain . . .'

'But it's no more than I deserve,' Lilian mumbled. 'It was always going to happen, one way or another.'

Jessica blinked. 'What are you talking about? None of this is your fault.'

'Not this, no, but things have a way of working themselves out.'

Jessica was still confused. 'Lily . . .'

'It doesn't matter,' Lilian cut in. 'Nothing does any more.' Then her eyes came anxiously to Jessica's. 'Have you told him about the baby? When he came here last night, did you tell him?'

'He didn't come here last night.'

Lilian's eyes stared into hers. 'I wish I could believe you,' she said. 'I want to, but I . . .' As the impact of it all hit her again, she covered her face with her hands.

'He didn't come,' Jessica repeated. 'And no, I haven't told him about the baby. It's your place to do that. He's your husband . . .'

'Did you think about him being my husband when you took your clothes off for him?'

Jessica said, barely audibly, 'I tried not to.'

Lilian's voice sounded ragged and weak as she said, 'You made love with him that day, didn't you? Tell the truth, Jessica . . .'

'No! I swear on the children's lives. He drew me that way because I asked him to, for my book. I wanted to know how it felt to be an artist's model.' In spite of it being partly true, the excuse sounded so feeble that she felt embarrassed even saying it.

Lilian was shaking her head. 'The night I came back . . . You were making dinner for him.'

Though Jessica didn't answer, her eyes showed the truth.

'The flowers, the candles . . . And you're asking me to believe you've never made love . . .'

'We haven't.'

'. . . that you weren't intending to that night? It explains why you were both so shocked to see me, why you were shaking and Luc couldn't seem to focus . . . In my naivety I thought you'd be pleased to see me . . .' As her voice faltered, she let her head fall forward. 'God, what a fool. What a sad, pathetic fool, but it serves me right.'

'Lily . . .'

'He won't want this baby now . . .'

'Don't say that,' Jessica cried. 'Of course he'll want it . . .'

'. . . it'll be my punishment.'

Jessica frowned. 'What do you mean? Punishment for what?'

'The second baby,' Lilian whispered, her eyes gazing at nothing. 'I couldn't go through with it. I just . . .'

Jessica was staring at her in bewilderment. 'Are you saying you terminated it?' she said.

'I had to. The timing . . . It was all wrong . . . There was so much . . .'

'Oh my God, Lily, you let work push you into a decision like that? Does Luc know?'

'Of course not. I couldn't tell him.' Her eyes went beseechingly to Jessica's. 'Please don't tell him either. It's in the past, I have to try to forget about it, but I'll never forgive myself, and now this . . .'

Still stunned by the idea of Lilian taking such a step, Jessica struggled for something to say, but all she could manage was, 'It's not my place to tell him anything.'

After a while, seeming not to know what else to do, Lilian walked to the door and stared out towards the horizon. 'I feel as though I should tell you to leave,' she said hoarsely, 'but I can't.'

Jessica watched her, her heart so weighted with love and guilt she no longer knew what to say.

'I should hate you,' Lilian stated tonelessly, 'but I can't do that either. You mean so much to me. I don't want to lose you, even now.'

'I don't want to lose you either,' Jessica said, going to put her arms around her. 'And it's not going to happen. We've always been there for one another, and we always will be, even through this.'

As Lilian held her too, she said, 'I wish it could work out that way, but if you and Luc . . . If you want to be together . . .'

'He wants to be with you. He loves you. We both do, which is why nothing happened between us.'

Lilian put her head back as she inhaled. 'Even if I believed you . . .' Her eyes closed as more pain washed over her.

'Lily, you have to.'

Lilian was shaking her head, and as she turned away she said, almost dully, 'I've destroyed the drawing, and the sculpture, just like I destroyed my baby.'

Jessica's head started to spin, until realising that the destruction of Luc's work was hardly of consequence in the face of everything else, she said, 'You were hurting and afraid, that's why you did it. And you've been given another chance. You're pregnant again, so it's important that you forgive yourself and make a good life for this one.'

Lilian nodded, but she looked so dejected, so defeated that Jessica wasn't even sure she was thinking about the baby any more. 'I didn't mean any of this to happen,' she said, huskily, 'but I should have known it would.'

'Why? What do you mean?'

Lilian only looked at her, then away again. 'Does Charlie know about Luc?' she asked.

Jessica frowned in confusion. 'Of course not,' she answered.

'Are you going to tell him?'

'There's nothing to tell.'

Lilian's smile was sad as she looked at her. 'We both know there is,' she said softly. 'So the question now is, do I try to keep my marriage together for the sake of the baby, or do I let him go to you?'

'Lily, you're talking nonsense. I love Charlie . . .'

'Of course, but not in the way you used to.'

Jessica started to protest, but the way Lilian was shaking her head stopped her.

'Maybe you haven't faced up to it yet,' Lilian said, 'but I can read you too well.'

Determined to prove her wrong, Jessica said, 'It's true things haven't been easy since we lost Natalie, but we'll get through it. That's what happens in marriages, you get through the bad times. You and Luc will too.'

Tears began to roll down Lilian's cheeks. 'I love you so much,' she whispered brokenly. 'You're the family I never had.'

'I still am,' Jessica insisted, also in tears. 'The children and Charlie think of you that way too.'

Lilian's eyes closed, then seeming to have no more to say she turned away and walked out onto the patio. 'Thank you for not telling Luc about the baby,' she said, staring absently ahead. Then without looking back she continued out to the lane and on up through the vineyard towards the house.

Luc was standing in the pergola waiting when Lilian returned to the *manoir*. The moment she saw him she knew from his expression that he'd discovered what she'd done in the studio, and since there was no way of avoiding it, she tried to summon what resources she had left to face him.

'I know how angry you must be,' she said, struggling to hold back more tears. 'It's too late to say I wish I hadn't done it . . .'

'It doesn't matter,' he told her.

'I'm sorry . . .'

'I'm the one who should be saying that. I never wanted to hurt you . . .'

His eyes were so full of compassion, so dark with feeling, that it seemed to tear her heart in two. 'Oh Luc . . .'

'Ssh,' he said, drawing her into his arms as she started to break down. 'It's going to be all right.'

After a while she lifted her head to look up at him. 'I spoke to Jessica. She says nothing happened. You never made love.'

'We didn't.'

She continued to search his eyes. 'But you wanted to?'

The strain showed in his face as he gazed down at her.

'Are you in love with her?' she asked, her voice breaking with her heart.

He took a breath, then pulling her back into his arms, he said, 'I love you. That's all that matters.'

Realising he was unable to deny it, her eyes closed in pain and horror. She couldn't let him go, she just couldn't, so the only course open to her now was to tell him about the baby and then pray with all her heart that Charlie, even against the odds, managed to prevent the secret she shared with him and Veronica from ever coming out, because if it did it really would be the end for them all.

Chapter Twenty-Four

Charlie was at the wheel of his Jaguar, heading out of the airport. Having already called Jessica to confirm Harry was on his way, he was now ready to ring Maurice, who'd left a typically formal message earlier confirming their four o'clock appointment for tomorrow.

'I've been trying to contact you all weekend,' Charlie told him, when Maurice answered at his number in Kent.

'I'm afraid we haven't been here,' Maurice informed him unnecessarily. 'Are you wanting to change our arrangement?'

'I was trying to make it sooner,' Charlie replied, 'but I can't now. The thing is, I need to speak to Veronica. Is she with you?'

'Not at the moment, but I'm bringing her home in the morning. If she's not too tired you can probably speak to her a little later in the day.'

Charlie frowned at the beat of unease in his heart. 'Home from where?' he asked cautiously.

'The same clinic I moved her to the last time she was unwell.'

Remembering the slurred voice, and collapse in Bond Street, Charlie said, 'Has she started drinking again? I know she used to, but that was a long time . . .'

'It's not alcohol-related,' Maurice assured him. 'It'll be for her to tell you any more than that.'

More alarmed than ever, Charlie said, 'She's Jessica's mother. If she's ill, we have a right to know.'

'And Veronica has the right to choose who she tells. But please don't worry, it's not as serious as it could be, or they wouldn't allow her to come home.'

'So what do I tell Jessica?' The words were out almost before he considered them, and as a terrible silence followed, he turned cold to his very core.

In the end Maurice said, 'You have the letter, Charlie, it's all there. Don't you think it's time now to let Jessica see it?'

'No,' Charlie said, almost without thinking.

'Then tell her in your own words.'

Charlie swerved to avoid the central reservation, then realising how dangerous it was for him to keep driving, he pulled over to the hard shoulder. 'You understand what it could mean if I tell her?' he said.

Maurice's voice was still unnervingly calm as he said, 'Yes, I think so, and if you ask me it's a pity no-one told her at the time. The consequences might not have been half as bad as anyone feared. Whereas, leaving it this long . . . Well, what's done is done. We have to face the future now, and while it's my job to take care of Veronica, it's yours, Charlie . . . Well, I guess it's yours to start facing up to the truth.'

Jessica was waiting with Antoine as Harry came bouncing into the arrivals hall with all the exuberance that was so typical of him. The instant he spotted her he abandoned his escort and dashed straight over, leaping into such a bruising hug that he started to gasp for air.

Laughing, Jessica put him down again, and wondered how she could have stood to be without him for so long. 'So how was the flight?' she asked, tilting his adorable face up to hers.

'It was really cool,' he told her chirpily. 'You look tanned, Mum. Everyone talked to me. Dad said I wasn't to talk to anyone, but that's just rude . . . Hey! Antoine!' and Jessica was abruptly forgotten as he high-fived Antoine, then grappled with the dog who'd insisted on coming along too. *'Où est Elodie?'* he wanted to know, breaking straight into French.

'À la maison. Elle aide Maman à préparer ton lit. Tu vas rester avec nous, n'est pas, Jessica?'

Harry's eyes rounded with excitement as he looked at Jessica. 'We're going to be staying at the chateau?' he cried. 'Awesome. And will Rousseau be there too?'

'Yes, he live with us now,' Antoine told him, making a good attempt at English. 'Tonton Luc say he is him, but really he is us. Jessica, can we take Harry to the water park?'

'Of course,' she replied, starting to usher them towards the exit, 'not right away, though. Maman's waiting for us at home now, and later I think Papa is taking us all somewhere for a special treat.'

'Where?' both boys cried at once.

'It's a surprise,' she laughed, and finally getting them all outside, and into the car, she began the forty-minute drive back to the chateau.

Since there hadn't been much time to explain things to Daniella before coming to the airport, she still wasn't entirely sure whether both she and Harry were expected to be staying there, but she'd decided during the drive here that she needed to remain at the cottage for now. It wasn't exactly what she wanted, but she was afraid if she moved over to the chateau that it might end up hurting Lilian even more to think that Luc's family was befriending her and perhaps taking sides, even though there were none to be taken. Besides, she didn't want to start involving Claude and Daniella in a way she felt sure they wouldn't like, and booking into a hotel wasn't an option either, because Charlie would certainly want to know why.

'Mum?' Harry said, leaving Antoine to get to grips with some new gadget he'd brought with him.

'Yes?' she replied, glancing at him in the rear-view mirror as he rested his elbows on the seatbacks to get close, and wishing she could kiss his puzzled little face.

'You know the cottage,' he began pensively. 'Well, am I going to be staying there at all?'

'You can stay tonight, if you like,' she answered. 'In fact, I wish you would, because I've really missed you, and you know Antoine and Elodie would be welcome to come too. And Rousseau.'

'Mm,' he responded, not really seeming to pick up on that. 'When I get there,' he continued, apparently still in his own train of thought, 'well, is Natalie going to be there? I mean, I know she's not, not for real or anything, but is she like a ghost now? Will I see her?'

Feeling her heart twist, while wondering at the workings of his little mind, she said, 'No, darling, you won't see her.'

He gave that some deliberation, then said, 'I think it would frighten me a bit if I did.'

Smiling, Jessica said, 'She wouldn't do anything to frighten you.'

At that his eyes rounded with indignation. 'Oh yes she would. She was always doing stuff to frighten me.'

In spite of the emotion, Jessica had to laugh. 'Not like this, though. She's gone to Jesus now, sweetheart, but there's a little dove called Solange who comes to visit, and sometimes I like to think . . . Well, not that it's Natalie exactly, but that maybe Natalie's telling her to come.'

'That would be so like her,' Harry declared earnestly. 'She was always really bossy, telling everyone what to do.' Then, with a little sadness in his voice, 'I wish she was still here telling me what to do. I didn't mind it very much really.'

'I know,' Jessica whispered, wishing they were alone and she wasn't driving, 'but you're going to have a lovely time with Antoine and Elodie – and Rousseau, of course. I just hope I'm going to see something of you.'

'Oh you will,' he assured her, suddenly brightening. 'I'll be driving you nuts soon enough, the way I always do because I don't know how to be quiet, or sit still, or tidy up after myself, but you love me more than anyone else in the world, except Dad and Nikki who you love the same – and Nat, who we all love a little bit more now she's not here any more.' With that he sat back to check on Antoine, leaving Jessica to laugh at the very close recital of her own words, with the exception of those about Natalie, which he'd so lovably tacked on himself.

Lilian was at her desk in the office, staring blankly at the emails in front of her. Since telling Luc about the baby it was as though she'd slipped into some kind of parallel existence, where she'd begun watching the world as though no longer quite a part of it. She was aware of feeling and thinking and speaking, but no matter how lovingly and attentively Luc responded, she was unable to make herself believe it was real. Perhaps if her conscience weren't so burdened she might not be doubting him, or herself, this way, but there was no escaping it, and even though he had no idea of the truth, she couldn't help feeling she was finally being punished for the terrible decisions she had made. She had her wish, she was pregnant again, but now she had to live with Luc no longer wanting her, or their child.

Knowing it was a dangerous mix of guilt and hormones making her think this way rather than anything Luc had said, or done, she tried to push it from her mind, but it wasn't easy. Even if she managed it, she was left with so many images of him with Jessica that her suffering only became worse.

She knew, because Daniella had told her, that Harry had arrived safely the day before and that he and Jessica had spent most of yesterday at the chateau, going for a picnic with a couple of other families in the evening, before Jessica had returned to the cottage alone. As far as Lilian knew Jessica was still alone, and the very idea that she couldn't go to her, that they couldn't give one another the support they both needed right now, felt almost as bewildering as being the cause of one another's pain. Nothing like this had ever happened between them before. Though she knew how easily love could turn to hate when there was so much jealousy involved, and that maybe she should be seeking all kinds of revenge, when she thought of Jessica's own suffering, and what she still might go through, she could summon no hate towards her, nor anger. She could only feel sorrier than she ever had in her life that any of it had happened.

Hearing footsteps outside, she turned away from her computer and looked up as Luc came in.

'I thought I'd find you here,' he said, stopping on the way to his own computer to kiss her. 'Daniella's just brought the children over, and a message from Claude to remind you about the chairs for the concert on Saturday. You were going to ask Madame Bouvier if she had any suggestions.'

'Of course, I'll bring it up at the meeting tonight,' she said, and wondered how they were able to behave so normally when she knew he must be thinking about Jessica possibly even more than she was. 'Is Daniella staying for lunch?' she asked.

'I don't think so. She seemed about to get back in the car when I came over here.'

At the sound of running feet outside he turned round, and an instant later his niece, nephew and Harry came bursting in through the door with the dog in tow.

'Found you!' Harry cried delightedly, and bounded straight up to Lilian, arms outstretched.

Lilian's eyes shone with love as she hugged him to her. 'How are you, my darling?' she said. 'I heard you were here.'

'I came yesterday, and I've been staying at the chateau, but we're staying with Mum tonight, at the cottage. I asked her if Natalie was there, you know, like a ghost or something, but she said no, and anyway I wouldn't have minded really, except it might have been a bit scary. Dad's coming tomorrow.'

Smiling in spite of the ache in her heart, Lilian said, 'So I believe. What do you have planned, all of you?'

Harry shrugged, then looked up at Luc. 'I'm going to ask Mum and Dad if I can have a dog like Rousseau, so can you tell me where you got him, please, and what kind of make he is.'

'I told you, he's a retriever,' Antoine piped up.

'A flat-coat retriever,' Luc added.

Satisfied, Harry shouted, 'Come on! Let's go and ask Mum now. We might be able to get her on our side before Dad arrives.'

'Yes, and we've got our secret to show you,' Elodie was saying, as they started running out. 'Antoine only told me about it last week, so even I haven't seen it yet.'

As they disappeared, Lilian got up from her chair and walked over to the door to watch them charging down through the vineyard. How wonderful to be their age, she was thinking, so innocent and pure, no fears, no crimes, no guilt, only secrets they were bursting to tell. She thought of Natalie, and how she'd tried to tell Jessica her secret but hadn't been able to – and as the darkness of it all began filling her up again she closed her eyes and tried not to think any more.

Charlie's mouth was set in a grim line, and his eyes looked

tired and strained as he listened to Veronica at the end of the line, telling him that she understood, of course, why he hadn't shown her letter to Jessica yet, but he must surely understand why she wanted him to now.

'I know my relationship with Jessica can't be considered as important as yours,' she was saying, her normally flighty tones still trying to make it through the tiredness and slurring, 'but I always was a teensy bit selfish, as you know, and though these little turns I've had aren't supposed to be serious, I really don't want to pop off without seeing her. And Maurice is adamant she can't come unless she knows the truth, or she'll start shouting at me and upsetting me and who knows, I might end up having another little turn. You do see that, darling, don't you? Please try to understand. I know she'll never forgive us, but I can't go on hiding things from her. Not any longer, and if she's going to shout at me, at least I won't have to keep worrying about what I'm saying if I'm not having to hide anything any more.'

'She's going to be very worried once she knows you've had a stroke,' Charlie told her, feeling he'd rather deal with that for now than anything else.

'Two strokes,' she corrected, 'but only little ones. Hardly anything to worry about at all, though I'm having a bit of a problem seeing at the moment. Everything's a bit blurred, but they say that will probably get better. And they might operate, apparently, because there are things they can do these days to stop the embolism . . . I think that's what it's called. Is that right, Maurice?'

'Yes, that's what it's called,' Charlie told her.

'Anyway, we're waiting to find out. I go back again next week for more tests . . . But you don't want to hear any more about that. I know how upset and worried you must be. Is Jessica still in France?'

'Yes, I'm going there myself tomorrow.'

'Oh dear. That'll probably be difficult for you. I was going to go back myself, but then I couldn't face it. How has she managed while she's been there? She must have found it very hard.'

'Yes, I think she has, but she felt it was something she had to do.' Then, after a pause, 'She's spoken to the paramedic.'

There was a moment's silence, until understanding the significance of what he'd just told her, Veronica said, very gently, 'Then it would seem to me, darling, that you don't have very much choice but to tell her now.'

'No,' Charlie responded bleakly, 'no, I don't suppose I do.'

'*Oh là là*, brace yourself,' Daniella warned as the sound of thundering feet coming down through the vines reached them. 'I'm just dropping off Antoine's toothbrush and pyjamas for tonight,' she told Jessica. 'I'll come back later for Elodie – she's going to stay with her friend who has a pool. The boys are invited to join them tomorrow, so you can drop them off on your way to collect Charlie from the airport, if you like.'

'Of course,' Jessica replied, a smile appearing in her eyes as the children came charging across the patio and in through the door.

'Hey Mum,' Harry cried, going to throw his arms around her waist. 'I just saw Lilian and Luc, and Rousseau is a flat-coat retriever.'

'Really?' Jessica responded, wanting only to go on holding him.

'Yes, so can we have one, please, because he's a really nice dog and I promise I'll take care of him myself. You won't have to walk him, or feed him, or anything, because I'll do it . . .'

'Darling, we're in the middle of London and look how big Rousseau is.'

'But other people have big dogs in London.'

'I'll wish you good luck with that one,' Daniella interrupted with no little irony. 'I'd better be off, Claude's waiting. I'll be back for Elodie around four.'

Letting Harry go and walking out to the car with her, Jessica said, 'Are you sure you don't mind Harry staying for a few days if Charlie and I go off to Provence?'

'Absolutely not,' Daniella assured her.

'There's always a chance he might want to come with us . . .'

'Mum! Can we go and play in the attic?' Harry shouted from inside.

Jessica turned incredulously. 'Do you have any idea how hot it'll be up there?' she said.

'We don't care. We're going, OK?'

Shrugging, Jessica turned back to Daniella. 'I'll see you at four,' she said, giving her a hug.

'Before I go,' Daniella said softly, 'I take it you know Lilian's going to have a baby.'

Jessica smiled as her heart contracted. 'Yes,' she said. 'Is Luc pleased?' Then, before Daniella could answer, 'I'm sorry, I shouldn't have said that. Of course he is.'

Daniella's sympathy showed. 'I don't know how he feels. He didn't say.'

As Jessica went back inside her heart was aching for Lilian and how hard she must be finding this, and knowing she was the cause of Lilian's pain was making it so much worse. She wondered how they were ever going to get past this, or if they even could, for Lilian would always be watching them and wondering if her husband and best friend still had feelings for one another. No friendship could withstand that kind of pressure and suspicion, not even theirs, and Jessica could hardly bear to think of how much she was going to miss her.

Becoming aware of Rousseau whining upstairs, she decided to go up and investigate, but had got only as far as her own bedroom door when the children started sliding down the attic ladder, bumping into one another and the dog who'd been crying because he couldn't climb up.

'Mum!' Harry cried breathlessly, the last to come down. 'Mum, look what we found.'

His face was pale and worried, and as Jessica looked down at what he was holding she felt her heartbeat starting to slow. Then the world outside seemed to quieten and recede, like a sea being sucked away from the shore.

'It's Natalie's,' he said.

Jessica could still only look at it. Somewhere in her mind was the memory of how determined she'd been to come here, how she'd known she should stay, and how she'd even felt Natalie's fear as though it were still in the house, but nothing was fully in focus yet, that would come later. All she could see now was a small pink book with a fake brass lock and odd little doodles scribbled into the flowers on the front. Natalie's diary.

A moment later it was in her hands, and the children were running off down the stairs, and out into the vines. She listened to their voices fading in the distance, then holding the book to her she went to the window to watch them.

Later she was unable to say how long it took her to open the diary and read it, because from the moment Harry put it into her hands – brother delivering message from sister – it was as though time itself slipped out of kilter. All she knew was that she was in the kitchen when she read the final entry, and as she stared down at the words blurring and slanting in front of her, and felt the horror of them gathering in her heart, she realised there was no longer any doubt about who had carried Natalie to the sofa that day.

Someone's just arrived. Think it's supposed to be a surprise so will pretend – but it's Dad cuz can hear his voice. Someone's with him I think, or maybe it's just Grandma. More later . . . (Need to have bigger mysteries in life, am determined to be exciting.)

Jessica put the book down and as she heard her daughter's perky, busy little voice echoing from the page she felt her entire world starting to crumble around her.

Charlie had been here when Natalie died.

Chapter Twenty-Five

As Charlie came into the arrivals hall Jessica was standing to the side of a large group of people, so he was unable to see her at first. She watched him looking around and felt an odd sensation that seemed to be a mix of nerves, anger and a kind of bewilderment. It was vaguely like watching a stranger, she was thinking, who bore a resemblance to someone she knew. Of course his appearance hadn't actually altered, he was still a large, robust man with a handsome face and shock of loose sandy hair, but the truth he'd kept hidden from her all this time had altered him in her mind. Now he seemed diminished, if not in stature then certainly in self, and all she could think was, *You were there when Natalie died, and you never said a word. Why? What are you hiding?* The answer seemed so blindingly obvious that were it not for the need to hear it from his own lips, she'd have turned around right then and walked away.

Instead, she stepped forward, saw his expression turn to one of pleasure, and attempted a smile of her own as he drew her into a hug.

'I was beginning to think you weren't here,' he said, holding her tight.

She didn't reply, merely allowed him to look down at her and wondered what he could read in her face. He must have sensed something, because his eyes showed a moment of wariness, but then he was smiling as he said, 'I'd almost forgotten I had such a beautiful wife.'

'Come on, let's go,' she said. 'The car's not far.'

As they walked out of the terminal he put an arm round her shoulders, while giving her all the latest news from home as well as passing on messages. '. . . and Suzie Collins is really keen to see you,' he was saying as they got into the car. 'She's heading down to Provence with her new man next week, so I've told her to give us a call when she gets there, in case we're there too. I wasn't sure if you wanted to go small and romantic,' he continued, as they drove away, 'or grand and expensive, so I've earmarked a few places to show you. You're using Lilian's computer, aren't you?'

'I was,' she replied.

Instead of sounding curious about that, he let a few seconds pass, then with a note of anxiety in his voice he said, 'So, do you still want to go, or have the plans changed again?'

'I'm not sure,' she answered.

He said no more and she wondered how deep his anxiety was, for the coldness of her manner must surely be setting off all kinds of alarms by now.

They continued in silence for a while, joining the autoroute and speeding north towards Macon. She thought about the secret he was hiding, and could only wonder how he'd found the courage to come here at all. Certainly it explained his reluctance, in fact it explained so much that she could barely make herself think of it, for the deception was so great, and had gone on so long that almost everything in the past few months seemed tainted by it. Including his inability to deal with his grief. Now she knew why he'd been blocking it all this time, trying to carry on as though Natalie's death hadn't happened, but it had come at him in other ways, and in amongst all the horror and confusion in her heart, she realised she almost felt sorry for how bitterly it must be destroying him.

'Have you spoken to Nikki today?' he asked, as they left the autoroute to begin driving through the countryside.

'No,' she answered. 'She's making a strike for independence, so we only speak every other day now. The rest of the time we text.'

'She seems to be having a good time up there.'

'Yes.'

'I miss her,' he confessed. 'The house is too quiet without any of you there.'

It's especially quiet without Natalie, she wanted to say.

'Harry's with Antoine and Elodie,' she told him, changing the subject. 'They're at a pool party so he won't be back until late.'

He had nothing to say to that, so she let the silence run on until he asked, 'What's this Harry tells me about a concert at the weekend? At the chateau.'

'Yes, Daniella's singing.'

He turned to her in surprise. 'And you want to go off somewhere without seeing her?'

'Not really.' She swung the car sharply to the left, and started heading down the road that would eventually lead to Valennes.

He turned to gaze out of the window, apparently still not willing to get into why she was being so uncommunicative. He must know I've found out, she was thinking to herself, he simply has to.

'So how are Luc and Lilian?' he asked, making another attempt to be friendly.

'Lilian's going to have a baby.'

He nodded, as though approvingly. 'They must be pleased,' he commented. Then, with an awkward laugh, 'I expect we'll be godparents. Do they have them in France?'

'Yes, but I doubt we'll be asked.'

To her surprise he said nothing to that, which annoyed her, for he surely had to be curious to know why Lilian might not want them.

Eventually he said, 'Have you and Lilian fallen out, or something?'

Instead of answering she simply glanced at him, and continued to drive.

Twenty minutes later she walked into the cottage ahead of him and turned to watch where his eyes went first as he came in the door. She wasn't entirely surprised when they avoided the stairs, nor was she sorry to see how pinched his expression had become.

Without even offering him a drink, she took the diary from a drawer in the table and handed it to him.

The moment he saw it the blood drained from his face.

'I want you to read the final entry,' she said evenly, 'and then I want you to tell me the truth.'

As he opened it she was aware of her heart starting a strange kind of beat, and could only imagine what was happening to his. Then for one awful moment she realised how close she was to tears. He was Natalie's father, for God's sake, he'd adored her, so surely it couldn't be as bad as she feared.

When finally he looked up from the page he appeared so haggard and grey that she was half afraid he might be on the verge of collapse. He tried to speak, but all that came out was a strangled sort of cry, and slumping into a chair he put his head in his hands.

'You were having an affair with my mother,' she said.

His eyes came up to hers, but before he could say anything she went on, 'Natalie found you together. She tried to call me, so you . . .' She couldn't say any more, she just couldn't. 'Please tell me you didn't push her down the stairs,' she gasped brokenly. 'Please tell me it wasn't . . .'

His eyes dilated with shock. 'No!' he cried. 'My God, how can you even think it?'

'Then what happened? For Christ's sake tell me how she fell. I need to know.'

He looked down at the diary again, and when his eyes came back to hers they were so full of pain that she couldn't remain unmoved. 'You're right, she did find me,' he told her, in a voice that rasped with grief. 'But not with your mother. It was Lilian.'

Jessica was so stunned that for a moment she didn't think she'd heard right. Then, becoming aware of the strangest swirling in her senses, she put a hand to her head. It was as though she was floating away from the shock, even as it held her to its core. 'But Lilian was in Paris,' she said stupidly.

He only looked at her, his expression telling her that her belief belonged to another place, another time, not to this horrible new world he was suddenly opening up.

A full five seconds or more passed before she could even inhale, and when she did it made her feel sick.

She continued to stare at him, all the time thinking, *he was here with Lilian, he was here with Lilian*. She repeated it over and over as though to make herself believe it. *Lilian. Her*

Lilian. It couldn't be true. She wouldn't let it be. Lilian's betrayal felt so much worse than his, not because of Charlie, but because of Natalie and the pretence they'd kept up all these months, lying to her in ways that made her head spin, even trying to convince her she was crazy for being unable to accept what she'd been told. How shamefully, wickedly, they'd deceived her, and so too had her mother.

She could feel herself starting to tremble, as though the shock was turning into some kind of attack. She tried to envisage the scenario, where he and Lilian might have been when Natalie found them, where her mother was, and how Natalie had come to walk in on them. Then suddenly she said, 'I want to know everything that happened here that day, from the moment you arrived till the moment . . .' She choked on the next words. 'I want to know everything,' she finally managed.

With his face drained of colour and his eyes heavy with pain he looked a different man to a few minutes ago, as though he was fracturing apart inside and unable to hold on. He tried to take a breath, then tried again. It was a while before she realised he was sobbing, dry, brutal convulsions, his whole body juddering as the beginnings of his grief broke free.

'You have to tell me,' she cried. 'Charlie, please.'

He nodded. By now his torment was so clear that she felt a stirring of pity, for whatever he had done, whatever madness had taken place here, she knew he would never have meant it to end the way it had.

'Lilian and I left Paris very early that morning,' he began, his voice cracked with emotion. 'I'd hired a car and . . .'

'How long have you and Lilian been involved with one another?' she asked, barely connecting with the words, they seemed so strange.

He shook his head. 'We're not. It was over before she moved to Paris.'

Jessica's eyes closed as another dizzying wave of shock came over her.

'I think it was why she went,' he continued. 'We'd been seeing one another for six months, maybe more . . .'

Jessica looked at him and wondered who he was. Who

Lilian was too, because suddenly her world seemed full of people she didn't know.

'We were terrified of you finding out,' he said, 'but we still couldn't seem to stop.' His gaze started to lose focus, as though he was no longer quite sure where he was. 'To be honest I don't think it was as serious as either of us thought, it just seemed that way at the time. I knew she was lonely and desperate for someone to love her, while I . . .' He took a breath, and for a moment it seemed he might break down again. 'I only ever loved you, but I didn't know how to end it. She was . . . It became . . . Oh God, it hardly matters now, because she came to France and met Luc, then finally it was over between us. I'm not saying I didn't have feelings for her, because obviously I did, but they weren't what she needed . . . I could never give her that.'

'I take it Luc doesn't know any of this,' she said, wishing he was there now so she could hold onto his hands, and feel as though something might keep her together.

He shook his head. 'Not as far as I'm aware. I'm sure she wouldn't have told him.'

No, of course she wouldn't, Jessica thought. How could she, and still hope to keep him? 'Go on,' she said.

'When we came here that day,' he continued raggedly, 'it wasn't with the intention of . . . I was coming to surprise Natalie, and she was going to surprise Luc.'

'What happened when you got here?'

As he started to answer his face contorted with the effort of not breaking down. 'Your mother and Natalie were about to go for a walk,' he said, barely able to speak. 'I was going to go with them, but then I had a call from the crew in Paris that I had to take, so they went on without me. Lilian was on her mobile too, talking to someone in Dubai, and we ended our calls around the same time. Then I asked her if she'd like a drink, and I guess . . . one thing ended up leading to another . . .' His voice gave out on him then, and as tears spilled from his eyes and the breath shuddered in his lungs, Jessica tried to understand how Lilian had been able to make love with another man when she and Luc had only been married for a few months. It didn't seem to make any sense. It was so out of character for the Lilian she knew, but clearly it had happened, and now she had somehow to accept that Lilian was more capable of betraying their friendship – and her husband – than she, Jessica, would ever have imagined.

After giving himself a moment to recover, Charlie forced himself on. 'We went upstairs,' he said, 'to the room Natalie was using.'

Jessica almost flinched at the thought of him making love to her best friend amongst his own daughter's soft toys, and on the sheets she would later use . . .

'When it was over,' he continued, 'I guess because of the early start, we fell asleep, and the next thing we knew Natalie was . . . Natalie was . . . there.' His head went back and in a voice that was so anguished it sent chills through her, he cried, 'Oh God help me! God help me! Why did it have to happen? Why? Why? Why?'

As Jessica looked at him her own heart was breaking apart, yet she realised his pain and horror must be far greater than anything she would ever know.

'She started . . . started shouting at me,' he stammered, pushing himself on, 'saying, "You can't do this. It's not right. I'm going to tell Mum." She had her phone in her hand and as she ran out onto the landing . . .' He gulped for more air. 'I leapt out of bed. I . . . I had no clothes on, so I grabbed . . . grabbed my shorts, and by the time I opened . . . opened the door she'd got through to you.' He pushed the heels of his hands into his eyes. 'Then she realised I was coming and started to run. She didn't see . . . the . . . newspapers at the top of the stairs, nor did I, but . . . but your mother did. She was in her room, and she shouted but it was too . . . too . . . *late.*' His voice was high-pitched with horror, as saliva and mucus mingled with the stream of his tears. 'She fell and . . . Oh God! Oh God!'

Jessica was crying too, and put out her hands as though to block the impact of those terrible moments.

'It was all over so fast,' he finally spluttered. 'One minute she was on the landing, and the next . . . Oh no, no, no. My baby . . . My girl . . .' he sobbed. 'And it was all my fault . . .' He tried to push the tears away, but they were coming too fast, and he was shaking so hard that Jessica grabbed his hands to try to hold him together.

It was some time before he was able to go on, but finally he said, 'Your mother was the first one down here . . . She came so fast that she fell herself when she reached the bottom.' He dashed his hands into his hair and clenched them tight. 'It was already too late,' he said, having to squeeze the words out. 'The way she was lying there . . . We could see . . .'

He took a breath, and then another. It didn't help, he still couldn't control himself.

'Just keep breathing,' Jessica told him, realising he couldn't get past the image of Natalie at the foot of the stairs. 'That's it. That's right,' she said, not knowing where her own strength was suddenly coming from.

'Your mother went to the phone,' he finally managed, 'but she didn't know the emergency number. She kept shouting for Lilian to tell her and Lilian was trying but your mother was hysterical, so . . . in the end Lilian made the call. I was on the floor with Natalie, holding her, trying to make her wake up, but she . . . Her eyes were . . .'

'Just tell me what you did,' Jessica broke in, unable to deal with how her baby must have looked.

'I picked her up . . . I picked her up . . .'

Realising he was starting to lose it again, she squeezed his hands so hard that she could barely take the pain.

'I took her to the sofa,' he said. 'She was on my lap and I was holding her . . .'

Finding it too easy to picture them, the big man racked with despair, holding his little broken daughter, Jessica let go of him and buried her face in her hands.

'Then the phone started to ring and I realised . . . it must be you, trying to find out why she . . . Why she'd called . . . I didn't know how I was going to tell you . . . I was . . . I couldn't . . . I started to panic . . . I didn't know how to tell you.'

Jessica was unable to look at him now, she was too afraid of what was coming next, for she knew it would be this that she was going to find the hardest of all.

'In all my life I will never understand what happened to me then,' he said. 'I'll never forgive myself, never. It was as though I lost control. I couldn't think straight. I know I was in shock, we all were, but it doesn't excuse . . . Nothing will ever . . . I was so afraid of what it was going to do to you . . . Losing Natalie and then . . . I couldn't let you find out like that I'd been unfaithful. It was too much . . . Your daughter, your husband, your best friend . . . I don't know if I thought it would be better to lie, or if I was so afraid that I just wanted to run . . . It was as though . . . If I got out of there and went back to Paris, it might turn back the clock. I know that sounds crazy, but it was how it seemed . . . Or what I was telling myself, I don't know. I only know that . . . That . . .'

When he stopped Jessica lifted her head. 'So you left her there?' she said hoarsely. 'You got in the car and drove away?'

His face seemed to collapse. 'Nothing you say or do now can make me feel any worse than I already do,' he told her, choked with pain. 'If it weren't for Nikki and Harry . . . I've thought so often about ending my life, because I can't bear what I've done . . . I'll never forgive myself. Never.'

Knowing that would almost certainly prove true, Jessica said, 'And Lilian went with you?'

He nodded. 'I think she was afraid to let me drive on my own, and she didn't want Luc to find out she was here . . .'

'So both of you drove away leaving my little girl and my mother . . .' She could still hardly make herself believe it. 'And when I called Lilian to get Luc's number . . . Where were you?'

'On our way to Dijon. We thought the time it would take to drive there and back would be about the same as it would have taken me to get here from Paris. So I dropped her at the station, where she waited for the next train . . . Then I . . . I drove back here.'

'Oh my God, so calculated,' she murmured in horror. 'You weren't thinking rationally, and yet you managed to work out how long it would take . . .' She closed her eyes, as though that could somehow shut out the madness. 'And all these months you've kept the lie going,' she said. 'You've let me doubt myself, and even think I was going crazy, when all the time . . . Oh my God, I feel as though I'm talking about strangers, not the people I love . . . Did you really think you were going to get away with it? Yes, you must have . . . You almost did, because if Harry hadn't found the diary . . .'

'I was coming here to tell you anyway,' he said. 'Your mother's already tried . . . She wrote you a letter . . . She left it to me to decide when to give it to you, so I've brought it with me, but I thought I should tell you myself first, and ask you not to blame her. She never wanted to deceive you . . .'

'She never wanted . . .? Jesus Christ, the whole thing . . . Even down to the tourists losing their way. It was obviously your car Luc saw. So when did you work that out? Was it your idea, or my mother's?'

'It must have been hers, because we didn't discuss it. I think it did happen though, but the day before, which was what put it into her mind.' His eyes looked pleadingly into hers. 'Try not to be too hard on her. She really didn't want to lie, and it's made her ill, which is why we've had such a hard time getting hold of her.'

Jessica's expression changed. 'What do you mean, ill?' she demanded, and feeling a distant panic starting to well up inside her, she said, 'She's not . . . Oh God, Charlie, please don't tell me . . .'

'She's OK,' he assured her. 'She's at home with Maurice now, but she's had a couple of strokes . . . Minor ones . . .'

This was becoming all too much. Her mother had collapsed in Bond Street, had suffered a stroke, very probably because of the stress the lies had put her under, and no-one had ever seen fit to tell her. 'How long have you known?' she asked. 'Is this something else you've been keeping from me?'

'Only since yesterday when I spoke to her on the phone. She wants to see you, but Maurice won't allow it until you know the truth. He's afraid of how much it upsets her.'

She turned away, racked with guilt for the way she'd treated her mother, accusing her of the most terrible crimes, blaming her for everything imaginable, when all the time Veronica's suffering must have been extreme. This was what Charlie's and Lilian's deceit had done, because she understood her mother well enough to know that she always thought everyone knew better than her, particularly men, so she wouldn't have had the confidence to stand up for what she thought was right. Except in the end, she had, because she'd written it all down . . .

'I want the letter,' she said to Charlie.

'It's in the car, in my bag.'

'I want it now.'

While he went to get it she found her mind going round and round, searching out memories, looking for more lies and treachery, which seemed to have worked their way into almost everything now. Then she was remembering Lilian's cryptic remarks the day before about being punished, and deserving what was happening to her. They made sense now, in the light of this horrible truth, and for a moment Jessica almost couldn't bear it, because she'd always trusted Lilian in a way she'd never trusted anyone else in her life. She'd believed so completely in their friendship and what they meant to one another, had never even dreamt she could deceive her that way . . . It was too hard to take, too difficult to understand, because no matter how many excuses Lilian might have made to herself, or how afraid she must have been of what would happen if Jessica ever found out, to have left Natalie the way she had was beyond anything Jessica could ever comprehend.

'I need to speak to Lilian,' she said to Charlie as he came back. 'Please call her and ask her to come here. You can tell her why, or I will, it's up to you.'

There was an expression of such helplessness in his eyes that she realised he was barely thinking about anything beyond her, and how he could possibly make this right.

'When you've done that,' she said, 'you can call my mother, or Maurice, to let them know we're coming back. We'll leave as soon as I've packed.'

'You mean today?'

'Yes, today. I want to see her for myself, to make sure it's not more serious than they're telling us.'

'And then?' he said, bleakly.

As she looked at him she found herself thinking of Harry who looked so like him, and Nikki who adored him, then of how crushed he was inside, how full of shame and grief and fear, so that in the end all she could say was, 'I don't know, Charlie. I just don't know.'

*

'Charlie,' Lilian cried brightly as his voice came down the line. 'How lovely. Are you here yet?'

'I'm at the cottage,' he replied.

His very tone caused the warmth to seep from her smile as she glanced nervously at Fernand, then at Luc. They were still sitting at the table in the pergola following lunch, but even though the meal was over, it was going to seem odd if she stood up and left now, particularly when they knew she was speaking to Charlie. 'Is everything all right?' she asked, managing to make it sound like a casual question. 'Good flight?'

'Jessica wants to see you,' he told her.

Lilian's heart missed a beat, but somehow she kept on smiling. 'Oh, I'd love to come and see you right away,' she responded, 'but I promised Daniella I'd help at the chateau this afternoon. You know about the concert at the weekend, don't you? I hope you and Jessica are coming.'

'We're driving back to England tonight,' he said. 'Veronica's unwell.'

'Oh my goodness,' Lilian murmured, able to lose her smile now. 'What's wrong with her?' Aware that both Fernand and Luc were looking at her, she put a hand over the receiver to tell them about Veronica.

'You need to come here,' Charlie said. 'Jessica's saying that you can use her mother's illness as an excuse if you like, but if you don't come she'll speak to Luc instead.'

'Oh gosh, of course I'll be there,' Lilian replied feelingly. She was about to say more when she realised Charlie was speaking to Jessica.

'She wants you to wait for an hour,' he said, coming back on the line. 'She wants to read a letter from her mother first.'

Lilian swallowed anxiously. 'Will you be there?' she asked, forgetting herself for a moment.

'I don't know,' he replied. 'I guess that's up to Jessica.'

As she put the phone down Lilian looked at Luc and Fernand, then pressing her palms to her cheeks she said, 'Poor Veronica.'

'We must ask Jessica if there's anything we can do,' Fernand said, reaching for his own phone.

'I'm sure she'll appreciate that,' Lilian responded. 'But I've said I'll go down there in an hour, so I can ask her then.'

Luc continued to look at her, but his expression was unreadable.

'Apparently they're driving back to London tonight,' she said, her eyes moving away.

'Oh, Daniella will be disappointed,' Fernand replied, 'but I am sure she will understand.'

Lilian got to her feet. 'I think I'll go over to the office and see about sending Veronica some flowers,' she said. 'They should arrive by Friday if I order them now.'

As she left she heard Luc saying something to his father, then he got up too, but instead of coming after her, as she'd half-hoped he might, he went into the house and closed the door.

'Are you all right?' Luc said into Jessica's voicemail. 'Lilian told me about your mother. She said you're leaving tonight, so I want you to know . . .' He stopped and started again. 'Please don't go without calling,' and ringing off he kept his phone in his hand as he walked over to the *cave* in the hope of losing himself in some work as he waited to say goodbye.

Chapter Twenty-Six

Needing to be alone when she read her mother's letter, Jessica waited until Charlie had gone to find out if Harry wanted to come back with them now, or stay with his friends, then sitting down at the table she took the small bunch of handwritten pages from their crumpled envelope and unfolded them.

As she read she could almost hear her mother's voice, sultry and breezy, deep-throated and occasionally girlish, but mostly there was anguish and pain, and heartfelt regret for the way she'd let her down as a mother, and for the lies that she could no longer keep up.

By the time she'd finished reading her vision was blurred by tears, but at least she knew now that Charlie was holding no more back. However, she'd read it very quickly, so drying her eyes, she went back to the first page and started again . . .

My dear Jessica,

I'm not sure if you will read this, because I think I must let Charlie decide whether or not you should see it, but even if he does give it to you, I know you're so angry with me that once you see my writing you're likely to throw it away anyway. But just in case here goes, my darling.

You've always known that we weren't telling you the whole truth about what happened to Natalie, and you were right. I never wanted to lie, but at the time no-one was thinking straight, least of all poor Charlie, and now we've all got ourselves into the most terrible mess, at least I have, so I have to try to unburden my heart.

What happened that day . . . Well, to tell the truth darling it all happened so fast that it still makes my head spin. I don't mean when Charlie and Lilian turned up, that was all normal, and slow, and to be honest, I didn't think anything of them arriving together. Natalie was thrilled to see her daddy and Lilian was off to surprise Luc (or so I thought), then the two of them got embroiled on the phone with all their work things, so Nat and I went off for our walk. It had started to rain, but we had to go because we'd found a nest the day before that had fallen out of a tree, and we thought the little chicks might be starving by now, so we took them some crumbs of brioche that we'd saved from our breakfast that morning. We looked for a long time but we didn't find them, and we both felt very sad to think that a fox or a badger might have got them.

So we came home again, and that was when everything became very fast. There was no sign of Charlie or Lilian, so Nat and I went upstairs to take off our wet clothes, and then I heard Nat shouting in her room, which really scared me, so I grabbed a big candlestick that was next to my bed, because I thought we had an intruder. I was just dashing out of my room when Natalie came flying along the landing with the phone in her hand, and, may God forgive me for not being quick enough to stop her. I swear I tried, Jessica, but there was a pile of newspapers at the top of the stairs, which she didn't see, and the next thing I knew she'd tripped on them and then she was gone. I couldn't see her any more.

Oh Jessica, Jessica. I should have saved your baby angel. I should have been faster. I shouldn't have left the papers where they were, I should have done a thousand things differently, but most of all I should have gone down those stairs instead of our little braveheart, anything rather than you have to lose her.

I think I'm taking a long time to tell this now, but it's still really fast in my mind, because I ran down after her, and then Charlie was there trying to make her wake up, and I was shouting at Lilian, and Lilian was crying . . . I think I might have screamed, but it could have been Charlie, or maybe I'm just imagining that, because every time I think of our dear little angel lying there with her eyes open, I want to scream.

I kept dialling 999, even though I knew it was wrong, and then Lilian took the phone and she made the call while Charlie carried Nat into the sitting room. Then the phone rang and Charlie said it would be you, and he started to cry. It was terrible to see. I tried to comfort him, but he just kept saying you didn't deserve this, and he was right, of course, but nor did he. It wasn't anyone's fault, but he was blaming himself, and of course he shouldn't have been up there with Lilian . . .

Anyway, I tried to stop him from going, but he seemed to think it was the only thing he could do. I could tell he wasn't in his right mind, but nor was I, and when he kept saying you didn't deserve this, and we had to think about you . . .

Jessica looked up from the page. Since she'd read the letter once before she didn't want to go over again how Charlie and Lilian had abandoned Natalie and her mother, so flipping over the next two pages she started to read again.

I knew, when you came to Fernand's house the day after it happened that you would blame me, tell me I hadn't taken good enough care of your girl, and because you were right I hardly had a way to defend myself. I could see how broken up Charlie was – I've never seen a man sorrier or more afraid than when he brought you from the airport – and Nikki and Harry were there, so I couldn't tell the truth then, and so time went on, and I didn't know what to do for the best. I wanted to go back to the cottage to have a little chat with Natalie, and to see if I could persuade Lilian to tell you the truth, but I couldn't face it in the end. Then I had a little turn in Bond Street, which is what put me where I am now (I'm in a clinic that Maurice moved me to, but I can't call to let you know, because I'm not supposed to have any stress, and I don't want to lie to you any more, so that's why I'm writing this letter).

All I wanted when I took Nat to France was to do something to make up for being such a bad mother, by trying to be a good grandmother, and now you must be wishing me straight to hell. It's what I deserve, but please try not to think too harshly of me, darling, because I swear if I could have given my life in place of hers, I would have. It really was a terrible accident, that never should have happened – and now Charlie, Lilian and I have learned how one deception leads to another, and to another. I can't let that go on. I'm sorry for them and what effect this letter might have on their lives if you ever see it, but now you are my only concern. I can't have you driving yourself crazy any longer trying to find answers no-one will give you.

If you really are reading this then I'm going to hope that you won't be too hard on Charlie once you learn the truth, because you know in your heart that he's not a bad man, he was just a very silly one, and he's ended up paying the kind of price no man ever should for a moment of weakness. And I'm sure that's all it was, sweetheart, a little moment of weakness, because I know he's always loved you very much. And so has Lilian.

Most of all though Nikki and Harry are going to need their mummy and daddy now, because their young lives have been shattered terribly by Natalie going, and I know you won't want to make it even worse, any more than Charlie does. Of course getting past this will be an enormous test to your marriage – how can it not be – but you've always been very close, you two, and I'm sure that's what will see you through.

Anyway, I hope you understand that I'm writing because I love you, and because our baby girl deserves to rest in peace, and I don't believe she can until you know the truth. As I said before, I don't expect you to forgive me, but I have to admit I'd like it very much if you could consider giving it a try.

God Bless my darling,
with all my love,
Mummy

Jessica smiled sadly at the 'Mummy', for it had been a long time since she'd called her that. Then putting the letter aside for now, she reached for her mobile, which kept bleeping to say there was a message, and pressing in the number to pick it up she felt her heart filling up all over again as she listened to Luc's voice coming down the line.

By the time Charlie came back, having left Harry at the chateau, Jessica was upstairs halfway through packing, so he began to carry her computer and books out to the car. He didn't ask what she was thinking now she'd read the letter, nor did she attempt to tell him. For the moment she wanted only to be quiet as she tried to take in all that had happened, and how it was going to affect where they went from here. Right now it was impossible to know anything for certain, but tempted as she was to see this as a way for her and Luc to be together, she knew it wasn't – not only because of the baby, but because she had Nikki and Harry to consider. She needed to be there for them while their father tried to come to terms with what he'd done, and she could sense already that Charlie's journey was going to be a long and hard one, and would be far too much for them to cope with at the same time as their parents breaking up.

Hearing voices below she realised Lilian must have arrived, so she stopped what she was doing and took a moment to collect herself, for as strangely calm and even detached as she seemed to be feeling, she was aware of how utterly devastated she was inside. These were the two people she'd loved and trusted most in the world, the very mainstay of her life to whom she'd always turned in a crisis. To find herself having to face them like this, knowing how unforgivably they had behaved towards both her and Natalie, felt so disorienting that she was suddenly afraid to take even one step into a future that was going to be so changed in the light of their betrayal. Yet she knew what had to be done, and though a part of her could hate them for bringing her to this, and even want to harm them in some way, another part was reminding her that no amount of anger or vengeance was ever going to undo what they'd done, any more than it was going to help her now.

They both looked up as they heard her footsteps and she wondered how they must be feeling, watching Natalie's mother coming down the same stairs Natalie had fallen from. They must have lived in such dread of this day, surely always knowing it would come, while still trying to deny it. Given the time over again, she felt certain they'd never act the same way. Perhaps because of this certainty, something in her sympathised with them, for time's inexorability ensured their mistake could never be unmade, only lived with for the rest of their lives.

By the time she reached the bottom she was managing to make herself think of her own guilt in the way she'd fallen for Luc. Desire and passion had made her reckless and selfish, and her feelings could have led her still further, but she knew with an absolute certainty that she and Luc would never have made love in her daughter's bed, nor would either of them have driven away and left Natalie and her mother the way Lilian and Charlie had.

It was with that thought in her mind that her eyes went to Lilian's once dear, now stricken face, as she said, 'I'm not going to try and make this any worse for you. I know you loved Natalie enough to have suffered terribly over this, and I think you love me too . . .'

'Of course I do,' Lilian broke in. 'Oh God, Jessica, if you only knew . . .'

'I don't want to know.' Jessica's voice was cold, but her eyes were full of pain. 'Your conscience is your own, Lilian. I can't take on the burden of it.' She swallowed hard as a wave of emotion came over her. 'I never imagined myself ever saying something like that to you,' she whispered. 'It's as though we've all become strangers, and it's not how I want it to be . . .'

'It doesn't have to,' Lilian cried. 'Somehow we can . . .'

'No,' Jessica interrupted. 'No, Lily. There's no going back from this. You sleeping with Charlie, having an affair with him even, would have devastated me – and our friendship – if I'd known about it at the time. Now, nothing can be worse than the way you left Natalie, and the lies you've told since.' She stopped and put a hand to her face as her heart faltered again, but her voice was steady when a moment later she said, 'Of course I understand now why I've seen so little of you since it happened, why you've thrown yourself into work the way you have, even to the point of not being here these past two weeks. It wasn't only too hard to face me for long, you've hardly even been able to face yourself.'

As Lilian started to sob, Charlie turned to comfort her, but it was plain from the haunted look in his eyes that he was so tormented by his own inner demons he barely knew what he was doing.

'I deserve everything you're saying,' Lilian wept, 'and you're right, I do hate myself. I wish to God I could wipe out that terrible day . . .'

'It didn't stop there though, did it?' Jessica interrupted.

Lilian looked at her, seeming unsure what she meant.

'Natalie wasn't the only child to pay for what you did, was she?'

Lilian's eyes were suddenly frightened. 'I don't know . . . Why are you saying . . .?'

'Does Charlie know about the baby?' Jessica asked.

Lilian's face turned white.

'You were afraid it was his, weren't you?' Jessica said. 'You couldn't bear the idea that a baby might have been conceived out of that day, so rather than take the chance you got rid of it.'

Lilian's mouth opened, but no words came out.

'You see,' Jessica said, 'maybe I read you a little better than you think.' She looked at Charlie and wondered how he was reacting to the fact that he might have fathered a child on the same day as he'd lost one, but from his expression she couldn't be sure he'd taken it in.

'I can't say any more,' she murmured, realising how close she was to breaking down. 'Going over everything that happened . . . Trying to make some sense of it . . . It's never going to make sense to me, so we have to try to think of the future now . . .'

'Are you going to tell Luc?' Lilian blurted.

Jessica looked into her eyes, and almost felt herself being drawn into the depths of her fear. She'd always known how desperate Lilian was to be loved, so desperate that maybe she didn't really understand the meaning of it, for Jessica could think of no other reason why she would have put her marriage at risk the way she had. In the end, though, she'd clearly been prepared to do anything to hold onto it: that had to be the real reason she'd been willing to go along with Charlie's madness that day, out of fear of losing Luc, not because she'd wanted to spare her best friend. So it would be the easiest thing in the world to ruin everything for her now, to destroy what was left of her dream, but Jessica knew she wouldn't do it. Not because she pitied Lilian, even though she did, but because she wanted the memories she shared with Luc to stay intact, untouched by this terrible betrayal, and unsullied by a useless act of revenge. For that was what it would mean if she told him, and neither he, nor his unborn child, deserved that. So finally she said, very quietly, 'No, I'm not going to tell him.'

'Oh God,' Lilian spluttered, sobbing into her hands with relief. 'Thank you. Thank you. I know . . . I realise . . .'

'I'm doing it for him, not for you,' Jessica told her.

'I understand that, but if there was some way I could make this up to you . . .'

'There isn't.' She took a breath, slightly shaken by her own sharpness. 'We have to go our separate ways now,' she said. 'I'm going to miss you, almost as much as I miss Natalie . . .'

Lilian's eyes flooded with panic. 'Don't say that . . .'

Jessica turned away. 'You have to leave now,' she said, struggling to hold back the tears.

'Jessica, please . . .'

Jessica shook her head. 'I'm sorry,' she whispered. 'This is the way it has to be, because no matter what happens, I'll never be able to forgive you for this, Lily. I wish I could, but I can't.'

As she walked back up the stairs she could hear Lilian sobbing and Charlie murmuring to try and comfort her, but she wasn't thinking about them any more. She was closing them out now, pretending they didn't matter, because there were too many other painful things she must try to resolve in her heart before leaving.

Once she got to the bedroom she left her open bags to go and gaze out at the vineyard, as luscious and still as a Renoir. After a while the brightness of the sun began to dazzle her eyes, blinding her to what was there, but she was no longer looking, only remembering . . . She was seeing him the first time he'd shown her how to taste the grapes, and tilting her face to the light. She'd felt such a thrill of anticipation when he'd asked if he could sculpt her, but it seemed so mild in comparison to the sensual pleasures she'd experienced when he'd drawn her naked and happy in a hat amongst the vines. She didn't feel guilty about that now, she had no reason to, she only wished they'd given in to their desire while they'd had the chance.

Her eyes moved on to the *cave* where he'd tried to teach her about wine and they'd laughed and felt the magnetism of one another as potently as the *pinot noir*. Then she looked at the pergola, where she'd read to him and his father from *Suite Française*, and felt her heart trip on how he'd chosen the chapters about Lucile and the German. He'd known so much more than she had already, and had more or less told her that the next day at Issy-l'Evêque, when they'd quoted from the book. Then there was the studio where she'd watched him work and felt the heady sensation of being touched, yet not. After that her gaze wandered on to the woods that led to the lake where he'd come to stand behind her, and she'd let him take off her dress. She recalled how they'd recited de Lamartine's poem together, and wondered what would have happened if instead of choosing the first verse they'd spoken the chorus:

Oh favourable hours, hold your flight
O time, pause on your way!
Let us enjoy the transient delight
Of this, our fairest day!

She thought of their time in Paris, the agony of resisting him and joy of just being with him. There was the music they'd listened to, the art they admired, the literature they loved, and she realised he was so much a part of her own book that it was going to be almost impossible to continue without him.

Then she thought of him up at the house now, and wanted to go to him so much that she almost couldn't bear it. She needed to feel his arms around her, the tenderness of his mouth, the warmth of his breath, and knowing she never would now made the longing so terrible that her head fell back as she sobbed out loud. She didn't want to leave without saying goodbye, but it would be too hard to speak to him now. She needed his strength, his courage, his unwavering calm, but it wasn't hers to take, so she must find her own and let him go.

'Forgive me for not calling,' she whispered, looking up at the *manoir*. 'Please try to understand.'

Hearing Charlie coming up the stairs she turned to carry on with her packing, knowing she must try to detach herself from everything she was feeling – the way he and Lilian had, over Natalie.

For a while he only stood in the doorway watching her, then, as he started to help, she saw how his hands were shaking, and could almost feel his despair. It was as though he'd been cast adrift in an ocean with no hope in sight, nothing to hold onto and no-one to save him. And knowing how that felt, because it was what had happened to her when she'd first lost Natalie, she said, very softly, 'It'll be all right. I won't let you drown.'

For a moment he appeared confused, then he seemed to understand and tears began rolling down his cheeks. 'I don't deserve you . . .'

'Come on,' she said, squeezing his hand, 'let's take this out to the car.'

Twenty minutes later, with everything loaded, they were driving away from the cottage, up the hill towards the top road. Overhead the sun was blazing in a deep cerulean sky, while the grapes were glistening in their clusters and almost bursting from the vines.

Then finally the valley was behind them, lost from view, sliding quietly, inexorably into the past, much like a dream, yet not, because if it was only a dream she wouldn't be leaving a best friend for ever, nor would her heart be breaking over a man it was wrong to love. Most of all, though, she wouldn't be mourning a daughter she should never have lost.

Chapter Twenty-Seven

'Yoohoo! Cul-*ture* vul-*ture*! What's her name?'

'I dunno. Jocelyn, or Jasmine, or something.'

'Oi, Jasmine. Want to come and critique this?'

'In't she married to that bloke what does the news?'

'Yeah, think so. Haven't seen him for a bit though.'

'Yeah, like you watch the news.'

'It's you who's the frigging muppet, not me. Oi! Beautiful! Fancy a drink?'

At that moment, to Jessica's relief, a taxi came round the corner, and running into the road to wave it down, she jumped in and slammed the door.

After giving the driver her address, she sank back in the seat and closed her eyes. The goldfish bowl of London. Even after eight months of not appearing on TV, this still happened. Rarely as bad as this, it was true, but to be recognised at all had never been a pleasure for her. Now it was anathema, mostly because it made her long for France and the freedom she'd known there, the joy of anonymity . . . Quickly pushing the memory aside, she looked out of the window. It did no good to dwell on it. It was over, this was her life now, as it had always been.

Eventually the ghastliness of the last few minutes began to trickle away, like the rain down the windows, and as she gazed out at the slate-grey sky and snarling traffic she began going over the meeting she'd just come from, which had transported her to turn-of-the-century Paris and all the chaos and colour of the Bateau-Lavoir . . .

Her mobile rang and seeing it was Nikki she quickly clicked on.

'So how did it go with your publisher?' Nikki demanded straight away.

Pleased that she'd remembered, Jessica said, 'Well, the good news is she liked the draft of the first few chapters.'

'See! I told you she would. You're brilliant.'

'And you're not biased?'

'I'd tell you the truth, and you know it. So what's the bad news?'

'There isn't any. Or none I can think of.'

'OK, so don't stretch yourself, because I've probably got it for you.'

Jessica's heart immediately contracted. She was so afraid of any more disasters befalling her family that she was almost constantly on edge now.

'Freddy and I have been invited down to Somerset at the weekend, and I think I'm going to go. I know that's leaving you on your own with Dad, but not really . . .'

'Darling, you have to go,' Jessica told her. 'You're entitled to your life, and I promise you, I can cope.'

'Are you sure? Has he gone to work today?'

'He went in for a few hours, but he's probably at home by now.'

'Well, at least that makes three days in a row, and he was talking to Freddy last night about reading the news again. So I really think things are starting to look up.'

'They are, and you have to stop worrying, darling. He'll make it, he's already the best part of the way there, and now you're at uni, that's where you need to be focusing.'

'Yeah, well, he's my dad, so I can't help worrying, can I? Oh hang on, someone else is trying to call me, it'll probably be Freddy so I'll ring you back.'

After clicking off the line Jessica sat with the phone in her lap, thinking about Nikki and how hard Charlie's breakdown had been for her. Never in her life had she seen her big, strong daddy even cry, never mind fall apart, and that was virtually what had happened these past three months.

The first sign of how serious it was going to be had come about a week after they'd returned from France, when Charlie had been rushed to emergency with what they'd feared was a heart attack, but had turned out to be an acute stress reaction. He'd then remained in hospital for several days until they'd managed to reduce his blood pressure, and run tests on his other organs. All the results had been satisfactory, but since that time he'd been unable to work, or even function at his normal level.

'OK, I'm back,' Nikki said, when Jessica answered her phone again. 'What was I saying? Oh well never mind, I just wanted to find out how you got on . . . Oh yes, and to let you know that actually you won't be on your own at the weekend because Grandma's coming up with Maurice, so I don't need to feel too guilty about leaving you.'

'You shouldn't anyway,' Jessica responded. 'You've been wonderful these past few months, I don't know what I'd have done without you, and I know they haven't been easy for you.'

'They haven't been easy for you either, seeing Dad like that, but he's getting better . . .'

'Of course he is. Everything will be back to normal in no time at all now, but I wish you'd agree to some counselling too. You've seen how much good it's done Dad, talking it all through . . .'

'I knew you were going to do that,' Nikki cried. 'But like I keep telling you, I'm cool, OK? I don't need it . . .'

'There's nothing to be ashamed of. You lost your sister, and now all this with Dad . . .'

'Yeah, and what about you? Do you think it's doing you any good, talking to someone about what you're going through?'

'Of course it is, I'd probably have gone off my head by now, if I weren't.'

'OK, so what do you talk about?'

'Natalie, of course. And you, and Harry and Dad.'

'What about Lilian? Do you ever discuss her?'

'From time to time, naturally.' There was no need to tell Nikki any more than that. It was already enough for her to know what Charlie was trying to come to terms with where Lilian was concerned, without complicating the issue any further with Luc. 'Anyway, the kind of things I'm discussing are personal to me,' she said. 'You need to talk about you, and your feelings and fears and . . .'

'I know, I know, but I've got you, and I can tell you anything, so I don't really want to talk to a stranger.'

Jessica sighed, but decided not to push it any more for now, even though she knew how hard Nikki was finding it to accept what her father had done to her mother, as well as to her sister. Had Charlie not suffered such a severe reaction to it himself, Jessica doubted Nikki would have been anywhere near as forgiving as she had. Even so, his actions were almost certainly taking their toll on her in ways that neither of them were fully aware of yet. 'OK,' she said. 'Will you be home for dinner?'

'Yes, but I don't want to discuss anything like this with Freddy there, or he's going to think we're all nuts.'

'From that,' Jessica said with a smile, 'I take it he's coming for dinner too.'

'Yeah, but he won't be over till nine. Is that too late for Dad?'

'I shouldn't think so.'

'Cool. I have to go now. Love you. And well done about the book. I'm really proud of you.'

Still smiling, Jessica rang off, then finding her thoughts drifting where it would be better not to let them go, she began debating whether or not to ring Charlie. In the end she decided not to. If he was already at home she'd find out soon enough, and right now she'd rather remain hopeful that he'd managed to stay even longer at the office today than he had on the previous two days.

To her surprise, and relief, she found the house empty when she got there, but within minutes she was starting to worry. She hadn't spoken to Charlie since he'd driven away at ten that morning, and it was unlike him not to be in touch for so long.

'Oh hi darling,' he said when he answered his mobile. 'Sorry I haven't called, I got a bit caught up here. I'm at the studios, talking about my big comeback.'

'Really?' she said warily. 'Was that a planned meeting, or just something that came up?'

'A bit of both. We're thinking I could do a couple of shifts as early as next week. Nothing major, a mid-morning or mid-afternoon slot.'

'Do you feel up to it?'

'I've been trying to tell you for a while that I do, but you all keep worrying about me. Not that I don't appreciate it, because I do, but there has to come a time when I start taking care of you all again.'

Pulling away from that, Jessica said, 'Have you spoken to the doctor about this?'

'If you mean the GP, no, but I will. And the shrink says it's time I started asserting myself. So that's what I'm doing.'

Having to concede that he really had seemed stronger lately, which might be thanks to some new antidepressants, she didn't argue any further. In fact, if she only had herself to consider, she had to confess she was more than ready for him to go back to work.

'Have you spoken to your mother today?' he asked.

'No, but I hear she and Maurice are coming for the weekend.'

'With a surprise, apparently. My guess is he's popped the question. What's yours?'

'Since he's been popping it for years, the surprise would be that she's accepted.'

'Good point. She wants us to go down there for Christmas, by the way.'

Once again Jessica felt herself backing away, not because she didn't want to spend Christmas with her mother, but because she simply didn't want to think about Christmas at all. 'Why's everyone talking about it already, when it's still seven weeks away?' she grumbled.

'And when you've got a fortieth birthday between now and then. Don't think anyone's forgotten, because we haven't.'

Even though she knew it was meant to boost her, it simply made her feel worse. 'I'm more concerned about you than birthdays or Christmases,' she told him. 'What time will you be home?'

'In about an hour, I should think. I'll call when I'm on my way.'

After putting the phone down she replayed the voicemail messages, then realising she'd have to go and pick Harry up soon, she began making a list for the supermarket.

It wasn't until she was halfway through that it occurred to

her Charlie hadn't asked about the meeting with her publisher. Not that she was particularly surprised, but it did annoy her, for it was another example of how self-absorbed he'd become. Or perhaps the omission was deliberate, since he now knew about her feelings for Luc, after she'd admitted to them during one of their joint therapy sessions. Being aware of how much help Luc had given her in the early stages of the book, there was every chance Charlie was viewing it as some kind of threat. If she was right, then he clearly wasn't ready to tackle the issue, since he'd never mentioned it again. It was as though the subject had never been raised, and a part of her wished it hadn't, for she'd only ever wanted to keep her feelings private, in the way they'd always been with Luc.

Still, at least she wasn't hiding anything now. No secrets, no lies, which was what had got them into this terrible mess in the first place – and why the therapist had encouraged her to be truthful. Nevertheless, she hadn't confessed to how much time she spent with her book, or how important it had become to her. What happened during those solitary hours when she allowed herself to recall how her ideas had first come together, and how much else she and Luc had shared, was hers and hers alone.

Seeing the time, she quickly grabbed her purse and ran out to the car. As pleasurable, and sometimes even vital, as her memories were, keeping her family together and making sure they all got through this must come first. And it did, she made certain of that, but there were times when she had to admit it wasn't anywhere near as easy as it should be, in fact it was so hard she often wondered how she made it through a day. However, no-one had any way of knowing what was going on inside her, so, mercifully, only she knew just how desperate she sometimes felt.

An hour later, Harry came bounding out of school, socks bagging around his ankles, coat half off, and mud all over his legs, which he hadn't had time to shower off, because . . . He couldn't remember why, but anyway, he needed to get home really quick, because Dad had sent a text to say he was thinking about reading the news.

'He doesn't mean today, darling,' Jessica told him, as she began reversing between all the other mothers' cars out onto the street, 'and we have to go to the supermarket now.'

'Oh no!' Harry protested. 'I hate going there.'

As he folded his arms and scowled Jessica threw him a look, knowing he wouldn't stay mutinous for long, and sure enough before they even reached the end of the road he was telling her more about his busy and challenging day.

As he chattered – and shouted – on, full of triumph or indignation or bafflement, she reflected on how, in his innocent and lovable way, he'd got her through all the terrible moments of loneliness and self-pity that had crept up on her when Charlie was at his worst. Without Harry she wasn't entirely sure anything she was doing now would even make any sense, for his unfailing happiness and ready affection was the only real joy in her life. His was also the energy that kept the house alive, and the humour that held them all together, and even the love that made them all one. Unlike Nikki, he seemed unaware of the tension between his parents, and therefore was only concerned with reading to Charlie, lying beside him to watch TV, or simply being himself with his mother. *Préjugée* as she might be, Harry was the most adorable little person in the world.

'Mum, can we have cabbage pizza for dinner?' he asked, as they drove into the supermarket car park.

Jessica looked at him askance.

He struggled not to laugh.

'How about marmalade pasta?' she suggested.

'Oh no! Yuk, yuk, ugh. I'll be sick.'

'But cabbage pizza would be fine?'

'No! I'm just joking to make you laugh. I love it when you laugh.'

Since that could only mean she wasn't doing nearly enough of it, she scooped him into her arms and kissed him hard. 'I promise to laugh all weekend when Grandma and Maurice come to stay,' she told him.

'Oh! Are they coming? Cool. Your phone's ringing, Mum. Shall I answer? Hello. Jessica Moore's phone, her son and hair speaking.'

His cheeky little smile started to wane as he listened to the voice at the other end, then passing the phone over he said, 'It's someone called Desmond. He wants to speak to you. Oh look, there's Mark Greenaway, can I go and see him? I'll come straight back.'

As he leapt out of the car Jessica put the phone to her ear. 'Desmond,' she said, to Charlie's agent. 'What can I do for you? If you're looking for Charlie . . .'

'I wanted to speak to you first,' he interrupted. 'Is this a good time?'

'I don't know until you tell me what it's about.'

'OK, here goes – now it's out that he's been going into the office . . .'

Cutting in right away she said, 'What do you mean "out"?'

'There's something in the *Standard* tonight,' he warned her. 'Not a big piece, but someone's obviously got hold of the fact that Charlie Moore's on the mend, so I wanted to find out from you how he really is before I start filling up his days.'

God, how she hated the way the press took such an interest in every little detail of their lives. 'It's true, he's improving,' she responded, not prepared to go any further than that.

'Enough for me to approach him with all the usual kind of stuff, guest-hosting news quizzes, chairing debates . . .?'

'Why don't you put it all in an email,' she interrupted, 'and I'll discuss it with him later.'

'Will do.' He took a breath. 'There is something a bit, well, different,' he went on cagily. 'I don't think you're going to like it much, but here goes . . . I've had a call from the exec producer of *The Morning Programme*, asking if you and Charlie will consider being interviewed about how you've coped with losing a child. You know, the initial shock, the grief, what Charlie's just been through, how you've kept your marriage together when so many don't in these situations . . .'

'Desmond,' she cut in sharply, her head already spinning with rage, 'there is absolutely no way in the world I am ever going to appear on TV to discuss my family's difficulties . . .'

'I thought you might say that, but I'm just the messenger, remember, and I wouldn't be doing my job if I didn't put the whole package to you . . .'

'I'm not interested . . .'

'They're offering full editorial control, network transmission, obviously, and a fee that's well into five figures.'

'I don't care if it's into ten figures, the answer's still no. Now please don't let's discuss this any more. Harry's about to get into the car and I don't want him listening to any of this.'

'OK. I'll send the email to Charlie, and sorry if I've upset you.'

After ringing off she waited for Harry to collect a trolley, then bracing herself for the usual go-round of unwelcome recognition while doing her shopping, she followed him in through the automatic doors. Why the heck, she was asking herself angrily, was everyone so damned determined to pry into her private life – publishers, producers, analysts? Didn't they understand, for God's sake, she just wanted to be left the hell alone?

Charlie's sunken eyes, with their tired, purplish shadows and bloodshot whites, seemed both bemused and defiant as Jessica turned to him in amazement. 'Are you out of your mind?' she cried, trying to keep her voice down, since they were in the study and Nikki, at least, was somewhere nearby. 'You can't seriously be thinking about doing it.'

'I don't see what the problem is,' he replied, trying to sound assertive. 'I mean, I understand why *you* wouldn't want to do it, because you've always been publicity-shy, but it's not the same for me. And they're right, it might help others to know what we've been through.'

Jessica could hardly believe her ears; she felt so enraged that she had to turn away and go to stare out at the rain for a moment in an effort to calm down, or she might just have hit him.

It was Saturday morning now, which meant he must have been thinking this over since the email had arrived on Thursday. Realising that this was the direction his mind had been taking, when he had to know how strongly opposed she'd be to it, was making her angrier than ever.

'Darling, I'm sorry if this is upsetting you,' he said, from where he was sitting at his desk, 'but if you try to see it from my point of view . . .'

Jessica spun round, eyes flashing. 'I think it would be a good idea for you to see it from my point of view,' she told him furiously. 'Do you really imagine I want the whole world to know what happened when my daughter died, how her father was in bed with another woman, and not just any other woman . . .'

His face was turning very pale now. 'I know it'll be hard,' he cut in nervously, 'but look at it this way, it might make other men – and women – think twice before they cheat on their spouses again, because this is a terrible example of how one snatched decision, driven by selfishness and lust, had the worst possible outcome.'

Jessica stared at him, dumbfounded. 'I can only think that the drugs you're on have addled your brain,' she told him frankly. 'You're not some kind of one-man crusade to save the world from infidelity. Your only job is to save yourself from the depths you've sunk to.'

'I know that, but if I can help others along the way . . .'

'Charlie! For heaven's sake, listen to yourself. You'd *never* have thought about it like this before.'

'I'd never been to hell and back before.'

Jessica's eyes closed as despair and frustration descended on her in a cloud of helplessness. 'Look, I know you've been through a rough time, but it hasn't been easy for the rest of us either. So how do you think it's going to be for Nikki and Harry if you go announcing to the world how you left Natalie for others to take care of? Harry doesn't even know, so is this how you want him to find out?'

Charlie's eyes fell away. 'I wasn't actually going to discuss that part of it,' he said. 'I just feel as though I have to make amends somehow . . .'

'Well this isn't the way to do it, and anyway, no-one says you have to. What's important is that you try to forgive yourself, not go out there seeking a pardon from your great viewing public, because you won't get it. Take it from me, Charlie, people won't understand . . .'

She broke off as the door opened and Nikki came in. 'I'm sorry, Mum, but I couldn't help overhearing,' she said, appearing both determined and anxious, 'and I'm not going to let him do it either.'

Charlie looked at her in confusion, then as his eyes went back to Jessica he seemed to slump inwardly, and rubbing his hands over his face he said, 'I'm sorry. I didn't realise it would upset . . . Maybe I'm not thinking straight.'

'What you're doing is thinking about yourself all the time,' Nikki told him brutally, 'and it's just not fair when Mum's been carrying the burden around here. You hardly think about her at all, and what she's been going through . . .'

'That's enough,' Jessica said gently. 'I thought you were leaving at twelve.'

'I am. It's still only ten to.' Then, turning back to Charlie, 'Promise me you're going to turn this interview down,' she said, her tone uncompromisingly firm.

Charlie looked at her.

'I'm telling you, if you do it, she'll leave you,' Nikki informed him as though it were a foregone conclusion, 'and I for one won't blame her.'

Charlie's anxious eyes went to Jessica.

Jessica only looked at him, letting her silence speak for itself.

'Oh God,' he groaned helplessly. 'Of course I won't do it if you feel that strongly.' Then, pressing his fists to his head, 'What's happening to me? Am I losing my mind?'

'No, of course not,' Jessica said. 'You just have to try to understand that the rest of your life isn't going to be about your grief, or your guilt, or even some kind of penance. You're focusing too much on it now. You need to start letting go a little, which is why it's a good idea for you to read the news a couple of times next week. It'll help get you back in the swing, and restore some proper perspective, because this isn't the only time you've lost sight of it lately.'

He nodded slowly, then apparently sunk in the disgrace of his other confusions, he looked from Nikki to Jessica as he said, 'I know I'm a waste of space, and I don't deserve either of you . . .'

Jessica turned away. 'If you're going to start down the self-pity route,' she said crisply, 'then you're on your own.'

There was a rare twinkle in Charlie's eyes as he looked back at Nikki. 'Well that told me, didn't it?' he said.

Nikki came to embrace him. 'Get rid of that email and do as Mum says,' she murmured, giving him a kiss. 'Now I have to go, so behave yourself with Grandma and Maurice, and call if you need to chat.'

As she left the study, Charlie turned back to Jessica, who was sitting at her computer now. 'I'm sorry,' he said again. 'I should have realised how much it would upset you without putting you through all this. Maybe it is the drugs. They seem to be helping in some ways, but . . .' He sighed and wiped his hands over his face. 'They're not doing much for me in other parts either,' he went on hoarsely, 'so I'm letting you down all over the place.'

'Don't worry about that,' she told him, keeping her eyes on the screen. 'All that matters is to get you fully well again so you don't have to take them any more.'

Getting to his feet he came to stand behind her, and put his hands on her shoulders. 'I know I probably shouldn't ask,' he said in barely more than a whisper, 'but is there a chance you'll consider coming back to our bed some time soon? I miss you, and I think I might sleep better if you were there.'

Resting her cheek on his hand, she said, 'It'll happen, don't worry. Just don't try to rush things.'

Accepting that for now, he stooped forward to press a kiss to the top of her head, then turned at the sound of a car pulling up outside. 'That'll be Freddy or your mother,' he said, going to the window. 'Your mother,' he announced. 'I'll pop out and help them in with their bags.'

For a moment Jessica carried on with what she was doing, finding it easier to absorb herself in the household accounts than to make a swift transition from angry and confused wife to forgiving and welcoming daughter. Not that she wasn't pleased to have her mother and Maurice staying for the weekend, in fact she'd rather spend time with them than the so-called friends in whose circle she and Charlie were supposed to belong. That kind of pretentiousness and one-upmanship was something she never wanted back in her life, though she guessed it would be hard to keep refusing it once the ever-popular Charlie was back on form. Still, that was a problem for another time, she wasn't going to worry about it now. She was simply going to make sure everyone had a lovely two days, and hope they managed to get through it without too many references to what had happened before.

She found her mother in the kitchen a little later, busily unpacking all the food and champagne she and Maurice had brought with them and loading it into the fridge.

'I thought I'd find you here,' Jessica said, dropping down from the last step.

Veronica turned round, joy lighting up her blue eyes which had managed to remain bewitching, and even sultry, in spite of her sixty-something years and the slight droop of a left lid. Her youthfully ruffled hair was a vivid shade of silver, while her small heart-shaped face and pretty mouth were as exquisite and childlike as a doll's. They were also, Jessica was aware, along with her vivacity and curvy figure, what had made so many men want to take care of her over the years, as well as full and frequent advantage.

'How are you darling?' she said, having to go up on tiptoe to embrace her daughter. 'You're looking a little tired, if you don't mind me saying so. You know my offer of a day at the spa stands for any time you'd like to go. Or two or three days. Or we can take a holiday together, because I'm sure you need one, and there's always Maurice's house on Capri.'

'I'll bear it all in mind,' Jessica assured her. 'Now tell me how you are. Happily, you're not looking tired. In fact you're looking rather good.'

'Oh I'm just scrumptious,' Veronica responded with an airy smile. 'No more nasty little turns, they all seem to be in the past now, thanks to you and Charlie, of course.'

Jessica's smile faded, for she sensed where her mother might be going next and she really didn't want to revisit the excruciating scene of apology and forgiveness the therapist had put them all through several weeks ago. 'Where's Maurice?' she asked, before her mother could continue.

'Still upstairs with Charlie, I expect, having a bit of boy talk. I must say Charlie seems to be looking much better today. Has he put a little weight back on?'

'Some, but he's still a long way off regaining what he lost.

Has he told you he's thinking about going back to work?'

Veronica clapped her bejewelled hands. 'Oh, that's excellent news. Apart from anything else it'll be a load off your mind, I'm sure. So how did the meeting go with your publisher? Nikki told me the bits she read were excellent.'

'Nikki's nothing if not loyal,' Jessica responded dryly, 'but it went very well. I'm looking forward to carrying on with the rest of it now.'

'I imagine she was very impressed by how quickly you came up with the first chapters,' Veronica commented, returning to the fridge. 'You don't have a deadline until the middle of next year, do you?'

'No, but I love doing it, so I spend a lot of time at it. What on earth have you brought all this for? Or are you planning to stay a month?'

Veronica gave a chirp of laughter. 'Would that I could, but between us I'm sure Maurice and I would have driven you completely insane by then.' She turned to look at Jessica, then came to put a hand on her face. 'Is it very hard?' she asked gently.

Jessica immediately shook her head. 'It's fine,' she said. 'We're getting through it.'

'I always felt sure you would, but I have to admit . . . Well, there aren't many women who could forgive what he did, and with your own best friend.'

'Yes, well, let's not keep going there,' Jessica responded, a little more abruptly than she'd intended. 'Charlie tells me you have a surprise, which I guess is what the champagne's about. He thinks Maurice has popped the question, is he right?'

Veronica chuckled. 'There would be no surprise in that,' she told her, 'but I want to wait until we're all together before I tell you what it is.'

'Grandma! There you are,' Nikki cried, bouncing down into the kitchen. 'I'm just off, but I couldn't leave without saying hi. How are you? You look fab, as usual.'

'So do you,' Veronica assured her, gulping at the crushing embrace. 'Is Freddy outside? I should go and say hello, but be warned, once he sees me in this gorgeous new pants suit you might have lost him for the weekend.'

'She's incorrigible, isn't she?' Nikki laughed as Veronica wiggled off up the stairs. Then, turning quickly back to Jessica, 'Are you OK? Have we talked him out of that madness?'

'Yes, I think so. I shouldn't have got so angry . . .'

'Oh, like you weren't justified? Anyway, the important thing is that he's thinking about doing the news again, and he was talking to Freddy about a really interesting documentary idea the other night, so his brain is functioning normally on some levels, which means he'll be out from under your feet soon enough.'

'Am I that obvious?' Jessica said with a smile. 'First Grandma, now you . . . And actually, I'm fine with him here, just as long as he lets me get on with my book and . . .' *Doesn't try to make me sleep with him*, she was thinking, but she could hardly say that to Nikki, so instead she said, '. . . doesn't try to take things too fast.'

Nikki smiled fondly into her eyes, then hugged her.

'I'm glad you've gone blonde again,' Jessica told her. 'Dad's right, it always suited you better.'

'Yeah, and Freddy's like treating me to all the jokes, so I'm thinking, duh, should have stayed dark. Anyway, are you going to ask Grandma who your father is?'

Jessica rolled her eyes and laughed. 'Darling, that's the last thing on my mind . . .'

'You told me last night that the therapist said you should. It's time for clarity, or something like that . . .'

'And maybe he has a point, but I've never got a straight answer out of her yet, so I really don't expect one now.'

Nikki shrugged. 'Your call, but personally I'm dying to know, so if you do get round to it and she tells you, just text GST, or MR, and I'll know it means Greek Shipping Tycoon, or Minor Royalty. Oh my God,' she cried with a splutter of laughter, 'I've just realised what it is right now – Father Unknown.'

'Charming,' Jessica replied. 'Now, if I were you I'd go and rescue Freddy before she manages to get herself invited to Somerset for the weekend. Where's Harry, by the way?'

'In his bedroom showing Dad and Maurice some new computer game. OK, loving you and leaving you . . . Let me know what Grandma's surprise is as soon as she tells you – and if she's planning to wear white at the wedding, tell her from me, she's got a nerve.'

Laughing, Jessica watched her go, and was just turning to carry on unloading her mother's shopping when out of nowhere she found herself thinking of Lilian. It often happened like that, thoughts flying up from her psyche and bringing a pang of emotion with them, but they were soon gone again. They were no more than old habits taking a while to fade, she told herself, but this time instead of brushing it aside she allowed herself to think of Lilian for a while, and how much she missed her. Then she imagined her at the *vignerons'* ball this evening, flushed with happiness at almost seven months pregnant, dancing in Luc's arms and loving the feel of the baby kicking inside her. Then she banished the thought, knowing it never did any good to go there, for it only made her more unsure than ever about the direction her own life was taking.

A while later Charlie was pouring champagne into everyone's glass as Jessica and her mother continued laying out the picnic lunch Veronica had brought, and the adorably myopic Maurice with his thick, creamy white hair and ruggedly handsome face, was trying to understand the mysterious world of mobile phones that Harry was teaching him. Outside the rain continued to drum on the conservatory roof, making the windows all steamy and wet, and bringing a sense of cosiness to the kitchen that Jessica found almost as pleasing as she used to.

'So, time for our surprise, I think,' Veronica announced, once all the glasses were full.

'Oh cool!' Harry declared, bounding into the chair next to her. 'Dad reckons you're getting married.'

Veronica's eyebrows rose. 'Then Dad would be wrong,' she informed him haughtily.

'Not that I haven't asked,' Maurice piped up.

'Oh, everyone knows that,' she chided, 'and I've told you, we will, one of these days, when I can find the right dress. No, our important news is that I am going to move in with Maurice on a permanent basis, so . . . and here comes the surprise . . . I'm going to sell my house and give all the money to Nikki and Harry. That way, we can avoid all those nasty tax men getting hold of it when I pop off.'

Harry's eyes were almost as big as Jessica's. 'Am I going to be a millionaire?' he asked.

Veronica laughed delightedly. 'Not quite, darling, but we do think we'll get around four hundred thousand for it, so even with the way things are that should provide an excellent start for both you and Nikki when you come to buy places of your own.'

'Nikki's already thinking about it,' Harry informed her earnestly. 'She wants to move in with Freddy, but she hasn't told Mum and Dad yet, because she thinks . . . Huh,' he gasped, clasping a hand over his mouth as he realised he'd let the cat out of the bag.

'Oh, I'm sure Mum's worked that out for herself,' Veronica told him. 'So, now, shall we all drink to my decision? I hope you're not going to argue, darling, because you're looking very like you might . . .'

'But Mum, you can't. What if you need the money . . .?'

Maurice cleared his throat.

'You see, I'm very well taken care of,' Veronica reminded her, 'and I know you and Charlie already have the company flat, as well as this house, so why shouldn't I try to help the children?'

'You don't have to,' Jessica said, suspecting the gesture was, at least in part, to try to make up for what had happened to Natalie.

'I'm aware of that, but I want to. So, it's all decided. Now let's drink to windfalls, shall we, because I do so love them, and none of us ever have enough of them.'

Jessica looked at Charlie, but he appeared as stuck for any more protests as she was. Then a mischievous look came into his eyes as he said, 'You know, it's giving me an idea.'

They all waited expectantly.

'No, I want to give it some more thought before I tell you what it is,' he decided, 'so come on, drink up. To windfalls.'

'To windfalls,' they echoed, and after they'd all taken a sip, including Harry, Charlie went to slip an arm round Jessica's shoulders and whispered, 'I know it's not your birthday until next week, but I want to tell you today how much I love you, not only for the way you've stood by me through all of this, but just for being you and making me the luckiest man alive.' He kissed her briefly on the mouth. 'I hope, on the day itself, I'll be able to show you, as well as tell you, just how much you mean to me.'

Chapter Twenty-Eight

The week passed in much the same way as all the other weeks, the only difference to this one being Charlie's return to the screen for a few hours, and the impromptu party afterwards to toast the successful comeback. The celebrations didn't last long, since Charlie wasn't allowed much alcohol, and Jessica, who'd driven in for the event, soon realised how much it was tiring him so whisked him off home. However, there was no doubt it had boosted his morale no end to be back in the world he knew, surrounded by cameras, lights, friends, and at least some of the attention he craved. For her part, she could hardly have been more relieved when she'd turned on the TV to see him looking so normal and in control, and even able to handle an acrimonious Israeli–Palestinian interview during his first ten minutes. In fact, if it weren't for the weight loss and extra lines around his eyes no-one would ever have guessed at the black despair he'd been through, or the self-loathing, or the longest, darkest hours of all when he hadn't wanted to go on.

Thinking back on it, she realised that supporting him through his grief had almost been worse than going through her own, for he'd become so dependent on her, and so needy, that she'd sometimes felt he was draining the very life from her. Though she was always there for him, ready to comfort and reassure, his weakness and insecurity had done little to soften her heart. On the contrary, it had often repelled her, for he was so changed from the man she'd respected and loved that she could hardly connect with the stranger he'd become. Just thank God the worst part seemed to be over now, though she was under no illusion that there was still a long road ahead. She only wished the mere thought of it didn't weary her so much, for the reality could surely only be more trying still.

Now, it was Saturday morning and being under strict instructions to have a lie-in, she was gazing up at the ceiling while allowing her thoughts, just for a few brief moments, to escape their prison and go where they always longed to, back to Valennes and Luc and those two precious weeks they'd shared. She was seeing his dark eyes watching her as she'd relaxed amongst the vines, hearing his voice, then feeling herself responding to the warmth of his smile. She didn't wonder what he was doing now, she only thought of him as he had been during that time, humorous, attentive, self-possessed and always seeming to want her in the way she wanted him. Then, knowing she had to, she gradually let him go.

A moment later she became aware of excited whispering outside the door, but even as she smiled to hear Harry, she felt disheartened to think that this was the last time she would wake up here in the guest room. She'd promised Charlie she would return to their bed tonight. Already she could feel herself rejecting the thought, as though if she ignored it the reality might go away, but of course it wouldn't. Unhappy as it was making her, she had to accept that if they were ever going to repair their marriage this next step had to be taken.

'OK, are you ready?' she heard Charlie murmur.

'Yes,' Harry said breathlessly.

'One, two, three . . .'

The door opened and a moment later Harry appeared with a heavy tray wobbling about in his hands and a look of fixed concentration on his face as he started to sing. 'Happy birthday to you, Happy birthday to you, Happy birthday dear Mu-um, Happy . . . Huh! I nearly dropped it. Birthday to you.'

Smiling, Jessica sat up against the pillows, then held out her arms to catch him as Charlie whisked away the tray and Harry launched himself onto the bed.

'Happy birthday, Mum!' he cried, snuggling in and giving her a big kiss. 'I made your breakfast all by myself, well, Dad opened the champagne, and I've got a present for you that I chose myself and wrapped myself. It's like, really cool and I know you're going to love it, because I know it's something you want. Well, Nikki says it is, so if it's not then it's her fault, not mine.'

'I'm sure I'm going to love it,' she told him, as Charlie put the tray down.

'Happy birthday, darling,' Charlie said. 'I'm sorry it's so early, but Mr Impatience here couldn't wait any longer. Nikki is still in dreamland, as you might expect at seven o'clock on a Saturday morning.'

Jessica ruffled Harry's hair, then stopped as he suddenly cried, 'Oh Dad! We forgot the flower. Don't worry I'll get it,' and with a bounce, a jump and speedy dash, he took off back down the stairs.

'This is lovely,' Jessica said, looking down at the three bowls of cornflakes and two racks of toast. 'I take it I'm not eating alone.'

'He insisted, and I thought you wouldn't mind.'

'Of course not. Come on, sit down.'

'I was wondering,' he said, 'if it would be permissible to give my wife a kiss for her birthday?'

Hoping her dismay didn't show, she said, 'Of course it would,' and raised her mouth for him to plant a gentle, lingering kiss on her lips.

'Here it is!' Harry cried, charging back into the room with a bud vase and single yellow rose.

'Beautiful,' Jessica declared as he plonked it down on the tray.

'Dad says you can't open your presents until Nikki's up, or she'll get mad with us all, and you know how scary she is. Well, I'm not scared of her, but Dad is, because he's just a wuss.'

Charlie gave him a playful punch, which made him shriek and roll over on the bed.

'Can I take my cornflakes to my room?' he asked, bouncing up again. 'I have to watch my programme, and there's no TV in here.'

'Harry, this is Mum's birthday . . .'

'Oh, let him go,' Jessica said.

Charlie watched him carry his bowl carefully out to the

landing, then getting up he went to close the door behind him.

Jessica reached for her Buck's Fizz, hoping the closed door didn't signify anything she'd rather not get into.

'Happy fortieth,' he murmured, picking up his own glass and clinking it to hers.

Grimacing, she said, 'How did I get to be so old?'

He smiled and took a sip of his drink. 'I wanted to tell you about your present while we were alone,' he said. 'I don't have it yet . . . You'll understand why when I explain what it is, I just thought you should know about it before Nikki and Harry, rather than at the same time.'

Realising she was closer to dreading what it might be, than feeling excited, she forced a playful look of intrigue as she said, 'I can't wait.'

'I've decided,' he began, 'to buy your mother's house for you. You've always wanted a place in the country, and I thought it would be perfect to . . .' He stopped as he registered how her expression had changed. 'What?' he said anxiously. 'Have I got it wrong?'

'No, it's just . . .' Grasping at anything, 'We don't have that kind of money.'

'I do if I take out a mortgage, and I thought it could be somewhere just for you, a kind of bolt hole where you could go to write, or get away from us, or even invite us if you felt in the mood.'

'Charlie, no,' she said, trying to hold back the panic. 'You can't. It's too much . . .'

'Nothing's too much for you,' he said, taking the glass from her hand. 'I want to try . . . Oh God, Jessica, please don't cry . . .'

'I'm not,' she said, closing her eyes as she put her head back against the pillows. 'I'm fine. It's just . . .' She didn't say any more, because her heart was too full of words and feelings she could never speak aloud, especially not to him.

He continued to look at her, confusion and helplessness clouding his expression. 'Jessica?' he whispered, reaching for her hand. 'Why are you crying? What have I done?'

She shook her head and turned her face away. 'I'm not crying, and you haven't done anything. It's just me . . . I guess I'm tired and . . .' She shook her head again, knowing it was safer to keep her thoughts inside.

For a while he simply held her hand loosely in his, not sure what more he could do, until finally he said, 'It's him, isn't it? You're thinking about him.'

Just that one small allusion to Luc caused her heart to fill up with so much longing that there was no more she could do to stop the tears. 'Yes. No,' she answered, still trying to fight them back. 'It doesn't matter. It's a lovely present, Charlie. I wish I could take it, but . . . Please, don't do it. Apart from anything else it's something we need to discuss and think about, not jump straight into.'

'But I thought you loved the house.'

'It's very nice, but . . . The thought was enough. You don't have to buy it. I don't want you to. I just . . .' Once again she couldn't go on.

He looked away, then as though he were staring into a void he said, 'We're not going to make it, are we? I know you're trying, but in your heart you can't forgive me, and I don't blame you.'

'Ssh,' she said, reaching for his hand. 'Of course we're going to make it. It's just not going to be easy. We always knew that, but now you're starting to feel better . . .'

'You don't want me near you. I can tell . . .'

'That's not true,' and pushing aside the tray she pulled him down into her arms so that his head was resting in her lap.

For a long time neither of them spoke again, and as she stroked his hair, feeling the silky softness of it running through her fingers she thought of all the years she'd loved him, all the wonderful times they'd shared, and how blessed they had been in so many ways. It had never seemed possible that one day she might feel about him the way she did now, but then she'd never dreamt that one day they would lose a child, or that he would behave the way he had. However, they had to put that behind them, because though she no longer loved him the same way, and knew she might never truly forgive him, for her own sake as well as for his and the children's, she had to continue to try.

*

It was a bitterly cold day as Daniella left her father in the kitchen and went outside to find Luc. The vineyard was shrouded in a fine silvery mist, making it impossible to see much further than the first dozen or so rows, and the ground was damp and peppered with frost. Most of the vines had been brutally pruned by now, reducing them to short, gnarled stumps, devoid of leaves and fruit, and the woods on the horizon were blurred and skeletal like winter ghosts.

She found him just inside the *cave* talking to Jean-Marc and Phillippe Court, the oenologist, who'd come for a blending of the *pinot noir*. All three men were wearing padded jackets to keep out the cold, and their mouths were stained red from the morning's tasting.

As they turned to see who was coming Daniella smiled and went to greet Phillippe and Jean-Marc, then waited for Luc to say goodbye before linking his arm to start back to the house.

'So how was Paris?' he asked, gazing down over the valley into the mist.

'Paris was fine,' she answered. 'I got back last night.' Then coming straight to the point, 'I saw Lilian while I was there.'

He only nodded, giving no indication of whether he was surprised or not.

'She's not coming back, is she?' she said.

'No,' he replied.

She cast him a look, but his expression was impenetrable.

'She told me what happened at the cottage before Natalie died. And after. Is that why you asked her to leave?'

His eyebrows rose. 'She told you I asked her to leave?'

'No. I just thought you might have, considering . . .'

'It was her decision to go.'

'But you didn't try to stop her?'

'No.' They walked under the bare frame of the pergola. 'When she lost the baby,' he said, 'even before that, things were no longer the same between us. You must have noticed, or she must have told you.'

'Yes, she did.' She stopped before they reached the door. 'She says it's because you're in love with Jessica.'

At that his expression became more withdrawn than ever.

'Is it true?' she prompted.

Looking at her, he said, 'When Lilian told me what had happened at the cottage, how she and Charlie had run away, and then lied . . .'

Daniella interrupted him gently. 'Lilian left because you're in love with someone else,' she said. 'If she's prepared to face it, then you should too.'

His eyes showed only how closed he was to her words. Then, seeming to understand what this was really about, he said, 'Daniella, I don't want you to interfere . . .'

She took a breath to protest.

'No, I know you,' he said, 'and I won't have it, do you hear me? Jessica's married . . .'

'Yes, but . . .'

'Let's stop this, Daniella. For Jessica her children have to come first, and that's an end to it.'

'So what are you going to do, shut yourself away here?'

'What I do is my concern, and believe me I have plenty more to do than shut myself away. Now, I want you to swear to me that you will not interfere in this.'

'I am only saying . . .'

His eyes darkened.

'OK, I swear,' she said, reluctantly, 'but if I should find out . . .'

Then she jumped as he said, '*Mon Dieu!* This is hard enough already, can't you see that? And you're just making it worse.'

'I'm sorry. I . . .'

'That's what it'll be like for Jessica if you go behind my back and contact her,' he cut in. 'You'll make it worse. So remember you've given your word,' and pushing open the door he walked into the house.

'Wow, look at you,' Nikki said admiringly, coming into the bedroom to find Jessica in a chic black evening dress and two small diamonds in her ears that matched the solitaire around her neck. 'Where are you going?'

Jessica held up a hand to show she was on the phone. 'Yes, Mum, the turkey's ordered, and the smoked salmon and the ham,' she was saying. 'OK, I'll make a pudding if you want me to . . . Yes, yes. You know we've been over this . . . All right, all right, I'm listening . . .' She glanced at Nikki, who was shrugging off her coat, and winked.

In the end, deciding her mother had run through the Christmas shopping list enough times for today, she said, 'I'm sorry, I have to go now, but I'll be available for the same call from about ten o'clock tomorrow, and every day for the next eighteen days until you've driven me so crazy I'll end up coming down there to stuff you in the oven, never mind the flaming turkey.'

'Oh, we're getting along so well these days, aren't we?' Veronica laughed at her end. 'Have a lovely time wherever you're going. Love to everyone.'

'So where are you going?' Nikki asked, sinking down on the bed as Jessica rang off.

'I'm meeting Dad and Ernest Schultz for cocktails and dinner,' Jessica answered, applying a delicate shimmer to her lips.

Nikki's eyes rounded. 'You mean *the* Ernest Schultz, who practically owns America?'

'Only in a news sense,' Jessica responded.

Nikki shrugged. 'Well, that's enough, isn't it? Anyway, it's good that you're going out. You haven't been anywhere for ages, you two. I take it Dad's going straight from work?'

Jessica nodded as she began hunting round for her purse.

'He really seems a lot better now, doesn't he?' Nikki said. 'It's like everything's back to normal.'

Detecting something odd in her tone, Jessica looked up.

Nikki tried to smile, but her mouth couldn't quite make it.

'What is it?' Jessica asked softly.

Nikki shook her head. 'Nothing. I mean, it *is* all back to normal, isn't it?'

'I think so, more or less,' Jessica replied carefully. Nikki didn't need to know that in spite of sharing a bedroom again, and putting on a united front where necessary, she and Charlie were as far from properly reconciled as they'd ever been. 'Why do you ask?'

Nikki took a breath, and said, 'I just wondered . . . I mean, I'm not planning to do anything yet . . . But well, like, Freddy's really keen for me, you know, that we . . . I just wondered, how would you take it if I said I wanted to move out?'

Though Jessica's heart turned over with dread, she managed to keep only tenderness in her eyes as she said, 'You're eighteen now, so I'd expect you to want a place of your own.'

'But would you be all right if I went?'

'Darling, you must stop assuming responsibility for me and think of yourself. I can cope, honestly. You've seen how well Dad's doing, and I've got my book and Harry – and *my mother* . . .'

Nikki smiled, but it was soon gone again. 'I'm just worried about you being lonely,' she said.

Jessica laughed. 'How can I be lonely when I've got Harry and Dad?'

'I don't know. You just seem it sometimes, and I think . . .' She hung her head.

'What do you think?' Jessica prompted gently.

Nikki shook her head.

'Come on. Out with it. Remember, you can tell me anything.'

Nikki's eyes came up to hers. 'I think you miss Lilian, well you're bound to, in spite of everything, because you two were like sisters, and if I go it'll be like you haven't got anyone . . .'

'Oh darling,' Jessica said, going to kneel in front of her. 'I take it you're not intending to cut me off, and never come to visit. In fact, we'll probably end up seeing even more of one another.'

Nikki inhaled deeply and looked down at their joined hands. 'Do you ever hear from Lilian?' she asked.

Jessica shook her head, and wondering if Nikki's bleak mood might have something to do with how much *she* was missing Lilian, she said, 'You know, she's still your godmother, so if you want to be in touch with her . . .'

Nikki recoiled. 'No way! Not after what she did with Dad. I hate her for that, but even worse was the way she left Natalie . . . I can't ever forgive her for that.'

Jessica sighed. 'I doubt she's able to forgive herself either,' she responded gently.

Nikki averted her eyes. 'Anyway, she'll have her own baby soon, so she won't be thinking about us,' she said tightly. '*If* she's managed to stay pregnant, and she hardly deserves to when we've lost Natalie . . .'

'Darling, you mustn't think like that,' Jessica broke in. 'Whatever Lilian's done, it's not her baby's fault, nor Luc's, and he counts in this too, remember?'

Nikki sighed. 'Of course,' she said glumly.

'And I'm sure,' Jessica continued, 'if Lilian had lost the baby we'd have heard, because bad news has a way of travelling, so let's try to wish her well, shall we?'

Nikki looked into her eyes. 'I wish I was more like you,' she said.

Jessica smiled as her eyes twinkled. 'It wasn't so long ago you were dreading being anything like me,' she reminded her, glancing over her shoulder as the doorbell rang. 'That'll be the taxi,' she said. 'Did Freddy come home with you?'

'No, he'll be here in about an hour. Where's Harry?'

'At the Critchleys for the night. Are you going to be OK? I can always cancel if you'd rather I stayed with you.'

'Don't be daft. I'm fine. We can chat any time, I'm not leaving home yet.'

'Well there's a relief,' and with a quick kiss on her cheek, Jessica slipped into her black velvet coat and Jimmy Choo slingbacks and went downstairs to answer the door.

An hour later she was at the edge of a very elegant crowd in a private function room at the Ritz, where several recognisable faces were mingling with the less well known, though in many cases far more powerful. Since she'd lately started to prefer these kinds of affairs to the more intimate occasions where well-intentioned friends kept grilling her about what she was doing now, how she was coping, or whether Charlie really had fully recovered, she was reasonably at ease. Just as long as no-one told her how marvellously brave they thought she was, or how fabulous she was looking, considering, or what an inspiration she could be to others, the evening should go well, she decided.

Though Charlie had come to meet her as soon as she'd arrived, sweeping her proudly into the midst of the crowd, he'd abandoned her again soon after to carry on mingling, and watching him now, blending so effortlessly with the crème de la crème of the media world, she felt a fondness for him much like when she watched Harry mixing with his friends. He was so at home with all these people, while she felt she had almost nothing in common with them.

Catching him watching her and realising he was concerned about her standing alone, she found her way to his side and smiled up at him.

'Are you OK?' he asked anxiously.

She nodded. 'Are you?'

'Pretty good. This is an amazing turnout, isn't it?' His eyes swept the crowd. 'Just about everyone who's anyone is here.' Then drawing her to one side, he spoke quietly so as not to be overheard. 'Have you been introduced to Ernest yet?'

'No, not yet,' she whispered, glancing over at the stocky billionaire whose newly woven hair and gleaming capped teeth were not exactly, she felt, a testament either to taste, or wealth. 'But don't worry, when I do I'll be sure not to mention either his coiffeur or his dentist.'

Once that would have made Charlie laugh, tonight it seemed not to click, as he said, 'He's taking us for dinner later.'

'I know,' she reminded him.

'I mean, just us.'

Jessica looked at him curiously. 'How generous,' she commented, not entirely sure why she wasn't thrilled.

'I had a quick meeting with him before the party,' he said. 'He wants me to take over the running of his Premium Channel in New York.'

Jessica became very still.

'I know, it was a big shock to me too,' he said, 'but I've had a bit more time to get used to it, and frankly, darling, it could be exactly the kind of fresh start we're looking for. Away from here, no more memories, a totally new environment . . .'

'Stop,' she said breathlessly. 'Just stop.' For one awful moment, as the room started to tilt and fade, she thought she was going mad.

'Are you OK?' he said. 'What is it?'

'Please tell me you haven't accepted,' she said.

'Not without talking to you first, obviously, and nothing's official yet, but think of it, darling . . .'

'No Charlie, I can't,' she said. 'I don't even want to have this conversation.'

'No, obviously now isn't a good time,' he agreed. 'I'm sorry. I just wanted to warn you what we're probably going to be talking about over dinner.'

'I'm glad you did,' she said, 'because I really need to go home now.'

'For God's sake, you can't.'

'I can, and I will. Try to stop me and I'll scream,' she warned as he made to grab her arm.

Immediately he let her go, then seeing Ernest Schultz's wife heading their way he quickly assumed his boyishly charming smile as he held out a hand towards her. 'Flora, I don't believe you've met Jessica. Darling, this is Flora Schultz.'

Out of politeness Jessica abandoned her flight and allowed herself to be drawn into a few minutes of small talk, dimly realising that she might actually like this slightly overweight, gregarious woman with an irrepressible twinkle and flashy red lipstick, were she not still so stunned by Charlie's news.

In the end, once she'd managed to stop reeling, she agreed to go for dinner as arranged, and to her relief the subject of Charlie's new position didn't come up – she suspected because he had asked Schultz to postpone it – so the evening passed in a reasonably enjoyable way.

It wasn't until they arrived home that Charlie mentioned it again, as she'd known he would. 'I understand it came as a shock,' he said, undressing for bed, 'but once you've had some time to think about it, you might feel differently. And there's no rush.'

Unable to imagine feeling anything but even colder to the idea, Jessica decided not to respond.

'He's invited us both to New York in February,' Charlie continued, from the bathroom, 'staying at his Upper East Side apartment, or at a hotel, if we prefer, and I suspect no expense will be spared. I can't see any harm in accepting that, can you?'

Jessica continued to stare into the mirror.

'OK. Let's not discuss it any more tonight,' he said, coming back into the room. 'We're both tired and I've got a seven o'clock start tomorrow.'

As they got into bed Jessica turned her back and allowed him to pull her against him as he often did. They never made love, as far as she knew his medication was still making it difficult for him, and she could only feel thankful for that, because she really didn't want to. However, tonight it seemed he wanted to kiss her, or maybe even take it further, because he was pressing his mouth to her neck and trying to ease her over onto her back.

'Charlie, I'm too tired,' she said and moved away.

For several minutes he lay still, saying nothing, then rolling over to his side of the bed he whispered goodnight in a way that brought an ache of guilt to her heart. However, it was never easy pretending an affection, or a passion she didn't feel, so tonight, at least, she wasn't even going to try.

Chapter Twenty-Nine

'There are not many people I'd allow to drag me out of doors this early in the morning,' Veronica grumbled, as she and Jessica trudged away from Maurice's grand old Georgian house towards the open countryside. 'Or in this freezing weather,' she added dismally. Then, eyeing up an approaching stile with marked distrust, 'Do I have to climb that?'

'Unless you want to jump it,' Jessica retorted.

Veronica couldn't help but laugh, and allowed Jessica to take her hand as she gingerly mounted the rickety wooden bars to manoeuvre herself down the other side.

It was just after ten o'clock on Boxing Day morning, and though the temperature was hovering around zero, sunlight was streaming from a clear blue sky and pooling over the meadows, making everything look fresh and vibrant as though nature was painting itself in oils.

'I think lunch went very well yesterday, don't you?' Veronica commented chattily, as they fell into step on a hard, muddy trail. 'We certainly had plenty to eat, and it was a lovely idea of yours, darling, to send goats and chickens to Africa for the people there, I didn't feel half so guilty about our little feast once you told me that. I must make sure Maurice and I do the same next year. Did you say it was through Oxfam?'

'That's right,' Jessica confirmed, linking her mother's arm and watching her breath puff out in small white clouds. 'So now, come on, spill the beans,' she said, keeping the pace going. 'I've waited all these years to know the truth, so I'm not going to let you fob me off any longer. Who is – or was – my father?'

'Oh dear.' Veronica instantly sounded troubled. 'It's that therapist of yours, isn't it, making you ask.'

'He thought it would be a good idea, yes, but honestly, Mum, it would be nice to know.'

'No, it wouldn't,' Veronica assured her.

Jessica almost laughed. 'He can't be that bad, surely?'

'I don't know. I mean, I couldn't . . . Oh dear, Jessica . . .'

'Just tell me his name,' Jessica prompted.

'What good do you think it's going to do?'

'I can't answer that without knowing who he is, but if you're afraid I might go knocking on his door and disrupting his life, that's really not my intention. I'm just trying to get some clarity, as the therapist put it, and shake out all the skeletons . . .'

'Ugh!' Veronica responded with a shudder.

Rolling her eyes Jessica said, 'OK, let's try this another way – I'm intrigued to know who he is and why you never named him.'

Sounding very unhappy now, Veronica said, 'I couldn't. I mean, I really couldn't, because I haven't lied to you, darling, I honestly have no idea who he is.'

Jessica's heart gave a beat of shock. 'Do you mean you were raped?'

'Heavens no.'

'So it was a one-night stand while you were drunk?'

'No. No. Nothing as sordid as that. It was much more . . . Well, much more fun.'

'I'm listening,' Jessica said dryly.

'Well, if you're sure you want to know . . .'

'I am, so keep going.'

'OK. It happened one crazy summer – well, it was February, actually, but it was very hot where we all were, in the Caribbean, so it seemed like summer. It was a week-long party at the most marvellous villa owned by some South Africans, I think, or maybe they were Australian, I can't really remember, because there was lots of marijuana going round, and alcohol and all kinds of other drugs, and no-one was really taking any notice of who was popping into bed with who – well, often we didn't bother about the bed, because no-one was wearing any clothes anyway, so we just did whatever took our fancy wherever we were . . .'

'You mean it was an orgy.'

Veronica seemed startled. 'Yes, I suppose it was, now you come to mention it,' she said. 'And it was immense fun. We were all so young and beautiful and liberated and it was so very hot . . . I remember this one particular day in the pool . . .'

'I don't think I need any details,' Jessica interrupted. 'So what you're saying is that my father could be any of a dozen or so men whose names you never knew even at the time?'

Veronica blinked with dismay. 'Put like that it doesn't sound very good, does it?' she said. 'But they were all jolly nice and whoever he was he was obviously very tall and good-looking and intelligent, because look at you. You hardly resemble me at all.'

Jessica was shaking her head in amusement and despair. 'I should have known it was something like that,' she said. 'I suppose the real mystery is why you decided to keep me.'

'Oh, there was never any doubt about that,' Veronica assured her. 'Once I knew I was pregnant . . . Well, I have to admit, it did shock me a bit at first and I did wonder if I could cope, but then I thought of how lovely it would be to have a baby, and I was right, because I had you and you were more than lovely . . .' Her voice dropped a little as she added, 'And I was worse than useless. Just thank goodness for Grandma and Gramps, or I dread to think what a mess I'd have made of you.'

Though Jessica laughed, there was a tightening in her heart as she thought of what a mess she was inside.

They walked on in silence for a while, watching birds flitting in and out of the hedgerow one side of the path, while everywhere else remained perfectly still.

'Has Charlie mentioned any more about New York?' Veronica finally ventured.

Jessica's spirits sank. 'Only insofar as he thinks we should book flights soon, if we're going to go in February.'

'It's a marvellous opportunity for him.'

'Yes.'

'But you don't want to go.'

Jessica sighed. 'No, I don't,' she replied. 'I like New York, but not to live. And there's Harry's schooling to think of – do we really want him growing up in America? Then there's Nikki. I know she's thinking of moving in with Freddy, but I'm not sure either of us could bear being so far apart. Not yet, anyway.'

Veronica pursed her lips thoughtfully.

'On the other hand,' Jessica went on, 'I can hardly say I'm happy in London, so maybe I should give it a go.'

Veronica cast her a glance. 'What do you really want to do?' she asked quietly.

As Jessica thought about all the answers she could give to that – to write, be a good mother, repair her marriage – she knew there was only one that was true, but there was no point admitting to it when it could never be.

'Mm, I thought so,' Veronica said.

Jessica blinked. Had she spoken without realising?

'You want to go back to Valennes,' Veronica said. It wasn't even a question. 'Charlie told me a while ago about Luc. He wanted to know if you'd confided in me. You hadn't, of course, and I think he took that as a good sign, but he was wrong. You're finding this very hard, I can tell.'

'No, not really,' Jessica responded, needing to deny it. 'Luc and I became close while I was there, I admit, but we didn't have an affair, at least not as such.'

Veronica's eyebrows rose. 'If you ask me, it's the "as such" that's causing the problem,' she commented sagely. 'If you'd slept together, got it out of your systems, you probably wouldn't still be pining for him now and wondering what it might have been like.'

'I'm not pining,' Jessica protested. 'And actually, it was more than just physical, so if we had slept together I think I'd be finding it even harder now.'

Veronica didn't point out the contradiction, she merely said, 'Have you had any contact with him since you left?'

'No, of course not. It wouldn't do any good. Lilian's baby is due soon, and I've had my own family to sort out.'

'So what are you going to do?'

Jessica shrugged and sighed shakily. 'There's nothing I can do except try to forget it.' Then realising how desperately she needed to talk to someone, she said, 'The trouble is, time doesn't seem to be making it any better. I felt sure I'd be over it by now . . . But I have to make myself let go. And I will. I'll go to New York with Charlie . . . I'm going to tell him that he has my support. People do get past these crises and find one another again. So maybe we can too.'

Veronica glanced at her, but remained silent.

'In fact, I'm going to tell him on New Year's Eve that I'll go with him,' Jessica decided. 'It'll mark the end of this year, and the start of a new one, so yes, that's what I'll do at midnight, let go of the dream of last year, and embrace the life that I have as we go into the next.'

As it turned out none of them celebrated New Year's Eve as the entire family, with the exception of Jessica, was struck down by flu. Since it was a particularly virulent strain, it wasn't until a full week into January that she set about preparing a special dinner in order to make her announcement.

On the chosen day both children were still in bed suffering, but Charlie managed to struggle into his office for a few hours, so Jessica spent as much time as she could reading *Suite Française* as well as Keats and de Lamartine, and dipping into the many other authors and poets she and Luc had discussed or quoted. After tonight she would have to put it all behind her, so like someone about to be deprived of air she was taking in as much of it as she could before the oxygen ran out.

By the time Charlie came home she'd set the table and the lamb casserole was in the oven. It seemed a very long time since they'd used the dining room upstairs, but she'd decided not to this evening. The kitchen wasn't exactly unromantic with the lights down low and no children around, and it would save them the trouble of carrying everything back and forth.

Hearing him moving about up in the study she began running through her announcement again, not that it was particularly difficult to remember, she just needed to inject the right amount of enthusiasm into her words. There was, of course, the alternative announcement which she'd practised several times, really just to see how it felt, but she'd put it aside now. No matter how many times she rehearsed it, she wasn't going to crush him by telling him that she wanted them to try some time apart.

'Everything OK?' she asked as he came down into the kitchen. 'How are you feeling?'

'Not too bad,' he answered, sounding hoarse and blocked. 'Mm, something smells good.'

Touched, since he probably couldn't smell a thing, she said, 'I've opened some wine. Do you feel up to any?'

'I'm sure I can manage a glass. Do I have time to shower and make myself more human?'

'Of course. Pop in and see the children while you're up there and remind them we're not to be disturbed.'

As he started off up the stairs she was thinking of how much they would once have enjoyed being alone together, feeling the anticipation of what was to come swirling around them, but there was no doubt the spark had gone now, leaving her with a disconcerting mix of sadness and pity – and a lingering contempt for what he had done. She kept telling herself she'd get past that one day, and it wasn't as if she wanted to punish him, or even make him unhappy, but she really didn't want to go to New York, and if she wasn't careful she might start resenting him for the way his needs once again seemed to be coming first.

However, after a fortifying glass of wine and a stern reminder of how good it would be for her to move on with her life, she was ready to start serving dinner, and even to give Charlie a kiss when he came back downstairs looking sprucely over-shaved, and not nearly as bleary-eyed as when he'd come in.

'They've been bribed to stay where they are,' he told her, going to pour himself some wine.

Jessica glanced at him curiously. He hadn't sounded as humorous about that as he might have. Over the next few minutes she began to realise that he was either feeling much more worn down by his flu than he was admitting, or his solemn, even edgy mood was about something else entirely.

'Is everything all right?' she asked, carrying the first course of asparagus and vinaigrette with Parmesan to the table.

'Yes, of course,' he answered, not meeting her eyes. 'What about you?'

'Fine,' she said, sitting down and unfurling her napkin.

As they started to eat she waited for him to say more, but he didn't, so she asked him about his day. He was less than forthcoming, and when he made no effort to ask about hers it didn't as much irritate as perplex her. Clearly he had something on his mind, but for the moment he was keeping it to himself. Wondering if he was afraid she was about to tell him it was over between them, she began considering doing just that. After all, why force herself to go along with his plans just to prove she was letting her own dreams go? If she was being totally honest with herself, the only reason she was still trying to keep them together was for Harry's sake, so if Charlie wanted his son perhaps he should be giving as much thought to staying in London as she was to going to New York.

Then, realising she was being too harsh, and that a trip to New York in February was hardly too much to ask, she put her cutlery down and picked up her glass. 'I have something to tell you,' she said.

At the same time he said, 'You don't have to go through all this, really. I've been expecting it . . .'

'Charlie listen, I want to tell you . . .' She broke off and started again. 'Well, I've been thinking . . . Maybe we should try a separation for a while.' She stopped breathing. She really hadn't known until the words came out that she was going to say them, but she had now, and in spite of the tension she couldn't deny how relieved she suddenly felt.

On the other hand she was never going to feel good about hurting him, but before she could attempt to temper her suggestion he said, 'Well, you've certainly taken your time.'

She blinked in surprise.

'Ever since Lilian rang I knew that sooner or later you'd want to go to him,' he continued tersely. 'Of course, I can't stop you, I understand that . . .'

'Lilian rang?' she echoed in amazement.

It was his turn to look surprised. 'Just before Christmas. She wanted to speak to you, but you weren't around so she said she'd call back.' The expression on her face prompted him to say, 'Clearly she didn't.'

'Why did she call?' she asked, feeling slightly dizzy and breathless.

With a cold edge to his voice he said, 'She's left Luc, she's lost the baby . . . What more can I tell you? What more do you want to hear?'

She sat back in her chair, too stunned to know what to say.

With a bitter laugh he shook his head as he realised what this meant. 'You didn't know he was free again, but you wanted a separation anyway. Well, isn't that great?'

She pushed her hands through her hair. 'I'm sorry,' she said, 'everything's suddenly . . . I thought . . .' She looked at him and for the strangest moment she felt as though she was drowning. Then realising there was air, only air, all around her, she took a deep, exhilarating breath.

'So what next?' he asked. 'I suppose you'll be moving to France.'

'For heaven's sake,' she cried. 'I haven't even had time to absorb this yet.'

'What is there to absorb? He's available now, it must be what you want . . .'

'Oh Charlie,' she said, realising his hostility was to hide the pain he was feeling, 'please don't be angry. I know this isn't easy . . .'

'The company flat's coming free at the end of the month,' he broke in. 'I could move over there . . .'

'If you're going to New York . . .'

'I'll tell Schultz it's not on,' he said curtly. 'It was only to give us a fresh start, but I guessed when Lilian called that wouldn't be what you wanted, so I'd rather be in London. It's where I belong, with the people I know.'

She nodded. 'For what it's worth I think it's the right decision.'

'And you? You'll want to take Harry with you, I suppose?'

Seeing the tears in his eyes, she had to swallow hard before she could reply. 'Charlie, I haven't seen or spoken to Luc in months, so I can't tell you anything until I do.'

He nodded and looked down at his glass. 'I suppose

there's always a chance, when you do see him again, you won't feel the same way,' he said bleakly.

She knew how unlikely that was, but she didn't have the heart to crush his hope, small though it was, so all she said was, 'I guess you never know.' Then finally realising that she might be seeing Luc again, and soon, she could hardly contain all the emotions that began flooding into her heart.

The following morning Jessica spent a long time on the phone talking to Daniella, then after checking Charlie's schedule to make sure he'd be around for Harry, she went online to book herself a flight. She didn't speak to Luc. She knew if she told him she was coming he'd insist on meeting her at the airport, and she didn't want the first time they saw one another with the freedom to touch and embrace to be in a public place. She had to admit that there was also the possibility she might end up cancelling, or at least postponing, for she needed to tell Nikki where she was going and why, and she had no idea how Nikki was going to react.

'Do you want to talk to her with me?' she asked Charlie, when she told him what she intended to do.

'No,' he replied. 'I'll be around if she wants me to join in, but I think you need to talk to her on your own.'

Understanding his reluctance was in part because he didn't want to hear her discussing her feelings for Luc, she didn't press the issue. She merely chose an evening when he was at home, and Nikki was more or less recovered from her flu – and when Harry was engrossed in one of his programmes. She would tell him, of course, that she was going to Valennes, but he was too young to take in the full complexities of why, the way Nikki could and since she still had no idea what the outcome would be once she saw Luc, she didn't want to start confusing him now.

'So, what's the big mystery?' Nikki asked, all intrigued, as Jessica came into her room. She was sitting cross-legged on the bed, dressed in a pink lacy tank top and pyjama bottoms, and with her hair scraped back behind her ears. She looked so much younger than her eighteen years, Jessica was thinking as she went to sit on the bed with her. It seemed a very poignant sort of irony that today of all days she should look so very like Natalie.

Smiling, she lifted a hand to Nikki's cheek and brushed it softly. 'I'm afraid there's no easy way to tell you this, darling,' she began.

Immediately Nikki's eyes filled with alarm. 'Oh my God. You and Dad are breaking up, aren't you?' she cried. 'I knew it was going to happen. Oh Mum, I don't want you to. I want us all to stay together.'

As she threw her arms round her, Jessica held her close and stroked her hair. Then after a while she said, very gently, 'You're right, we are, but there is a little more to it.'

Nikki pulled back to look at her, full of suspicion and fear.

'When I was in France last summer,' Jessica said, 'Luc and I . . .'

Nikki's eyes rounded with horror. 'Oh no, don't go there. Please don't go there,' she protested, backing away.

'We didn't have an affair,' Jessica told her, 'but we did become close.'

'Oh my God,' Nikki groaned into her hands. Then her head came up sharply. 'You're doing it to get back at Lilian, aren't you?' she challenged. 'That's what this is about . . .'

'No, it isn't. It happened before we knew anything about Dad and Lilian, and it wasn't something we planned, or even really wanted to happen . . . I guess it was . . . Well, like when you fell for Freddy, you didn't consciously decide you would, you just did, because there was an attraction between you . . .'

'But I wasn't married to someone else!' Nikki cried wildly. 'Nor was he. And what about Lilian's baby? Or have you conveniently forgotten about that?'

Jessica's eyes went down for a moment. 'Apparently she lost it,' she said. 'Dad only told me a couple of nights ago. Lilian called just before Christmas, and broke the news to him then. She's not with Luc now. She said she'd call back to tell me, but she never did.'

Nikki's eyes were still bright with hostile confusion. 'So what? Luc slings her out because she can't carry a baby . . .'

'No, of course not. He's not like that, and you know it. I spoke to Daniella yesterday and apparently Lilian left of her own accord. She didn't feel . . . She thought he probably didn't love her any more, and when there was no longer a baby to consider . . .'

'Does she know about you?'

Jessica nodded.

'So he doesn't love her, because of you?'

'Only he can answer that.'

'Oh God,' Nikki seethed, covering her face again. 'I hate this. I hate it. Please make it go away.'

'Nikki, listen to me.'

'No, no, I can't,' she cried, blocking her ears. 'I don't want to hear any more . . .'

'Darling, I'm speaking to you as an adult, so please try to behave like one.'

'Well I don't feel very adult when my mother tells me she's going off with another man, like the rest of us don't matter . . .'

'That's not what I said, so stop putting words in my mouth and please listen.'

Nikki's expression turned sullen.

Sighing a little, Jessica said, 'One of the hardest things we ever have to deal with in our lives is change, especially when it means having to let go of things that have made us feel safe. You've had a lot to cope with since Natalie died, trying to get used to her not being around, then finding out what happened at the cottage, what Dad's been through since . . . It's been too much already, I understand that, and with all my heart I wish I wasn't having to make you go through any more . . .'

'Then don't,' Nikki wailed. 'No-one's forcing you to. I mean, I know what Dad did was terrible, but you've forgiven him now . . .'

'I'm still trying,' Jessica corrected gently, 'but even if I manage to, my feelings just aren't the same for him any more. I know how hard that is for you to hear, and I promise, it's hard for me to say. Obviously I care about him . . . I still love him in a way, but it's not the kind of love that's going to keep us together.'

'It might if it weren't for Luc.'

Jessica shook her head. 'Even before I found out Lilian had

left Luc, I'd already decided that Dad and I need to separate. He's not going to New York now, so you don't have to worry about that, and nothing's going to change right away. I need to see Luc first to find out if the way we felt about one another last summer is still how we feel now.'

'So it might not be?' Nikki said hopefully.

Jessica's smile was sad. 'No, it might not,' she said, but only because it was what Nikki wanted to hear. 'I'm going over there on Friday . . .'

'For how long?' Nikki jumped in.

'Until the following Thursday, unless I decide to come back earlier. I definitely won't stay any longer though.'

Nikki turned her face away as more tears welled in her eyes.

'Oh darling,' Jessica said, gathering her in her arms. 'No-one will ever matter more to me than you and Harry, but I don't think, in your heart, you want to make me stay somewhere I don't want to be. Especially when you're starting out on your own life now.'

'Yeah, well, maybe I've inherited Grandma's selfish gene, because I do want you to stay here. I don't want you to go to France, even for a few days.'

'So you want me to cancel?'

'Yes!'

Jessica looked at her.

Nikki's expression became more mutinous. 'Yes!' she repeated. Then, banging her fists into the bed, 'What about Dad? He's just been through a terrible depression, a virtual nervous breakdown, this could set him off again . . .'

'I don't think it will, but if it does, we'll deal with it then. I'm not going to abandon you, any of you.'

Though Nikki was trying with all her might to stay angry, Jessica could see it starting to drain out of her, until finally, looking bewildered and dejected, she said, 'Oh God, Mum, this is all such a mess. How am I going to leave Dad here on his own, if you go? I can't move in with Freddy then, can I?'

Thinking of the selfish gene, Jessica only smiled as she said, 'Of course you can. I've told you enough times, you have to stop assuming responsibility for me and Dad and live your own life. He'll agree with me on that, I can promise you . . .'

'He might *say* it . . .'

'Listen,' Jessica interrupted more firmly. 'You're getting far too ahead of yourself. No decisions have been made yet, about anything, nor will they be until I go to France. Then when I come back we'll talk again. OK?'

After a while Nikki nodded, then sighed heavily as Jessica got up to leave. 'Mum?' she said.

Jessica turned back.

'I know I should probably wish you good luck, but I'm sorry, I can't.'

Jessica smiled. 'That's all right.'

'I mean, what I really, really hope is that you find out you don't want to be with him, or he doesn't want to be with you.'

'I know,' Jessica whispered, and opening the door she left the room.

Chapter Thirty

Daniella was waiting beside the car when Jessica walked out of the arrivals hall on Friday afternoon. Seeing her beautiful, welcoming smile brought such a rush of emotion to Jessica's heart that she clasped her straight into her arms, while the feel of French rolling off her tongue as she greeted her was even more delicious than she remembered.

'You look wonderful,' she told Daniella, wondering why she'd never noticed before how like her brother she was. 'As gorgeously exotic as ever.'

Daniella laughed and rolled her eyes. 'It is a miracle with three such dreadful children that I have not yet turned into a hag,' she declared. 'But Claude, he would divorce me if I did, so I must keep myself together. And you, Jessica, you look beautiful, *chérie*. Your hair is longer, and your eyes are very lovely and . . . *mystérieux*. I think you are happy, no? It shows in your face.'

Knowing how sunken and shadowed her eyes had become over the last few months, Jessica had to laugh at the 'mysterious'. 'I am very happy to see you,' she told her.

Daniella winked, then loading Jessica's bag onto the back seat she waited until Jessica was buckled up before starting out of the airport. 'This is so very exciting and romantic,' she declared, as they sped away from the *payage* onto the autoroute. 'I have told Claude that I am finding him very boring now, so he must do something like this for me. Do you know what is his answer? He tell me that *you* are doing this for Luc, so it is time I do something for him, and if I need any ideas, he will very much enjoy to have a slave in the bedroom, and he is prepared to give me the job, but only if I pass the exam.'

Jessica's eyes were dancing. 'Dare I ask what the exam is?'

'I don't know yet, but I am sure I will find out soon. He is in Paris until tomorrow but when he comes back maybe you and Luc will find some time to come over to the chateau. It is all right, you do not have to give me an answer now. I know you will have a lot of . . . er, catching up to do.'

Jessica's eyes closed as a wave of anticipation and happiness washed over her. Then belatedly realising what Daniella had said she cast her a look, wondering how much she knew – and seeing the mischievous gleam in Daniella's eyes she started to laugh.

'It was not hard to work out,' Daniella declared. 'When you tell me you do not want him to kiss you for the first time at the airport – *oh là là*, if you have not kissed before, then how can you have done anything else? But it is none of my business . . . Ah, I think this must be Claude,' she said as her mobile started to ring. 'He will want to know if you have arrived. *Oui, c'est lui,*' she confirmed, glancing at the number that came up. Then clicking on she said, *'Chéri. Elle est arrivée.'*

As Daniella continued to talk, Jessica turned to gaze out at the passing countryside, and wondered how she could feel such a sense of belonging to a country that wasn't her own. Of course she knew it was because it was Luc's, but even in the murky light of a tepid January sun she could feel its magic embracing her. It was as though something palpable was emanating from the scattered patches of snow on the hills, and from the trees, stripped of their glossy summer foliage now to twist and jut like gnarled, skeletal fingers against the relentless grey backdrop of the sky.

'Oh là là, this is very interesting,' Daniella said, when she rang off. 'Claude has lunch with Lilian today and she happen to ask if you have seen Luc yet. So I think we were right in what we said on the phone, *chérie,* she was never going to ring back, she was expecting Charlie to tell you that she and Luc were no longer together.'

'And eventually he did,' Jessica said, wondering when Charlie might have got round to it, had it not come up when it did.

'I am afraid it is very typical of a man not to understand

the subtleties,' Daniella commented. 'Still, what is important is that he did tell you, and you are here.'

Jessica smiled, and because she genuinely wanted to know, she said, 'So how is Lilian?'

Daniella grimaced and shrugged. 'Personally, I am not sure,' she replied. 'I have seen her only once since she leave Valennes, but Claude sees her sometimes in Paris, and so does Luc when he is there. I think they are trying to become friends, which is very like my brother, because he hates to have bad feeling, or to think he is the cause of someone's pain. He has given her the apartment, did you know that?'

Jessica shook her head, and thought of how hard all this must have been for Lilian, and how normally she would have been there to see her through it. She wondered if a day might come when they could be friends again. She hoped so, but it was still too soon to try, for she hadn't yet found it in her heart to forgive the way Lilian had left Natalie, and nor, she imagined, would Lilian be anywhere close to getting over her break-up with Luc.

'Tiens,' Daniella said, when finally they pulled up outside the chateau. 'I will leave you to drive on now, and maybe you should go quickly, because if the children see you, you will not be able to get away.'

'Are you sure you don't need your car?' Jessica said.

'I have Claude's. He take the train to Paris.'

Jessica glanced at the black Mercedes, then seeing a silver one next to it she said, 'Isn't that Luc's?'

'Papa drove it over,' Daniella answered. Turning in her seat to look at Jessica, she pulled an apologetic face as she said, 'Now it is time for me to confess, *chérie*. I hope you will not be angry with me, but Luc knows you are coming.'

Jessica's heart stopped as her eyes widened.

'I had to tell him,' Daniella went on quickly. 'He would never forgive me otherwise, because he would want to make the house ready for you, and it was difficult for Papa to say he was coming here for the weekend without him . . . Of course he wanted to meet you at the airport, but when I told him why you didn't want him to . . . Well, I think he understand.'

Jessica smiled at the expression in Daniella's eyes, too

bound by nervous tension to respond in any other way.

'Alors, bon courage,' Daniella said, pulling her into an embrace. 'I will not expect to see you again very soon.'

As Jessica drove away, back down the leaf-covered drive and out into the narrow country road that led towards Valennes, she was so full of apprehension that the stiffness in her limbs made her movements clumsy and wrong. Twice she crunched the gears, and once she almost carried straight on when she needed to turn. Though she could hardly wait to get there, she found she was driving slowly, almost as though she was becoming afraid of what she was doing. And in a way she was, for it seemed that she was only now beginning to realise that being here, going to him, could very easily be the first step towards changing her life completely. The enormity of it swelled in her heart. Though she felt certain it was what she wanted, she hadn't truly understood until now just how much courage it was going to take to get through the weeks and months to come, leaving London, giving up everything she knew, taking Harry from Charlie . . . If indeed that was the way it all went . . .

By the time she arrived on the top road to Valennes dusk was settling over the valley like a grimy veil, but there was still enough light for her to see how bleak and forlorn everything looked with its brutally clipped vines and winter-torn fields. It seemed so changed from the valley she knew that it could almost be another place, belonging to another lifetime where strangers had lived and loved. Yet, as she turned down the hill, she felt the familiarity of it starting to stir inside her, as though an old friend in shabby clothes was welcoming her back. When she reached the grape-picker's cottage she found she wasn't really seeing it as it was, all closed up and in darkness, instead she was recalling the tranquil air inside and the bittersweet memories it had given her.

After pausing outside for a while, she drove on up towards the *manoir*, where she could see a light in the kitchen, and two more in the pergola. No flowers or foliage at this time of year, only the naked brown sticks of midwinter that were still three months or more from their slow, exquisite burst back to life, and a fine mizzle descending over the *combe* and coating the windscreen to make everything distorted and blurred.

Then she saw him, standing outside the *cave* waiting for her, and there was such a surge of joy in her heart that she could only wonder how she'd experienced even a moment's doubt, when merely to look at him was enough to tell her that all she wanted was to be with him.

As he pulled open the car door she saw the sardonic look in his eyes and tried to smile, but then she was biting her lip, for too much happiness and relief was starting to swamp her.

'I'm getting wet,' he told her, unromantically, and pressing the buckle to release her seat belt he took her hand to help her out.

Even the feel of his fingers closing around hers, the hard flatness of his palm, the easy strength of his grip, was causing a gentle turmoil inside her, and as he walked her across the pergola into the house she almost felt afraid of her own reactions.

After closing the door behind them he took her coat, and she walked forward into the wonderfully familiar kitchen with all its handmade pots and painted cupboards, the overhead beams and the long table down the middle where two glasses and an ice bucket containing a bottle of champagne were waiting. She watched him walk over to it, then went to stand between the two large armchairs in front of the fire. All the time they kept looking at one another, and she could feel herself smiling, unable to stop. She wanted him to touch her, to kiss her and hold her, but she waited for him to pour the champagne, then watched him bring a glass to her.

As he handed it to her, he said, 'I was trying to decide, before you came, whose words I would use to greet you, de Lamartine, Keats, Irène, *n'importe qui*, but now you're here I find they are all letting me down.'

Her head went to one side as her expression challenged him playfully.

'The best way I can say it,' he whispered, 'is that it's as though the light has come back into my life.'

Her smile faded as her heart expanded with the meaning

of his words, then he touched his glass to hers and said, 'To us.'

'To us,' she echoed in a whisper.

His eyes stayed on hers as they sipped, then taking her glass he put it with his on the mantelpiece. When he turned back she felt her heartbeat starting to slow, for she knew he was going to kiss her now and she had never wanted anything more in her life. Her breath caught in a gentle gasp as he took her in his arms, and in the first moments that his mouth covered hers it was as though all the love she had ever felt began to gather in her heart, while all the desire she could know swelled quietly, potently into life.

His kiss was deep and tender and full of the words neither of them had yet spoken, and all the pleasure yet to come. She could feel it moving into her as though to bring her even closer to him, and as she gave herself completely, feeling the pressure of his lips and strength of his arms, she wanted it never to end. Then his tongue entered her mouth and inflamed such need in her that it made her murmur for more and still more.

When he lifted his head to look at her she felt unsteadied and dazed, and so full of longing that her voice was barely a whisper as she said, 'I know there's a lot we need to say, but please don't let's wait any longer.'

Though amusement glinted in his eyes, their darkness showed the force of his own desire, and taking her hand he led her out of the room. When they reached the first landing he stopped to pull her into his arms again, and as she clung to him she knew if he wanted to take her right there she would be happy to let him.

They continued up to the second floor and into his bedroom. It seemed more masculine than when she'd last seen it, but being warmly lit by a small log fire in the hearth, and the lamps either side of the bed, it couldn't be anything other than romantic and inviting.

As he closed the door she turned to look at him, and continued to look at him as he began slowly to undress her. His eyes were intense, while his fingers were steady, and the air around them seemed gently but powerfully charged with their need.

Then her clothes were gone, leaving her fully revealed to him, and she stood watching him as his gaze moved like a languorous caress over her firelit shoulders and arms, her breasts, her abdomen, and the slender length of her legs. '*Tu es plus belle que je me rappelais,*' he said softly. You're even more beautiful than I remember.

'I want you to see you,' she said, and taking his hand she pulled him to her.

As she unfastened his shirt he unbelted his jeans, and when finally he was naked too she stepped back to take in the hard masculinity of his chest, the firmness of his thighs, but most of all the uncompromising might of his desire.

She gave a gasp of longing and as her eyes went back to his he pulled her quickly to him, and the sensation of his skin on hers was like nothing she'd ever known before. She could feel him all over her, the strength of his arms, the pressure of his mouth, the power of his legs and the hardness of his cock. Her hands moved over his back and his buttocks, pulling him even closer, and as her tongue sought his she felt as though she was struggling to stay afloat in a sea of irresistible need.

With his mouth still on hers he scooped her up and carried her to the bed. Then he was lying over her, covering her body with his – and her legs were circling his waist, bringing him to her. She needed him inside her, he had to come to her now, but he only touched the tip of himself to her, pushing and probing, until the brutally teasing contact sent her to the very brink of a climax.

'Oh Luc,' she gasped, clutching him hard.

'It's all right. I can feel it,' he told her.

'Please,' she begged. Then she cried out as he suddenly pushed all the way in and joined them completely. 'Oh my God,' she choked.

'Let it go,' he urged. 'Just let it go.'

There was nothing she could do to stop it, and as the exquisite release began to pound and clench around him he rode her and held her and she clung to him sobbing and gasping, and never knowing if she could take any more.

'It's all right, I've got you,' he murmured, and putting his mouth to hers he drew her orgasm on and on, taking her to realms of such impossible sensation that in the end she could only turn weak in the thrall of its power.

It was a while before she opened her eyes, and looking dazedly up into his she ran her fingers over his mouth as she said, 'I've tried to imagine what it would be like to feel you inside me, but I could never have imagined anything like this.'

He smiled, and as his lips came to hers it was as though she could feel his love moving right into her heart.

Soon after he was taking her gently again, easing her back from the stupor, bringing her to him until he was making love to her in ways no-one ever had before. She hadn't known it was possible to feel so much pleasure in her entire body, or that she could move from one orgasm into another and then another. He seemed to know every part of her even better than she knew herself, how to touch and kiss her, when to be gentle and when not, and even the very moment to compel her over the edge into oblivion.

Then finally, when she really could take no more, he allowed himself to let go, and the force of his release was so intense that they both cried out. And as he pounded her harshly, then gently, then harshly again, she could feel the sheer power of him as though it was becoming a part of her.

It was a long time later that they lay gazing into one another's eyes and feeling the bruising tenderness of their bodies. The remains of the fire sighed and shifted in the hearth, while the rain pattered rhythmically over the eaves. Her heart was so full that tears were wet on her cheeks, and when she tried to speak the words couldn't make it past the tightness in her throat.

'Ai-je pensé te dire que je t'aime?' he murmured softly. Did I remember to tell you I love you?

Her mouth trembled as she laughed, then moving even closer to him she kissed him with all the love she felt was consuming them both.

Late the following day they were in the kitchen listening to a recording of Claude conducting the Orchestre de Paris in Mendelssohn's *Symphonies for Strings*, when Daniella rang to invite them over for dinner.

'Dinner?' Luc repeated, as though it were a forgotten concept. He was sitting at the table reading a printout of Jessica's book, and wearing only a thick navy robe which he'd changed into after they'd walked over to the lake in the rain. 'Yes, I think we'll come for dinner,' he said, 'but maybe on Tuesday.'

Jessica smiled as she heard Daniella laugh.

She was standing at the window staring out at the drab, motionless day now that the rain had stopped, her hands buried deeply in the pockets of another of his robes, her senses responding gently to the smell of him each time she inhaled. Though nothing could make her want to be anywhere other than where she was now, it still felt bewildering to be this new woman, as though she were fulfilling a dream that she'd almost lost the courage to have. And yet it was all real, because he was right there behind her, and she knew if she went to him now he would make her believe it all over again.

Her eyes moved across the dankly misted vines to the cottage, and as she thought of Natalie an all-too familiar ache cleaved through her heart. She knew nothing would ever replace her precious girl in her life, she wasn't even expecting it to, any more than she was expecting to make sense of why she'd had to die. Maybe one day she would start to come to terms with the loss, even though it was hard to imagine now, but the future was impossible to predict, as she'd come to learn very well. Whether Charlie could ever truly live with himself again, she guessed only time would tell. There was no more she could do to help him. She'd tried to forgive him, and to an extent she had, but the way he had left Natalie that day would always be there between them, as it had since the moment it had happened, which was why they'd started to come apart even before she'd known the truth.

She could only wonder now why fate had used such a senseless tragedy to pull a family – and friendship – apart and send them all in new directions. Since they were still on the threshold of this unplanned future she knew she couldn't possibly know the answer, and accepted that very probably she never would. She wouldn't even ask herself if the price was worth paying, because nothing would ever be worth Natalie's life, and she knew Luc would understand that too. Anyway, she'd been made to understand in the most brutal of ways that life didn't bargain, or discuss, or even hesitate with its plans, it only delivered. So all she could do now was try to let go of the bitterness and pain, and embrace the love she was still lucky enough to have.

Feeling him coming to stand behind her, she sank back into his arms as he wrapped them around her.

'What are you thinking?' he asked, resting his cheek against hers.

Smiling, she said, 'Lots of things, but most of all about Natalie and how lovely it would be to put a little dovecote down at the cottage for her. Do you think your father would mind?'

With a wry tone he said, 'I'm sure he'll love the idea, but the cottage is mine and Daniella's so I can tell you we wouldn't mind at all.' Then after a moment, 'Do you think Harry would like to help build it?'

Hearing that, her heart contracted, and as she turned around to look up into his eyes, she whispered, 'He would love to. Knowing it was for Natalie . . . It would make him feel so important.'

He kissed her softly on the mouth as she linked her arms around his neck.

'Can it work?' she asked, wondering why she was suddenly doubtful again. 'Can we really be together?'

As his eyes swept her face, he said, 'You're looking for answers that aren't yet there to be found. All we know for certain is how we feel about one another now, which means we'll do everything we can to make it work – and over the next few months we will find out how possible it is.'

Though it wasn't exactly what she'd hoped to hear, she knew he was right. She was under no illusion, making the break from Charlie and Nikki, and London too, was going to be far from easy. Just thank God she wasn't having to let go of Harry, because she knew in her heart she'd be unable to. Instead she was going to start bringing him here as often as she could, first of all to get him used to seeing her and Luc together, and then to thinking of Valennes as home. Luc had even suggested letting him have the puppy he wanted, and allowing it to sleep in the room that would become Harry's – so they were planning to do everything they could to make the break from his father as painless as possible. However, it was still going to be traumatic, on both sides, Jessica was in no doubt about that, but since it wouldn't happen until summer, when Harry had finished this school year, she wasn't going to make an issue of it now. After all, anything could have happened by then – she might even be pregnant, which was something else they'd discussed when they'd walked over to the lake, and weren't going to do anything to prevent.

Turning in his arms to gaze out at the vineyard again, she gave a sigh that was part contentment and part frustration. 'I feel such a sense of freedom and happiness when I'm here,' she told him, wishing the next few months were already over and she didn't have to leave at all. 'It's as though I'm really being myself in a way that I almost seem to have lost a sense of.' Then, leaning her head back on his shoulder, 'But it's not the place that makes me feel like that,' she whispered. 'It's you, because life isn't about places, is it, it's about people, especially those we love.'

Tightening his embrace, he kissed her neck, then taking her hand he led her back to the table. 'We haven't talked about my father at all,' he said, as they sat down. 'You know that this is his house, and he is very happy for you and Harry to be here, but maybe you would prefer me to find somewhere close by for us.'

She shook her head. 'You know I adore your father,' she said, 'so if he's prepared to give it a try with us all being under the same roof, so am I.' She smiled as she saw the relief in his eyes, and sat forward to kiss him. 'You're right to be happy with that decision,' she told him, 'because your father is a far better cook than I will ever be. My talents, I hope, lie elsewhere.'

His eyebrows rose, and she laughed as she realised what he was thinking.

'I was meaning my book,' she said.

'Ah. Then let me tell you that you have two exceptional talents, and the other one is writing. Of course you may have even more that I am not yet aware of, but the work you have done here is *exceptionel*. Your style is so fluid it is almost melodic, but very suddenly it becomes arresting or impetuous, like an arabesque or capriccio. And you have evoked a very seductive and real sense of the period, as well as the passions of the characters. I warm to them all in different ways, and find myself already feeling sad to lose them. You have only now to write the final chapter?'

She nodded and smiled as she sighed. 'A very tragic end, but a real one,' she said, 'because it is death.' Her eyes went to his. 'Lucile and her German didn't have a happy end either, because she found she didn't love him after all.' Her expression showed some anxiety that the same fate might be awaiting them.

He appeared amused. 'It was the plan for her to fall very deeply in love with a Frenchman,' he reminded her. 'If Irène Némirovsky had lived, that is what she would have written. It is in her notes.'

She laughed at having been read so easily, and put right so wonderfully. 'So are we very deeply in love?' she asked playfully. Then, more seriously, 'That's how it feels to me.'

'It is how it feels to me too,' he said, linking his fingers through hers.

She looked down at their hands, then raising her eyes back to his she smiled as she remembered the line he'd once written on a card for her, reminding her of what the quotation in *Suite Française* should really have been. '"*A thing of beauty is a joy for ever*,"' she said, speaking the words aloud.

Recognising them and realising how appropriate it was now, his eyes remained on hers as he continued the verse:

> '"*Its loveliness increases; it will never*
> *Pass into nothingness; but still will keep*
> *A bower quiet for us, and a sleep*
> *Full of sweet dreams . . .*"'

As the beauty of the poem and its promise stole over her, she went to put her arms around him and said, very softly, 'Whatever the future might hold, *mon chéri*, I need to be with you now . . .'